THE IMPERFECTION OF US

NICK ALEXANDER

Storm
PUBLISHING

To request permissions, contact the publisher at rights@stormpublishing.co

Ebook ISBN: 978-1-80508-001-5
Paperback ISBN: 978-1-80508-004-6

Cover design: Beth Free, Studio Nic&Lou
Cover images: Shutterstock, Beth Free, Studio Nic&Lou

Published by Storm Publishing.
For further information, visit:
www.stormpublishing.co

ONE

BILLY (BY DAWN)

My mother was a bit of a goer in her youth – 'goer' being my preferred euphemism. If you asked Mum she'd probably say she was a 'liberated woman' or something, while Wayne – my brother – tends to use more basic language, favouring terms like 'slapper' or 'slag'.

If Mum overheard him talking about her like that, she'd always whack him around the head, but Wayne didn't expect anything less. Her smile, as she hit him, gave the game away: her son's insults were just part of the fun. I don't think anyone's ever found a way to upset Mum, not really.

Anyway, the result of Mum's so-called 'liberation' was that neither of us ever knew our dads. Mine, the family myth has it, left before Mum had even 'come' – something she considers to this day as proof that it was a case of 'good riddance to bad rubbish'.

The story of my conception, then, goes as follows:

Mum and Bert – her minicab driver boyfriend – were busy doing it on the sofa, when our St Bernard decided it was the perfect moment to join in, jumping up and starting to hump Bert's leg.

Bert, I suppose quite reasonably, was outraged, but not enough to actually pause the sex act. Instead, and without interrupting his thrusting, he requested that Mum control her 'bloody dog'. But Mum, in addition to being pinned down by the combined weight of both Bert (who apparently wasn't skinny) and her beloved Benjy (who was massive), was too busy laughing to intervene. Mum laughed, she always says, until she wept that day, and I believe her on that one. Even now, tears of mirth well up whenever she tells the story.

Bert, who, I gather, felt humiliated both from having been humped by a dog and by Mum's failure to take his humiliation seriously, stormed out, leaving Mum and the dog together, both sexually frustrated, lying on the sofa.

But luckily, or unluckily, depending on how you look at these things, Bert had managed to *finish off* before *storming off*, so, nine months later, I was born.

Did Wayne and I miss out by not having dads? It's kind of hard to say, really, because how do you miss something you've never had? How would you even know what you might be missing?

Plus, it's hardly like there were no father figures around – there were lots and lots of boyfriends. In fact, I'm not sure Mum, who was tall, blond and pretty – funny too – ever went more than a week between one man and the next.

She dated bartenders and BT engineers; policemen and criminals... Some of these boyfriends were fun, and some were mad, but mostly they were just kind of repetitive – an endless stream of not-quite-good-enough men.

All the same, David taught me to play poker and roll a cigarette one-handed, and Pete to ride a motorbike, long before I was old enough for that to be legal. Jeremy – who was a gardener by trade – planted spuds in our tiny front yard, potatoes we harvested long after Mum had broken up with him. And Andy, whingy Andy, not only taught me the meaning of 'passive aggressive' but also demonstrated the flammability of cheap furniture by setting light to our new sofa with a cigarette. The remains are still in the front garden today.

Mum even went out with a bank robber for a bit, an actual proper bank robber called Pablo, and even he had his good points. Because, of course, Pablo always had plenty of cash in his wallet and he didn't mind splashing it around, either.

So, though Wayne might not agree, I'd have to say that I, at least, never felt short-changed. Some of my schoolfriends came from stable two-parent relationships, and it never struck me as something to be jealous of. If anything, it seemed to me that, compared with our varied adventures, they'd missed out. There always just seemed to be so many things they'd never tried, so many things they'd never even *thought* of trying.

Of course, sometimes a guy would stick around long enough for us to get attached and, when he packed his bags, we'd feel sad. But we were so fusional with Mum that we'd either be furious on her behalf, or we'd be as relieved as she was that it was over. In our house, sadness never had much space to hang around for long.

Years ago, I read a silly column in *Smash Hits* that said something about absent father figures making for girly sons. And I suppose that's proof of a kind that we didn't miss out too badly. Because though our Wayne might have some issues – and he really, really does – being girly definitely isn't one of them.

As for me? Well, I suppose you'd say I'm a bit of a chip off the old block. I gave my first blow job to Patrick Stevens behind the bike shed at fifteen, something that, because I didn't know the cheesy topping was optional, I didn't do again for a decade. I had my first full-on bang on the morning of my sixteenth birthday in an abandoned house out in Westgate. That was with drop-dead gorgeous (and clean as a whistle) Andy Copeland, so no regrets there. Thanks to my brilliant upbringing, I never felt guilty about any of it.

In my opinion, people make way too much fuss about sex. I mean, I really don't get why it should be more or less complicated than swimming or cycling or any other physical activity. If it's fun, and you like it, then do it, that's my motto. And if it's not fun, or you don't, then don't.

That said, the one aspect of our upbringing that was lacking was any detailed education about pregnancy, Mum's theory seeming to have been that the best protection was ignorance.

'Dawn!' she'd snap. 'Cross your legs! There are boys present!'

'Why, Mum?' I'd whine – I didn't much like crossing my legs.

'When you're old enough to know why, you'll be old enough to decide,' she'd say, a Rothmans Menthol wobbling as she spoke.

Trouble was, by the time I was old enough to know why, I was at an age where I was incapable of deciding anything other than 'Yes.'

It's not that information was hard to come by, either. It's just that the gossip we relied on, in the days before the internet, was no more reliable that the fake news kids get nowadays. Thus, we all 'knew' you couldn't get pregnant if your period was due, and that you couldn't get pregnant if you peed right after, either. The doggy position was clearly safer than missionary because the tadpole thingies had to swim upstream, plus Julia Biggin's sister said you only got pregnant if, deep down, you really wanted to. As I really, really *didn't* want to get pregnant, I figured I didn't have much to worry about. Plus, if the worst came to the worst we all knew we could just take a pill the way Tracey Judd had, and the problem would be solved in a flush.

But I was lucky and for a while, for quite a while really (especially considering how much sex I was having), it didn't

'Me?'

'Yes, I'm assuming you have a name?'

'Oh, Dawn,' I said. 'Dawn Weaver.'

'Cool,' Billy said, dragging so hard on his cigarette that it crackled. 'And how old are you, Dawn Weaver?'

'I'm eighteen,' I lied.

'Cool,' Billy said, breaking into a grin. And it was a grin that I understood was good news.

To avoid having to fake smoking again, I dropped my cigarette and, concentrating on accentuating my hip movement, ground it out with my foot. 'So the jumpsuit thing...' I said, sounding, I thought, rather sassy. 'Admit it: it's just part of your pop-star persona.'

'My pop-star persona?' Billy repeated, looking amused.

'Yeah, for your band.'

'No,' he said, with a sigh. 'It really is just practical. I'm kind of lazy. About laundry and shit. You know.'

'Right,' I said, trying to hide a smile, because I didn't believe for one minute he'd chosen to wear a US Air Force jumpsuit for practical reasons. He'd chosen it because he thought it looked sexy, which, by the way, it really did. I couldn't stop wondering if he was naked underneath it.

'I like your thing, too,' Billy said, appraising me.

'My thing?'

'Yeah, the boots. The skirt. The jacket.'

I was wearing purple Doc Martens boots, olive-green leggings and a tartan skirt, an outfit I'd carefully selected so it would appear to have been carelessly thrown together.

'You could be a singer in my band like that, no problem,' Billy said, nodding and grinning salaciously as he scanned my body from top to toe.

'If I could sing,' I said. 'Only I can't.'

'Oh, anyone can sing.'

I laughed genuinely at that because Billy had no idea quite how wrong he was.

Looking back, I'm a bit embarrassed at how superficial I sounded, but it wasn't superficiality, honest it wasn't. It was fragility, really, that was driving me.

Despite the sexually liberated side of me, which, admittedly, was well developed for a seventeen-year-old, I was desperate, achingly desperate to be loved, to be appreciated – to be respected as different and individual and above all cool. I wanted to *not* be like my schoolfriends, who for the most part were what, round our way, we called bus stop girls — those youngsters you see hanging around the bus stops of small towns, smoking, drinking lager and swearing. But inexorably, that's exactly what I knew I was becoming.

My problem was that my ideas about who I *didn't* want to be were far clearer than my thoughts about who I *did*. I'd prepared for adult life by ruling out all the obvious Margate clichés: chav, fashionista, skinhead... I'd determined that I'd never be right-wing or racist or boring or conventional, because these were the things I hated most. But these self-imposed limits had only served to create an emptiness – a sort of void that left me feeling self-conscious and scared in almost all situations. The only side of me I felt confident about was the fact that I was sexually attractive. Boys liked me, I knew that much. They liked my blond hair and my long legs; they liked my precocious boobs. And I knew how to flirt, that's for sure. I'd mastered that one by watching Mum. But otherwise, the truth of the matter was that I hadn't the faintest idea who I was.

Billy seemed to have self-assurance and personality to spare, and, if I could just get into his inner circle, I hoped I'd soak up some of that cool myself.

So when, flicking his cigarette into the darkness, he said, 'Time I got back for the second half. Will you still be around when we finish?' the only possible answer was 'yes'.

. . .

Billy's parents had a huge red brick house overlooking Dane Park, but Billy lived in the garage. It had been converted into a sort of studio flat, with a shower cubicle in one corner, and fluffy insulation that peeped out from the tops of plasterboard walls. But you could tell that that's what it had been: a garage.

He had a messed-up sofa-bed in one corner that I never once saw folded away, and a drum kit and a keyboard at the back. He had three guitars hung on the walls, a hi-fi, racks of records and fridge-sized speakers. I thought it was the coolest pad I'd ever seen.

We lounged on his bed, drinking rosé from a box, until I found the courage to ask him if he was wearing anything beneath that jumpsuit. This led directly to the big reveal: he wasn't. And I mean, not even underpants.

After sex – which was OK if not exceptional – I felt miserable. I'd decided halfway through that Billy was out of my league and that if I wanted to hang out with him and the rest of the band, I should have played hard to get rather than serving myself up on a platter.

But then Billy, still naked on the bed, picked up a guitar and started strumming, and instead I decided I was in love.

As he played, he asked me about myself, so I told him about growing up on the Millmead estate, and about my mum, and her boyfriends, and about Wayne.

Billy said he thought that was all 'really cool', which was a bit of a shock. He said the working classes 'knew where it was at' while people like his parents had their 'heads so far up their own arses they could barely tell night from day'. But his approval gave me the courage to refuse a third cigarette. I didn't, I finally admitted, smoke.

'So why d'you take 'em before?' he asked, still strumming, still smoking.

'Dunno.' I shrugged. 'Peer pressure, maybe? I think I wanted you to like me.'

'Because how could I ever like a non-smoker?' Billy laughed.

'Sorry.'

'Oh, don't apologise,' he said, then, more seriously. 'And don't *ever* do that.' He gave me a sad shake of the head, then dropped his gaze to a new chord sequence he was trying to master.

'Don't do what?' I asked.

'Don't say yes to things you don't really want,' he said. 'Saying "no" is as important as saying "yes". More important, maybe. What you say "no" to defines who you are.' He stopped playing momentarily then, and reached to a shelf behind him for a notebook and a Biro. Once he'd jotted something down and returned the book to the shelf, he looked up at me and smiled.

'Just notes,' he said. 'Ideas for songs. You see? You've inspired me already.'

My relationship with Billy lasted just one summer – the summer of 1990. But my God, what a summer that was!

Maybe there are just moments in a life that are special – moments when you're changing from one thing to another, the way caterpillars change to butterflies – moments when you're open and ready to become someone new. So perhaps it was just luck that Billy happened to be there at the right time for me. But it's always felt like more than that somehow. It's always felt like he was *meant* to be there right then, like he was the one person on the planet I needed to meet.

Billy taught me everything, really, and by the time the summer was over I'd filled that gaping void of mine, and built a whole new personality.

He introduced me to his parents, that was the first thing. They were these incredibly calm, cultured dope smokers and were unlike any parents I'd ever met.

His dad was a schoolteacher, and his mother a freelance copy-editor – intellectuals, I suppose you'd call them. They listened to classical music and read books and drank too much wine, letting Billy do pretty much whatever he wanted. His mum actually gave me a copy of *The Life and Loves of a She-Devil* to read, and it was the first novel I ever read out of choice rather than because it was on the school syllabus.

Of course, if you're a literary snob kind of person, then you might turn your nose up at *The Life and Loves of a She-Devil*; you might not consider it to be 'proper literature'. I've met plenty of people who seem to think anything that's been adapted for TV is automatically rubbish. But to me, Fay Weldon was a revelation. Her books were funny, sassy, opinionated and tragic all rolled into one, and I realised for the first time how reading let me peep into other lives, lives I'd never see otherwise. I was hooked, and by the end of the summer, I'd read *Puffball* and *Praxis* as well.

Billy introduced me to new music, too. My friends rarely ventured beyond Radio One, a burst of Madonna or, at a stretch, just maybe an album by Sinead O'Connor. But Billy listened to Pink Floyd and Siouxsie and the Banshees. He made me listen to David Bowie, the Stone Roses and Prince.

I remember one night in particular. Billy had stolen some weed from his dad's stash in the sideboard and convinced me to take a hit from his bong. Predictably, I'd coughed my guts up, but afterwards I did feel super-mellow.

It was a hot summer's evening so, item by item, we undressed, ending up naked together, on his bed. Billy put *Horses* by Patti Smith on the turntable and it was one of the strangest collections of songs I'd ever heard – raucous and screechy, then suddenly, *unexpectedly* soft, melodic and beautiful.

At first I ignored the music. I was too busy revelling in the sensation of Billy's fingertips running rings around the edges of my nipples. For a moment, because the rhythm changed, and Billy's finger stopped, I hated Patti Smith with all my heart.

But then something strange took place, something that had never happened to me before. Perhaps the weed was part of it, but mainly I think it really was just the music.

I got lost in sound, that's the thing. I was *absorbed* by it until everything else around me disappeared. Patti Smith's melodies, and her lyrics – which were like poetry – were alternately beautiful and nightmarish. For forty-five minutes I just floated there, on that bed, held in Billy's arms, soaking up an alternate world that the music seemed to be creating inside my head.

When the second side came to an end and the needle lifted clunkily from the vinyl, neither of us were able to speak. For ten or twenty minutes we just lay there together, stunned by whatever had just happened, and in my case shocked that music could even do that. I'd always loved music to dance or to sing along to, but this? This was on a whole different level. It was a revelation.

Finally, Billy gently turned my head so that I was looking up at him and said, 'Wow! Did you get that? Did you just, like, trip on that album? Cos I swear I went to Planet Patti.'

I nodded and swallowed and tried to think of something coherent to describe how I was feeling, but I couldn't. Instead, by way of reply, a tear trickled from the corner of my eye. Billy saw it and smiled, then leaned into me and kissed it, and I thought, *I love you!* And then, you guessed it, we had sex.

There were times, of course, when I hated the music Billy played, but even the bands I couldn't stand opened up glimpses of different ways to be. And that experience of listening and choosing and asserting my tastes made me feel like I was finally growing up.

Another time, with a huge band of biker friends, Billy took me to the New Forest, camping.

We rode down in a swarm of roaring motorbikes – plus a Ford Transit van – terrifying the sleepy towns we drove through. Once there, we got drunk, smoked more weed (also stolen from his parents) and got lairy around the pool tables of local pubs. Late at night, after a drunken ride back to the camp-site, we'd sit around the campfire and someone would inevitably start strumming a guitar. Billy's friends were older and wiser than mine – they discussed music, art and politics, but without ever being stuck up about it. They talked, just as often, about life, or drugs, or shagging.

I'd lie back in Billy's arms and listen to the music, and feel so happy. Actually, it was more than happy: I felt as if, for the first time, I was right where I was supposed to be.

I'd notice how Billy's friends paid attention to him when he spoke, and I could hear how they laughed at his witty one-liners, and these things made me feel proud I was his girl. Everyone wanted to sit next to Billy; everyone wanted to *talk* to Billy. But at the end of the evening it was little old me who he'd take by the hand and lead to his tent where, without fail, we'd have sex. Sometimes this was discreet, soft, romantic lovemaking, but more often it was carefree, naughty and noisy. In those moments Billy actually seemed to be proud of what we were doing – it was as if he *wanted* the others to know. So instead of feeling embarrassed, I'd think *yeah, suckers, he's with me!* I could hardly believe it was true.

We got back to Margate late one Sunday evening, and Mum, who just loved to be around youngsters and who also had Mondays off, convinced half of them to stay the night. They pitched their tents in our front garden and, while Mum heated oven chips and sausages for everyone, Billy's friends lit a bonfire.

Then, there, in the middle of the estate, surrounded by grubby tents, she and I sat on the old singed sofa, like some queen from the Middle Ages with her bride-to-be daughter, demanding that the musicians entertain us.

Billy and his friends did just that, with Billy playing the guitar and singing, Siobhan on backing vocals, and boyfriend Jake drumming with sticks on a Tupperware. They all loved the vulgar devil-may-care madness of my mother, and Mum loved their youth and freedom right back. A few neighbours came to complain about the noise, or the tents, or the smoke from the bonfire, but for the most part they ended up joining in the fun. The moment was impossible to resist.

The next morning, once all the bikes had roared off, Mum and I went around the muddy garden with a bin bag, picking up empty beer cans.

'Now that Billy, darlin', is a keeper,' she said. 'And if you don't want him I might try my hand myself.'

I laughed. 'I know,' I said. 'He's great, isn't he?'

'He's better than great,' Mum said. 'That boy, mark my words, is gonna be famous.'

'You think?' I asked. I was in love with Billy. I thought Billy was amazing. But famous?

'He's got star quality,' Mum said, definitively. 'Like Trevor Howard. The actor.'

'Yes, I know who Trevor Howard is, Mum,' I said.

'But did I ever tell you, my mum used to know him?'

'Yes, Mum,' I said. 'You did.' She had told me many times.

'Well, my point is, you could tell, even back then. Mum always said that the minute you laid eyes on Trevor Howard, you could tell he'd make something of himself. Like your Billy. It's like an aura some people have around 'em.'

'An aura,' I said. 'Right.'

'So just make sure you don't lose him. Cos that Siobhan's got her eye on him, too. Just so's you know.'

'She hasn't,' I said, emptying a Tennent's can into the weeds before binning it. 'She's got her own boyfriend, Mum. She's with Jake – the drummer.'

'You just keep an eye on 'im,' Mum said. 'Cos a bloke like that... they don't crop up every day. And frankly, he's out of your league. So you'd better be on your best.'

'Huh!' I said, hesitating between agreement, amusement and outrage. 'Well, Billy doesn't seem to think so, does he?'

'Think what?' Mum asked. 'What doesn't he think?'

'That he's out of my league... so rude! And as for Siobhan, well, maybe she does fancy him. I wouldn't blame her. But Billy, for your information, prefers me... So maybe he's not as *out of my league* as you think.'

Mum rolled her eyes and gave a little shake of her head. 'That ego's gonna get you into trouble one day, my girl,' she said. 'How old is he, anyway?'

'He's twenty,' I told her, for some reason deducting a year from his age.

'Well, I hope you're being careful,' Mum said.

'Of course I am,' I told her. 'Of course we are.' After all, Billy wore condoms most of the time.

'Good,' Mum said. 'Because Premier League or not, we don't want him getting you up the duff.'

* * *

Mum, unfortunately, had been clairvoyant about Siobhan and, one week exactly after our wonderful council-house camping extravaganza, I caught them in bed together.

The whole scene, from me opening the side door of Billy's garage, seeing his bare buttocks and Siobhan's boobs, to turning and running away, must have lasted less than ten seconds.

Billy came hobbling after me, simultaneously trying to run and hop into a pair of jogging trousers, but I was too fast for him, and by the time he got them on I was gone, cutting diagonally across Dane Park, crying as I ran.

I walked all the way to the seafront and sat staring out at the grey swell until I started to feel cold, upon which I trudged miserably back to our house.

Mum was out at work that evening and Wayne was upstairs playing, I could hear, *Teenage Mutant Ninja Turtles* on the Nintendo, so I knew the likelihood of him interrupting my misery was low.

I switched on MTV and stared blearily at the screen.

I thought, momentarily, about calling Shelley, but the truth was that I hadn't seen her since the night I'd met Billy and, in fact, had been actively avoiding all my friends.

It wasn't that I was embarrassed by Billy's poshness, nor was I embarrassed about the relative chavviness of my schoolmates. It was just that they came from different worlds really, and it seemed given that if I tried to combine them then... Actually, I don't think I had any clear idea what would happen if those two worlds met. I just knew that it couldn't possibly work.

So I sat alone and stared at the TV screen, with Mum's words banging around my head: *He's out of your league.* And he was, after all, wasn't he? Siobhan was living proof of that.

Wayne came downstairs just after eight. I heard him light the gas under the kettle and pull a Pot Noodle from the cupboard.

'All right?' he asked from the doorway.

I shrugged, and, because it wasn't actually a question, Wayne neither noticed nor cared that I hadn't answered.

'She's such a donkey,' he said. 'God knows where they dug her up. Looks like someone you bump into in Tescos.'

Hazell Dean was singing on MTV, and I assumed she was

the person Wayne was currently choosing to insult. 'You know he's a Margate boy?' he added.

'Who?' I asked. There were no men currently on screen.

'Mike Stock. From Stock Aitken Waterman. Born and bred in Margate. Our only claim to fame. Until me, of course.'

'Oh,' I said, uninterestedly. 'OK.'

The kettle started to whistle then so, our socialising for the day apparently over, Wayne returned to the kitchen to hydrate his dinner.

Billy's motorbike roared up shortly after that, and I hid in the corner of the room so he wouldn't be able to see me through the lounge window. But Billy just went to the kitchen door and, finding it open, let himself in.

'Dawn,' he said, pulling off his crash helmet.

I'd just hurled myself onto the sofa facing away from him and towards the TV.

'Dawn?' he said again, moving into my line of vision. He was wearing his jumpsuit underneath a leather jacket.

'Go away,' I told him, stretching my neck to peer around him at the TV screen.

'We need to talk,' Billy said.

'Yeah, but we don't,' I replied, sulkily. 'What we need is for you to sod off back where you came from.'

'I will go away, if you want me to,' Billy said softly, perching on the arm of a chair. 'But I honestly think it would be better if we talked.'

'Oh, just, go and talk to Siobhan or something,' I said, wincing at how adolescent I was sounding even to myself. What can I say? I was seventeen.

'You *know* I don't do monogamy,' Billy said, sounding reasonable, or at least trying to sound like someone who was being reasonable. 'We talked about this, didn't we? We had a conversation about it down in the New Forest.'

This was true, but also not true. Because, yes, Billy and his mates had chatted about monogamy, around the campfire, down in Bodmin. And yes, I'd heard him say what a stupid medieval concept he thought it was.

But no one could call that a conversation, could they? Because no one had asked me how *I* felt.

'Aren't you going to say anything?' Billy asked.

'I thought we were boyfriend/girlfriend,' I said, and again I hated myself for how immature the words sounded.

'We are,' Billy said. 'If you want us to be, we are. But like I said, I don't do exclusivity. I don't believe in it, and I don't think you do either, not really.'

I shrugged because I didn't know whether I believed in it or not. 'I don't know what that's even supposed to mean,' I muttered, still staring straight past him at the screen.

'It means you're free,' Billy said, and the thought of being free made me want to cry. I didn't want to be free. I wanted to belong to, to be owned by, him. He was so beautiful, so clever, so creative, so confident, so unlike anyone else I'd ever met. What was the point in being free to meet other people?

'It means you're free, and I'm free,' he continued. 'Free to see each other whenever we want, and free to see other people too. Don't you want to be free?'

I shrugged again and swallowed with difficulty.

Billy sighed deeply. 'D'you still want me to sod off?'

I shrugged again, but topped it off with a vague nod, not because I wanted him to leave so much as because I wanted this confusing, upsetting conversation to end.

'OK then,' Billy said. 'Sure. Whatever. Just let me know when you're ready to talk.'

He walked to the doorway then, but returned and laid one hand on my shoulder, giving it a squeeze. 'Don't look so glum,' he said. 'It's not the end of the world. You'll see that once you've calmed down. It's not the end of the world, at all.'

I shrugged beneath his hand so he released me.

'Bye then,' he said.

As he opened the front door and stepped outside, I started to cry again, because I realised that I didn't want him to leave at all.

Mum woke me up the next morning. She didn't say a word, simply letting herself into my bedroom and perching on the edge of the bed. She vaguely rearranged the items on my bedside table and then, saying, 'Shove over,' she lay down beside me.

'What?' I asked. This was not a regular occurrence.

Mum sighed. 'Wayne says you've been moping around.'

'Wayne?' I snorted. 'He never leaves his bloody room. He never stops playing Nintendo.'

'No? Well, he left it for long enough to notice you were moping around,' Mum said. 'And long enough to tell me. So what's happening? You got trouble in paradise?'

I groaned and rolled away from her. For a moment, when I'd first woken up, I'd forgotten how wrong everything had gone. But now here it was – my misery whacking me around the chops like a wet towel.

Mum followed my movement and rolled so that she was spooning me. She laid one arm across my chest and pulled me tight.

'Stop it,' I said. 'You're scaring me.' But she could tell from my voice that I secretly liked it, I think. At any rate, she didn't move.

'So is this just a tiff, or...?' she asked.

I shrugged, but then started to cry, and Mum tutted and pulled me tighter.

Eventually, I told her everything, and her response was predictably unpredictable.

'I think I agree with your Billy,' she said. 'I don't think we're made for monogamy at all. It's just an invention, innit, by society, and the Church and that, to make us all feel guilty. It's bollocks, really, is what it is.'

I thought about this for a while and then sat up and plumped a pillow behind me. 'But what if I am?' I asked.

'What if you're what?' Mum said.

'What if I *am* made to be with one person? What if I don't want to shag around?'

'Oh,' Mum said. 'Right.'

'You see?'

Mum shrugged. 'Then maybe Billy's not the one,' she said, thoughtfully. 'Maybe you need to find yourself someone more boring. Not boring – I don't mean boring. Normal. Maybe you need to find yourself someone more normal.'

I thought about it all day, swinging violently between two extremes, thinking in one moment that Billy was right, and that freedom surely meant the best of both worlds, and then the next thinking, *It's bullshit. It's just a way for Billy to have his cake and eat it.*

At six-thirty, Mum came into the lounge and switched the TV off.

'Oi!' I said. 'I was watching that.'

'Yeah, well, it's time you got your glad rags on,' Mum said. 'Cos tonight, you're coming with me.'

'I'm not,' I said, laughing at the craziness of the suggestion.

'You are,' Mum said, nodding seriously.

'I'm *so* not.'

'You so are,' she said, reaching out one hand to drag me to my feet.

'No,' I said, refusing to budge.

'C'mon!' Mum said. 'Get up! Get out! Just move from that little rut you're in!'

TWO

BIG FRIENDLY GIANT (BY DAWN)

Mum worked as a barmaid in the Wheatsheaf, a rough community pub sat bang in the middle of our estate. Though it wouldn't have been my choice of drinking venue, the truth was that I'd never spent a bad evening there. Between the free drinks she'd slip me and the fact she knew absolutely everyone, it was impossible to stay miserable for long.

So I sat at the end of the bar and, between customers, she'd sidle over to whisper all the local gossip in my ear. Mrs Burston was having an affair with that new young postie, and Jim Dean's daughter was plucking up the courage to tell him she was gay. Mike, the man who ran the darts club, suspected that Bill, the Kent County darts champion, was stealing from the cash box in order to buy drinks... And—

'Hello, Rob!' Mum said, interrupting a fresh story to serve a massive squaddie type who'd popped up beside me.

'A pint of the usual, please,' Rob said, and, as Mum reached for a glass and began to pull a pint of IPA, she said, 'That's my daughter you're standing next to there, Rob, so watch yourself. And she's on the rebound, too, so be nice.'

Rob frowned at her and then turned to steal a glance at me,

but we were so close it was almost impossible to do so politely. He blushed visibly, then turned back to face the bar, and I sensed myself blushing in sympathy.

Once Mum had served him and bustled through to the other bar, Rob said, without turning towards me, 'Hello.'

'Sorry about that,' I said, sourly. 'She's an embarrassment.' I shook my head and turned away to look at a rowdy group coming in through the street door.

When I finally looked back, I was hoping that Rob would have taken the hint and returned to his seat, but he was still there beside me, sipping his beer. I shifted my seat back a little, and glanced up at him. He was big, surprisingly so – well over six feet tall. His bulk, combined with something uncalculated about his smile, made him look younger, I thought, almost verging on simple. There was a naivety about that big, round face of his that made you want to say, 'Ahh,' the way you might to a girlfriend's gurgling baby. I thought about Billy and mentally compared them, thinking that Rob was a teddy bear while Billy was a fox.

'*What?*' I asked, resisting my desire to mother him and forcing an aggressive tone instead.

'I... Erm...' Rob said. 'I just thought, maybe, I could get you... you know... a drink or something?'

I raised my glass of snakebite. 'Got one.'

'Maybe later then?' Rob said, sending me a clumsy, matey wink.

'I'm not sure if you noticed this, Rob, but my mum's the barmaid,' I said. 'So my drinks are on the house.'

'Right,' Rob said. 'Well, in that case, you could buy me one.'

'Yeah, but why would I?' I said. 'I don't even know you. I don't even *want* to know you.'

'Oh. Oh, OK!' Rob said, his smile fading as he blushed deeply once again. 'I only... never mind.'

Once he'd left the bar, I felt awful. I'd been rude to him, and

I knew it. But in a pub like that, you kind of had to be, really. Otherwise the men never left you alone.

'W'happen?' Mum asked, during a pause. Rick Astley was belting out of the jukebox, so she had to shout.

'W'happen with what?' I asked.

'What did you do with my lovely Rob?' she asked, peering around the room in search of him.

'Mum!' I whined. 'Jesus, I haven't even split up with Billy yet, and you're already trying to set me up.'

'Yet...' Mum repeated, with meaning. 'So you've decided then. It's over.'

'No I haven't,' I told her. 'I haven't decided nothing.'

'Anything,' Mum said. 'It's I haven't decided *anything*.'

'That's rich, coming from you. My grammar teacher, now, are you?'

'Well, anyway, you should talk to Rob about it,' Mum said. 'That's why I introduced you.'

'Mum,' I said. 'Just stop.'

'Serious,' Mum said. 'He's clever. Wise, like.'

I rolled my eyes as she leaned closer. 'Plus,' she murmured in my ear. 'I think he's probably, you know...'

'Probably what?' I asked. I took a sip of my cider.

'I suspect,' Mum said, 'he's a bit poofy.'

I laughed so suddenly, I spat my cider out. Because the idea that massive, squaddie Rob might be 'a bit poofy' was laughable.

'Talk to 'im,' Mum said. 'You'll see.'

So I did. The next time he came to the bar, I abandoned my stool and went over to apologise. 'Sorry if I was rude before...' I started.

'If?' Rob repeated, laughing.

'OK, I'm sorry I *was* rude before,' I said. 'It's just, I thought you were trying to chat me up, and I'm really not in the mood.'

'I got that,' Rob said. 'And the thought never crossed my mind.'

'Well, good,' I replied, allowing myself to smile. 'All forgiven, then?'

'If you buy me that drink,' he said. 'Seeing as you said they're free and all...'

* * *

I woke up the next morning feeling dreadful.

There was something wrong with my pillow — that was the first thing I noticed. It had a strange embroidered relief that was digging uncomfortably into my cheek.

I fidgeted until I found a smooth patch and almost fell back to sleep, but then I realised something wasn't right and moved my hand so that I could run my fingertips over the unfamiliar pattern. Not my pillow.

I rolled onto my back and tried to open my eyes, but the light in the room was so blinding it took me two or three attempts before I could focus. *Abnormal amount of light. Not my ceiling.*

I slid a hand across the thick cotton sheets. *Not my sheets, either.*

I sat bolt upright and looked around to see that I was in a bright, modern studio flat. There was a gloss red kitchen along one wall and a big sunlit bay window at the front. It was then I remembered, I was at Rob's.

'Oh shit,' I murmured. It was all coming back to me now: the drinks, the laughter – Rob's jokes, which had been so awful they'd been funny. His invitation – irresistible to drunken me – to come back to his place for cheese on toast.

The wobbly walk up the hill: he'd given me a piggyback halfway, and had actually dropped me because he'd drunkenly tripped over a bollard. I had a bruise on my elbow to prove that and another memory of us laughing ourselves silly as he'd tried to pull me to my feet.

Then... what? I couldn't remember. Oh! The cheese on toast (heavenly), in the kitchen. Quite probably the best cheese on toast ever made. Then we'd sat on the sofa talking about... Mum, maybe, and how much fun she was? There was a vague memory of us agreeing that Pernod and ouzo should be banned because they were taste crimes. Rob had put Bananarama on his stereo, which had made me laugh some more because it seemed so camp.

Then... a gap... followed by the two of us on the sofa kissing. That had felt lovely and I'd been the one – blush – to initiate sex by reaching down and unbuckling Rob's belt. Rob, bless him, had been shocked by that. Next up from my unreliable memory bank: his fumbling lack of technique before suddenly – before I'd even got going – unexpectedly arriving at the finish line. Even more surprising had been his tears on pulling out. Because, no, in the end, Rob had not turned out to be gay. What Rob had turned out to be was a virgin.

'Shit!' I said. 'Shit, shit, shit!'

I threw the quilt aside and stood. The room spun for a moment but then settled.

I looked down at my naked body. If proof was needed that this wasn't merely a bad dream, there it was: five foot eight of sweaty, naked skin.

I moved to the lounge end of the room, where I found my clothes in a pile, neatly folded, and, at the sight of the sofa, more memories: the kissing, the grappling... casting my clothes off as we moved towards the bed. And the memory of a decision, too. Because, though I'd been drunk, I remembered deciding quite clearly. Billy would be proud of me, I'd thought. He'd see that I was able to claim my freedom as well. What stupid, drunken logic had *that* been?

'Rob?' I called out, just to confirm that he really had gone out. *Silence.*

I slid a door open and peeped in on a blindingly white-tiled bathroom. I closed the door behind me and sat down to pee, taking in the wet-room shower design, the ginormous chrome shower head, the folded fluffy towels... It looked like a hotel bathroom or... No, actually, what it looked like was one of those TV makeovers. The whole place looked like it had been redone by Laurence Llewelyn-Bowen. Perhaps Rob was gay, after all.

Though a shower was tempting, I merely splashed my face with water and pulled my clothes on. I'd get out of here before Rob came back, and we could all just forget this had ever happened. But as I reached for the bathroom door handle, I heard a key in the front door.

'Dawn!' Rob called out. 'Dawney? Are you still here, Dawney?'

I stepped out into the bedroom area and grimaced at him.

'Oh there you are,' Rob said. 'I thought you'd done a runner on me.'

'I was about to,' I admitted.

'I just went to get a few bits,' he explained, jiggling a Happy Shopper bag around. 'Crumpets and stuff. Coffee, too.'

'I really should just go,' I said, avoiding eye contact. 'This was—'

'Dawn,' he said. 'Stay for coffee.'

'I can't,' I said. 'Sorry. I... I have a... Look, I just need to go, OK?'

'I know,' Rob said. 'You told me. You told me all about Billy last night. I'm not asking for anything. But stay for some coffee. Please? Last night was a big deal for me.'

My stomach rumbled. I was hungry – *hangover* hungry. 'Crumpets, you say?' I asked.

'Yes, yes! Crumpets!' Rob said, nodding with childlike enthusiasm and digging into the bag. 'I got Marmite and marmalade, too. I didn't know which one you'd want, so...'

'Wow,' I said, doubtfully.

Rob made proper coffee and toasted crumpets, and as he

did so he burbled on excitedly, telling me random things about his life. He was an electrician, he explained. He had his own business, rewiring people's houses. His parents had moved back to Wales, but he'd decided to stay on in Margate. He hadn't got on with them anyway... His business had been working out well, so why move? He had a van now and everything. So life was great really. Well, except for the romantic side of things. But that had never been his strong point...

'I'm sorry about last night,' he said, suddenly, unexpectedly. 'I know it's not meant to be... I know it's not a race or anything. It's just, you're so beautiful, I couldn't stop myself.'

I laughed at this sourly and pulled a face.

'You are,' Rob said. 'But you know that, right? Of course you do.'

I fidgeted on my bar stool and looked down at my swinging feet. Though I knew I was no monster, I wasn't used to compliments. 'So was that...?' I asked, then, 'Look, I'm not sure if I dreamed this... And I don't want to offend you or anything... But did you actually say that was your first time?'

Rob bit his lip and nodded. 'Sorry,' he said.

'God, don't apologise,' I said. 'We can't all be precocious slags, like me.'

'You're not a slag,' Rob said. 'You're beautiful. I think you're amazing.'

'Yeah, thanks,' I said, thinking, *Well of course you do. You've never shagged anyone else.* 'How old are you, Rob?'

'Twenty-five,' he said. 'I know it's late. It's just... I don't know.' He handed me a cup of coffee.

'Wow!' I said. 'Twenty-five? How come you never...?' I reached for my coffee, then paused. 'Sugar?' I asked.

'Oh, God!' Rob said, looking suddenly panicky. 'Shit! I tried to think of everything. But I didn't... Shit! Sugar! Of course.'

He was standing, lifting his keys from a key-peg behind the kettle.

'Rob,' I said. 'Wait, it doesn't matter.'

But he'd already crossed to the front door. 'Five minutes,' he said. 'Not even.'

'Rob!' I shook my head in disbelief.

Men, the men I'd come across – my mother's men, boys from school, Wayne's friends, even Billy – they did not behave like this. They didn't make breakfast, and they didn't go roaring out the door because they'd forgotten the sugar, either. I was shocked, but in a good way. I wondered briefly if there was a whole world of helpful eager-to-please men out there I'd never, for some reason, met. Or maybe it was just Rob.

The crumpets popped up but they were still squidgy, so I pushed the lever down to give them a second toasting and wandered round the flat looking at things. I'd never seen a man who lived so tidily, either.

By the time the crumpets popped up again, Rob was back. 'It's only on the corner,' he said, looking ridiculously young again, looking like a child desperate to please. 'It's really handy, actually.'

'You didn't have to,' I said. 'But thanks.'

He dropped the keys over the hook again and handed me the bag of sugar. 'There you go, Dawney,' he said.

'Um, you can stop calling me that right now,' I told him. 'I hate it.'

'Dawney?' he asked, grinning so broadly he looked like the face on his Happy Shopper bag. 'Your mum told me to say it. She told me to keep saying it until you lose the plot.'

'Oh,' I said. 'Of course she did. Well, believe me, you do not want to see me lose the plot.'

Rob nodded and handed me a teaspoon. 'She likes a joke, your mum.'

'She does,' I agreed.

'She tried to teach me to pour beer once,' he said. 'Did she ever tell you about that?'

I shook my head.

'Yeah, she showed me how to do it on one tap – like to demonstrate – and then got me to do it on the other one, but it was impossible. I just couldn't do it. D'you know why?'

I shook my head.

'It was the end of the barrel. And all you get at the end of the barrel is froth. But I kept on trying. "Come on, Robby," she kept saying. "You'll get it right next time." It was so funny.'

'It sounds it,' I said, suspecting that he was burbling to avoid returning to our previous, far more interesting discussion. 'So anyway, how come, Rob?'

'How come what?'

'How come you've never shagged anyone before? I mean, you're a good-looking bloke. You're not religious or anything, are you?'

A cloud crossed his features and I felt bad about having asked the question.

'It's...' he said. He coughed, then cleared his throat. 'Yeah...' he said, looking away towards the front door, and for the first time I felt like he wanted me to leave.

'It's OK,' I said. 'Forget it.'

'Yeah... Thanks,' he said, turning back. 'I...' He shrugged.

'Mum actually thought you might be gay,' I said, hoping to lighten things up a bit. 'But you're clearly not, are you?'

'No,' Rob said, folding a tea-towel with surprising precision. 'No. Everyone thinks that, yeah... But no. Not gay at all, as it happens.'

* * *

'What's that saying, about apples not falling far from trees?'

I'd barely made it in the door and my little brother was being snarky.

'What's that, honey?' Mum called out as I hung my coat on

a hook. 'Oh, hello!' she said, appearing in the kitchen doorway. 'You're home.'

'Yep,' I said, flatly. 'I am.'

'And what was that, Wayne, honey?'

'Ignore him,' I told Mum. 'He's just insulting me, as usual.'

Wayne started to climb the stairs, but then paused and turned theatrically to look back. 'Actually,' he said, 'I was rather cleverly insulting both of you.'

'That boy!' Mum said, returning to the kitchen. 'I swear there's something wrong with his brain.'

'It's just that I've actually got one!' Wayne called out from upstairs. 'You're not used to that round here.'

I followed Mum into the kitchen, where she was busy greasing a frying pan with margarine. 'I half expected you to come home with a whole new look,' she said, shooting me a cheeky smile.

'What?'

'They're supposed to be good at that, aren't they?' she said, sounding amused. 'Fashion and make-up and stuff...'

'Mum!' I said. 'He's not gay.'

'Oh, I'll bet you anything you like that he is,' she said. 'Eggs?'

I shook my head. 'I ate already.'

'At Rob's?' Mum said, visibly struggling not to crack up. 'Good cook, is he? What'd he make you, a soufflé? Eggs Florentine?'

'Mum!' I protested again, by now struggling not to laugh myself. 'He really, really isn't.'

'Oh, OK...' Mum said, cracking an egg. 'Sounds like some-one's done her research.'

I ignored her and licked my finger before dipping it in the sugar bowl.

'Was it fun, though?' she asked, then, 'Please don't do that.'

'No, Mum,' I said, sucking my finger. 'No, it was not fun. And I wish you hadn't let me go.'

Mum raised an eyebrow. 'Hardly *my* responsibility,' she said. 'I can barely look after myself.'

'True enough,' I said. Then, to avoid any further questions, I went upstairs to run a bath.

As I lay there flicking at the suds, I couldn't help but compare my night with Rob with all the other nights I'd spent with Billy. Sex with Billy had certainly been on a whole different level, but Rob's ineptitude actually made me feel an unexpected warmth for him. Was that pity or perhaps empathy I was feeling? Billy was so confident, so exciting, so sexy and full of himself, but in a way wasn't that precisely Billy's problem? Whereas Rob? Well, he was a mirror-image opposite – so unsure of himself and so inexperienced he'd do anything and everything to make you like him. I thought, absurdly, of how good that cheese on toast had been and how he'd run back to the shop for sugar. As an antidote, I compared my Patti Smith moment at Billy's with Rob blasting out Bananarama. I shook my head at the endearing hopelessness of Rob, and the thought made me smile. Then I switched to thinking about the fact I'd lost my hold on biker/musician/sex-machine Billy and felt sad. Perhaps he *had* been out of my league all along.

The flowers arrived during lunch and, to my horror, it was Wayne who answered the door. 'Dawney!' he called out, camply. '*Dawneeeeeey*! I think this one is for you.'

I groaned and levered myself from my chair. Mum looked at me enquiringly, so I shrugged by way of reply.

Beyond the open front door, a young delivery guy was waiting, holding a bunch of red roses.

'Looks like Dawney has a new fan,' Wayne said. 'Unless it's

for a funeral, maybe? In which case, I suppose it could be more of a warning kind of thing.'

I rolled my eyes and pushed him back toward the dining room before forcing a fake smile for the delivery guy as I signed for the flowers. Before returning to join the others, I lingered in the hallway just long enough to take a peek at the card.

I think you're amazing!!!

With the thought, *If only they were from Billy*, my heart sank, because I could tell from the number of exclamation marks they weren't.

The flowers continued all week. Every day a fresh bunch of roses would appear with another one-liner ending in exclamation marks. 'I need to see you again!!!' 'You're so beautiful!!!!' 'Please, please can I see you again!!!'

By Thursday it was clear that something needed to be done, and I found him outside his flat next to his van. He had spread the contents with mathematical neatness across the pavement and was methodically loading it all back in.

'Oh, hello!' he said brightly, when I tapped on the roof.

'The flowers have got to stop,' I told him.

His smile faded. 'I'm just organising the van,' he said. 'I have to do it regularly, otherwise I spend all my time looking for things.'

'Did you hear me, Rob?' I asked. 'The flowers. They have to stop.'

He started clipping screwdrivers to a tool-board that had the silhouette of each tool drawn round a clip.

'Rob?' I prompted.

'OK, but why?' he said.

'Because it's embarrassing. Because I have a boyfriend called Billy, who'll go crazy if he sees them.'

Rob nodded. 'You're back together, then?' he asked, without looking at me.

'Yeah,' I said, and I wondered if it was a lie. 'Actually, we never split up.'

'Oh,' Rob said. 'OK.'

'So, no more flowers, OK?'

He shrugged.

'Rob!' I said, and he turned to me again, looking almost as if he was going to cry. 'Just let me finish this and I'll make you a coffee or something,' he said.

I snorted. 'No, Rob,' I said. 'Just no. I'm going to go home now. So just, you know...'

I gave him a little wave and started to walk away, and as I did so he spoke, quietly saying, 'But I love you.'

I pretended I hadn't heard.

* * *

The next day, at lunchtime, the doorbell rang again.

'Ooh!' Wayne said. 'More flowers. Just what we need!'

'Shut it, Wayne!' I said, exiting the room.

'Get him to send chocolates or something useful,' he called out as I opened the door. 'Or bog roll. We're almost out of bog roll, so get him to send some of that!'

On the doorstep I found not a delivery guy with flowers, but Billy holding his crash helmet. I stifled a gasp.

'Hi, I was, er, wondering if we could talk?' The sunlight was making his blond curls shimmer and he looked as beautiful as ever. Just looking at him gave me a strange fluttery feeling deep in my chest. It felt a lot like hunger.

'Sure,' I said. 'Come up.'

'Which one is it this time?' Wayne called out as we climbed the stairs.

Billy glanced back at me enquiringly but I just shook my head. 'Ignore him,' I said. 'He's in his own stupid world.'

We sat at opposite ends of the bed, cross-legged. I thought about how much I wanted to have sex with him and then forced myself to think about Siobhan until the feeling faded.

'So, how have you been?' Billy asked.

'Fine,' I said, avoiding eye contact. 'You know...'

'You haven't missed me?' he asked.

I shrugged.

'Not even a bit?'

I nodded vaguely. 'Maybe a bit,' I said.

'I wrote a song,' he said. 'About us.'

'Oh,' I said. 'OK.' I wanted to ask to hear it, but I didn't.

'It's over, by the way. That thing with Siobhan.'

'Over?' I repeated. It hadn't really crossed my mind that the thing with Siobhan was a thing. I'd assumed it was a one-off event rather than an ongoing process that could be over.

'Yeah. Flash in the pan, really. She told me to sod off this morning. She's gone back to Jake.'

'A week,' I said, staring at my fingernails. 'You've been seeing her all week.'

'Yeah. On and off.'

'OK.'

'More on than off, I s'pose. It was hot. Till this morning it was, at any rate.'

'That's nice.'

'Yeah. While it lasted, it was.'

'And now here you are,' I said.

'Yep. Here I am.'

Despite my best intentions, I thought about sleeping with him again, and had the disgusting thought that he probably hadn't showered since he last pulled out of Siobhan. I tried to think of something witty or clever or even just something sarcastic to say to him, but nothing came to mind.

'I just think it's good we can be so honest about it all,' Billy said.

'Right,' I said, frowning. Then, before I really knew I was going to do so, I found myself saying, 'Actually, I had a *thing* this week, too.'

'Oh!' Billy said, sounding taken aback. 'You did?'

'Yep.'

Billy covered his mouth with one hand.

'What?' I asked.

'Nothing,' he said. 'I just didn't think you were like that.'

'Like what?'

Billy shook his head and shrugged at the same time. 'Dunno,' he said.

But I knew what he meant. I could hear Wayne's voice in my head saying *slutty*.

'Is he nice? Do you like him?' He looked like he was trying really hard to smile, but the result was closer to a grimace.

I shrugged.

'Or was it just a sex thing, like with me and Siobhan?' I thought he sounded hopeful, but it was probably just wishful thinking.

'Yeah,' I said. 'I suppose it was something like that.'

'Not as good as with me, though,' he said.

I frowned at my fingernails a little longer until a flash of anger rose up in me, the devil possessing me just long enough to make me say, 'Actually, it was pretty amazing.'

'Oh!' Billy said. 'OK.'

'Hung like a donkey,' I said, 'which helps, of course.'

'Oh!' Billy said again, his eyes widening. 'OK then.'

I nodded and sighed. 'Anyway.'

'I should probably go,' Billy said.

'Yeah,' I agreed. 'Probably.'

'I'll, um, see you around.'

I raised my fingers to mimic a gun and said, 'Not if I see you first!'

It was pure habit; in fact it was one of Wayne's favourite put-downs, and I'd hoped it would lighten the mood. But Billy looked quite heartbroken, and it was only once he'd left that I thought, for the first time ever, about what the phrase implied.

* * *

Mum actually knew before I did, which was weird.

It was about six weeks since my night with Rob and five since that final conversation with Billy. I was heading out the door to meet Shelley when Mum called me back.

'Come in here and sit down,' she said. 'You and me need to talk.'

I grimaced as I put my coat back on the hook. I was pretty certain I knew what this was about.

I'd been kicked off my A level courses for non-attendance the previous March, and the deal had been that Mum would refrain from kicking me out of the house if I got a job. At the time she'd generously given me until September to work out what I was going to do. As tomorrow was the end of the month, the subject of our talk was a no-brainer.

She made two cups of tea without asking me if I wanted one (I didn't) and then sat opposite me at the Formica kitchen table and lit up a menthol cigarette.

'So,' she said, speaking in smoke as she pulled the ashtray towards her. 'I suppose my first question is, have you told him?'

I frowned. 'Have I told who, what?' I asked.

'Or aren't you going to? Because, of course, you don't have to. You don't have to do anything you don't want to.'

'Told who what, Mum?' I asked again. 'I'm really not...'

'That... you know...' Mum said. 'That you're...'

'That I'm?' I asked, wide-eying her and shrugging exaggeratedly.

'That you're pregnant, silly.'

I gasped and sat back in my chair, grinning. 'I'm not,' I told her.

Mum laughed at that. She actually laughed out loud. 'Oh, I think you are!' she said.

'I'm not!'

'Look, if you're going to get rid of it, then that's fine too. You know me. I've no objection to anything, me. But if you are, well, you're going to need some support. Either way, actually, you're going to need some support. So it's best if you just tell me what—'

'Mother!' I said. 'I am not pregnant.'

'Oh God,' Mum said. 'You don't know, do you?'

'And now you're just being silly,' I said.

'Look at you.' Mum laughed. 'Your tits are huge!'

I glanced down at my chest. 'Are they?' I asked, noticing that she was right, that my chest was looking unusually perky. 'They've been a bit weird, actually. You know... sore. Maybe that's why. Maybe I've got an infection or something.'

'Oh, you silly sausage,' Mum said, reaching across the table to take my hand in hers. 'You're preggers, love. Trust me. I can spot it a mile off.'

'I...' I said, chewing my bottom lip as I counted backwards in my head, hoping to prove her wrong. I looked nervously out at the hallway, worried that Wayne might be listening in. A dose of his sarcasm was the last thing I needed.

'He's at school,' Mum said. 'He's out all day. It's just us. When was your last—?'

'OK, I am actually late,' I admitted. 'I hadn't thought about it, but I am. But only ten days or so. That doesn't have to mean I'm pregnant! I've been late before. You know I have.'

'Honey,' Mum said. 'You've been an absolute nightmare lately. You've been all over the bloody place.'

'But that's just because of Billy,' I said. '*And* Wayne. Wayne's been extra-annoying.'

'He has,' Mum agreed, softly. 'But you've been *really* funny too, sweetheart. Emotional, like. Crying at films and stuff. Look. I can just tell. It's a woman thing.'

It was then I started to cry.

Mum went into town and came back with a test kit, which, trembling, I peed on. By the time I unlocked the door, I knew.

Mum was sitting at the top of the stairs, waiting for fresh confirmation of her clairvoyant abilities. 'OK,' she said, not even needing to ask me the result. 'So come and sit next to me for a bit.'

'I might be better off throwing myself down there,' I said, as I squeezed in next to her.

I looked at the sunlight coming through the front door and realised I'd never once sat on the top step before. Our hallway looked strange and unfamiliar but I wasn't quite sure if it was the vantage point that was new, or whether it was because my life had changed so fundamentally in the last few minutes that everything simply looked different.

'So what now?' I asked.

Mum shrugged and put one arm round my shoulders. 'What do you want to do?' she asked.

'I don't know,' I said, again, fighting back tears. 'I can't even...'

'Well, the options aren't that complicated, sweetheart. You can have it on your own, or you can tell Billy and try to have it with him. Or you can... you know... get rid of it. You're nice and early on, so...'

'Billy,' I said.

'I'm assuming... I mean... It's his, yeah?'

I couldn't bring myself to reply. Tears dribbled from the corners of my eyes, then ran down my cheeks.

'Oh,' Mum said. She gave my shoulder a squeeze, and I started to cry properly again.

'Is it Rob's?' Mum asked. 'Is that it? Or is it someone else's? Maybe there are others? I mean, what do I know?'

'Mum!' I spluttered. 'No, there aren't any others! But I don't know. I can't be sure.'

'You had unsafe sex wiv 'em both?'

'It was only once or twice,' I whispered. 'With Billy, I mean. It was just, you know, when we were drunk, or one time we were almost asleep and... Sometimes it just slipped in.'

Mum fanned herself with her fingers. 'Lordy,' she said. 'OK.'

'And Rob, well, it was just that one time.'

'And no condom then, either?'

'I was going to tell him to pull out. I was going to tell him to stop. It's just...'

'Hey, I'm not telling you off,' Mum said. 'I'm just asking what happened.'

'With Rob, it just happened really fast,' I said. 'I wasn't expecting him to... you know... come that fast. I don't think he was either.'

'Right,' Mum said. 'Well, that's a bit messy, really, isn't it.'

I would have laughed at Mum's accidental double entendre. Because *messy* was exactly what it had been. But I felt too ashamed to laugh. I could feel my skin burning up.

Mum gave my shoulder another squeeze and then released me.

'Look,' she said. 'Listen. These things happen. If anyone knows that, I do.'

Because I loved her so much in that moment, I dropped my head onto her shoulder. I'd seen this scene hundreds of times, on TV and in films. I'd seen silly girls tell their parents they were pregnant over and over, but I'd never seen a parent say, 'These things happen.' In that moment, I thought my mother was amazing.

'Was Gran this cool when you got pregnant with me?' I asked. I wasn't sure quite where the question had come from. We never talked much about Mum's own single-parent childhood. Perhaps I was trying to work out why she'd reacted so well.

Mum laughed at that. 'No,' she said. 'No, your grandmother wasn't cool *at all*. She threw me out of the house.'

'God, really?' I said. 'That's outrageous.'

'It *was* outrageous. Especially seeing as she wasn't exactly a paragon of virtue herself, as you know.'

'Um, well, no I don't really,' I said. 'I mean, I know she wasn't sure who your father was, but—' The shock thought that I was *exactly* like my awful grandmother popped up, shaking me to the core.

'And that kind of tells you everything you need to know about her, don't you think?' Mum said.

'I suppose,' I said. 'If you say so.' Then, as the implication of what she was saying hit me, 'Actually, no. What does it mean? Because I'm in the exact same situation.'

'Oh God, honey. I didn't mean...' Mum said, reaching out and gripping my arm. 'I didn't mean nothing by it. It's just, well, Mum used to bring men home all the time. I suspect some of them even paid her. They certainly used to give her "money for bills".' Mum made air quotes with her fingers.

'Oh,' I said. 'Wow.'

'We *were* very broke,' Mum said. She suddenly looked like she might cry. She had always been edgy when talking about her childhood and I worried I'd spoiled the moment by forcing the subject on her now.

'Did she really kick you out?' I asked, trying to move the conversation back to safer ground.

'She did. But, well... She was religious. Or at least, she liked to say she was. *Pretend* she was. I was never that convinced myself, what with all the men and everything. I think she went to church about twice. But she was religious when it came to other people, put it that way. She could get very judgey very quickly. I think it was a way of avoiding thinking about herself really. Anyway, all you need to know is that *no*, she wasn't cool. She was an absolute bloody nightmare.'

I nodded as I thought about this. So my mum was cool not because her parents had been brilliant, but because they'd been bloody awful. That somehow seemed to make her an even better person. 'Where did you go? When she threw you out?'

'Oh, I... sort of moved around a bit,' Mum said, looking uncomfortable again. 'I stayed on a friend's sofa for a while. I even spent some time in a shelter. Then... a guy I met... put me up for a while. It was messy.'

'God,' I said. 'Poor you.'

'It was OK,' Mum said. 'I was young and full of beans. But anyway, come downstairs and we'll make some lunch and work out what we're going to do with you.'

'What *I'm* going to do with me,' I said, reaching out for the bannister and pulling myself upright.

'No, what we're going to do,' Mum said. 'You're not alone with this one, Dawney. Not for this one and not for nothing else, neither.'

'Anything else, either,' I corrected her. Correcting each other was a sort of running joke in our family.

Mum laughed. 'Ooh, speaking proper now so the little one doesn't pick up bad habits, are we?'

Downstairs in the kitchen, she lit another cigarette while I opened the fridge in search of sandwich ingredients.

'So wh'happen with you and Billy?' she asked. 'Cos I have noticed he hasn't been around, but I didn't like to ask.'

'He said he *doesn't feel the same about me anymore*,' I said, using a silly, middle-class voice to mock him. 'He says *something's been broken*.'

'Because?'

I shrugged.

'Oh come on, Dawn,' Mum said. 'You were all loved up and then suddenly you wasn't no more. Something must've happened.'

'Rob,' I said, so quietly, I wasn't sure she'd heard. 'Rob happened.'

'You told him?' Mum said, so shocked that she actually put her cigarette down so that she could put her hands together in prayer. 'You *told* your Billy about Rob?'

I paused buttering the bread just long enough to look up at her and nod sheepishly.

'Why?' she said. 'Why the hell would you do that, Dawn?'

'Well, he was shagging Siobhan, wasn't he?' I explained. 'He said he wanted us to have a free and easy relationship.'

'Free and easy,' Mum repeated. 'Of course. It was him who said he doesn't believe in monogamy, right?'

'Yes,' I said. 'Not for him, he doesn't, at any rate.'

'Meaning?'

'Meaning that when he found out about Rob—'

'But you said you told him...?'

'OK, as soon as I *told* him about Rob, he went off me,' I said.

'Of course he did,' Mum said. 'Bloody hypocrites.'

'Who are?' I asked. I was scared she was including me.

'Men!' Mum said. 'Why d'you think I never let one stick around? They're bloody hypocrites, one and all.'

'I thought you were in love,' I said. She'd been seeing a new guy called Martin for the last few days, though I hadn't yet met him.

'I am,' she said. 'But that doesn't mean I will be this time next week.'

We talked about it all morning, over numerous cups of tea.

Mum was convinced I was too young to have a baby on my own. That was something I could trust her about, she said, because at my age she'd done exactly that and it had been an 'absolute bloody nightmare'.

'So you regret having me,' I said, feigning outrage. 'That's lovely, Mum. Cheers!'

'No, I don't,' she said. 'Not one bit. But I *do* wish I'd waited a few years.'

I could see the logic of what she was saying. There were plenty of single girls my age pushing prams around Millmead, and none of them made it look fun.

'What it all boils down to,' Mum said, summing up, 'is whether you want to snag that Billy. If you love him enough to have a baby with 'im and settle down and everything.'

I reminded Mum, yet again, that Billy wasn't necessarily responsible, but she insisted it didn't matter. 'If you tell him it's his, he'll believe you,' she said. 'And if he's daft enough to want to be a father, then you're sorted. But like I say, he probably won't. He'll probably just bugger off anyway.'

And I'm ashamed to say that I toyed with the idea – I seriously gave it some thought. But after a cheese and Branston sandwich and another cuppa, I realised that not only did I not believe Billy could be fooled, but, even if he could, I didn't want to 'snag' him. What I *wanted* was for him to be head over heels in love with me. And that boat, sadly, had sailed.

* * *

At first, the consultation went well enough.

Mum, who was with me, took it upon herself to answer all of the questions, so I sat there in a weird spacey trance, merely nodding to agree with Mum's answers.

But then the doctor lifted up my T-shirt and spread cold slimy gel over my belly, and I was forced to understand that this was about me.

'So, we're just going to check how far you're gone,' the woman said.

'She told you,' Mum said. 'It's six weeks.'

'Yes,' the doctor replied. 'But that's something we need to check.'

She turned the screen a bit further away from me and slithered around with her scanner. I looked over at the rain dribbling down the window and thought, for some reason, about sledging down the hill in Tivoli Park.

'Yes, I'd say six weeks is about right,' she said. 'You can barely see the heartbeat.'

'So just pills?' Mum asked. 'No need for any sort of surgery?'

But that word 'heartbeat' had jerked me back into the room.

'The baby's heartbeat?' I asked, tensing up. 'Or d'you mean mine?'

'Yes, the foetus has a heartbeat,' the doctor said. 'But it's barely visible at this stage.'

'Show me,' I said, trying to sit up so I could lean towards the screen.

'Dawn,' Mum said. 'Don't. Trust me. Really. Don't.'

'But I want to see,' I said.

'Really, darlin',' Mum said. 'It won't help.'

'It's entirely up to you,' the doctor said, actually turning the screen a little further away from me.

'Show me!' I insisted.

And so with a sigh she turned the screen back towards me.

At first, I sighed with relief. Because the thing on the screen was far more dumpling than baby. I'd had this terrifying idea that he'd be looking out at me, staring right at me. I'd even imagined him waving.

'So that's the head,' the doctor said, pointing at part of the grey on-screen blob. 'Or at least, where the head will be. *Would* be, if we let things continue their course.'

'Right,' I said, relaxing. 'It's fine. When you said heartbeat, I thought you could actually see it.'

'Let me just...' she said, clicking on her keyboard and sliding the scanner head a little lower on my belly.

'OK, can we just...?' Mum said, trying to quit while we were ahead. 'I think that's enough.'

'There!' the doctor said, proudly. 'You see that? That's a pulse of about 120. It sounds fast, but at this stage it's perfectly normal.'

'Dawn,' Mum said. 'Enough! Let's just get the prescription and get out of here.'

'Shh!' I said, peering in at the screen. 'Can you move that closer?' I asked, and the woman frowned at me and then with a shrug moved the screen so that it was right next to me.

It was nothing really, just a fluffy grey image of something pulsing at about two beats per second. I don't really know how to explain this to you, but an unfamiliar, warm, wonderful feeling washed over me. I once read something about how bonding hormones flood your body when you're pregnant, and maybe that's all it was. But I remember thinking, 'A heartbeat! My baby has a *heartbeat!*' And in those few seconds, my pregnancy ceased being a problem to be solved and became a potential baby – a potential with a heartbeat!

My next thought was, *Billy's* baby, though of course that was something I didn't know. But in that moment, as I looked at the blob on the screen, it seemed like I knew. I felt, in that moment, 100 per cent certain that I was looking at Billy's blob, Billy's baby – Billy's baby with a heartbeat. And for some inexplicable reason, I realised that I loved it already, that I loved it more than anything I'd ever loved.

'Is it a boy or a girl?' I asked, absurdly imagining it with curly blond hair in a tiny green jumpsuit.

The doctor laughed and turned the screen back away from me 'You can't tell that yet!' she said. 'You wouldn't know that until at least fourteen weeks.'

'Right,' I said. 'So is that when I have to come back?'

At the bus stop outside the hospital, Mum was chewing the inside of her cheek, a surefire sign that she was worried. 'We'll just go home and think about it all again,' she said.

'I can't,' I whispered. 'I'm sorry, Mum, but I can't.'

'I know what you mean,' Mum said, 'But you just need to sleep on it. You'll see things more clearly once you've had time to think. Luckily you still have a few weeks before things get messy.'

'Sure,' I said. 'Whatever.'

'She shouldn't have showed you the ultrasound,' Mum said.

And though I was thinking that the moment I'd seen that ultrasound was one of the most amazing moments of my life; even though just the thought of that beating heart made me want to smile, I faked a shrug. 'Maybe,' I said. And then I added, in my head, *But she did.*

THREE

DAWN (BY ROB)

Girl, wooden bench, tears.

The first thing I noticed was that she was crying. What I mean is that at first I didn't realise it was her at all.

Because my mate Andy was sunning it up in Majorca, I was walking his poodle in Dane Park. As I rounded a corner, I saw a girl on a bench, crying. It was only when we got closer that I realised it was Dawn.

I let Choupi off his lead, knowing that he'd run up and give her a good licking. I figured that some dog-love was exactly what she needed and, by the time I'd reached the bench, she was no longer crying, but instead laughing as she tried to push the dog away.

'Your dog...' she said, as she struggled. 'Your dog is out of control!'

'Choupi! Heel!' I shouted, then, 'Sorry, he doesn't seem to listen to me at all.'

'Rob!' she said, shocked to discover it was me. She continued to wrestle with the dog.

I clipped the lead onto Choupi's collar and dragged him away. 'Sorry about that,' I said again.

'He's made my face all wet,' Dawn said, wiping away what I knew were, in reality, tears.

I slid in beside her on the bench and asked, 'So what's up?' I'd meant it in the English sense, as in *what's wrong*, but Dawn thought or chose to think I'd meant *what's new?*

'Nothing much,' she replied. 'Other than being licked to death by your dog.'

'Not my dog,' I said, raising my palms. I took a ball from my pocket and threw it across the green to gain a few seconds of calm. 'I'm just walking him for some friends who are away on holiday.'

'Oh,' Dawn said. 'Right. I was struggling to imagine you with a poodle.'

'And yet,' I said, 'if I was gonna have a dog, I'd want this one. I love him to bits. But anyway, what's going on with you? You looked like you might be a bit upset?'

'Oh?' Dawn said. 'Upset? Me? Nah!' It was a half-hearted sort of denial, one that seemed to say, *Let's pretend I wasn't, OK?*

She turned to look across the green at Choupi, who'd abandoned the ball in favour of some pigeons he was chasing around. I suspected she was struggling not to cry all over again.

'Tell me,' I said, placing one hand on her shoulder. 'I can take it.'

She sighed and looked back at me, smiling weakly. 'Oh, it's nothing. Just a bit of bad news. It's nothing. Really. I'm all over the place at the moment. Girly stuff.'

'Choupi! Here!' I shouted. He'd started harassing an Alsatian being walked by a man who looked too old and frail to control him. 'So come on!' I urged. 'Tell me. I'm good with people's problems. Everyone says so.'

Dawn smiled half-heartedly. 'Mum actually said that about you.'

'She's OK, is she? Your mum?'

Dawn nodded. 'She's fine. Mad as ever, but...'

'Then it must be Billy,' I said. I hadn't wanted to say his name, but I couldn't think of another way to find out. 'I'm assuming you're still together?'

That started her crying all over again, and a glimmer of hope rose up in me.

'He's gone,' she said, struggling to speak, and, evil git that I am, I felt ecstatic. 'I just went round there and he's gone.'

I took her to Andy's house for coffee. It was near the park and I had to take Choupi back there anyway. It was a sunny day, so we sat in his tiny back garden while Choupi went sniffing around the edges, just in case something might have changed radically during our walk.

Between sips, Dawn explained how she'd been going to Billy's place for over a month. She always told stories in a very literal step-by-step sort of way. 'So I said this... and he said that...' She never missed out a step.

There had never been anyone at home, she explained. She'd phoned the house in the evenings too, but no one had answered.

Until today, that is, when she'd arrived to find Billy's mother in the garden.

They'd been away at their holiday home in France, Dawn explained, using a silly posh voice when she said *holiday home*. Dawn had asked Billy's mum if he'd come back with them and if she could see him, and Billy's mother had laughed because Dawn had got the wrong end of the stick. Billy hadn't been on holiday with them at all. *Billy* was back at college in Manchester.

'College?' I repeated.

'I know. He never told me he was at college,' Dawn said. 'Can you imagine that? He's in his third year, apparently. Doing Architecture.'

'So he always knew he was going back at the end of the summer?'

Dawn shrugged. 'I suppose he must've,' she said.

'But he didn't tell you? He never mentioned it? Not once? Not even a hint?'

'*No*, Rob,' she said, sounding annoyed. 'He didn't.'

'Sorry,' I said. 'But it sounds like—' But then I stopped myself and petted Choupi instead.

'Sounds like what?' Dawn prompted.

I shrugged. 'Sounds like the guy's a dick. Maybe you're better off without him.'

'Yeah, maybe I would be,' she said, visibly tearing up again and then turning away from me to hide the fact. 'But the thing is, Rob, I'm pregnant.'

I frowned, struggling to take her words in. I had a lump in my throat before I could work out why, and, when I opened my mouth to speak, nothing came out. An unfamiliar feeling was sweeping through me – a sense of warmth seemed to be welling up from some previously unknown place, deep within. It'll sound a bit weird I suppose, because it's kind of hard to explain, but it seemed like it was physical before it became mental, like a sort of weird lovely full-body rush. A new emotion, a new feeling, a new sense of hope, but for the time being without any kind of thought process as to why I was feeling that way.

Unable to speak, I patted Dawn's back and waited until she continued, telling me in dribs and drabs how she felt. She spoke to me like a mate, or perhaps a brother, definitely not like someone she'd slept with, and not like someone who might be madly in love with her, either.

But I was in love with her – that's the thing. She was pretty and she was funny and she was clever. Just sitting next to her made me feel warm and deep-down happy. Now that she was pregnant as well, she represented everything I'd ever wanted and everything I was terrified I'd never have.

'So how far gone are you?' I finally asked. She'd started talking about how it wasn't too late to 'get rid of it'.

'Ten weeks,' she said. 'So it's still an option. If I can get my head around it.'

'Ten weeks,' I said, scratching my ear as I worked out the dates.

She looked at me questioningly, then laughed. 'Oh, Rob!' she said. 'We did it once and it wasn't even... C'mon.'

'Once is enough,' I said. 'I mean, do you know it's Billy's? Is there actually some way you can tell?'

'Yes,' she said, 'It's Billy's.' But because she looked away again, I could tell that she was lying and she didn't know at all. It was as much as I could do to stop myself from breaking out in a grin.

I reached out to take her hand in mine. I half expected her to pull away, but she didn't. She let me do it, which had to be a good sign, didn't it?

'Billy's a knob,' I told her. 'You know that, right?'

'Yeah,' Dawn said. 'I'm slowly working that out.'

'You deserve better,' I said, squeezing her fingers. 'You deserve much, much better.'

She turned back towards me then, and as her eyes searched my face I could tell she was considering it for the first time.

Once I'd fed Choupi and washed up our cups, I gave her a lift home, and by the time I drove away the decision had been made to woo her.

I'm a very organised, logical kind of guy – something my friends often joke about – so I did what I always do when faced with a complex problem. I sat down and wrote out a plan.

Phase one was dealing with Billy. I figured that if he hadn't even told her he was at uni, he definitely wasn't going to give it all up to become a dad. But until Billy was done and dusted, there was no space in Dawn's head for Yours Truly. So I'd encourage her to contact him. Hell, I'd drive her up to Manchester if that's what was needed to get him out of her system.

Phase two was to make myself seem essential. I was good at listening to people's problems, and lord knows Dawn had a few of those. I was good at talking to girls generally in fact, just not so good at seducing them. Dawn would need help, and she'd need support, and she'd need problem-solving. These were skills I reckoned I could make work for me.

As for phase three, well, that was the biggy. Because phase three meant moving out of my flat. There was no way we could bring up a baby in my place, so it was obvious what needed to be done.

Phase one went perfectly to plan. I went to the Wheatsheaf on Monday evening and asked Tracey – Dawn's mum – if she could get her out for a drink the next night. Tracey loved me to bits, so that worked out a treat. Dawn and I sat in the corner while I listened to all her Billy-shaped woes.

Dawn declined my offer of a drive to Manchester, choosing to write to Billy instead. And just two days later he phoned her, apparently both panicked and angry. He'd pay for her to get rid of it, he said, something Dawn laughed about, saying he'd obviously seen too many films set in America where the NHS doesn't exist. But that was the limit of Billy's involvement. He was young, he was having fun, and he had his whole wonderful life ahead of him, he said. The last thing he wanted was marriage or babies.

I commented that some people sure had a weird idea of what a wonderful life looked like, because without kids or love, what was left? Dawn gave me that gentle searching gaze all over again, and I reckoned I'd gained a few points.

But then she asked me if I could drive her somewhere that

Wednesday. Her mum was having to work that day and she had an appointment at three she couldn't miss.

'Sure,' I said. 'Where's the appointment?'

'The hospital,' she said. 'I've decided to take the pill that ends this nonsense once and for all.'

* * *

I picked her up just before two. I had to 'pop in' somewhere first, I said.

The place I had to 'pop in' to was a house in Cliftonville, up by the lido – one of those washed-out bed-and-breakfast places that had been used, for some years, as temporary housing for DSS recipients, but which now had a battered for-sale sign outside.

I knew the inside was going to be rough, but I could just about borrow enough to buy the place and if there was one thing I had mastered it was DIY. The estate agent, young, smug, dandy, was standing outside fiddling with the enormous knot of his tie.

'So this is the hallway,' he said, as he let us in.

I winked at Dawn and murmured, 'Just in case you didn't realise,' but she didn't react. She was, understandably, thinking about other things.

The place was basically a wreck, all cracked lino, boarded-up windows and mouldy silicone joints. It had a leaky roof over the top two bedrooms, a bathroom that had been beyond cleaning for decades, and a chipped seventies Formica kitchen. But it was big – five bedrooms in all – and had a sea view from the upstairs front bedrooms, along with a surprisingly well tended backyard.

Once the tour was over, I led Dawn back to the van.

'So?' I asked, once she'd buckled up. 'What d'you think?'

'About what?' she asked. She hadn't realised where I was

going with this and her naivety actually made me feel a bit gooey about her.

'The house,' I said, softly.

'Oh, it's huge,' she said. 'A huge, three-storey shit-hole. It's like a hotel from the 1930s or something. The 1830s, actually. Who's it for? They doing a remake of *Friday the 13th* or something?'

'It's for us,' I said, ignoring the joke. 'And it won't be a shit-hole once I've fixed it up.'

'Us?' she repeated. She seemed more startled than outraged.

'You, me, and the baby,' I said.

'Oh, for fuck's sake, Rob,' she said. 'I'm on my way to get an abortion here. Or did you think we were going to Dreamland?'

'Yeah, I know,' I said, calmly. I'd expected to meet resistance. I'd even noted it in my bullet points. 'But what if you didn't?'

'It's not yours, you know,' she said. 'It's Billy's. The baby's Billy's, Rob.'

'You don't know that,' I told her. 'No one knows that.'

'Oh, I do, though,' she said. 'That's the thing.'

'How?' I asked.

'I can just tell,' she said, glancing at her feet. 'I can sense it.'

'And what if I can sense that it's mine?' I asked. I tried to reach out to touch her belly, but it was a bad move – too much, too intimate, too soon. She pulled away, and I felt bad. 'What if *I* can sense we'd make a bloody amazing family together, Dawn?' I asked.

'Oh...' she said. And then she made a strange *pfff!* noise, waved me away like a fly, and let herself back out of the car.

I caught up with her in Dalby Square by the green, and grabbed her sleeve to make her stop. 'Get off me,' she said, then louder, 'GET OFF ME!'

A passing guy with tattooed knuckles crossed over to ask Dawn if she was 'having trouble'.

'Oh, just fuck off!' Dawn told him, making me smirk.

His sympathy switched immediately to me. 'Good luck with that one, mate,' he said, shaking his head and trudging off.

'You were *supposed* to drive me to the effing hospital, Rob,' she said, and I saw that her eyes were shiny with tears.

'And I will, Dawn,' I said, grabbing her arm again as she tried to move away. 'I promise you, I will. We've still got...' I checked my watch. 'See, it's only two-thirty. We've got loads of time if that's what you really want. I just want to be sure—'

'What I really want?' she spat. 'Jesus, Christ, what planet are you on, Rob? Planet bloody... Zorg?'

'Planet Zorg?' I repeated. I loved everything she said so much it was hard not to smile whenever she spoke. 'Where *is* planet Zorg, Dawney?'

'Oh shut up,' she said.

'Just think about it,' I persisted. 'Think about what I'm offering here.'

She tried to pull away again, so I grabbed her sleeve and held on tight. 'I love you, Dawn,' I said. 'I know you don't believe that's true, but it is. I've loved you since I first laid eyes on you. And I'm not perfect, but I am one of the good guys. Really, I am. And I want to make a home for you and our baby in that big house back there.'

'Even if it's not *our* baby?' she asked, sounding like she was intentionally being cruel. But that 'if' was music to my ears. 'Even if it's *Billy's* baby?'

'We'll never know, will we?' I said. 'So that's something we can just decide for ourselves. If we decide that it's ours, then it's ours.'

'Just drive me to the hospital, Rob,' she said. 'Or if you don't want to do that, then at least let go of my effing arm so that I can walk.'

So I drove her to the hospital. She sat beside me in stony silence.

I stopped at the bus stop outside the hospital and asked her if she was sure about this.

'Yes,' she said. 'Yes, I'm sure.'

So I pulled into the hospital car park and bought a ticket at the pay-and-display. 'I got two hours,' I told Dawn, 'but if it's not enough I can get more.'

'Two hours?' she said. 'Are you getting an abortion too?'

I shrugged. 'I assumed you'd want someone to hold your hand. Someone to drive you home afterwards?'

Dawn shook her head as though I'd said something crazy and then started to stride towards the main entrance. 'All they do is give me a stupid pill, Rob,' she muttered over her shoulder. 'And then another one I take at home and it's done.'

'OK then,' I said, trotting to catch up. 'Well, I can drive you home after your pill.'

When we reached the main entrance she paused and took a deep breath. 'Here goes,' she said. And then she stunned me by grabbing my hand.

We had to wait in a queue at the main desk for almost ten minutes and holding hands started to feel awkward and sweaty. I'd hardly ever held hands with a girl in public before and it made me feel self-conscious. I thought about this as we stood there, and realised that I couldn't even dig up a memory of having held hands with my parents. I was actually a bit relieved when she released me from her grip.

'I've got an appointment for a medical termination,' Dawn announced, when it was finally our turn. 'But the thing is, I think I've changed my mind.'

I'm pretty sure I gasped out loud. I turned to look at her, but she was rigidly avoiding my gaze.

'Is it today, your appointment?' the receptionist asked.

Dawn nodded. 'It's right now, actually,' she said. 'Well, in four minutes.'

'But you're not going through with it.'

'No,' Dawn said. 'No, I don't think so.'

'Then you should probably go through and tell them that yourself,' the woman said.

'Yeah...' Dawn said, glancing in the direction the woman was indicating, and then back towards the entrance. 'Sorry,' she added. 'No can do.'

And then before I understood what was happening, she was striding back across the hall.

'Your name?' the receptionist called out. 'Miss? Your name!' But it was too late. Dawn had slipped through the doors.

'It's Weaver,' I told her, turning back to face the counter and pulling an embarrassed grimace. 'Dawn Weaver.'

'Thank you!' the woman said, then, scrunching up her nose. 'Don't worry, it happens all the time. Most of them don't even bother to cancel.'

'Right,' I said. 'Of course.'

'You don't look *too* devastated,' she said, giving me a friendly wink.

'I'm sorry?' I asked, realising as I said it that I was grinning stupidly. I tried to wrestle my face back under control.

'... about Ms Weaver's change of heart,' the woman said. 'You look pretty happy about it, actually.'

'Yeah,' I said. 'Yeah, I'm... yeah...'

Out in the car park, Dawn was sitting on the bonnet of my van.

'I'm not living with you,' she said, swiping tears from her eyes and sounding feisty. 'Just so you know.'

'OK,' I said, still struggling to look serious. 'Fine.'

'In fact this is nothing to do with you at all. I just couldn't go through with it, that's all.'

I nodded enthusiastically. 'That's fine,' I told her. 'I'll be here as much or as little as you need.'

'Right,' Dawn said. 'As long as that's clear.'

'It is,' I said. 'Crystal.'

'And what I need now is for you to take me home.'

I nodded. 'Sure,' I said. 'I can do that.'

'But can we call in at the pub, on the way?'

'The pub?'

'Yeah,' she said, with a sigh. 'We need to tell Mum what's just happened, and she's really not gonna be thrilled about it. You'll be good at calming her down.'

We, I thought, as I unlocked the door. No word had ever made me happier.

FOUR

LUCY BOOP (BY DAWN)

Rob's campaign to woo me was more a war of attrition than a classical attempt at seduction.

Mum, I suspected, was giving him intelligence reports, so that if I needed to go to a clinic, or a gynaecologist, or the DHS, he'd magically pop up to drive me there. Rob was everywhere, every time that I could even think about possibly needing him, and often a few minutes before I'd even realised I needed him. Sometimes I'd see him drive up and think, *Shit! What have I forgotten I have to do today?*

I wasn't falling for the whole thing though.

I mean, the idea that someone could worm their way into being your partner – I even suspected Rob was aiming for *husband* – through ambition and sheer endurance was just silly. But I'd come to admit that he was, as he'd said, 'one of the good ones' and had accepted him into my life to the point that if, for a few days, he was too busy with jobs to be around, it would cross my mind that I missed him. I'd ask Wayne to do something basic like make me a cup of tea or nip to the shop for a Yorkie bar and realise, when he snarkily refused, that the only person I knew who'd say 'yes' – the only person I'd ever met who would never, ever refuse – was Rob.

Sometimes I'd be out shopping and remember one of Rob's silly jokes and find myself grinning stupidly in public. Or I'd find myself running bits of conversations I wanted to have with him through my mind, working out my own replies in advance so I could impress him with my wit. So no, I wasn't falling for the whole thing. But Rob was definitely worming his way into my psyche.

Mum was definitely on his side, there was no doubt about that. She and Rob got on so well – laughing together and dancing around, even pinching and tickling each other – that I sometimes wondered if it wasn't my mother he fancied.

'That boy,' Mum would say, 'is smitten!'

'Yeah, but with you or with me?' I'd ask.

'And he's so practical,' she'd say, ignoring the question. 'Everything in this house, everything what was ever broke, he fixed it!'

It was true, too. The wobbly kitchen cabinet doors were no longer wonky. The S-bend under the sink no longer dripped. Even the bathroom heater worked, something that, until Rob's arrival, had never happened in living memory.

There was something incredible about Rob's energy levels too, something almost otherworldly, because he managed all of this – mending Mum's council house and driving me back and forth to appointments; doing his day job of rewiring other people's houses – while buying and fixing up his own new house in Cliftonville.

'I'll sell it,' he said, when I asked him what the point of buying such a big house was. 'If you don't change your mind, then I'll just sell it. I'll make a packet. And then you'll want to be with me, cos I'll be rich!'

I laughed at that and told him I wasn't going to change my

mind. That I was never going to change my mind no matter how rich he became.

But Rob just shrugged and I wasn't sure if it was because he didn't believe me, or because he no longer cared. Despite my protests to the contrary, I hoped it was that he didn't believe me. Because being cared about definitely felt good.

As my pregnancy progressed, I'd call round to his new house more and more often and sit on a box to chat while Rob sanded or painted or rewired. I'd take the Pretenders or Sonic Youth CDs that (thanks to Billy) I now listened to, and force Rob to turn off Radio One. Once or twice I even picked up a paintbrush or some sandpaper to chip in. Getting involved in Rob's project felt nice, but – and I'm not sure if this will make sense to anyone except me – it felt nice in a melancholy sort of way. It was as if that time with Rob was a demonstration of what I *could* have had if only life had been different. I'd wonder, inevitably, if Billy was also painting a wall somewhere, in another house in another town with another girl. I'd wonder if he ever thought about me.

* * *

The baby was due mid-June so, at the beginning of the month when I went to visit Rob, I was waddling more than walking. I'd remained super-skinny, so my pregnancy made me look like I had an exercise ball stuffed up my jumper. My back ached *all* the time.

Rob was in the garden using an electric sander, and when he failed to hear the doorbell I went round the back to let myself in through the gate. He had the radio on and was singing along to Cher's 'It's In His Kiss', so I crept up behind him and then said loudly (intentionally making him jump), 'Are you *sure* you're not gay, Rob?' It had become our standard joke and, once he'd re-composed himself and switched off the sander, he gave his stock reply: 'Nope, still not gay. And unfortunately, still in love with you.'

'So what are we doing today, Rob?' I asked in my *Blue Peter* voice.

'Um, this,' he said, waving the sander at me. 'I did one without sanding it down, but it looked shite, so...' His hair and eyebrows were white from the dust and it made him look as if he'd been disguised by a make-up team to look old. Despite myself I wondered if I'd still be hanging out with him when he was.

'I'm assuming that's not something I can help you with,' I said. 'So shall I just make tea?'

'Tea would be brill,' he said. 'I'm gasping.'

As I turned to leave, I actually peed myself a bit, something that had happened from time to time since I was pregnant. I glanced back at Rob but he was lost to his sanding, and under the circumstances that seemed just as well.

I wobbled across the garden, picking my way between doors and power tools, and went straight inside to the bathroom, where I sat and did my best to wee.

Within a minute or so I began to suspect that something else was going on, and when a cramp stabbed at my insides it seemed to confirm my fears. But for a while, I didn't move, just sitting there as if paralysed, waiting to see what would happen next. I'd thought this final episode of pregnancy would begin in another two weeks, and I'd expected a more dramatic opening too – something more tidal, not lukewarm wee dribbling down my leg.

Eventually I stuffed a wad of bog roll down my knickers and tried to stand, but things were speeding up and even Rob's extra-soft three-ply wasn't up to the job. 'Shit!' I muttered. *Why here? Why now?*

I grabbed a thick towel from the pile in Rob's bathroom, regretting that they were all white, and rolled it and wedged it between my thighs before waddling back to the door, feeling scared – because I was early – and embarrassed, or rather mortified, by my uncontrollable leakage.

'Rob!' I called out, but my voice came out weaker than I'd intended and the sander was too loud for him to hear. 'ROB!' I tried again, but he still couldn't hear me.

'Jesus,' I muttered, and I considered leaving through the front door; maybe calling for a cab and vanishing before he'd even noticed I was gone. But the truth was that a taxi seemed even more embarrassing than involving Rob, so I reached indoors and yanked the extension lead from the socket.

Rob peered at his sander comically before tracing the path of the cable to my hand.

'Tea ready?' he asked, then, noticing the rolled towel, 'Oh! Are you OK?'

'This is...' I said, shaking my head. 'It's kind of embarrassing. But I need you to take me to the hospital, Rob.'

'But is it...? Isn't it...? I mean, isn't this too...?' he stammered, dropping the sander and jogging to my side.

'Yeah, it's too early, but I think this is it.' I gasped, grabbing at Rob's arm, as a stabbing cramp gripped my insides. 'Oh God,' I said when I could speak again. 'I don't know if this is normal, but if it is... *fuck!*'

'Looks like the sanding will have to wait,' Rob said, his expression ecstatic in a way that made him look as if he'd just found Jesus. 'We're going to have a baby!'

Even then, even in that state of fear and embarrassment and pain, I made myself correct him. '*I'm* having a baby, Rob,' I said. 'Not *you*, not *us*... me.'

'Sure,' Rob said. 'Whatever. I'll get the van.'

* * *

Giving birth is bloody awful, and anyone who tells you otherwise is either lying to you, or themselves, or most probably both. Arguably, it's all worth it in the end, and our brains are made to help us forget just how awful the whole thing was, but that's just as well, really, because otherwise no one would *ever* do it twice. But don't be fooled: in the moment it's simply the most dreadful, painful, endlessly excruciating thing most women will ever have to live through.

Natural births were trending by the early nineties and, thanks to Thatcher's cutbacks, NHS resources were stretched. So I was repeatedly asked just how much medical involvement I actually wanted. Doctors asked me this; nurses asked me this; friends asked me this. Everyone seemed to be hoping I'd say, 'Oh, it's fine, I'll just get some evening primrose oil or whatever and sort it myself.' Shelley, who since Billy's disappearance I was seeing again, seriously wanted me to have it in a paddling pool in our lounge. 'We could film it all on Dad's camcorder,' she said. 'Wouldn't that be great?'

But I wasn't having any of it. Madonna might like to mix up the pain and the pleasure, but pain wasn't my thing at all. I wanted doctors and nurses and drugs, lots of drugs – all the drugs – and I wasn't embarrassed to say so repeatedly as the months went by.

Naively, I'd assumed this would mean my birth would be painless. I mean, I understood it would be *uncomfortable*, but the year was 1991, after all. We had shuttles flying to space stations and home computers and video games and carphones... Surely all those clever scientists had managed to solve something as everyday as the pain of having a baby.

But whether all the *men* who dominate science simply hadn't been that interested in what women go through in order to keep the species going, or whether the team in Margate hospital were just extra-stingy with their medication, the result was that, 1991 or not, it really, *really* hurt.

Eventually, after hours and hours and *hours* of snotty weeping and sweating and screaming at people to 'do something', they finally gave me an epidural, and almost immediately the whole nightmare sailed off over the horizon. I remember sinking into a soft, warm sea of pain-free exhausted nothingness and being furious about the fact they hadn't done it twelve hours earlier.

Rob did his best to be present at the birth. He actually seemed to think I might let him watch a baby, an actual, massive baby, push its way out of my fanny, I mean, *as if!* I had to get a nurse to eject him from the room so that in the end it was just me and Mum present for the greatest show on Earth.

Once it was over – something which, thanks to sheer exhaustion and the epidural, I was only vaguely aware of – they wiped her clean and handed her to me, and, oh my God, I was shocked at how beautiful she was. That's the moment you forget the pain. It happens pretty quickly.

In films people always seem to be worried there'll be something major wrong with the baby – missing arms or legs or what-have-you – but I'd believed the gynaecologist when she'd told me my baby would be fine. No, what I'd been worried about was having one of those ugly babies, the ones that look like they've popped out of a horror film.

Trudy Rogers – a friend of Shelley's who lived in the Arlington flats – had given birth to a baby who looked like Shane MacGowan. Actually, it was worse even than that. He was so wrinkly and wizened that he looked how you might imagine Shane MacGowan's *grandfather*.

We'd all told her he was beautiful – as you do – something Trudy must have realised was a lie. And then we'd all laughed ourselves silly about it as we walked home. So I knew that ugly babies could happen. They could even happen to pretty girls like Trudy. And, superficial as it might sound, that was the terror I obsessed over.

But, like I say, even straight from the oven Lucy was a stunner, and I was so relieved I burst into tears. Sometimes I'd have the beginning of a thought, wondering *why* Lucy was so stunningly pretty and who, if anyone, she looked like, but I'd manage to cut that thought process short every time. It really was best not to go there.

Rob was our first visitor. He'd been waiting in the lobby all night.

'She looks like Betty Boop,' he said, and, with her little wisp of hair and her big eyes, I knew exactly what he meant. He bopped her on the nose and said, 'Hello, Betty Boop.'

'It's Lucy, actually,' I told him.

He nodded. 'Cool,' he said. 'I like it.' Then, 'Hello, Lucy Boop.' He glanced over at me with tears in his eyes. 'You must feel so proud,' he said. 'I know I do.'

I started to smile at this but then my smile slipped into a frown. Something about what he'd said troubled me but I was so shattered it took me a moment to figure it out.

'Rob,' I said. 'You're not to... you know...'

He frowned at me and gave a tiny shake of his head.

'... to claim this,' I finally said. It sounded cruel, saying it out loud, but I felt it needed to be done. 'Don't start claiming her as your own. We're not a couple here and you know we don't know—'

'Yeah, yeah,' Rob said, interrupting me. 'Sure. I know all that.'

'So don't go telling people, all right?' I was imagining him calling round the houses telling everyone he was a dad.

'Telling people?' he repeated. 'Of course I'm going to *tell* people.'

'Sure, but I mean, not like you're the father,' I said, thinking it sounded even crueller. 'Don't go phoning all your mates. Don't go announcing it to your parents, either.'

Rob snorted at that. 'Like *that's* gonna happen...' he said.

'Oh,' I said, a little surprised. I'd have hated it if he'd said he *was* going to tell them, or, worse, that he already had. But I was also quite shocked that he had no desire to.

'Is it bad?' I asked. 'With your folks, I mean. Have you fallen out big-time?'

'Yeah, something like that,' Rob said. He'd stopped looking at me and returned to staring at Lucy in her cot.

'*What* did you fall out about?' I asked. 'I don't think you ever told me.'

'Yeah, I'd rather not talk about them, right now,' Rob said, still without even looking at me. 'I'd rather talk about lovely Lucy Boop here if it's all the same to you.'

And I was too tired to pursue the subject anyway. We could have that conversation another time.

* * *

Back home I had an endless stream of visitors.

'I can't believe you went through with it,' Shelley said. 'You're so brave!'

'I can't believe you went through with it,' Wayne parroted. 'You're an unmarried teenage mother. Congratulations!'

But compliments or insults, it was all the same to me. I was so in love with little Lucy Boop that nothing and no one could touch me.

I was exhausted after giving birth – more than I'd ever been before. And as those first days and weeks went by, that tiredness got worse, not better.

Lucy would wake up screaming for milk every three hours 24/7 and on a bad day it could be as often as every two. I was so shattered from lack of sleep that I felt as if I'd been hollowed out and turned into some kind of mothering feeding robot. My brain seemed to have stopped working, and I was left stumbling from room to room like a zombie, the baby clamped to my breast.

Mum and Wayne, who were also constantly woken by Lucy's nocturnal terrors, were looking pretty red-eyed too. 'If I fail my exams,' Wayne told me, 'It'll be entirely because you couldn't keep your legs together, Sis.'

'Thanks, Uncle Wayne,' I said flatly. 'That really, really helps.'

Rob called in roughly every other day, delivering nappies or babygrows or chocolates – I don't think he once turned up empty-handed.

'You're the best husband any woman never had,' Mum told him.

'Thanks,' he said. 'I try.'

And then, on the last Saturday of June, Mum declared that I needed a break. 'You're smelly and so out of it that you're more hindrance than help,' she said. 'Plus, you need a haircut.'

I was so numb from lack of sleep by that point that I couldn't even begin to think about whether what she was saying was fair. But through the fog I conceded that the smelly part, at least, was true, and that, even though I couldn't really remember what the point of them was any more, it *had* been months since I'd had a haircut.

'Are you sure about this?' I asked.

'I'm sure,' she said, quite literally wrenching Lucy from my arms.

'But she'll need feeding,' I countered, reaching out to try to take her back.

'I can give her a bottle,' Mum said. 'Believe it or not, I do know how.'

I went to my bedroom first for a lie-down. If I could just get twenty minutes' kip, I reckoned I'd have the energy to at least decide what to do next. But then Lucy started screaming down-stairs, and it was a noise that seemed to have been designed by God to be utterly impossible to ignore. It bit into the core of me and the only possible reaction was to run to her.

'Give her here,' I told Mum flatly, once I'd resigned myself and returned downstairs.

'She cries with you too!' Mum replied, feigning offence.

'I know,' I said. 'But still. Give her here.'

'Just let her cry,' Mum said. 'Let her cry in *my* ear for a change. Run a bath. Put some music on. Or even better, go to Rob's and do it there.'

'Rob's?' I repeated, frowning at her. 'Why would I want to go to Rob's?'

Mum restrained a smirk and nodded sideways at the lounge window, beyond which Rob's white van was pulling up.

'Jesus,' I murmured. 'It's a set-up.'

'Go!' Mum said, using her special no-nonsense voice. 'It'll do you good. It'll do us all good, believe me. I'm sick to death of the sight of you.'

Separating from Lucy was a form of trauma. Not in any logical way – nothing I could reason with myself about – it was more just physical really. It's hard to describe that sort of angst if you've never felt it, but I'll try. You know when you have a nightmare that you've lost your purse with everything in it, or your passport, or your keys or whatever? Well there's that moment when you realise it's gone and the bottom sort of drops out of your stomach. It's a deep, empty sickening feeling that lasts for a few seconds, and leaving Lucy, even with Mum, felt like that. Only it didn't last for a few seconds. It was a perma-nent gaping emptiness that lasted as long as we were apart.

'She'll be fine, you know,' Rob said, patting my knee as he drove.

I hadn't said a word but he'd somehow worked out my state

of mind from the simple fact I was gripping the roof handle in the van as if my life depended on it.

By the time we got to his place I felt lost and deathly, as if being anywhere else, being anywhere without Lucy, was something I'd forgotten how to do. 'What now?' I asked, standing on the polished floorboards of the newly decorated lounge.

Rob shrugged and took his bomber jacket off. 'Run yourself a bath,' he said. 'Have a look around the house. Sit in the sun and read a book. Do whatever you want. And in a bit I'll make you brunch.'

'I need to call Mum,' I said. The second I'd spotted his phone on the shelf, the desire to call home had become urgent.

'She said she'd call you if there's a problem,' Rob reminded me, but he was already handing me the phone.

Once Mum had reassured me, I went upstairs to run a bath. I was shocked by how much the house had changed over the past few weeks, and the bathroom had been entirely remodelled. Rob had tiled it in glossy white and installed one of those old-world standalone baths with poncey gold taps. 'There's a shower on the top floor if you prefer,' he called out from downstairs, so I went on up to the top floor to see what he'd done there.

The front bedroom had been painted in a pleasant dusty-red colour, and simply furnished with a single bed and a wardrobe, both of which looked second-hand but recent. At one side of the room he'd built a half-length wall and behind this a minimal en suite bathroom had appeared. 'Wow,' I murmured. 'Someone's been busy.'

I returned to look out of the window at the grey swell of the sea beyond the lido and for a minute or so I got lost in my own tiredness. But then the clatter of a saucepan downstairs dragged me back to the present moment.

I returned to the landing and, as I pushed open the door to the rear bedroom, I gasped.

Rob had redecorated it as a nursery, painting the walls baby blue and installing a pink cot in the middle of the room. He'd even suspended a mobile above it.

The room was basic but struck me as beautiful just for existing. His gesture was breathtakingly generous but, I quickly decided, also super-presumptuous.

I stood on the landing in a daze, glancing back at the front bedroom with its sea view and then in at the nursery and back again as I tried to work out what it all meant.

And then I leaned over the bannisters to listen just long enough to check that Rob was still in the kitchen before creeping back down to the bathroom so that I could pretend I hadn't seen any of it.

By the time I got home, late afternoon, not only did I feel desperate to see my daughter, but my body was demanding access to her as well. My boobs were actually leaking, leaving damp patches down the front of my T-shirt.

But when Mum greeted me at the front door, she raised one finger to her lips. 'She's only just gone down,' she whispered, 'and if you wake her, I swear, I'll brain you.'

Wondering if my boobs might actually burst, I pulled my cardigan more tightly round me and followed Mum to the lounge, quietly closing the door behind me. 'And Wayne?' I asked.

'In his room catching up on homework,' Mum said softly. 'He's been really struggling, what with the baby crying and everything.'

'Yes,' I said. 'He told me. Repeatedly.'

'So how was it?' Mum asked, smirking.

'How was what?'

'Your day?' she said. 'Wha-cha-get-up-to? Anything nice?'

'Not really,' I said. '... had a bath, ate brunch and had a

snooze on the sofa. That's about it really.' I was being deliberately nonchalant about it all, but the snooze had, in fact, been amazing. I hadn't slept so deeply since Lucy was born, and I'd woken to the sun on my face and the sound of seagulls squawking. It had felt like being in a dream.

'And what did you think?' Mum asked.

'About what?'

'Well, about the rooms.'

'The rooms?'

'The top floor,' Mum said. 'The ones Rob's done up for ya. I chose those colours, by the way. That red... that was me. It's called Tufted Killim.'

'Tufted Killim...' I repeated. 'What the buggery is *Tufted Kilim* when it's at home?'

Mum shrugged. 'It's just the name of the colour, I think.'

'But you chose it?'

'You do like it, don't you? I know you always like the warm colours best. I told Rob, I said, make it something warm and she'll be fine. He wanted green, but I said no! And the blue, what about the blue in the nursery? It's called Sky Dust or something. Did you like it? I mean, I know everyone says it should be pink, but I've never had much truck with all that pink-for-girls nonsense.'

'I don't...' I said, shaking my head, then turning to the TV screen, where Jimmy Savile's mouth was silently blabbering away. 'Look, what's this all about? Why are you advising Rob on colours I like? What are you two up to?'

'Well, you must have... I mean, I'm assuming you two talked, right?'

I shook my head and pouted.

'You didn't?'

'Nope,' I said. 'At least not about anything we haven't talked about before.'

'Oh,' Mum said with a sigh. 'God, I didn't think he'd leave it up to me. That boy can be such a wimp...'

'Well, whatever it is, it looks like he *did* leave it up to you,' I said. 'So go on.'

I pretty much knew what was coming even before she started. Rob had tried various ways of getting me to talk about my living arrangements at Mum's, enquiring how things were 'working out' with the baby, and suggesting it must be a 'bit of a squash'.

'No,' I'd told him, heading him off at the pass every time. 'It's working out great, actually, but thanks for asking.'

He'd offered me that top room for my siesta, too, and when I'd refused he'd tried to give me a tour of the house. But I'd said my legs were tired and I'd just have a kip on the sofa if it was all the same to him.

'We can't go on like this,' Mum said, at the end of her speech. 'You know we can't, Dawn. We're all shattered. Wayne's worried about failing his exams and I don't want him ending up...'

'Like me?' I said.

'That's not what I was going to say at all.'

'You're right,' I said. 'Can't have that.'

'But look... I'm dead on my feet at work, cos I'm so tired. You look more dreadful every day—'

'Thanks.'

'But you *do*, sweetheart. You really do.'

'*Really*, thanks!' I said.

'So...'

'So?'

Mum shrugged. She couldn't bring herself to say it.

'You're kicking me out,' I said. 'That's lovely, Mum.'

'I'm not kicking you out at all,' she said.

'Good, then that's settled, I'll stay.'

'But it makes sense, sweetheart,' Mum insisted. 'Just think about it. Rob's got that huge place all to himself and—'

'I'm not sleeping with Rob just so that you and Wayne can get a good night's sleep!' I exclaimed.

'Oh, who said anything about *sleeping* with him?' Mum asked, looking shocked. 'You silly sausage! Honestly! No, it's just he's got that big place and he's out all day, every day, and there's a room for you and a lovely room for Lucy and a garden and the seafront and everything. You... we *all* need some space and peace and quiet. Rob needs the cash—'

'Cash?' I said. 'What cash? I don't have any cash.'

'But if you move out of here you can get housing benefit, can't you? So that helps Rob with his mortgage too.'

'Are you aware, dear Mother, that he's in love with me?' I asked.

'Of course I'm aware, I'm not stupid.'

'So...?' I said, shrugging and raising my eyebrows in a way that invited her to think it through.

'I'm... Is... Look... is that supposed to be a downside?' Mum asked. 'Is the fact that you've got a lovely bloke – because I think even you'd have to admit, he's a lovely bloke...'

I waited for her to continue. 'Go on,' I said, eventually.

'Admit it,' she said, 'and I'll go on.'

'OK, he's a lovely bloke! So what? He also happens to be the ultimate creepy stalker!' I glanced back at the TV. On the screen Jimmy Savile was sliding his arm round a teenage girl on *Top of the Pops*, and I admitted to myself that Rob perhaps wasn't *the* ultimate creepy stalker.

'So you need somewhere to live—'

'Only I don't,' I interrupted.

'Only you do!' Mum said, nodding at me insistently. 'And you've got this lovely bloke who absolutely worships the ground you walk on, who loves Lucy to bits, offering to rent you some rooms.'

. . .

That conversation was repeated incessantly, albeit with slight variations, and it was repeated multiple times daily. But because it was what Wayne would call an 'unsolvable equation' it never got us anywhere new.

In the end, ten days later, I threw some things in a bag and chucked it down the stairs into Rob's waiting arms.

Both he and Mum looked so pleased with themselves that I'm sure they believed they'd finally won, that they'd finally convinced me. Rob definitely thought he'd gained far more than he had, and I saw him hide his surprise when, on arrival, I carried my bag of clothes up to that top room rather than to the master bedroom, in which he'd generously offered me 'wardrobe space'.

But the truth of the matter is that I was exhausted from not sleeping, from breastfeeding and dealing with nappies and puke. I was sick, too, of arguing with Mum and Wayne about the same things over and over again. I was feeling miserable about my life, about how radically things had changed since that exciting camping trip with Billy.

In my absence, my brother would doubtless excel in his exams and go to college and do just about whatever the hell he wanted – just like Billy, who was at college learning stuff, having fun and doing whatever the hell *he* wanted.

But me? I actually shrugged as I thought about it all. I'd become Little Miss Zero Options, stuck with an angsty crying baby in someone else's house, with no excitement, no joy, no surprises coming my way at all. I thought of Wayne's jibe. 'You're an unmarried teenage mother. Congratulations!' he'd said. Congratulations indeed!

The only thing easing any of this was the fact that I was so utterly exhausted and so thoroughly depressed that I was beyond caring *where* I lived.

* * *

Living at Rob's turned out to be wonderful. It took me about a week to let myself admit it, but it was truly, totally brilliant.

I was vaguely suspicious of his motives at first, so I took Lucy in with me and locked the door. But Rob didn't try to sneak into my room to ravish me during the night and, if anything, it seemed his interest in me actually waned. It was as if all he'd ever wanted was for us to be safe and sound under his roof and, now we were, he could relax.

He was incredibly busy, too, those first few weeks, and that no doubt relieved some of the pressure. He'd been flat out getting the house ready – ultimately, for *us* – but now he was working fourteen-hour days trying to catch up with all his normal jobs.

So during the daytime, and for much of the evening, I'd find myself alone, in that big house, with Lucy.

I'd actually been scared of being alone with her, I realised, but surprisingly it turned out to be easier than sharing with Mum and Wayne. I could negotiate with myself about just how long I could get away with between feeds or nappy changes without the shame of knowing I was being judged. Even Lucy's crying became less stressful once I knew the only person it was bothering was me.

We quickly settled into a routine, the three of us. I'd get up and eat the breakfast Rob had laid out for me before leaving for work, and then I'd put Lucy in the pram and take her for a push along the blustery seafront. After that, we'd have a snooze together, and then I'd tidy the house a little and do my best to rustle up an evening meal – my way, I suppose, of thanking Rob. I was a pretty rubbish cook back then but, as Rob's tastes went no further than a fry-up or a reheated pizza, I coped, and he was always grateful no matter how bad the result.

Shelley, who visited often, once joked that we were like an

old retired couple. None of them had sex either, she said; and in a way that was exactly how things felt.

In the evenings, we'd sit and watch *Have I Got News For You*, and we'd laugh together at some joke and I'd glance across at Rob and think a warm sort of *this is all right, isn't it?* feeling, and then have to fight myself to avoid the thought going any further.

But love's a funny thing, really, isn't it?

I remember once, in school, they taught us that in French there's only one word for both *like* and *love*, and there was some discussion in the common room about how stupid the French must be to not even have come up with a proper word for *like*.

But I've thought about it from time to time since, particularly during those first few weeks at Rob's, and in a way it made sense to me. Because what was the difference between the way I felt about Shelley – who I loved to bits and who made me laugh so much I'd almost wet myself – or my mum, who I'd die trying to save – or calm, collected Rob, sat beside me chuckling at *MasterChef*?

When I thought of Billy, I'd think *no! That's bollocks!* Because real love, which perhaps really just means love + sex, is a completely different kettle of fish, isn't it?

* * *

In August, Lucy had an endless bout of colic, and she screamed for ten days solid. The doctor prescribed Infacol, which didn't help, and told me to come back in two weeks' time. I was shattered.

Mum had promised to take Lucy off my hands on Monday, her day off, so that I could have a break from it all, but I wasn't sure I could make it to Monday. By Saturday night I was almost in tears from lack of sleep.

I'd juggle her and burp her and rock her. I'd push her along the seafront and bounce fluffy toys in her face. But nothing worked at all. She screamed and screamed, and sometimes she screamed so much that she actually went a bit blue.

That Saturday night Rob got home late to find me at the end of my tether. He'd been out for a pint with his friend Andy and looked glassy-eyed from a combination of tiredness and beer.

'Sorry about this,' I said, speaking loudly to be heard over Lucy's screams. 'She hasn't stopped once all day.' I stood and vacated the lounge so that poor Rob could watch the television in peace, taking my bundle of angst up to my room at the top of the house.

'Please stop, Lucy,' I said, closing the door firmly behind us.

I paced the small room, rocking her in my arms, squinting at the pain her screams were provoking inside my head.

I laid her down on the bed, but, though I hadn't thought it possible, she got louder, so I picked her up again and crossed to the window and looked out at the moonlit sea. I thought about the three-storey drop to the road below and though I truly didn't consider throwing her out of the window, it would be a lie to say that the thought wasn't somehow present in the air, that night.

I sat on the bed and rocked her in my arms. 'Please, please, just stop,' I said, looking down at her furious little face. I began to cry, silent tears of utter hopeless exhaustion, trickling down my face. 'Lucy, I can't do this,' I told her. 'I just don't know what you want.'

I offered her my breast – she pushed it away. I put the dummy in – she spat it out.

There was a gentle rap on the door, but I didn't want to see Rob, so I pretended not to hear it.

It came again, so I shouted out, angrily, 'Yes, Rob, *what?*'

'Can I come in?' he replied, the door easing open a crack. 'Are you decent?'

'Yes, I'm decent, Rob, and I'm sorry, and I know it's late, and there's absolutely nothing I can do about it, so go and put earplugs in or something.'

His big round face appeared between the door and the frame. 'You must be exhausted,' he said so softly that above Lucy's screams he was barely audible.

I started to open my mouth to reply, but nothing came out. Instead, I started to cry again.

'Oh, oh, oh...' Rob said, crossing the room and sitting beside me on the bed. He laid one hand on my shoulder and I started to sob properly.

'I don't know what to do, Rob,' I told him. 'I've tried everything and I'm just... I don't know what to do. I'm no good at this.'

'Here,' he said, reaching out. 'Give her to me and go downstairs and sleep. Have a kip on the sofa. You can hardly hear her in the lounge.'

'But...' I protested weakly.

'Lucy Boop and me will be fine,' he said. Nestled in his arms she looked smaller, and instantly less terrifying.

I scanned Rob's features and I wondered how drunk he was. I wondered if I was a bad mother for handing my baby over to a man who'd been drinking. But then, after taking a deep breath, she started screaming again and I just couldn't stay in the room a second longer. 'Maybe just for half an hour?' I offered.

'Whatever,' Rob said. 'Take as long as you need.'

I went downstairs and made myself a cup of tea and then attempted to watch TV. But I couldn't concentrate on anything anyone was saying. I was too busy listening for Lucy's screams.

Finally, I switched the TV off and crept back upstairs until I could peep through the banisters. Rob was sitting on the bed in a nest of plumped-up cushions, eyes closed, with Lucy clamped against his chest. She was still crying, but with considerably less gusto than before. Rob was alternating between humming and quietly singing the words to that summer's chart hit: 'Gypsy Woman (la da dee la da da)'. Something about the sight of them together made me tearful all over again, but in a good way.

I woke up about five the next morning when the first daylight began to creep through the lounge windows. The house was silent, which made me panicky, so I quietly sprinted back upstairs to check on them. The thought that *Rob* might have lost the plot and chucked Lucy out of the window did actually cross my mind.

But I found them in my room, pretty much as I'd left them: Rob still fully clothed on my single bed, nestled round Lucy, finally silent, sleeping with her little rosebud mouth open. Something big shifted within me at that moment, something that's kind of hard to describe.

Looking back, I think that maybe the whole thing about *liking* and *loving* isn't that having one word is better, or worse, than having two. It's more that, perhaps, we actually need loads more words. It's that we really need *so many* words to properly describe all the different kinds of love that having one, or just two, is neither here nor there.

Because there's the love you feel for your mother, the woman who gave birth to you, who you depended on, and the love you feel for your father, and they are entirely different kinds of love. There's the love you feel for a brother or sister, and the fierce protective – *hurt them and I will kill you* – love you feel for your kids. There's love for friends, who make you laugh and feel good about yourself – and love for just about any other human you see suffering on the news. There's romantic, sexy love, that makes you want to get so close that you end up making babies, and the inexplicable love you have for an old cat or dog you've had for years. My point is, I suppose, that the list just goes on and on.

And somewhere in that rainbow list of things we don't have words for there's a special kind of hormone-swamped love that a mother feels for a man when she sees him curled protectively round her sleeping child. That one's a particularly nice kind of love. And a bloody powerful one, too.

FIVE

COUNTING IN THREES (BY ROB)

Orange light in the windows, the smell of sausages, a smile looking up at me in the kitchen. Just her presence made me feel happy.

That will sound like a daft thing to say maybe – and it wouldn't be the first time I've been accused of saying daft things – but it was true. I never knew how much I hated coming back to an empty house until I didn't have to do it any more.

I'd pull the van up in Dalby Square and walk round the corner to see the orange glow spilling out of our lounge window, and I'd smile.

I'd put my key in the lock and push the front door open and hear Lucy crying, smell Dawn's dodgy cooking and feel as fulfilled as I ever had.

I'd wanted this from the get-go and only now I had it did I really understand why. Because it was perfect. Not perfect as in some non-existent perfect baby that never cries, and not perfect as in some non-existent woman who isn't in an inexplicable mood half the time. No, it was all perfect in its imperfection, that was the thing. It was perfect the way the weather's perfect even though you never know what's coming next.

Surprisingly, I didn't much mind that Dawn didn't love me and I didn't even care a great deal that she didn't want sex. My imagination and my right hand managed to plug that gap just fine. I'd become an expert, over the years.

Obviously, either or both of those things would have been nice, but I've always been a glass half full kind of guy, me. And if I'm honest, romance-wise, my glass had been empty for so long that I think I'd traded it for a smaller size. So coming home to Dawn and the baby, well, it was enough to make my little glass overflow.

Then, one Saturday night, she let me take care of the baby. Lucy had a cold and colic and was wretched. She'd been screaming herself into a frenzy all week, to the point where I worried she might actually run out of breath at some point and simply, somehow, expire.

I'd had a right shitty week myself, working on a rewire in a posh place over in Broadstairs – supposedly a house that Charles Dickens had once lived in. The snobby old couple who lived there were like something from a Dickens novel them-selves. She smoked all the time using a long black cigarette holder, and he wore those silky cravat things stuffed down his shirt.

Anyway, they were never happy with anything I did. They were bored with their lives I reckon, to the point where having someone to hassle made a change. They buzzed around me like a couple of bluebottles and by day three they were doing my head in. Did I really need to run the wires through the walls? Did the carpets really have to come up so that I could run them under the floorboards? Did the drill really need to be so awfully noisy?

It all came to a head on Saturday afternoon when I walked dog-shit over their deep-pile white rug. I cleaned it up, of course I did, but the bloke, who was even worse than his missus, just banged on and on about it until eventually I did something I'd never done before: I packed up and walked out on the job. I suppose, in retrospect, that I was shattered. Lucy's screaming fits had been mucking up my sleep patterns too.

Not wanting to roll up at home with all that anger, I'd gone for a pint and a pie after work. But Andy had been in a right mood too – there are days like that sometimes, no doubt something to do with the positions of the stars – and he'd gone off on one about the poll tax.

It wasn't as if I didn't agree with him, either – the poll tax was clearly a nightmare for just about everyone except the likes of the Queen and Thatcher herself. But it was all over by then, anyway. Thatch had resigned and Major had announced it would be replaced and I just couldn't see the point of getting het up about it any more. In any case, it was the last thing I wanted to talk about that Saturday.

By the time I got back home I was feeling overly tired – that special tired that makes you wonder if you're ill. I was even feeling depressed about the state of the world, not something that afflicts me too often. But then I saw the lights on and heard the baby crying and none of that other stuff seemed to matter.

Dawn looked like she'd died and been barely resuscitated. She was losing it over Lucy's tantrums and I worried she might actually whack her one if the screaming didn't stop. There was something erratic, almost violent, about the way she kept striding up and down the room. So I offered to take a turn. I was so tired myself that I didn't think even Lucy could stop me nodding off.

But Lucy calmed down, slowly at first, and then progressively more and more, and within an hour she was fast asleep in my arms. She smelled milky and warm and vaguely of baby poo, and snuggled against her I felt inexplicably happy. I remember wondering how my parents had managed to remain so cold to their own child, because I had no recollection of ever being cuddled, not even as a toddler. And they *are* kind of irresistible, toddlers, aren't they? At any rate you'd have to be a strange kind of person to resist, or even to *want* to. But then my parents *were* strange kinds of people. Understatement of the century really, that one.

I'd always worried that I'd end up being like them, that I'd be incapable of loving a child. But that cuddle with Lucy felt so wholesome, so natural, that it seemed like proof in a way. Perhaps not everything was genetic after all.

We slept like that for five or six hours solid and by the next morning something had changed. I could see it in the way Dawn looked at me. We never once discussed what had happened, me because I didn't want to jinx it, and Dawn because I think she was embarrassed. After all, she'd promised repeatedly that she would never ever change her mind.

But the next night she put Lucy down and, for the first time in two weeks, she stayed down. The cold and the colic were over.

I watched to the end of the news and went up to bed, to find that Dawn had gone to sleep in my double.

I slipped in beside her as discreetly as I could and lay there, like a plank, wondering if she'd made a mistake, and then whether it was OK that I was naked, and then wondering if Dawn was naked too.

But Dawn wasn't asleep after all. 'Is this OK?' she eventually asked.

'Uh-huh,' I said, too nervous to think what else to say.

'Don't sound so keen,' she said, and the laughter in her voice made me relax a bit.

'Oh, I'm keen,' I said, still rigidly lying by her side. It was true too. Every inch of me was rigid, even the bits that are usually squidgy.

'Show me,' she said, rolling towards me and slipping her hand across my waist. 'Show me how keen you are.'

* * *

God, we were happy that autumn. I suppose I should just speak for myself and let Dawn tell you how it was for her, but even though she did this thin-lipped smile all the time, doing her best to pretend she was unconvinced, I could tell. I'd catch her singing out of tune as she hung the washing out, or laughing with a friend on the phone. Even her cooking improved.

As for me, I felt suddenly at ease, as if I was finally the person I'd always meant to be. For the first time since I was a kid, my panic attacks stopped too.

They'd been ongoing – the attacks – since I was fourteen, and through seeing the school shrink when I was sixteen I'd worked out exactly where they stemmed from. Not that I'd told him. No way I was ever going to tell anyone about something like *that*.

But sadly, it turned out that knowing why wasn't enough to make them stop. What, unexpectedly, did make them stop was being with Dawn.

In the meantime, the therapist had taught me how to calm myself down. He'd called it counting in threes. 'One, name something you can see,' he'd say. 'Two, name something you can smell or hear. Three, name something you can touch.'

'Sunlight, woodsmoke, corduroy,' I'd reply. 'Window, after-shave, button...'

And it worked almost every time. After three or four rounds I'd find myself re-centred there in that room instead of lost in whatever childhood horror my brain had chosen to revisit. My heart would stop pounding and the oxygen would seem to return to the room.

My three, back then, were always, *Dawn, Lucy, happiness*. Yes, my happiness seemed solid enough to touch.

. . .

At first, the sex got better, too. Sex was perhaps the thing that made me feel the most panicky of all, but slowly, surely, we got there. I don't think I ever became the world's greatest lover, but Dawn knew what she was about and wasn't too embarrassed to explain. So within a month, I knew both to hold back as long as I could, and to carry on even after I'd caved in. 'Slowly, but surely,' she'd say, 'that's it. A slow and steady rhythm. Don't speed up... I know you want to, but just don't.'

That September was what people call 'an Indian summer' and I switched to working Saturdays so that on Mondays I could join my ladies on the beach. They liked to picnic near the clock-tower and on Mondays Dawn's mum was free, too.

Tracey was dating a new man back then, a hippy guy called Alan who'd had a ponytail since long before he'd started going bald. He was a weird-looking bloke with a beaky nose and slate-grey eyes. He wore cowboy boots, flares and patchwork shirts that Tracey seemed to be forever darning. I thought his grey, half-bald ponytail and white pointy beard made him look, for some reason, a bit unsavoury.

Still, Tracey was happy with him for a while, and they spent one very giggly summer stoned off their heads on Alan's home-grown weed.

'Funny-looking bloke,' I said to Dawn as we drove home after a picnic one day. It seemed strange to me that Dawn never commented on her mother's choice of men.

'Don't worry,' she said, 'it won't last.'

'How'd you know?' I asked. 'Experience?'

'Nothing ever does,' she said, sounding thoughtful.

'You mean for anyone,' I asked, 'or for her?'

Dawn giggled a bit at that – she'd taken a few hits of Alan's joint as we were leaving. 'It never lasts for anyone called Weaver,' she said, sending me a cheeky wink. 'There's a curse on the Weaver surname. You'll see!'

'We'd better get on with changing that surname, then,' I said. 'We'd better change it before the curse catches up with us.'

She started to frown at me but then understood what I was suggesting, and laughed so much that Lucy started to make gurgling noises too. 'Yeah,' Dawn said, when she could speak again. 'Like that's gonna happen.'

We got married in March '92.

It was a quick and dirty ceremony at Margate registry office followed by a meal in Giorgio's Italian, after which we went for drinks in a wine bar overlooking the bay.

Tracey, who was single again by then, ended up sexy-dancing with a DJ half her age, but other than that it was all pretty low-key. I wouldn't have been opposed to a more imposing wedding, but as I only had three friends I wanted present, and as we weren't exactly rich, any of us, it was enough. I was satisfied with our mini wedding. I was more than satisfied – I was chuffed.

Back home, I carried Dawn, who in turn was carrying Lucy, across the threshold.

'Your palace, Mrs Havard,' I said, and she laughed. 'Mrs Havard!' she said. 'Sounds ridiculous!'

Out of nowhere, for no reason I could name, the thought came to me that this couldn't last. It was too good to be true, wasn't it?

I kicked the front door closed behind us and my breath caught in my throat. I wondered if I was about to have an attack.

'The sofa, please, Mr Havard,' Dawn said, thinking my pause came from the fact that I was hesitating about where to dump them. So I carried them into the lounge, and laid them gently on the sofa.

House, wife, daughter, I thought. *Security, love, joy.* And the feeling faded, and my chest loosened and I thought, *perhaps we'll be OK after all.*

* * *

The years stuttered by in a surprising, unpredictable manner.

Apparently Einstein said that time isn't linear, and I can totally relate to that. Because some of those years had to be dragged like a cart with no wheels, while others slipped and slid and vanished before anyone even noticed.

Different events within a single year could feel both blindingly fast and painfully slow, so that Dawn's uncomfortable second pregnancy lasted, I'm pretty sure, at least three years, while at the same time Lucy went from 'Mmm' to verbal diarrhoea in what I remember as three or four days. That process of her learning to speak was so funny, so cute, so utterly adorable, I remember wishing it would last forever.

I truly doted on Lucy once she started speaking. I just couldn't get enough of her.

'You have to say 'no' sometimes,' Dawn would instruct me. 'You're making yourself into her slave.'

But I couldn't say 'no' to Lucy any more than I could say 'no' to Dawn.

'Daddy, can we go to the sweetshop?' Lucy would ask.

'No more sweets!' Dawn would say. 'We haven't had tea yet!'

I'd wink at Dawn and pull my coat on. 'We promise not to eat them until after tea, don't we Lucy?' I'd say, sweeping her onto my shoulders.

'Promsis promsis cross pants die,' she replied one time, making us all crack up laughing. She'd mixed up *Liar liar, pants on fire,* which she'd recently learned, with *Cross your heart, hope to die.*

Promsis promsis cross pants die became, for a while, my favourite catchphrase, a treasured gift from my daughter.

There were proud first days at nursery school that were over way too fast, and sleepless nights when Lucy stayed over at her new friends' houses for the first time. But gradually we got used to Lucy being an actual person with her own free will and at some point worrying about Lucy morphed into worrying how I was going to pay my taxes instead. Becoming a dad had made me take my eye off the ball and suddenly business wasn't so good.

* * *

In '94, just a week before Lou was born, I met a guy who imported cheap copper cables from Turkey, and by the time little Lou was running after his sister – something that also happened in the blink of an eye – two long, angst-ridden years had groaned past, during which I'd rented, then bought a warehouse, set up a business, and morphed from electrician to boss.

By '97, when Blair was elected, Lucy was already at primary. Dawn had learned to help with my accounts and we'd become rich enough for proper holidays. I was importing VCRs, CD players and phones.

But the sex, unexpectedly, had stopped, and I think we were both too embarrassed to discuss why.

Things had never really been the same after Lou was born, but though Dawn had claimed for a while that 'it hurt' I'm not sure I ever believed her that was the only thing going on.

My insecurities about sexual technique meant that I'd always suspected she forced herself to sleep with me. So when she began rolling away and murmuring that she was sleepy, I naturally assumed that she'd had enough of having to pretend.

But like I said before, I'm a glass half full kind of guy, and even that I managed to take as a compliment, albeit a back-handed one. Because if Dawn no longer felt she needed to pretend to want sex with me then didn't it mean everything else was fine? Didn't it mean that our marriage was now so rock solid that we didn't need the 'glue' of sex holding us together? It was true, after all: everything else really *was* hunky-dory.

Over the seven years together, we'd negotiated every aspect of our lives so that they overlapped perfectly, without any raggedy edges at all.

We preferred Bowie and the Stone Roses to my Duran Duran or Dawn's Sonic Youth – CDs that were banished to the Dusty Drawer of Oblivion. We liked Coldplay but not Oasis, preferred Indian to Chinese, and favoured Channel 4 News over the Beeb. We both voted for Blair (at least I think we did), and we definitely shared a bottle of champagne when he won. We liked Greece more than Spain, preferred Andy's ex to his stuck-up current, and raisin and biscuit Yorkie bars better than the plain ones.

We were parents who didn't slap their kids, *ever*, but not the awful friendless kind of parent who'd make a fuss when others slapped theirs. And like many, many other couples (according to the *Guardian*, which we both now read) we'd agreed not only to never have sex, but to never talk about the fact we weren't having sex, either.

So yes, we were pretty much in tune about everything.

SIX

CHOOSING HAPPINESS (BY DAWN)

I should probably have felt happier.

I don't mean that I felt *un*-happy – I wouldn't want to give the wrong impression... It's just that there were so many reasons to feel happy that I think I should have been happier. I should probably have been ecstatic.

Lucy was just... I can't even think of words to describe how amazing she was. She was cute and funny and smart and pretty... For a while she was my world.

On top of that – on top of being absolutely smitten with my daughter – everything else was good too. The house was lovely to live in and Rob was, as Mum liked to say, *the best husband any woman never had*. Living so close to the seafront and, in summer, to the beach, was brilliant. So yeah, all the ingredients were there, and I hated myself for the fact that I *didn't* feel ecstatically happy.

I suppose, if I'm honest, I felt cheated. It seemed as if I'd somehow been conned into a life that wasn't my own: a very, very nice life, and a very lucky one too, when you consider all the misery there is on this planet. It's just that it wasn't my life and I couldn't quite let myself relax into it.

Shelley, who often surprised me by revealing hidden depths, said that maybe I just needed to choose it.

'Sometimes you have to choose to let yerself be 'appy,' she told me. 'And maybe, in your case, you need to choose Rob. I know I bloody well would, given 'alf a chance.'

The thought crossed my mind that perhaps it might be Shelley's life I was living, because it certainly wasn't mine.

Anyway, I tried her words out in my mind, as I sat together with Rob, as we ate, as we made love, as I vacuumed the hall... *I choose to be happy*, I repeated like a mantra. *I choose Rob*. And sometimes, it felt, for a bit, as if it worked. But then I'd think of Billy, and sigh.

I hadn't seen or heard from Billy for years by then, but still he'd pop up in my thoughts uninvited.

Only once did I bump into his mother, outside Margate train station. She hugged me and asked me how I was and cooed a little over Lucy.

But she didn't ask any difficult questions and I found myself too scared to enquire after Billy. Knowing more felt, in that moment, terrifying. So I made my excuses and left, something I regretted afterwards for years.

Shelley was the only person I really talked to about deeply personal stuff, but I did try, just once, to discuss my doubts with Mum.

We were on Margate beach one sunny September lunchtime. Lucy, now two, was discovering the mysteries of sand, running it through her fingers, inserting it into her mouth, considering rubbing it into her eyes.

As even the concept of staying with the same guy for more than a few weeks was one that was challenging for Mum, I'm not sure what I was hoping for, but I tried.

She nodded thoughtfully and then said, 'Look, I know you've got a kid and everything, but you can still leave if you're not happy. It's not like you're stuck with him. This isn't the 1920s any more.'

'Mum!' I exclaimed. 'I'm not looking to leave him! I'm just trying to find a way to... I don't know...'

'If you don't know, I'm sure I don't,' Mum said, one of her stock phrases.

'A way to... I really *don't* know, actually. To feel like I belong, perhaps?'

Mum pushed her lips out and shrugged. 'Maybe you need to get married, then,' she said. 'Or maybe you need another kid.'

'How exactly would *that* help?' I asked.

Mum shrugged again, but started fiddling in her bag for cigarettes. I guessed there was something she wasn't saying.

'What?' I asked. 'Come on.'

A split second before she replied, I knew exactly what she was going to say. If I'd worked it out a bit sooner, I definitely wouldn't have asked.

'At least you'd know it was Rob's,' she said. 'At least you'd know he's the father.'

'Jesus!' I said, glancing at Lucy just in case she'd decided to tune in and understand a concept way beyond her years. I stood and brushed the sand from my bum. 'Leave him! Marry him!' And all in the same breath! I don't know why I even bother asking you for advice.'

'Someone doesn't like the sound of the truth,' Mum muttered, then, 'Anyway, now you're on your feet, how about you pop over there and get us all an ice cream. I fancy a '99.' At those words, Lucy looked up. Ice cream was definitely a concept she understood.

Her advice had hardly seemed useful, but, when I dismissively told Shelley what Mum had said, she nodded. 'It's not helpful how she put it,' she said, 'but in a way your mum's got a point.'

'A point?' I repeated, putting down my mug of tea. We were sitting in Rob's back garden on deckchairs.

'Yeah,' Shelley said. 'I mean, you didn't exactly *choose* to have you-know-who, did ya?' She nodded vaguely in Lucy's direction. She was playing with a washing-up bowl of water. 'And you never really chose to live here either.'

'So what I should do is get married and have loads of babies?' I said, sarcastically. 'Fantastic!'

'That ain't what I'm saying at all,' Shelley said. 'There ain't no shoulds and shouldn'ts in stuff like this, are there? But if you *did* choose to do that, and then you did it, then at least it would be something you'd actually chosen, instead of something that just, like, happened to you. D'ya see what I mean?'

And I *did* see what she meant.

I argued with myself about it all winter. I found I could sit with Rob and watch a film, or go for a walk with him or have sex, and all the time a part of my brain would be arguing with itself, trying to decide whether choosing to marry Rob, choosing to have another child with Rob – would these actually feel like choices at all?

Or would they feel like sort of Hobson's choices? Would they feel like imposed choices, like the only choices available because I was stuck in someone else's life?

And even if it did work, even if I finally convinced myself I'd chosen Rob, would that actually make me any happier? Or would I just feel as if I'd made yet another bad choice, because my phantom life with Billy (or with an imaginary man I could fall equally in love with) was still just out of reach, lingering beyond the frame?

* * *

The wedding definitely helped, and that was almost certainly because it was my decision. Mum had never mentioned it again (and I suspect she was secretly against), while Shelley had no real opinion either way. Though it was clearly what Rob dreamed of, he knew me better than to try to push.

Rob didn't want his parents present – once again wouldn't even *discuss* them – and that caused a fairly major tiff. But the end result was that in terms of family we only had Mum and Wayne. As we didn't have that many friends we wanted to invite either, it ended up feeling very low-key but, perhaps because of that, also rather lovely and intimate.

Once I was Mrs Havard, I definitely did feel more like I belonged. I'd look at Rob and think, *my husband*. I started referring to the place we lived as 'our house' instead of 'Rob's'. And sometimes, just sometimes, I managed to imagine getting old together.

I realised only once we'd done it that this was in fact the point of marriage. I'd always assumed that it was something showy, something you did for parents and friends to show off, or at the very least to satisfy their need for tradition.

But it was actually about saying, 'I choose this.' It was about saying, 'I give up on ridiculous dreams of perfect men I haven't met yet, perfect men with porn-star bodies, millions in the bank, and the wit of Ian Hislop. I accept I'm a perfectly ordinary human being, and I choose perfectly ordinary, sweet-hearted Rob.'

I got pregnant quite quickly afterwards, and we were happy when we knew it was a boy.

'One of each,' Rob said, 'that's perfect.'

'All we need now is a black one and an Asian, and we'll have the whole set,' I joked, but I think it went over his head.

Pregnancy, second time round, made me grumpy. I was like a gremlin who'd eaten chocolate after midnight.

To start with, unlike with Lucy, I had morning sickness –

the special kind that lasts all day. Looking after a three-year-old while suffering from all-day sickness did not put me in the best of moods.

Rob was in the middle of setting up a new business – perfect timing! – and was having to work sixteen-hour days. A year later, once the money started coming in, I finally took the time to understand what he'd been up to – and to appreciate his efforts – but at the time, I was resentful as hell. Banging me up and leaving me alone, vomiting with a three-year-old – how dare he?

But for a while, it seemed my daemons had been slain. I'd chosen Rob, I'd chosen pregnancy. I felt bloody awful, but there was no one else to blame.

Because Thatcher had done her best to make the NHS unusable, Rob signed us both up for BUPA. It was against all our principles, but at least this time I got my epidural right at the outset and a nice little dose of morphine once I was done. I suppose it's no surprise that when you're paying, the answer to any drug-related question is 'yes'.

Rob also, after extensive negotiation, got to watch. At least, he did until the head appeared, whereupon he almost fainted and had to be led from the room.

I didn't expect there to be so much blood,' he said, afterwards.

'Men,' Mum said, rolling her eyes. 'Other than shagging, what are they good for?'

When it was over and I had little Lou in my arms, I watched Rob and Lucy wave goodbye and promptly fell into a morphine pillow of sleep.

When I woke up, the shadows had moved halfway across the floor and a nurse was holding Lou just to my left.

'Feed time, I'm afraid,' she said, handing him over.

'Right,' I said. 'No worries.'

I took him from her and thought first how beautiful and then how much like Rob he looked, and this made an unexpected wave of love rise up in me for Rob.

Once the nurse had gone, I looked more closely and realised that Lucy didn't look like Lou, and by deduction, more importantly, she didn't look much like Rob either. Before we'd had a second baby who was his spitting image that fact had been easier to ignore.

I shook my head to try to get rid of the thought, and glanced up at the TV screen, which was silently showing Sky News. Landmines were going off somewhere in the world and a black kid was missing a leg. The world was such a miserable place to bring a kid into, wasn't it?

Another nurse stuck her head through the door and asked if everything was OK.

'Can you do something about that?' I asked, nodding at the telly, now showing a whole school full of amputees. The images were simply heartbreaking but I didn't feel I had the strength left to bear it. 'Isn't there a music channel, or something?'

'Sure,' she said, entering the room and lifting the remote control from its holder. 'MTV's on 337. Is that OK?'

She turned the sound up until it was just about audible and left the room. Ace of Base were bopping around on screen singing 'All She Wants', which made me smirk. 'That's apt,' I told Lou. 'She's singing about you and me.'

He continued to feed, through Meat Loaf and East 17, and then a new song came on I didn't know, prompting me to glance up at the screen.

I gasped. Because how was that even possible? I mean, seriously, what were the chances?

I reached for the remote and turned up the sound, and, yes, it was definitely Billy singing. He'd ditched the shiny green overalls and was wearing leather trousers and a dark-green satin shirt, but there was no doubting it was Billy. The song was more jingly-jangly guitars than the rock songs he'd liked in the old days, but it was good, it was catchy. I liked it.

Lou started to cry, so I jiggled him and asked him to keep it down at least to the end of the song. I remembered Mum saying that Billy would be famous one day, and I felt proud because I knew him and then silly for feeling proud, because, after all, what did it possibly have to do with me?

Transfixed, I stared at his gyrating leather-clad hips, his chest hair and new beard. I tried to listen to the lyrics, stupidly hoping they'd be about me. But Billy was singing something fun and vacuous about strawberry lollies and cherry-stained lips, lips that definitely had never been mine.

As the song approached the end, the title scrolled across the bottom of the screen. Billy and the Argonauts: 'Cherry Lips' (Island Records).

Island Records! I thought. *He's been signed to Island Records!* I wondered if he'd met Grace Jones.

The song started to fade, and Billy began to blur so that soon Kylie's lithe body had replaced his.

I reached for the remote and switched the TV off so that I could think. But think about what, other than the fact that what had just happened was so absurd as to be dreamlike?

I'd just given birth to a baby that looked like Rob, and I'd been specifically thinking about the fact that Lucy quite clearly *didn't* look like him. And like a twisted message from the ether, her probable father had appeared on TV – a sexy, nightmare vision designed to mess with my mind.

A nurse came in ten minutes later and I realised I'd dozed off while breastfeeding. 'Everything OK?' she asked. 'You look a bit funny.'

I shook my head. 'I'm fine,' I said. 'Just tired.' Though *tired* didn't really cover it. I was so exhausted I was barely conscious.

As she turned to leave, I asked, 'Have you...? Sorry, but have you heard of a group called the Argonauts? A pop group?'

She thought for a moment and then shook her head.

'Billy and the Argonauts?' I offered.

Another shake of the head. 'Jason and the Argonauts, maybe,' she said. 'But I think that was a film. Why?'

'No reason,' I said. 'I think it must have been a dream.'

* * *

The very first day I was able to, I dragged Lucy and Lou down to Woolworths.

Lucy was in a good mood. She associated Woolworths with Pick 'n' Mix, which she loved. But Lou, who was six days old, screamed all the way. And I do mean *all* the way.

I was suffering from months of compounded sleep deprivation by then and that simple walk to the high street felt like climbing Everest.

The only comfortable sleeping position before the birth had been on my back. Any other configuration had made my spine hurt. But sleeping on my back made me snuffle like a buffalo, to the point where my own gasps and grunts would wake me up every time. Add to that the constant pressure massive Lou had been putting on my bladder, and it wouldn't be an exaggeration to say I hadn't slept more than an hour straight for at least the previous three months. And as anyone who's had a baby will know, the birth did *not* usher in a period of calm serenity.

So I was shattered that morning, *utterly* shattered, and Lou's screams grated on me like broken glass. Sometimes the force and pitch of his tantrums could make me break out in an actual sweat, and that morning – with him being in a carrier, his mouth mere inches from my ears – I arrived at Woolworths drenched in my own icy sweat.

'Do you have anything by a group called the Argonauts?' I

asked the young spotty guy behind the counter, shouting to be heard over Lou's screams. I was fully expecting him to say *no such band,* revealing that it had been a dream. After all, I'd listened to the radio pretty much constantly since leaving hospital, and Radio One didn't seem to have heard of them at all.

'The Argonauts?' he said, wrinkling his nose and frowning momentarily at the back of blue-faced Lou's head. I realised I was embarrassed to say the full name.

'*Billy* and the Argonauts?' I said doubtfully, barely mumbling the word 'Billy'.

'Oh, yeah. Of course. *A Bit of Argy-Bargy.* Thirty-four,' the guy replied, shooting another disapproving glance at Lou.

'Thirty-four?' I repeated. 'Thirty-four what?'

'Album chart,' he said. 'It's thirty-four this week. *A Bit of Argy-Bargy.* But REM are better if you ask me.'

My heart sped up a bit at the realisation I hadn't dreamed this after all. I eased the pushchair along the racks of albums, but Lou was writhing in his carrier, gasping between shrieks, while Lucy was doing her best to worm her way out of the pushchair, her eyes fixed on the multicoloured sweets across the way.

'You've got your hands full there,' the lad said, his disapproval shifting to far-more-appropriate pity as he slid out from behind the racks. 'Here, let me help you.'

He walked smoothly to the far end as if on roller skates – it was almost a moonwalk, actually – and reached up to grab a fluorescent-pink gatefold album. 'Record, CD or cassette?' he asked, flashing the cover at me.

I hesitated. The album cover, featuring Billy in leather jeans, was glorious, but we didn't have a record player. Rob's tastes, technology wise, were decidedly modern. *Did I want to look at a big picture of Billy, or listen to him?*

'CD,' I replied abruptly, telling myself off for being so silly.

The lad slid the record back into the rack and grabbed a CD

from the shelf above. 'Chart stuff's £12.99,' he said. 'But if you like that, then you really should have a listen to this.' He briefly lifted REM's *Automatic for the People* from further along the same shelf, and then slid it back in.

'I will,' I told him, 'but not today. Just the Argonauts, please.'

As I fumbled in my bag for my purse, Lou, writhing with surprising force, managed to punch me in the chin.

By the time I got back home I was almost in tears myself. Lou hadn't paused for breath and once Lucy's sweets were gone she started to moan and throw things out of the pushchair too. *Why had I had another child?* I wondered. I could remember, now, what a nightmare baby Lucy had been. How had I let myself forget?

Having a newborn is a bit like being in an abusive relationship. You're stuck with someone who constantly mistreats you but you're not allowed to fight back, get angry or walk away. Not ever. Not even for a break.

I was feeling overwhelmed by it all and as nothing I tried – not feeding, not jiggling, not swaying, and definitely not shouting at him to shut up – would calm Lou down, I put him in the nursery, which was still at the top of the house. I needed half an hour of peace and quiet to relax. And I *needed* to listen to my new album. It seemed like if I could just steal a moment to do that, I might actually feel like myself again.

In the lounge, still wired but also a bit breathless with excitement, I slid the CD in and pressed play. Lucy looked expectant, then, once the music started, distraught.

'Lucy songs!' she said, and I could tell from her wrinkled brow she was about to get feisty. The sugar from the sweets was hitting her veins now, and was about to reach her little brain.

'No, we're going to play Mummy songs first,' I told her,

listening to the first few bars of the title track before skipping to track two, which was the single I'd heard on MTV.

'Mummy!' Lucy shouted angrily. 'Lucy songs!' She'd picked up the box that held her nursery rhymes – a CD she'd become addicted to the moment Rob had played it for her the first time – and was whacking my knee with it, hard.

'Later,' I told her. 'Now, shush!'

Second time round, the song was even better. The jingly-jangly guitars reminded me of the Smiths with maybe a touch of the Cure thrown in for good measure. Billy's multi-layered voice slithered over me like chocolate. It was like having five Billys sing to me at once.

I'd been right – this was what I needed! Just a moment to listen to the wonder of Billy's voice. It took me straight back to the sensations of that summer, to being young and free and in love. I'd actually been this guy's girlfriend! In a room filled with the music Billy had created, the memory felt like a shock.

God, it was good to close my eyes and just listen though, wasn't it? I'd forgotten how wonderful that simple pleasure felt. To be able to *choose*; to be able to enjoy something, just for the fun of it, just for me. Half an hour listening to some music – it wasn't a lot to ask.

A sense of relief washed over me. I was still that person after all. I still had the capacity to be happy. I'd actually been starting to doubt that.

The music stopped and I opened my eyes – to see that Lucy, incredibly, had managed to eject the CD from the drawer and was trying to insert her nursery rhyme box instead.

'Stop it!' I said, snatching the box from her and putting it on a shelf out of reach. 'You'll break it! That CD player cost Rob a fortune!'

Lucy started to wail full-on. There would be no slow build-up today. She'd gone straight to maximum meltdown.

'Lucy,' I begged. 'Please stop. *Please?*' Then, 'LUCY! I *need* you to stop.'

I was breaking out in a sweat again. Tears were welling up afresh.

'Look, Lucy, you're making Mummy cry!' I told her, pointing at my eyes. 'Please, please, just give me a bloody break here?'

My daughter glared at me, unmoved, and pinched her little mouth at me. I swear that in that moment she looked possessed. 'Good!' she said, trying to climb up my arm for the CD box. 'Bad Mummy! *Bad* Mummy! Hate Mummy!'

I cracked. Some dam within me gave way. I think I'd just run right out of reserves.

So I did a terrible thing.

It was only once, I promise, and it only lasted for just over an hour – long enough to listen to the album twice – but I carried her shouting and kicking upstairs, and locked her in the nursery with Lou. I left them to scream themselves silly.

Down in the lounge with the door firmly shut, I turned Rob's top-end Marantz up until the sound made the windows rattle.

As I listened, with no one there to see me, I ran my fingers over that tiny photo, all the while imagining that Billy was singing to me.

One song in particular hit me hard. It was called 'Where Did You Go? (Uncensored version)' and as I listened it was as much as I could do not to weep. I could almost have written it myself.

Where did you go?
Why did you leave me?
I thought it was love.
Where the fuck are you?
Free me!

* * *

I held off visiting Billy's parents' house for almost a month. Some days, I'd wake up thinking that I had to see him, that it wasn't a desire, but a need, and other days I'd wake up drenched in sweat from some nightmare about the horror of seeing him. On those days I felt convinced that seeing Billy would be like pulling the pin from a grenade – a grenade that could destroy my life. But the truth is that one way or the other I thought about Billy every day.

He could pop into my thoughts at any moment – I could be hanging out the washing, playing with the kids or sitting on the loo, and suddenly there he'd be. He even popped into my mind once or twice when I was nestled in Rob's arms, in bed. *How would that feel?* I wondered, despite myself. Snuggling with Rob felt as lovely as ever, but since Lou's birth any desire for sex had vanished. Would it have been the same had it been Billy's stiffy pressed against my buttocks instead of Rob's? The thought made me feel guilty; it actually made me feel like I was being *unfaithful*. But I couldn't stop myself from wondering all the same.

In the end I put together a lie that was intricate enough to make everything seem OK: I was happy with my life with Rob, Lucy and Lou. In fact I was so happy with the choices I'd made that there was no danger in pursuing a friendship with Billy. After all, that's all it was and all it could ever be – a friendship. I was lucky enough to know a pop star and it would be a waste not to make the most of it.

It was a Saturday when I finally cracked and went round there, and I'd convinced myself I was just going for a walk around Dane Park. I had baby fat I needed to lose, after all. It was time to get serious about getting trim.

Lucy ran around after the pigeons while, on a bench, beneath a shawl, I fed Lou. But all I could think about the whole time was Billy and how unlikely it was that he'd be there anyway.

And he wasn't there, either. To my dismay his parents had moved away, a year before. The open garage now housed nothing more than a rusty Renault 5.

A young woman, also with a baby strapped to her chest, answered the door. 'It's the Ruddles you're after then?' she asked once I'd explained.

'It's Riddle,' I said, 'but yeah, that's them.'

'No, it's definitely Ruddle,' she said. 'I remember from all the paperwork when we bought the place. Mr and Mrs D. Ruddle.'

'Ruddle,' I repeated. 'Gosh.' Even his name had been a lie. It *was* part of his pop star persona.

I asked if she had a forwarding address but she didn't. 'I think they did one of those redirection things,' she said. 'So maybe if you wrote to them here, it'll get forwarded. I'm not sure. It was a while ago.'

'And you've no idea where they went? Not even the town?'

'Yeah, it was...' She frowned and hitched her baby a bit higher. 'He's heavy!' she said as an aside.

'Your first?'

She nodded.

'They get heavy really fast,' I agreed.

'It's that place where they had them little steam trains,' she said. She pronounced little *lickle*, which in an adult seemed strange, but kind of touching. 'D'you know where I mean? I'm trying to think of the bloody name. Down near Folkestone.'

'Steam trains?' I repeated.

'Yeah,' she said. 'Oh! Hythe and Dymchurch, that's the one. Me dad used to take us there all the time. Obsessed with trains, he was. That's why I remembered it. The Hythe and Dymchurch railway.'

'So they moved to Hythe?' I asked. 'The Riddles – Ruddles. Or Dymchurch?'

'Dymchurch, I think,' she said. 'Yeah, I'm pretty sure it was Dymchurch.'

'Thanks,' I said. 'That's great.'

I started to walk away but she called me back.

'Just... I'm sorry. I know this is...' she stammered, looking uncomfortable. 'But does it get better? The crying thing? Does it stop? Because this one's been doing my head in.'

I smiled. 'I used to think about chucking her out of a window,' I said, tapping the handle of Lucy's pushchair. 'But I'm glad I didn't. So maybe don't do that.'

'Right,' she said. 'I didn't think it would be so exhausting, is all.'

'It gets better,' I said. 'Honest, it does. Plus you learn to look after yourself a bit better.'

She frowned at me when I said that, as if it was a whole new concept.

'Sometimes you have to hand 'em over and walk away. Sometimes it's the only thing you can do, so you don't crack up.'

'Right,' she said. 'Maybe I'll try that then.'

'It's hard,' I told her. 'It's really hard to hand them over, but not as hard as ending up in the loony bin. Or ending up in prison for murder.'

She smiled for the first time since opening the door. 'Thanks,' she said. 'That helps.'

I waited a week before I phoned Directory Enquiries – they came up blank – and another before I wrote Billy a letter. It was a simple, friendly, utterly dishonest letter, saying I had his album, and I was impressed, and if ever he was in town it would be 'cool' to hang out 'for old times' sake'. I rewrote that letter twice, with and without the phrase *for old times' sake*. I could hear my own dishonesty in those words, but in the end I included them all the same. And then I copied the letter out again and sent both, one to his old address, and one care of Island Records in London, copying the address from the back of the CD.

It took a crazy amount of time – years in fact – for me to stop waiting for his reply to drop through our letter box, but in the end I did abandon hope. Eventually, I realised it would never come.

By then, I'd bought and discreetly listened to his '94 album, *The Weight of Diamonds* (leather trousers and a T-shirt) and 96's *Death by Chocolate* (the return of the satiny jumpsuit) – albums I hid in a drawer beneath all the old ones, which, in the interests of marital harmony, we pretended we no longer liked.

But in '97, when *Ears, Nose, Arse* came out (no picture of Billy at all!), I didn't even get around to buying a copy. I thought the single was a bit rubbish, if I'm honest – there was something pretentious and self-conscious about it I didn't like. I probably wasn't being very objective, though. I was feeling pretty spurned by then.

But it seemed like time to move on anyway. The music on the radio suddenly sounded fresh and optimistic. And I – apparently like most of the country – decided that Billy belonged to the past.

* * *

Cool Britannia. That's what the papers were calling it. *Blair's booming Britain.*

We had a flourishing economy, the Millennium Dome and a high chance, some said, of hosting the Olympics; we had gleaming tower blocks (in London, at least) and the Eurostar; we had a new tax credit system splashing the cash to those who needed it most, and Blur, Radiohead and Coldplay; Britain was the place to be.

When we went up to London – a trip we took a few times a year to visit the wonderful and now free-to-enter museums – the wealth slapped us in the face. Angular skyscrapers were sprouting like mushrooms; rich men in suits climbed out of BMWs, Mercs and Rollers.

And yet Margate was going to the dogs. Nearby London's obscene wealth only made Margate's slide into poverty more unbearable.

The process was so gradual and had been going on for so long – since they invented cheap flights to Benidorm, really – that it took us a while to realise what was happening. But day by day, year by year, the place started to fall apart. The streets got dirtier and shops and pubs closed. I started to check the beach for syringes before I sat Lucy down.

BHS, M&S, Dixons, Woolworths… one by one they all shut down. With half the high street boarded up, the place started to look like The Specials' 'Ghost Town'. Even Dreamland – briefly rebranded Bembom's – went bust. An amusement arcade on the seafront caught fire and, because no one seemed to care, it was left that way, sooty, blackened, hollowed out.

Lucy's schoolfriends started moving away, and one by one the houses they vacated became refugee 'hotels' – the most efficient way of extracting money from the state anyone in Margate had come up with. Buy a place and fill it with asylum seekers. Fill it with people who are too desperate to complain about the rotting walls and the mould, and get paid by the government for doing so. And once there were buildings filled with Somalians and Serbs and Croatians, what could be more normal than filling another one with Albanians fleeing the Kosovo war?

I didn't resent these people in any way. I do just want to make that clear. In fact, my heart bled for them – they were fleeing wars, and misery, and famine. They were trying to stay alive, trying to build a new life, trying to protect their kids – and were even poorer than us.

But the refugee process was shot to pieces, and not even Tony seemed to care. There was no integration process to teach men with strange religions from the back of beyond that a woman in a skirt was not a prostitute. There was no attempt to ensure the houses were sanitary or safe, or even worth the money the government was paying. There didn't seem to be much of an effort to teach them English either, and the law even stopped them from working. Enforced poverty and dependence for all.

So Cliftonville slowly filled with sad, unhealthy, traumatised communities who not only had little in common with the working-class population who remained – they didn't much like each other either.

We got burgled.

It was normal, in a way, Mum said. Because who could possibly live on asylum seekers' allowance? She'd just got involved in a charity helping refugees called Home from Home and was in the process of roping me in too.

Rob's car got stolen, twice. My washing vanished off the clothes line.

'If you're stealing someone's old undies,' Mum said, 'then it ain't because you're rich. It's cos you can't even afford to go to Primark.' And I knew from the people I met at Home from Home that she was right. I'd seen grown men cry because I handed them some faded jeans. The security guard at Primark wouldn't even let them in the door.

And then one day, as I was walking Lucy and Lou home from school, a man asked me how much it would be for a blow job. He had a lovely big dick, he said, winking at Lucy. I was so angry, I punched him in the face.

'Mummy hit a man today,' Lucy told Rob, the second he got home. She'd promised me she wouldn't say anything and I'd been hoping to talk to Rob after she'd gone to bed. 'I'll tell Daddy about that later,' I told her again.

'What's a blow job, Daddy?' Lucy said. 'Mummy won't tell me.'

Rob dragged me through to the kitchen, where I explained exactly what had happened.

'He was drunk,' I told Rob. 'He was just drunk, I think. I punched him and he fell into somebody's garden.'

'Jesus,' Rob said. 'And this was in front of the kids? He said that in front of the kids?'

I nodded. 'It was pretty awful.'

'Do you think we can go for a drive and find him?' he asked. 'Because if you can point him out, I'll kill the...'

I believed him about that totally. 'Yeah... I don't think that would be helpful, hon,' I said. 'I'm not the prison visits type, me. But I do think – and I've been meaning to talk to you about this – I do think we maybe—'

'... need to move?' Rob said, finishing my phrase. 'I know. The place has gone to shit. You know they're calling it Little Kosovo here? Cliftonville is now officially a war zone, for God's sake.'

I nodded. 'It's been rough for a while,' I said. 'Decades, really. But with the kids it's just...'

'I know,' Rob said. 'I'm sorry. I should have dealt with it before. It's just the business... I'm all over the place these days. I barely have time to take a dump.'

'Don't apologise,' I said. 'I haven't done anything about it either. But I do think the time's come to look elsewhere. Before something bad happens. We *can* afford to move, can't we?'

SEVEN

THE JOSS BAY YEARS (BY ROB)

I found Dawn's Billy CDs during the move.

I'd actually seen him on TV late one night, long after Dawn had gone to bed, so I knew he was doing well. His music was OK so – despite the fact that he seemed like a bit of a knob – buying them wasn't altogether unreasonable. It was just the fact she'd hidden them that concerned me. I worried she was still attracted by more than his music.

I'd found the letter almost five years earlier, too – though *intercepted* is probably closer to the truth. Opening it had been a genuine mistake. It had been addressed to Ms Havard, which I'd misread as Mr, and stamped Universal Music Group. I'd optimistically hoped it was an enquiry about supplying some kind of audio equipment. Instead, inside I'd found a signed, A3 poster of Billy Riddle, along with a standard printed reply. I can't really remember what it said – I was too busy feeling pukey at the sight of all that chest hair – but it was something basic like *Thanks for your fan mail – have a poster*. That was the gist of it, anyway.

I'd sat on the letter for a week, not knowing whether to bring the subject of Billy up or not, and then finally I'd decided just to bin it. Let sleeping dogs lie and all that. I thought it was probably for the best.

Because living in Cliftonville had started to get lairy, we bought a new-build up near Joss Bay. Business at Havard Electronics had been flourishing for the last five years, and I'd got to the point where I was struggling to find time to even invest all the cash I made, let alone spend it. Sticking it all in a big house with a sea view seemed like a no-brainer, really.

It was during the great Unpacking of the Boxes that I found them, stacked between A-ha and Nirvana. I saw Dawn see me find them, and I saw her leave the room to make tea.

I added them to the CD racks a supplier had given me, and it became merely one more thing we didn't discuss. A week later I noticed they'd vanished and been replaced with old Velvet Underground CDs from another box. I hoped that was a good sign.

It took six months to settle into that house and by the time we had I felt as if I'd aged twenty years.

There had been something about parking in Dalby Square I'd liked, and something about walking around the corner to our first house that had been special. Parking on the drive of our new-build felt middle-aged and middle-class and it definitely didn't feel like me.

I'd sit there sometimes in the driveway, peering out through the rain-speckled windscreen at that alien house, and feel an inexplicable sense of unease. Occasionally I'd catch a glimpse of the family beyond one of the many windows and feel like a voyeur – like this was someone else's family, like these were people I didn't know at all. I'd have a queasy feeling in my stomach and a lump in my throat. Sometimes I'd even wonder if our relationship would survive the move.

Then, once I'd waited for as long as I thought I could get away with, I'd sigh and drag myself from the car.

Changing houses seemed to have changed the people I lived with, too.

Dawn stopped dying her hair. 'Embrace the grey!' That's what she used to say.

'You're looking more and more like Patti Smith,' I said one night. It was supposed to be a friendly nudge – an attempt at getting her to take more care about her appearance. I wasn't much enjoying her transformation to wild gypsy woman. But I'd chosen the wrong reference: she'd always worshipped Patti Smith.

'I know!' she said. 'I think she's incredible for her age, don't you?'

'Incredible, but not necessarily that sexy,' I replied, trying to sound like I was being a tease.

Dawn shrugged. 'Who cares about sexy any more?' she said. 'It's a whole new century, baby. Un-sexy's the new sexy.' I didn't know what to say to that.

The kids thrived through junior school and passed the eleven-plus without a hitch. But going to grammar school seemed to change them in ways that made them less and less like people I might reasonably want to hang out with.

They spoke better than we did, knew more about Maths, Geography and History, and occasionally even corrected our grammar. Perhaps it was just my insecurities about my own lack of further education, but it often felt as if they considered themselves superior. Sometimes I worried they were actually ashamed of us.

'Oh, don't be so stupid, Daddy!' Lucy would say, dismissively, if I dared to voice an opinion. I missed her calling me 'Dad'. I wondered when that had changed.

'It's just adolescence,' Dawn would say when I mentioned Lucy's dismissive tone. 'Don't worry.'

One day, at Dane Court's parents' day, Lucy introduced me to her friend Cecelia's father. She'd been nagging us to authorise a sleepover and her introduction was intended to facilitate a 'yes'.

He shook my hand and his palm was clammy and limp. His face was shiny and blubbery, as if he'd maybe used so much skin cream his head had swollen, and his blue suit looked top-end but outdated. To say I didn't take to him instantly would be an understatement.

'Edward,' he said, 'but my friends call me Ted. Jolly good to meet you.'

I thought I remembered his face from somewhere and said so.

'I don't think so,' Ted said, thoughtfully. 'But anything's possible, old chap.'

'Work, maybe?' I offered, thinking, *Old chap? Who the hell actually says old chap?*

'I doubt it, I'm a pilot,' Edward said.

I'd decided 'Edward' suited him better after all – we were never going to be friends.

'And you?' he asked. 'What line of work are you in?'

'I'm an electrician,' I replied. 'So maybe not. Unless you had a rewire a few years back.'

Edward shook his head. 'Sorry,' he said. 'I think I must just have one of those faces.'

* * *

'I wish you wouldn't say that,' Lucy said on the way home. 'I was mortified.'

'Say what?' Dawn asked, stretching to look back at our daughter.

'Electrician!' she said. 'It's so embarrassing.'

'Embarrassing?' Dawn repeated, sounding shocked. 'How the hell is being an electrician embarrassing?'

'Cecelia's dad's a *pilot*,' Lucy said.

'And?' I asked Lucy, glancing in the rear-view mirror. 'He's a pilot, *and*?'

'Oh, forget it,' Lucy said. 'There's no point.'

'Being a pilot's cool,' Lou said. 'D'you think he'll take us up in his plane?'

'No! Doh!' Lucy said. 'He flies big 747s and stuff, *stupid*.'

Dawn looked at me and shook her head in apparent despair, and I drove on in silence for a bit. But then she said quietly, 'I suppose you could say business owner if you wanted to. You haven't been an electrician for years.'

I thought about it as I drove, but 'business owner' didn't work for me. It crossed my mind that, in some strange way, changing from *electrician* to *business owner* would be like our move to Joss Bay. It would dissolve some essential part of my being and I'd be left looking in on myself the way I looked in on that house. I'd be left wondering who I was.

No, I was Rob, an *electrician from Margate*, and I was proud of it.

I didn't feel uncomfortable all the time, though – and, if I'm being objective, not even most of the time.

Generally we were so busy tumble-drying PE kit, making sandwiches and driving Lucy to dance class or piano or Cecelia's, there was no space left for feelings at all. We'd have strategy meetings about how best to get Lucy to Ramsgate for five, Lou to judo by five-fifteen and then Lucy back from Ramsgate to Cecelia's by seven. Half of parenting, it turned out, was logistics.

There were wonderful moments too, like when Lucy danced for us to *Swan Lake* or when Lou suddenly became geeky and wanted my help. He'd built a monorail out of Lego and wanted to know how to add an electric motor to make it run, something that, obviously, was right up my street.

I popped into work for components, and we stopped off on the way home for extra Lego. And by the end of that rainy weekend we'd built a working monorail capable of carrying an actual mug of tea from the kitchen to the lounge. I felt closer to my son than I had in years.

Holidays tended to be high points too, which reinforced my belief that Joss Bay was cursed. Surrounded by sand and sea, Dawn would stop looking pinched and start laughing again. The kids would forget themselves and have fun.

But the best holiday of all, the one that probably saved us as a family, was the summer of 2004. It was a holiday that was so good it made the whole family fall in love with each other again.

We'd been going to the Greek islands on and off ever since the takings at Havard Electronics had made foreign holidays possible.

We'd been to Milos and Paros, repeatedly, then Santorini (great, but not for kids) and Mykonos (a nightmare island-sized rave party). After Mykonos we thought that we were over Greece for life, but then Shelley recommended a place she'd been to on the island of Tinos. She raved about it so much, we thought we'd try again.

* * *

The journey to Tinos was complicated, apparently something Dawn hadn't given much thought to. I'd assumed she'd booked plane tickets at the same time as reserving the house, but it turned out she'd left it to me. When I started to look into it, I understood why.

We had to fly to Athens and then from Athens to Mykonos before finally taking a ferry to Tinos. Every changeover had the potential, through the slightest of delays, to make the whole thing fall apart. But by running with shrieking children through airports, we made it, arriving about six in the evening.

Tinos was a particularly un-touristy island, which, having visited Mykonos, was sort of the point. Other than us, the only people who seemed to want to travel to Tinos were nuns and priests. The port was overrun with them.

'They look like penguins,' Lou, who loved penguins, said, making us laugh. And he was right, they really did.

A battered taxi drove us out of town, past a dusty lunar landscape, and on over a big hill or perhaps a small mountain, to the far end of the island where our one-horse village was situated. Dawn and Lucy got car-sick.

The town was almost non-existent. There was a wide arc of empty beach, a few tens of white houses clinging to the hillside, and one small, family hotel. That was it.

Our rental was even more minimal than the town it was in, consisting of two tiny buildings linked by a small, pretty courtyard. One downstairs building comprised a basic bedroom with two single beds, and the other a tiny kitchen-cum-lounge-cum-bathroom. The second bedroom – our bedroom – was in a simple flat-roofed cube that had been constructed on top of the kitchen: four white walls around a bed, a dresser and a table. And you had to climb an outdoor staircase to get to it.

'How much did you pay for this?' I asked Dawn, once the taxi had driven away and we'd found the keys hidden, predictably, beneath the doormat.

'Not much,' she said. 'About twenty quid a night I think. I'm sorry, I should have realised it was going to be basic. I mean, I knew... but I didn't realise it would be like *this*.'

'There's nothing here,' Lucy said, spinning on one foot to take in the 360-degree vista of the beach, the hills, the hotel. 'What are we going to do?'

'D'you want to get a taxi and go somewhere else?' I asked

Dawn. I instantly started praying she'd say no, because I hadn't made a note of the number for the taxi. 'Or we can think about it in the morning,' I added hopefully. 'This is probably OK for one night.'

'I want to go somewhere else,' Lucy said definitively.

'So do I, I think,' Lou agreed, sounding less certain.

'Tomorrow,' Dawn told them. 'We'll find somewhere better tomorrow.' Then to me, she added, 'I'm too tired to even think about it now.'

'Look!' Lucy said, 'A cat!'

Peeping through the bushes on the far side of the courtyard was the face of a tiny cat, but as soon as Lucy ran towards it it vanished.

'Can we buy some cat food tomorrow?' she asked.

'We're going somewhere else tomorrow,' Lou reminded her. 'So there's no point.'

That evening, we walked up to the hotel. They had a small restaurant set up beneath a pergola, overlooking the bay.

There was no menu because they didn't need one. They had Greek salad and fish of the day or calamari served with rice or pasta. Dessert was ice cream or yoghurt; the wine 'red' or 'white'. But as these limited options covered everyone's needs – as Lou loved calamari and Lucy loved pasta; as everyone loved ice cream – it was fine. The waiter was friendly, calm and kind, and the food fresh, tasty and astoundingly cheap.

I woke up the next morning to the sound of the waves and sunlight creeping through the shutters. I checked my watch – it was after ten. I'd gone to sleep next to Lou, while Dawn had slept downstairs with Lucy. I hadn't slept so well in years.

When I stepped out onto the roof I was shocked by the beauty of the place. It stunned me to the point where I think I actually gasped. I couldn't believe that the previous night I'd been unimpressed: proof, if proof were needed, how tiredness can change your perceptions.

The sky was deepest blue, the beach, about a mile of it, empty, and the white hillside village so blindingly bright in the morning sunlight that, without sunglasses, it hurt the eyes.

Down in the courtyard I could see Dawn slicing watermelon. Lou and Lucy were playing with three kittens.

'Look, Dad, there's three cats!' Lou said excitedly when he saw me.

'There's actually even more,' Dawn said. 'They keep coming and going all the time.'

'We think they're hungry,' Lou told me.

'We're going to get cat food,' Dawn added, smiling up at me.

'Aren't we leaving?' I asked. 'Or did I miss something?'

'No!' Lou said, 'Don't be stupid. We're going to the beach!'

Those two weeks were bloody amazing.

The owner, a sun-dried farmer, brought us fresh produce every day. He'd ride up on his moped at about nine, and hand over a box with watermelon and tomatoes and cucumbers. Sometimes there would be bread, or fish, or cheese, and if we requested anything – sun lotion, a rubber ring, or ketchup – he'd bring it the next day, without fail.

We'd eat a breakfast of bread and local honey and then walk to the beach, where the kids were happy to spend the whole day.

Mid-morning, a couple of biker/hippy types would arrive on motorbikes and open the awning of a VW van parked on the beach, turning it into a bar. They played brilliant music all day, of all genres, from reggae to rock to techno. They served cocktails and beer, sandwiches and burgers, ice creams, iced coffees and chips.

Some evenings the bar got livelier and on others, unpredictably, it didn't. When that happened, when it was quiet, the owners would close shop and we'd sit on our rooftop and play cards, the gentle sea breeze welcome after the sweltering heat of the day.

One night – I think it was about day four – the kids asked if they could go for an evening walk along the beach. The waves were strangely fluorescent in the moonlight and they wanted to skim stones. As we could see most of the beach from our rooftop and were pleased that they wanted to do something together, we agreed.

Once they were gone, the clicking of their flip-flops fading into the distance, we sat sipping wine, staring out at the view.

'The holiday is doing them good,' Dawn said, nodding towards the kids, now making their way down the rocky staircase leading to the beach. 'Who would have thought it?'

'It's doing us all good, isn't it?' I asked, sending her a wink.

She nodded but, because I thought I'd seen a shadow crossing her features, I asked a question that had often crossed my mind. I'm not sure why I said it out loud at that moment – it just sort of slipped out. 'You don't regret it all, do you?'

'Regret what?' she asked, surprised. 'You mean this holiday?'

'No,' I said. 'All of it. Us. Me. *Choosing* me. Or rather, letting yourself get convinced.'

'Oh,' Dawn said, '*that.*' Momentarily I saw that regretting *all of it* was a far less unreasonable proposition for her than regretting the holiday itself.

'Not at all!' she added suddenly, having realised she was spending too long considering the question. 'Don't be silly.'

'Sometimes I think you do,' I said, softly. 'Sometimes I worry I'm too...'

'Too what?' Dawn asked.

'Too *ordinary*?' I suggested.

Dawn snorted gently at this and for a moment I thought this

too was something she was going to have to consider. Instead, she said, 'You're not *ordinary*, Rob. You're not ordinary at all.'

'OK,' I said. 'But—'

'Look, I'm not sure where this is coming from,' she interrupted. 'But don't let's spoil this moment, eh? It's gorgeous here, hon. It's so beautiful. It's amazing. The kids are having a good time. I'm having a good time. *We're* having a good time, aren't we?'

I nodded and forced a smile.

'So enjoy it, Rob. I am. Frankly, I'm loving it. I'm *loving* being here with you.'

I had a lump in my throat and tears were welling up. I smiled at her and I saw her see the emotion and respond in kind.

'Oh, Rob!' she said, her voice breaking. 'You silly sausage! Come here.'

I laid my cards on the table and moved from my seat to kneel before her, laying my head in her lap. 'I love you so much,' I mumbled into her shorts. 'I know I don't say it enough, but I do.'

'Me too, Rob,' she said, sighing and caressing my hair. 'And if you pick those cards up and let me thrash you, I'll love you even more.'

By the time the kids came back she'd beaten me seven times and we were tipsy. The conversation had all but been forgotten.

But some vestige of it must have been lingering in the air because Lou frowned at us and asked what was going on.

'Nothing!' we both said at once, and I laughed because it was as if we'd been caught in the act – the act of loving each other. Every adolescent's nightmare.

* * *

On both weekends, twenty or thirty youngsters rolled up on a collection of noisy scooters. The owners turned the music up and everyone got drunk, and smiled and danced together in the sand.

We grooved with our kids, that summer – the first time we'd ever done so – and for the first time ever, I suspect they saw us as something other than 'old'. When Dawn and I taught them the big box/little box dance, I think they might even have thought that we were cool.

One of the cats gave birth to six kittens, right in front of our children's eyes, and when finally we had to leave, and even though the owner promised to feed them, both Lou and Lucy cried about leaving them behind. Dawn and I got misty-eyed as the taxi drove us away, too, though in our case it was more about leaving that house in Tinos than the cats.

It's hard, really, to explain just how magical that holiday was, or why. Suffice to say that, by the time we left, we'd become a proper family again.

Our kids had become swimming, snorkelling children again, instead of snooty wannabe adults, and Dawn and I were briefly proper husband and wife. We'd even had sex, twice.

None of that lasted once we got home, but it did leave a sort of memory imprint that helped hold things together for a while. It enabled us to remember who we'd once been.

* * *

Back home in Joss Bay, it was prematurely dark, and raining.

'I hate this house,' I said, as I parked the car. 'I didn't think I would when we bought it, but I really really hate it.'

'Dad!' Lucy said. 'I love this house.'

'It's better than the old house,' Lou agreed.

'I know what you mean, though,' Dawn said, once the kids had climbed out. 'After Greece, coming home is depressing.'

Should we have moved homes back in 2004? *Very possibly,* is the most honest answer I can come up with, and I've thought about that one a lot.

But sometimes life just gets in its own way to the point that even the most important decisions don't get taken.

Early 2005 my business gained a new investor and we opened outlets in Bournemouth, Brighton, Maidstone and Redhill. As an aside, Maidstone was dreadful, taking up more of my time than the other three put together. But you get the picture: I was as busy as I've ever been.

Any time left over was taken up with Lucy, who, frankly, had become an absolute nightmare.

I'd be hard put to say when the problems with Lucy started; I'd struggle to name an exact date, or even a specific year. It was more of a slow slide into horror.

Until about ten, Lucy was mostly gorgeous. She was funny and pretty and loved. From when she was four to about eight years old, I was extra close to her. She'd follow me around the house and 'help me' with my DIY projects by sticking a screwdriver in my ear. Perhaps she was trying to kill me even then.

With hindsight, the signs had been there even when she was a toddler. Lucy had always been prone to inexplicable fits of rage and from the earliest age she'd had the ability to scream until she went blue, refusing any kind of solace and effectively cutting off her nose to spite her adversary's face. She soon learned to throw a few pointed insults into the mix, too, and quickly learned which ones hurt the most. When this happened – when she shrieked that she *hated* you or that you were a *nasty* Mummy or Daddy, or later, when she said she 'wished she'd just been adopted or something' – Dawn would say she *had the Devil in her*, a phrase that always made me uncomfortable.

Because of my own upbringing, I believed pretty firmly that some people really *did* have the Devil in them – and I don't mean that in an abstract way. So when Dawn said that about our daughter, I worried I'd somehow passed the worst of my inheritance on to Lucy, like some terrible regressive gene.

By twelve, Lucy was getting snarky and skipping school – being generally difficult to control. When she was fourteen, Dawn showed me a documentary about a boot-camp for problem teenagers in America and, horrific as it was, and without a word being spoken between us, I think we both wondered if something like that would help. Another time Dawn suggested an exorcism and we both had to pretend that she'd been joking.

The one thing that might have helped was moving towns, thereby forcing Lucy to change schools, but saving Lucy from her skanky schoolfriends would have amounted to sacrificing Lou. Because where Lucy was not doing well at Dane Court (and she really, really wasn't), her brother, calm, serious, geeky Lou, was consistently top of the class.

But the sad truth is that with me whizzing around the south-east opening new branches, and Dawn chasing around after Lucy (mainly) and (far more rarely) Lou, alongside the hours she put in at Home From Home, we were too busy to go house-hunting anyway.

We worried about Lucy constantly, though. When, at twelve years old, she vanished for a whole weekend, we called the police, and when she came home we grounded her for a month and took away her iPod.

Later, we tried switching off the internet or banning her from watching TV. We'd forbid her seeing this person or that (not that it ever actually stopped her), or lock her possessions in the naughty cupboard for a week. We docked pocket money and confiscated make-up too, but it was all pretty pointless. It was like giving a good telling-off to a terrorist. Nothing we came up with was ever anywhere near equal to the task at hand.

Lucy made me feel powerless, and that, for a man like me, was tough. I'd always liked to think of myself as The Great Problem Solver, you know, car broken? Rob'll fix it! Not enough space? Here! New shelves! Aching back? Try these pills. Or massage. Or swimming. Or yoga! But with Lucy I ran right out of solutions. Because nothing ever helped.

'I don't give a shit,' Lucy told Dawn, one time. She must have been nearing fourteen and we believed that life with her was at a low point – though, looking back, she hadn't got started.

'If you say that to me one more time, I'll take those boots I gave you for Christmas as well,' Dawn warned.

'Say what?' Lucy asked.

'That you *don't give a shit*,' Dawn said. 'You know full well we don't use language like that in this house.'

'Only we do use language like that in this house,' Lucy said, snidely. 'You just actually said *don't give a shit* yourself.'

'I was quoting... Anyway, that's it!' Dawn told her calmly. 'The boots are history. Carry on, girl, and see what gets confiscated next.'

'In case you didn't notice,' Lucy replied, her glossed lips curling – an expression she had already mastered, 'I really *don't* give a shit.' And then she flounced out of the front door and vanished to a friend's house for the weekend.

'Other than chain her up in her room like an animal, I don't know what I could have done,' Dawn told me that evening, when I got home late and shattered from work.

'I know,' I agreed. 'I'm not sure either. But I'm sorry I wasn't here to help.'

'And it's not like I could do that even if I tried.'

I frowned at her, so she explained. 'Chain her up, I mean. She's bigger than me now. She's taller and she weighs more. I'm pretty sure she's stronger, too. You know, we should never have let her take those self-defence classes. That was our one big mistake.'

'I could still come out on top in a fight,' I said. 'I've got a great right-hand jab, me.' I feigned boxing – an attempt at lightening the mood.

'Yeah, but you won't,' Dawn said. 'Thank God! I'd hate you if you started hitting our kids.'

'I'd hate that too,' Lou said, from the doorway. We hadn't known he was there.

'Hah, I could never hit either of you,' I told him. 'Or anyone for that matter. Come here and tell us what we should do about your immensely annoying sister.'

Lou crossed the lounge and sat down, looking thoughtful. 'I suppose it's too late for an abortion?' he said. He was eleven, so we tried not to laugh.

'Yeah,' Dawn said. 'Just a tad.'

'There's still time for you though,' I joked. 'The age limit's eleven these days.'

'Send her to live with Uncle Wayne then,' Lou offered. Wayne, who liked to say he'd 'dropped out and tuned in' (though what he'd tuned into, no one knew) was currently WWoofing on an organic farm in Portugal.

'Now that,' I said, 'is an excellent idea.'

'She'd never go for it,' Dawn said. 'She *hates* gardening. Plus there's no internet, apparently. She'd *die* without the internet.'

'Plenty of drugs, though,' Lou said. 'She'd love those.'

'Lou!' I exclaimed.

'What?' he asked, pulling his most innocent face.

'She doesn't do drugs, does she?' Dawn asked, suddenly serious. We'd repeatedly caught her smoking cigarettes but it hadn't gone any further – that we knew.

'More than my life's worth to answer that one,' Lou said, standing and leaving the room.

'See,' Dawn said. 'Lou's scared of her too.'

'He is. And rightly so. And I'm taking that answer as a yes.'

'Are we searching her room again?'

'Yes,' I said. 'I think we probably are.'

We tried shrinks, but she wouldn't turn up. We tried picking her up from school to take her to the shrink, but she'd leave by a fire door on the far side.

At fifteen it was the police who brought her home from Canterbury before we'd even known she was missing. She'd been picked up smoking weed in a bus shelter.

'How *classy*,' I remember Dawn saying.

'Well at least I've met my dad,' she replied. 'Unlike *you*. Talk about *classy*...'

We both forced ourselves not to react to that one. Because once you reacted, that was it. She'd use the same insult over and over.

We talked about Lucy first thing in the morning, and we talked about her last thing at night. We discussed her with school psychiatrists, with helplines and with friends, a couple of whom shocked us by asking if we'd ever tried 'giving her a good hiding'.

But violence wasn't the answer, something thankfully Dawn and I agreed on. And even now, even having lived through it all, I'm glad we weren't those kinds of people, because I'm certain it would have made things worse. We would have been just like the rest of her life: violent and sordid and awful. So I still believe that our pacifism was the one thing that enabled her to come back to us when the time finally came for her to be saved.

Anyway, slowly but surely, and despite our very best efforts, Lucy began to sink into the swamp.

She stole, and drank, and got arrested for drink-driving, under the influence of drugs without a licence – too young even for a licence. She got pregnant, had an abortion, and got pregnant again, this time by a guy who also beat her up.

By the time, aged nineteen, she finally 'moved out' – read, *ran off and didn't come back* – we felt guilty that we felt so relieved. The mayhem she'd been weaving through our lives had been exhausting and all three of us had been running on empathy reserve for years.

So we made the most of the sudden calm around the house and pretended not to know that Lucy was living in a squat in Hastings.

When she got arrested, we bailed her out. When she needed money for food, we sent her food, and, when she needed money for clothes, we took her shopping – all so that she wouldn't buy drugs.

When, the day before Christmas, she broke in and stole my computer, Lou's PlayStation and Dawn's purse, we called (after considerable angst-filled arguments) a mate of mine who happened to be a policeman. It was supposed to give her a scare, but Lucy seemed to think it was funny.

When, for burgling someone else *and* buying and selling drugs with the money she made, she got arrested by a proper on-duty policeman and sent to Maidstone Prison, we met her at the prison gates and drove her to a rehab facility in Rye. She later told us she'd got high half an hour after being released.

But eventually she did come back to us, turning up on the doorstop one evening dressed in filthy clothes. By the time that happened, she was twenty-two.

'Can you help me?' she asked, shaking as we helped her indoors. 'Because I think I'm actually going to die if someone doesn't do something to save me.'

'Only *you* can save you,' Dawn told her. 'We've been through this a thousand times.'

'Sure,' Lucy said. 'I want to this time. Really. But I need help. Will you help me?' Tears were rolling down her cheeks.

'Of course we'll help you,' Dawn said unconvincingly, sounding tired even at the thought of getting involved again. 'You're still our daughter, sweetheart.' She looked at me questioningly and I nodded. By then I believed that I hated her, though I still loved her even more.

'Yep, you're still my little Lucy Boop,' I said, trying to sound like I meant it.

Saving Lucy took another two full years out of our lives: years of therapy and community service and methadone; years of relapses and thefts followed by *more* rehab and tears and reparations.

But incredibly, unexpectedly, after her fourth stay in rehab, she got better. In the end she didn't have the Devil in her after all. And she really *didn't* want to die.

EIGHT

THE JOSS BAY YEARS (BY DAWN)

So now we knew, it was genes after all. And Lucy had inherited all the bad ones – the Weaver propensity for teenage sex and pregnancy plus the Ruddle fondness for drugs. She'd been blessed with Billy's arrogance, too – something I'd found inexplicably sexy in a man, but which was utterly repulsive in my child.

Lou, on the other hand, had been lucky in the great cosmic lottery. He had my edgy sense of humour, but everything else came from Rob. He was calm, diligent and kind – a carbon copy of his father.

Poor Lou got ignored for the best part of nine years, from about 2004 to 2015 – the downside to being normal and undemanding. Sure, we did our best to look like we were going through the motions: we remembered birthdays and Christmas; we celebrated good exam results, one after the other. But the truth was that Lucy consumed all the oxygen in the house and there was none left for anyone else.

Lou, bless him, thrived despite it all. He seemed to see his sister as a textbook case of everything he needed to avoid doing, being or thinking.

He told me, much much later, that she'd once tried to sell him drugs, offering him a pocket-money deal on E.

'She said it felt really great,' Lou told me. 'She said I'd feel the best I'd ever felt.'

'And how old were you, exactly, when this happened?' I asked.

'About twelve, I think,' he said. 'She was evil back then. I used to tell my mates she was possessed. She was like that kid in *The Exorcist*.'

'She was *exactly* like the kid in *The Exorcist*,' I said. 'And you just said "no", I take it?'

'Yeah, you know me. I was polite,' Lou explained. 'Plus she was kind of scary. So I just said I didn't really fancy it and thanked her for her kind offer.'

'I can totally imagine you doing that,' I told him.

'Anyway, I was saving up for a Wii,' Lou said. 'There was no way I was giving her my pocket money.'

Lucy was hard work for the whole family, but she drove me to my absolute wits' end. I cried over her so many times that I lost count.

Sometimes I'd go round to Mum's and sit in her kitchen for half an hour crying into a mug of tea, even though Mum rarely had much advice to give.

'I really don't know, hon, cos I was lucky,' she used to tell me. 'You two weren't like that at all. Neither of you was. You were proper little angels.'

'I *did* get pregnant at seventeen,' I pointed out one time.

'Yeah, well,' Mum said. 'People in glass houses... I mean, I was never likely to start chucking stones about that, was I?'

'No,' I said. 'I guess not.'

The only time Mum ever ventured parenting advice, it was because of something she'd seen on TV.

'Look,' she said one day, no doubt sick of listening to me

complaining. 'I don't want to... you know... tread on anyone's toes.'

'OK,' I said, intrigued. 'Go on.'

'Well, I was wondering, have you ever thought that maybe you're too hard on her?'

'Too hard on her?' I said, frowning.

'Yes,' Mum said. 'It's just...'

'Too *hard* on her?' I repeated, my outrage building as I digested her words. 'Have you actually been following any of this, Mum? Have you any idea what she's putting us through?'

'I know,' Mum said. 'It's just... Hear me out, OK?'

I laughed sourly, then, after forcing a deep breath, I threw myself back in my chair and clapped my hands. 'OK, go for it!' I told her.

'I saw a thing on telly,' Mum said. 'A shrink. On that *Supernanny* thing. He was a sort of consultant. And it made me think about you. Well, about Lucy.'

'Uh-huh?' I rolled my eyes skywards. *Supernanny!*

'He was...' Mum shook her head. 'Don't look at me like that. I'm not criticising you or telling you what to do. I'm just discussing ideas. You *were* asking for ideas, weren't you?'

'OK,' I said, steeling myself. 'Whatever. Go on.'

'He was saying – this young shrink – that some kids do more or less what you tell 'em to do, and others do the exact opposite. And the trick is working out what kind of child you're dealing with.'

'Pretty clear, that one!' I said.

'Exactly,' Mum said. 'And he was saying the ones like Lucy, the rebellious ones, sometimes *not* trying to control them actually works better. Cos they're left with nothing to rebel against.'

The idea struck me initially as a daft one, but as time went by, and as Lucy continued to do the opposite of everything we said, it came to sound less ridiculous. So eventually, after discussion with Rob ,we decided to give it a try.

For a few months, we let Lucy do pretty much anything she wanted and we did our best to pretend we didn't care. We were running out of other options, after all.

But sadly – Supernanny take note – it actually made things worse. Within a month we had a woman police officer on the doorstep asking us why we weren't controlling our daughter. Lucy, it appeared, hadn't been merely opposing us after all. She was following her own personal roadmap to hell.

Lucy used to get Rob worked up too – I know she did – but it was never quite the same for him, for the simple reason that he had an excuse to get out of the house. He even admitted to me once that even the worst days at work, even the worst of employees in their very worst moments, were nothing compared to dealing with our Lucy.

In 2010 in the middle of one of her many crises (she was dating a guy who'd started to hit her), I looked Billy up on the internet.

Initially, I was looking for proof that it was down to him, and, when I learned he'd been arrested on drugs charges in LA, it seemed to confirm my fears.

So I wrote to tell him so.

I couldn't really say what I was hoping for because I wasn't necessarily thinking that clearly. I'd dealt with nothing other than Lucy's various crises for the previous few months, and I hadn't slept properly for years.

But I do remember having thought, *Maybe he'll want to meet her. Maybe he'll tell us to put her on a plane.*

And I remember thinking, *Maybe he'll say, 'Send her to boarding school. It worked wonders for me. I'll pay.'*

And also – and this is the hardest one to admit – *Maybe he'll say, 'Run away and leave them. Come live with me in LA.'*

And that maybe, just maybe, I would. I was feeling pretty fed up with my life.

.   .   .

Billy did write back this time. He replied about two weeks later by email, including a photo of his wife, Candice Rayner (she was the spitting image of Naomi Watts) alongside his dimpled newborn son.

The text of the email wasn't long or even particularly interesting – he mainly talked about his career. But he finished with, 'I'm really sorry you're having trouble with one of your kids. We're hoping that Gandhi is going to be cool. So far so good, he sleeps like a log.'

I looked on AltaVista to see if they'd really called the kid Gandhi and it seemed, from what I could find, that they had. *Gandhi Ruddle*, I remember thinking. *The poor thing! What chance does he have with a name like that?*

Other than all the Lucy stuff – and as I say, Lucy took up so much space there was very little *other* than Lucy stuff – life in Joss Bay was fine.

The house was new and functional and you could see the sea from nearly every window. I passed my driving test early on and Rob bought me a little red Micra I used to bomb around in, though mainly I provided a taxi service for kids.

For rainy days there was a sunroom that didn't feel too claustrophobic, a room I used mainly to read in, and on sunny days (when the sun, ironically, made the sunroom unusable) you could cross the road and scramble down to the beach.

We got a cat – a gorgeous cuddly tabby Lou for some reason named Cedric, and when Cedric got tragically run over, five years later, we got a mean bitey kitten Lucy christened Blanche.

Rob had a vague belief that the house was somehow jinxed, but I never believed that to be true. The house was just a box really – a plain, reliable, weather-proof box. It was up to the owners to fill that box with love and fun, or alternatively with misery and hatred. Our jinx was quite simple: one family member consistently chose the latter.

But there were little joys and triumphs along the way that helped to make life bearable. No matter how bad things are, there are always those, in every family.

We had nice holidays where Lucy behaved herself, alternating with horrid holidays where Lucy did not. We even had – and Lou liked these best of all – holidays where Lucy didn't come at all, generally because she was in custody, or rehab, or in a squat.

There were lovely dinners without the kids where we got drunk and laughed until we wept, specifically when Mum and/or Wayne came to stay, and benefit fundraisers for Home From Home and parties and dancing and picnics. A couple of times, because Mum had invited one of her asylum seeker friends, we had beautiful, tear-jerking Christmas dinners, too.

And in the middle of the mayhem of family life there were moments when I'd unexpectedly fall back in love with Rob.

Sometimes there would be a trigger to cause this sudden shift – a gift, or a meal out, or some touching, thoughtful act. But other times it just seemed to come from nowhere, taking me by surprise.

One time, it happened while driving back from a weekend in the Lake District. We'd left Mum at ours looking after the kids so we could attempt to recharge our emotionally exhausted batteries, but the weekend had been an utter flop.

To start with, it had rained non-stop from the moment we arrived until we left. The heating in our Airbnb had been inadequate, meaning we'd felt cold and cheated all weekend, and the Michelin-starred local restaurant had been closed. The bed had been lumpy too, meaning we hadn't been able to catch up on lost sleep, either. By the time it came to go home we were both feeling more weary than when we'd left.

During the long drive back I fell asleep, and when I woke up we were on the M25.

Rain was pattering on the windscreen, being rhythmically swished away by the wipers, and light from the streetlamps was sweeping across Rob's face. The car felt cosy and safe, and on the radio they were playing a Massive Attack song, 'Protection'. It's the one that Tracey Thorn sings, and I've always really loved it. Rob was singing quietly along, unaware I'd woken up.

In that moment, for no reason I could name – perhaps the music, perhaps just sheer tiredness – something in me, some hard shell I used for *my* protection, cracked open and I felt this huge whoosh of love for him. Concentrated on his driving but half smiling as he sang, he looked as beautiful as I'd ever seen him. His massive hands were gripping the steering wheel, his fingers tapping to the beat... *The sheer beauty of another human being who just, God knows why, happens to love me*, I thought. *I am so lucky to have you.* It seemed like a whole new concept, like a thought I'd never had before. Tears rose to my eyes.

Rob put the indicator on to change lanes just then, and as he glanced in the wing mirror he saw I was awake. He smiled at me then, so softly, so gently, so *lovingly*, and he reached out and caressed my hair. 'Hello, sleepy head,' he said. 'Only about an hour, now.' He frowned then, at something in my expression. 'You OK?' he said. 'You look funny.'

'I'm fine,' I said, swallowing with difficulty. 'I love this song.' Then, 'I was actually watching you singing along and thinking how much I love you.'

'Gosh!' Rob said, performing a double-take before dragging his eyes back to the road. 'I shall sing to you more often!'

'Nah,' I joked. 'You're all right, thanks.' But I remember thinking that he was right – I didn't say that kind of thing enough.

These little bursts of love were unpredictable in their arrival, and never lasted that long – a week or two in general, tops, and sometimes less than ten minutes. But they *did* happen, that was the point. And the fact that they happened was important because, even once the moment had passed, my memory of it continued to provide *hope*. Because I knew the feeling could return at any time.

* * *

One day we were driving home from Westwood Cross, where we'd just seen a disappointing Bond film.

Lucy had finished her final rehab stay about three weeks earlier, and because we didn't know, or even dare hope, that it *would* be her final stay, we were having to keep an eye on her by taking her everywhere we went.

'*Skyfall* was way better,' Rob said.

'God, you sound just like Lou,' Lucy said. Her brother was back at uni, down in Bath, where, as ever, he was acing it. 'But it's only because we saw *Skyfall* at the IMAX.'

'I just think it's a better film,' Rob said. 'I'm allowed to have that opinion, aren't I? Even if it is an opinion I share with your brother.'

That's when Rob's phone began to ring. It was connected to the car's Bluetooth system, and a phone number appeared on the dashboard.

'Sorry,' Rob said. 'I don't know who this is, so I'm going to have to take it.'

'Rob?' a voice boomed out of the car speakers. 'Rob, is that you?'

A man's voice. Elderly. Maybe Welsh. The first time I'd ever heard it.

'Shit,' Rob muttered, pressing a button on the steering wheel to end the call.

'Who was *that*?' Lucy asked.

'No one,' Rob said. 'So what were we saying about *Skyfall*?'

'No one,' Lucy repeated, cheekily. 'If that was a call from your secret lover, Dad, I'm a tad concerned.'

'It's just some bloke,' Rob said. 'Work stuff. Someone I don't want to—' His phone started to ring again. '... to talk to,' he said, finishing his phrase as he took his phone from his pocket and handed it to me. 'Can you switch that to airplane mode or something?'

'Wow, you really *don't* want to talk to him,' I said as I did so. 'Is everything OK?'

'Yep!' Rob said sharply. 'Everything's great. Now can we just forget about it?'

Once we were home and Lucy was safely in her room, I challenged him. 'Was that your dad, Rob?'

I didn't know much about Rob's parents – the subject, I'd always known, was taboo. But the two things I did know were that they were elderly and Welsh.

'No!' Rob said, rolling his eyes and shaking his head theatrically. 'Why would it be my father?'

'OK, so *why* is your dad calling you?' I asked, ignoring his patent lie. Rob had always been a terrible liar, something I saw as a positive, endearing trait of character. 'Has something happened?'

Rob shrugged. He knew the game was up.

'Are you going to call him back?'

'I doubt it.'

'Why not?' I asked. 'What if something's happened to your mum?'

Rob grimaced. 'I don't want to, I guess,' he said. 'That's generally why people don't do things.'

'Rob, why don't you ever see them? Why won't you ever talk about them?' The question was dangerous and I knew it. You don't live with someone for that long without learning which subjects to avoid.

Rob shook his head as if he could shake my question from

the air around him, and reached for the TV remote. 'Wha'd'you wanna watch?' he asked. 'Any idea what's on?'

He'd responded exactly like this over the years, every time the subject of his parents had come up. But that day, for some reason, I didn't want to let it go. Perhaps I just fancied an argument.

'Rob!' I said. 'Don't do this. Talk to me.'

'He's a...' Rob said, with a sigh. 'The man's a...' He shook his head quickly.

'He's still your father.'

'He's... not a good person,' Rob said. 'Neither of them are. You don't know what they're like, so just...'

'Which might be because you've never *told* me what they're like,' I said.

'Yep,' Rob said. 'I know.'

'But what if she's dying?' I asked. 'What if your mum's on her deathbed? Or what if he is?'

'I dunno,' Rob said.

'You *dunno?*' I repeated.

'Good riddance, maybe?' he said, quietly.

'Rob!' I exclaimed, shocked. 'You can't say that. No matter what they got wrong in the past, they're still your parents.'

'Sometimes bad people have kids,' Rob said. 'What can I say?'

'But what if this is the last chance?'

'The last chance for *what?*' he asked, dismissively.

'For anything,' I said. 'I mean... when was the last time you spoke?'

'I don't remember.'

'Yes, you do.'

'OK... When I was seventeen, I think,' Rob said.

'Christ! I mean, I knew it was... but *seventeen?* So why now? Something must have happened.'

'OK!' Rob said angrily. 'OK! OK! OK! Jesus! I'll call him, all right?' And with that he stood up, threw the remote more at me than to me, and left the room.

Because getting anything out of Rob about his parents was like extracting a pearl from an oyster, I never did find out the exact nature of that conversation. But he did eventually reveal that the call had been about a box.

His parents were moving into a care home, he said, and his father had come across a box with Rob's name on it.

'What's in it?' I asked. We were side by side in bed, about a week after the phone call in the car.

'I don't know,' Rob said. '*Dad* doesn't know, or so he says.'

'Presumably your mum must know?'

'She's gone loopy, apparently,' Rob said. 'Dementia. So...'

'And he can't open the box and have a look?'

'He could,' Rob said, starting to sound irritated again. 'But he won't. And don't ask why he won't – please don't ask me that – because other than the fact he's a dick, I don't know.'

'Could he maybe send it, then? Couldn't he just post it to you? How big is it, anyway?'

'Jesus!' Rob said. 'It's like having the exact same conversation twice. I didn't enjoy it much first time round.'

'I'm sorry,' I said, actually feeling a bit tearful because of his snappy tone. I reached for my book and opened it at the bookmark, but then changed my mind and snapped it shut. 'You know, the only reason I have to ask you all these questions is because you don't just tell me what happened like any normal person would.'

'Yeah, well, maybe I'm not,' Rob said, rolling away from me.

'Not what?' I asked as he clicked off his bedside light.

'A normal person,' he said. 'Good night.'

* * *

'I'm going to go up there and get it,' Rob announced. It was seven the next morning and I wasn't yet awake enough to eat breakfast.

'I'm sorry?' I answered, then, 'Oh! The box?'

Rob nodded. He looked glum. 'It's probably full of shit – old clothes or something. But if I don't go, I'll never know. And Dad being Dad, he *will* bin it.'

'He probably just wants to see you,' I said. 'That's what it sounds like to me. He's using it as a hostage.'

'Maybe,' Rob said. 'Subconsciously, maybe, at any rate.' He took his tea off to the office then, leaving me to drink my coffee and come to. I'd had a night of Lucy-themed nightmares, and felt as if I'd been running through junkie-filled squats for a week.

Rob returned half an hour later and poured himself a mug of coffee before he sat down. 'Will you be OK on your own with Lucy?'

'When?' I asked.

'It takes a whole day to get there, and another one to get back, that's the thing. So I'll probably be gone two or three days.'

'Oh,' I said. 'Where the hell are they? The Outer Hebrides?'

'Wales,' Rob said. 'But North Wales. It's not so easy to get to from here. It's about an eight-hour drive.'

'Train?' I offered. '*Plane*, maybe?'

Rob shook his head. 'Even worse,' he said. 'Nine hours instead of eight. And about a thousand different changeovers on the way. Now you know why I've never taken you to meet the in-laws.'

'Um, I don't think it was because of the long drive,' I said.

'No,' Rob admitted. 'Probably true.'

'Do you *want* to see them, then?' I asked. 'Is that why?' Something about the journey he was planning didn't make sense.

'No,' Rob said. 'No, I really don't.'

'Not even a tiny bit? Not even after all these years?'

He shook his head solemnly. 'Not even a tiny bit. Not even the weeniest bit.'

'Then don't go,' I told him, simply. 'Tell him to open the damned box or bin it. Leave it up to him.'

'I kind of feel that I *need* to go,' Rob admitted, after a moment's thought. 'Or I *maybe* need to go at any rate, and if I don't I'll never know if I needed to or not.'

'You think you might regret it later on?'

'Something like that,' Rob said. 'It's messy.' He tapped his forehead with one finger. 'Up here,' he said. 'It's all messed up, really. None of it makes much sense.'

'No, it does,' I said, reaching for his wrist and giving it a squeeze. 'They're your parents. Whatever they've done or not done, they're still your parents.'

'Don't say that,' Rob said quietly. 'Please stop saying that.'

'OK,' I said, releasing his wrist. 'I'll stop. I'm sorry. You're right. I don't know.'

We were still expecting Lucy to relapse at any moment back then, and in the past such events had been spectacular – involving threats and theft or even violence.

Lou was down in Bath, Mum was working and I did not want to be left alone looking after our daughter. I could perfectly imagine Rob coming home and me having to announce that I'd lost track of her – or, worse, that she was dead. So we travelled to Anglesey as a family, the three of us, Rob and me taking it in turns to drive, the soundtrack provided by Rob's old Duran Duran and OMD CDs, which had, it transpired, migrated from the oblivion drawer to his car.

It rained all the way up the M2, around the M25, and even hailed a bit on the M1, half of which had been coned into contraflow damnation, seemingly for no reason. We never saw anyone with so much as a spade, never even a workman with a mug of tea. Lucy said the cones were maybe alien invaders, and no one realised they were about to attack – an idea that Rob said would make a great episode of *Doctor Who*.

It was nine in the evening and dark and blustery when we arrived in Red Wharf Bay. 'Lovely,' Lucy said, sarcastically. 'Anyone for a swim?'

Once we'd eaten a pub dinner and gone to our rooms, I asked Rob if he thought Lucy would be OK. 'Do I need to go sleep in her room, do you think?'

'Whether she'll be OK is up to her,' Rob said. 'But I think even she'd struggle to find a dealer here.'

'Lucy can find a dealer anywhere,' I reminded him.

He sighed deeply. 'She'll be fine,' he said. 'And if she isn't we'll just leave her with her lovely grandparents.'

The next morning, the weather had changed and in the morning light the bay looked stunning.

The tide had gone out, beaching fishing boats on the shiny mudflats. These were bordered by an autumn-leaved coast peppered with quaint cottages and low outcrops of cliff. 'Who knew Anglesey was like this?' I said. I couldn't believe that I'd never been there, that I'd never even known anyone who'd been there. It was stunning.

We walked half a mile in the morning sunshine and then sat, side by side, on a wall.

'It's gorgeous,' Lucy said. 'It's like a Turner painting.'

Rob and I glanced at each other. He discreetly raised one eyebrow.

Lucy had been unable to experience any kind of happiness for ages, that was the thing. Beauty, sunsets, music, joy – for years they'd passed her by. For most of the past decade the only comment she would have ever made about somewhere like Red Wharf Bay was that it was 'boring' and there was 'nothing to do'.

Eventually, we'd come to understand that what she meant when she said she was bored was merely that there were no drugs to take. And without drugs to enhance the experience, everything, to Lucy, looked grey. After years of drug-enhanced ecstasy her brain had rewired itself so that life without drugs just seemed interminably awful.

So she shocked us, that morning, with her simple, 'It's gorgeous.' I think we were both thinking that just perhaps, for the first time, something had changed. Either that or she'd managed to get hold of more drugs.

'What?' Lucy said. 'It is!'

I realised I'd been staring at her, trying to catch a glimpse of her pupils.

'She's right,' Rob said, raising his fingers like a picture frame. 'It's the mist that does it. It makes it look like a picture.'

'Do they live on the coast?' Lucy asked.

'My parents?' Rob said. 'I don't know.'

'You must have looked it up on a map,' I said.

'Yeah,' Rob admitted. 'Yeah, I think the house they're moving out of is pretty near the coast. Not so sure about the home.'

'You never lived here then?' Lucy asked.

'Wales, you mean, or here?'

'Either,' Lucy said. 'Both.'

'We lived in Cardiff until I was six,' Rob said. 'But then we moved to Margate. So Wales, yes, but never here.'

'Why Margate?' Lucy asked.

Rob shrugged. 'Why does anyone move anywhere?'

'But they moved back here and you stayed on?'

Rob nodded, then looked down at his swinging feet.

'How old were you then?' Lucy asked.

'How old was I when?'

'When they moved back?'

I swallowed with difficulty. She was pushing the boundaries and she knew it.

'Seventeen,' Rob said.

'Wow,' Lucy said. 'You were young.'

'Yeah,' Rob said. 'Anyway... What I suggest is that I leave you here to explore all this beautiful countrys—'

'I want to come,' Lucy said, interrupting him.

'Well you can't.'

'I want to lay eyes on my grandparents,' she said. 'At least once in my life. Surely that's not too much to ask, is it?'

'I'm going over there, getting the box, and then I'm leaving. In and out, that's it.'

'Come on, Rob, Lucy's got a point,' I said. I was thinking how this too – an actual desire on Lucy's part to do something that had nothing to do with drugs – was new. 'I'd quite like to catch a glimpse of them myself.'

'Please, Dad,' Lucy said. 'I never ask you for anything.'

Rob guffawed at that and I joined in with a snort, so Lucy changed her tune. 'OK, maybe I've asked for lots of stuff. But it's not like I'm asking for drugs here,' she said pointedly, pressing the most powerful button she had available. 'Or even money for drugs. I just want to see them. Just so I have a picture in my head.'

'Come on, Rob,' I said. 'Where's the harm?'

He sighed and looked out across the mudflats to where a fisherman was digging up bait. I knew he was weighing up what was best for him with what might be best for Lucy.

'OK,' he said with a shake of the head. 'Whatever. But I'm warning you, it's going to be in and out. I'm not staying more than five minutes, and I don't want either of you hassling me when I decide to leave.'

'That's fair, isn't it, Lucy?' I said.

'Sure,' she said. 'It's a deal.'

After lunch on the bay we drove along the coast to Moelfre, where Rob's parents' current house was located. He was silent and brooding during the drive.

'Why did you fall out with them?' Lucy asked unexpectedly. 'What did they actually do?'

I was shocked that she'd asked so directly. I felt sure that she understood just as well as I did that both the question and the answer were taboo. But then as we sat there in silence, as we waited to see how he'd respond, I thought, *Maybe he's going to actually tell us. Maybe someone just needed the courage to ask.*

But no, my first instinct had been the right one. 'I'll tell you some day,' Rob said. 'But not now. Not just before I have to look at them.'

'Wow,' Lucy said. 'It must have been bad.'

'Yeah, it was *haven't-seen-them-since-I-was-seventeen* bad,' he said.

Lucy reached forward and gave Rob's shoulder a squeeze. 'Poor Dad!' she said. 'That sounds shitty.'

'Lucy!' I said.

'No, she's right,' Rob said with a shrug. 'It was.'

When we got there, the row of houses looked a lot like Mum's street in Millmead – small two-up two-down pebble-dashed council houses with scrappy gardens. Instead of overlooking the wonderful seascape they backed onto a car park and an ugly public toilet block. My brief hopes of one day inheriting a pretty holiday cottage in Wales were dashed.

'Are you sure you don't want to go for a walk or something?' Rob asked. 'I'd be happier. It's not likely to be pleasant.'

'If it makes you really uncomf—' I started to say, but Lucy interrupted me.

'No,' she said, defiantly. 'I want to see them. And then one day soon, when you're ready, I want you to tell me what all the fuss is about.'

The Havards lived at number 76, which turned out to be the last – and shabbiest – house in the row. The roof was green with moss and a couple of aggressive-looking gulls were picking at it and squawking at each other as we opened the gate.

It was Rob's father who came to the door and my initial reaction was shock at how old he was. I'd been expecting someone roughly my mother's age, but of course, in addition to Rob being older than me in the first place, my mother had had me at seventeen. Rob's father looked well into his eighties. He had ugly out-of-date clothes – shiny school trousers and a shirt with a seventies collar – a bald head and a snowy beard, along with watery grey-blue eyes.

'Rob!' he said. 'Christ! When you said you'd come, I didn't believe it.'

'No,' Rob said. 'Me neither.'

They stood there on the doorstep eyeing each other up until eventually Rob's father said, 'I'd forgotten how tall you are.'

'Had you?' Rob said, nodding gently and sounding disdainful, then, more softly, 'I suppose it's been a while.'

There was a moment of edgy silence until Lucy stepped forward and held out her hand. 'Lucy,' she said. 'The daughter.'

'David,' Rob's father said, shaking her hand. 'The father.' I couldn't tell if he was mocking Lucy or simply copying her because he didn't know what else to do.

'Dawn,' I said, trying to make a joke out of it. 'The *wife!*'

David shook my hand but carried on looking at Lucy. I assumed he was searching for a resemblance between her and Rob, but then he said, 'Aren't you a pretty one, eh?'

'Don't!' Rob said sharply, making us all jump. 'Just don't, or I swear...'

David glanced at me then and pulled a face. 'He's always

been touchy, this one,' he said. 'But then I'm assuming you know that by now.'

'No,' I said, pointing a fake smile in Rob's direction. 'Can't say I do. Rob's never been touchy with me at all.'

'OK,' David said. 'Well, lucky you.'

Rob drew in a big noisy breath and then said, 'So! This box!' His voice was higher and edgier than usual and he sounded vaguely Welsh. I performed a sort of double-take.

'Yes, the box,' David said. 'It's in the shed. I'll just...' And then he closed the front door in our faces while he went looking for the keys.

'Gosh,' Lucy whispered. 'Welcome to Wales. Do come in!'

'I warned you,' Rob said. 'I warned you he's—'

The front door opened again sharply. David waved a key at us – it was tied onto the end of a shoelace.

'Found it!' he said, triumphantly. As he crossed the tiny garden to the dilapidated shed, he continued, 'I would invite you all in for a cup of tea, but there's not much furniture left. They took most of it last Monday. Plus we only kept two cups.'

'Sure,' Rob said. 'No problem.'

'But you can see your mother if you want to.'

'Right,' Rob said flatly. I wasn't sure if it was a yes or a no.

David struggled to open the rain-swollen door to the shed and eventually Rob stepped in to help him.

Inside, it was piled high with classic shed rubbish – a hosepipe, a rusty lawnmower, some tools, an old pedal bin... And in the middle of a small clearing sat the box.

'That's it,' David said, tapping it gently with the tip of one shoe.

We all stood looking at the box. It was about the size of a large microwave and had been taped up so thoroughly that it was impossible to tell what it had originally held.

'And you honestly don't know what's in it?' Rob said, crouching down.

'I do not,' David said, then, 'Open it if you want.'

Rob tested the box for weight – it looked pretty light. He hiked it up into his arms. 'No, I think I'll open it back home,' he said.

'It might just be rubbish though,' Lucy pointed out.

'Then that's something I'll find out back home.'

'So do you want to?' David asked, as he locked the door. 'Do you want to see Eileen, or not?'

Rob shrugged. 'Not sure,' he said.

'You do,' I told him. 'Now we're here, of course you do.'

'Maybe,' Rob said, then, 'Sure.'

'There's not much of her left,' David said, and for a split second I imagined the horror of her dead and rotting in one of the bedrooms.

'He means there's not much left of her *mind*,' Rob said, catching my eye. 'The dementia.'

The house smelled of something sickly and sweet – maybe porridge – but there was also a smell of piss. Most of the furniture had indeed been taken away and all that remained in the lounge were two armchairs, the TV and a horrible glass and rusted-chrome coffee table.

Rob's mother was sitting in one of the armchairs staring vaguely in the direction of the television, which was showing some kind of game show. The sound was turned down low.

Eileen was working her mouth silently and fiddling with the sleeve of her faded blue dress. She had a downy moustache and a few long white hairs sprouting from her chin that I immediately felt desperate to pluck. She looked even older than her husband.

At the sight of her, Rob paused and blew through his lips, and I wondered for the first time if it might be his mother who Rob had fallen out with all those years ago. For some reason I'd always assumed that it was his dad, but now I wasn't so sure.

'Hello, Mother,' Rob said, coldly. He crossed the room and

crouched down between her and the TV.

Eileen didn't react to his presence in any way, so he bobbed left and right, trying to catch her eye, before glancing up at his father. 'Can she see me?' he asked. 'Can she even hear?'

David nodded and blinked slowly. 'It's her mind that's gone,' he said. 'The lights are on but nobody's home.'

'It's Rob,' Rob said loudly. 'Do you remember me?'

'She doesn't remember anything at all,' David said.

'That must be convenient,' Rob muttered. 'Still, I bet you do.'

I bit my lip and shot a fleeting glance at Rob's father. He looked somehow blank, like he too had switched off his mind.

'Mother!' Rob said again. 'It's Rob!'

She moved her mouth silently for a bit and then quietly said, 'Rob.' She said it flatly, without recognition or any kind of intonation. I think she was simply repeating the word.

'This is...' Lucy gasped. And then she was gone, running out into the street.

'Go with her,' Rob said nodding at me. 'I'll only be a couple more minutes.'

I found Lucy pacing the car park, her eyes glossy with tears. 'That was just so awful,' she said, shaking her head. 'I'm sorry I ran out but...'

'It's OK,' I told her, grabbing her elbow and reeling her in for a hug. 'I know. It's horrific.'

'Can you imagine?' she asked, and though I didn't know if she meant, *Can you imagine how it feels, being like that?* or *Can you imagine being that distant with your parents?* or *Can you imagine seeing your parents in such a decrepit state?* I said, 'No, I can't,' because the truth was I couldn't imagine any of it.

'Can we go for a walk or something?' Lucy asked, glancing furtively back at the house. 'I don't want to even be near the place.'

'Sure,' I said. 'I'll go tell Rob.'

. . .

We walked to the seafront – it wasn't far – and then continued on along the coast. I checked my phone a few times and when there was still no news from Rob half an hour later I suggested we turn back. 'If he's still with them we can wait in that cafe we saw,' I suggested.

'Sure,' Lucy said. 'I'm starting to get hungry anyway.'

We'd walked in near silence until that moment, both lost, I think, in our thoughts. But as we started to head back, Lucy asked, 'What do you think happened, Mum? Or do you secretly know?'

'I don't,' I told her. 'I really don't.'

'But you must have an idea,' she said. 'You must have a theory after all these years.'

'Only I don't, really,' I said. 'Rob's never given me any clues. As you know he really doesn't like to talk about them. But I think it must have been quite bad.'

'Yeah,' Lucy said. 'I was thinking maybe...'

I braced myself because I thought she was about to put words to something so awful that I'd never even allowed myself to think it in any coherent way.

Instead she said, '... never mind. I really don't know,' and I was happy to leave it at that.

'I'm not sure I even *want* to know, if I'm honest,' I told her. It was an attempt at closing the conversation.

'No,' Lucy agreed. 'Just seeing them was bad enough. They were creepy. I know that sounds nasty and they're my grandparents and everything, but didn't you think they were creepy?'

'Maybe,' I said. 'Maybe a bit.'

'Dad *said* not to come,' Lucy said. 'Now I'm thinking he was right.'

'At least you've seen them,' I said.

'That's kind of my point,' Lucy said. 'I'm wishing that I

hadn't.'

When we reached the cafe, I texted Rob so that he could join us.

'You were with them a long time, in the end,' I said, once he arrived, looking red-faced and either flustered or angry – I wasn't sure which.

'Not really,' he said. 'I left just after you.'

'Oh,' I said. 'Then where were you? Why didn't you call?'

'I was just in the car, catching my breath.'

'Did you look in the box?' Lucy asked.

'Like I said,' Rob said, 'I'll do that back at home.'

We ate our sandwiches and paninis in thoughtful silence, and then drove back to the hotel at Red Wharf Bay. 'Siesta time,' Rob said as he switched off the ignition. 'I'm exhausted.'

'Me too,' Lucy said. 'That was intense.'

'I'm sorry,' Rob said. 'I'm sorry you had to see them like that, Luce.'

'It's OK,' she said. 'It's not like you didn't warn me.'

Once she'd gone to her room and Rob and I were side by side on the bed, he asked, 'It won't change the way you look at me, will it?'

I frowned, then rolled towards him. I laid one hand across his chest. 'No,' I said, then, 'How could it?'

'Seeing I've got such awful parents,' Rob said. 'You won't start to think that I'm like them?'

'They weren't *awful*, Rob,' I said. 'They're just very old.'

'Is that how it seemed then? Just old?'

'Yes,' I said, 'Of course.' It was a lie. 'They seemed old and frail and, in your mother's case, really quite ill. He was a bit crotchety maybe, but what eighty-year-old isn't?'

'He's nearly ninety,' Rob said. 'Eighty-nine, I think.'

'Well,' I told him. 'There you go. But nothing *awful*

happened.'

'Good,' Rob said, rolling away from me. 'I'm glad it seemed that way.'

I snuggled against his back and pulled him tightly against me and he raised one hand and placed it over mine to welcome the gesture.

I thought about his question and wondered if it *would* change how I felt about him, because, in a way, it already had. I was feeling a tenderness towards him, a sort of pity really, for whatever it was that he was going through and whatever had happened to him as a boy.

But it was also true that I'd noticed he had his mother's brown eyes and his mother's blobby nose, and I'd momentarily, despite my best efforts, imagined him old, with dementia, staring at some mind-numbingly stupid game show. Perhaps meeting the in-laws had been a dangerous game. Even I didn't know how my thoughts about it might pan out.

'What about Lucy?' Rob asked. 'Was it the same for her, d'you think?'

'I'm sorry,' I said. 'I don't really...?'

'Did *Lucy* just think they were old and a bit sad?'

'Oh, yes,' I replied after one complete breath. 'I think that's exactly what she thought.'

'Right,' Rob said. 'Good.'

'Why?' I asked. 'What are you worried about?'

'Just, you know...' Rob said. 'How she sees me. How she sees herself, now she's met her grandparents. I wouldn't want it to derail her recovery. Because she's doing really well this time round. Don't you think she's doing better?'

'I do,' I said. 'It feels different, doesn't it?'

'Yeah,' Rob said. 'Yeah it does. So this won't...?'

'No,' I told him, pulling him tight again. 'Of course not.'

But I remember worrying that maybe he was right. I thought briefly, as I lay there with my husband in my arms, that if it did upset Lucy too much then maybe the answer would be to tell her about Billy. And then I decided that would clearly be worse – that it was the sort of thing that could really send her over the edge.

God, I remember thinking. *Kids. The worry never ends.*

That afternoon, while the sunshine lasted, we visited Llanddona Beach, Penmon Point, and Beaumaris. They were all as pretty as each other and I almost suggested returning one summer for a holiday. Luckily I realised what a bad idea that would have been before I opened my mouth.

By the time we ate our evening meal, the rain had returned and was lashing against the windows. Because the next morning the weather remained unremittingly foul, we simply ate our breakfasts and left.

* * *

Rob did not open the box when we got home, and a week later it was still sitting on the workbench in the garage.

'I'm going to open the damned thing myself,' Lucy said, one day. 'It's driving me insane.'

'I know what you mean,' I said. 'But maybe *don't* do that.'

'Oh, I won't really,' Lucy said. 'Though actually, I just might.'

I'd already inspected the box closely myself, trying to find a way to take a peep inside. I'd considered peeling back the old masking tape, but it was ancient and un-peelable, and putting on fresh new masking tape would be a giveaway.

While Lucy was intrigued about the contents, I in some weird way feared them. If I could just get a preview, I thought, then I could prepare myself. I could work out the best thing to say when the time came.

But then, one day, I went out to the garage to look for a screwdriver, and I realised the box had gone. It was about a month after our trip to Anglesey.

Lucy got home first that evening. She'd been working part time in a beauty salon in Broadstairs, a job Ange, Shelley's sister, had fixed her up with.

'You didn't touch Dad's box, did you?' I asked.

'No. Why?' Lucy said. 'What's happened to it?'

'It's gone,' I said. 'So as long as that wasn't you, it must have been your father.'

'God,' Lucy said. 'He finally opened it, then?'

'I'll ask him about it later, if it's all the same to you. I'll wait for the right moment and I'll find out.'

'As long as you tell me,' Lucy said. 'As long as you tell me as soon as you know.'

But Lucy being Lucy, she couldn't wait. Instead she asked Rob at dinner. 'Mum says you opened your mystery box,' she said. 'So come on, Dad. What was in it?'

Rob, who was in the process of serving spaghetti sauce, didn't flinch. 'Nothing in the end,' he said. 'It was just junk. So I binned it.'

'Junk?' I repeated. 'What kind of junk?'

Rob looked me in the eye and blew through his lips nonchalantly. 'An old schoolbook of mine. An old teddy bear. One half of a pair of roller skates. *Junk*.'

'God,' Lucy said. 'All that driving for nothing!'

'Yeah,' Rob said, resuming his dolloping of pasta sauce. 'I know. Bummer, huh? Anyway, how was your day in Hairy Heaven?'

'It's Nail Nirvana, Dad, and you know it. And it was fine. I was just sweeping floors and shit.'

'They have a lot of that in Hairy Heaven, do they?' Rob asked, grinning lopsidedly. 'Shit?'

. . .

By retracing my movements over the last few days I was able to work out that the box had still been in the garage on Tuesday. It had rained and I'd used the tumble-drier, so I would have noticed if the box had been gone.

As bin day was Monday, I still had forty-eight hours left to investigate. So, on Sunday, I sent Rob on a fake mission to buy caster sugar so that I could rummage through the contents of our wheelie bin.

Perhaps you guessed this already, but I found nothing. There was no box and nothing strange that could have been in the box. Whether it had not really been binned, or had been binned far from home to prevent anyone discovering the contents, I didn't know.

On Sunday night I asked Rob again if he'd really just thrown it away.

'Yep,' he said. 'I told you. It was rubbish. Absolute rubbish. Random stuff left over from their last move.'

'All of it?' I asked.

'All of it,' he said.

Rob had never really lied to me before, or when he had he'd always caved in at the moment I'd challenged him. But this time he'd looked me in the eye and dug in. He wasn't going to tell me, and that annoyed me a bit really.

Perhaps it was understandable – though without actually knowing the contents it was impossible to be sure – but that lie festered a bit. It niggled me.

What upset me more than the lie itself was the way the lie had been delivered. Because for the first time ever – that I knew of – Rob had lied and been utterly convincing. Which made me wonder if his infamous inability to lie had been a double-bluff all along. Had he lied badly about all the small stuff so that he could get away with the big stuff? And if that was so, then what *was* the big stuff?

NINE

LOSING TRACK (BY ROB)

I got bored with it all.

I know how pathetic that sounds, how inexcusable, too, but it happens to be the truth.

Dawn and Lucy had been everything I'd ever wanted but though I could still remember that as a fact, my life with them suddenly bored me to tears. The reality of our family had been exhausting and I think resentment was probably quite a big chunk of it. Boredom and resentment can sometimes be hard to separate.

Whatever the cause, I felt chronically, depressingly tired.

Lucy had finally calmed down and was living with her Polish chap, Aleksei, in Ashford. He seemed nice enough, though, it has to be said, by then she'd set the bar quite low. As long as he wasn't hitting her or dealing drugs (and it appeared he did neither) it was OK with us. But now the brackets of her madness had closed, I felt more resentful about it than relieved. Because other than to ruin ten years of our lives, what on earth had been the point of all that?

As for Lou, everything was so perfect, I felt jealous. Jealous of my son. Yes, I know that's a bit pathetic too.

He had a job that he loved with a cool video game company, and a big room in a shared house with good people. He had a turntable and vinyls and a whole string of gorgeous girlfriends who, like a fashion show, appeared one after the other. He rode a motorbike and went to concerts and raves, and rode across Europe one summer with a curvy Norwegian girl who looked like Raquel Welch circa 1967. I did feel proud too, and I told him so, but the dominant emotion was jealousy.

I bought stuff, lots of stuff, and for a while it seemed to help.

I bought new clothes and a better hi-fi and – to be like my trendy son – a retro turntable for vinyls. I got just about every gadget Apple released and bought Ray-Bans and a cross-trainer and traded the BMW for a TT.

When Dawn jokingly called it my 'midlife crisis' I managed to laugh convincingly.

I could trace the beginning of these misery years – these years where I felt I had a gaping hole in the middle of me – to that trip to Wales. But identifying the start didn't help.

I'd seen my parents hurtling towards oblivion that day. I'd never really thought about death before, or at any rate not in a way that really got to me. But as I'd driven home from that dreadful visit, a veil of misery had settled on me, a deep damp blanket of imminent decay.

Because this was it, wasn't it? This was as good as it would get.

This was a wife who seemed to be doing her damndest to look like a witch – who didn't like sex – or at any rate not with me – and who, perhaps worst of all, I didn't even mind not having sex with. *This* was a daughter who'd wrecked the best ten years of our marriage and, though now she was perfectly fine, could still wreck the rest as well, if she merely decided that's what floated her boat. Beyond that, the future was aches and pains and dementia. My back was already playing me up and I had a twinge in my shoulder.

What was next? What was there to hope for? A piss-scented old people's home that would be so bad I'd actually welcome death?

I suppose we all have to realise this stuff at some point, but how anyone copes with it gracefully is beyond me.

As the weeks and then years went by, I tried to think myself out of the rut. I really did put serious effort into it.

I had a pretty daughter – now saved and reasonably sane – and a handsome, successful son. I was with the woman I'd always wanted to be with – a woman who I agreed with on just about every subject – and owned a business that ran smoothly, feeding multiple bank accounts with cash.

But for what? That was the thing I couldn't work out. What was the point of any of it?

Even the good-news fact of Dawn and me getting on so well, I found boring.

We'd tailored our thoughts and tastes over the years so that they fitted perfectly together. We now voted for the same party, listened to the same music and tended to choose the same foods, sometimes even the same wine. The few things we still disagreed about – nuclear power, whether Bill Gates was truly good, Nicola Sturgeon – we'd learned never to mention. And that was great, that made things run smoothly. Supposedly, according to Andy, it was proof that we were soulmates.

But where were the passionate discussions? Where were the new bands, the new foods, the new holiday destinations, the new experiences another person was supposed to bring into your life? Why did I feel like I was living with a doused-down version of me? More to the point, why did I feel like *I* was a doused-down version of me?

To jazz things up a bit, to try to step out of our routine, I bought a motorbike. It was an old, perfectly reconditioned XT 500. I bought a leather jacket and two helmets and some boots.

The Yamaha was the same model I'd owned when I'd met Dawn way back when, a bike I'd sold before she'd ever once climbed on behind me. At the time, I'd needed the money to put towards the deposit on our first house.

I rode the bike back from the seller's place, past Dungeness power station, a road Andy and I used to race down in our youth. And for a moment, just for a moment, it worked and the feeling returned. I felt young again. I felt free.

When I got home Dawn was mealy-mouthed and mocking. She had days like that, sometimes whole weeks.

'It's fun!' I told her, almost tearful at her lack of enthusiasm. 'We can go for rides! We can whiz out to the country for picnics! The kids are gone now so we can be ourselves again.'

'That's never who we were, Rob,' she said, shaking her head as if I'd lost the plot. 'If you want to be who we were before, then get yourself a little white van.'

A week later Dawn's mother came over for dinner. 'I'd *love* to go for a ride on your motorbike,' she said when Dawn mockingly told her about the bike.

'Now we've had the sports car, the leather jacket and the motorbike, I'm assuming the next step will be the mistress,' Dawn said.

'I'm up for that too,' Tracey said, with a wink.

'You see,' I told Dawn. 'At least your mum still fancies me.'

* * *

Her name was Cheryl, and she was the secretary in our failing Maidstone branch. And yes, I do know that's another cliché. At least she wasn't *my* secretary.

I rode over there one sunny July day on the Yamaha and, when I left, Cheryl, who'd already commented on my new leather jacket, came out to see.

'Lovely bike,' she said. 'My ex had a big Kawasaki. A Z900

or something. Start it up, then. I love to hear a throbbing engine.'
And when I did, 'Ooh, that sounds meaty. Will you take me for
a ride sometime?'

And what can I say? Dawn wouldn't go near it.

I was as careful as a husband can be. I even bought another
crash helmet so that Dawn wouldn't realise 'her' still unused
one was missing.

Cheryl was the exact opposite of Dawn in every imaginable
way, and I suppose that was the point. She liked rap music and
pizza and perfume. She dyed her hair platinum blond and had
glossy-red lips; she wore heels that made her bum stick out; she
smoked until her voice went husky and laughed until her boobs
wobbled. In many ways she reminded me of Dawn's mum and
that made me realise that I'd expected Dawn to become more
and more like her mum as she aged. It had been an idea that
suited me fine, but instead – and this is no doubt as much my
fault as it is hers – Dawn had become middle class. She'd
become a well-read, feminist, anti-make-up, anti-heels fan of
Fay Weldon, Sandi Toksvig and Patti Smith. Cheryl seemed to
fulfil some part of the bargain I'd missed out on.

Though there were multiple occasions for sex, I resisted for
almost a year.

I told Dawn I had to work one Saturday a month but
instead I'd pick Cheryl up, either in the TT or on the bike, and
we'd drive or ride out into the Kent countryside.

Cheryl had a boyfriend when I met her – though that didn't
last for long. She insisted he wouldn't mind. 'It's not like we're
doing anything anyway,' she said, and that was true, wasn't it?
So we had pub lunches and picnics on the River Medway. We
swam on Sheerness beach and ate Magnums.

For the most part, I managed to not feel guilty. Because
other than the fact I never once mentioned Cheryl to Dawn,
other than the fact I told Dawn I was working, other than the
fact I wore sunblock so I wouldn't go home looking too brown,

and washed it off before I went home so that I wouldn't go home smelling of sunblock – so basically, other than the almost constant deception, what was there to feel guilty about?

But then one day, Cheryl said, 'Pull over.'

We were halfway back to Maidstone after a day on Whitstable beach, and I assumed that she wanted to pee. 'There,' she said, pointing to a lay-by beneath some trees. 'There's perfect.'

'So I have something to ask you,' she said, once I'd turned off the ignition.

'Yeah?' I said. 'What's that?'

'D'you like blow jobs?' Cheryl asked, one finger raised to her pouty, glossy lips.

I sensed myself blush, but admitted that, as far as I could remember, I did.

'Good,' she said. 'Because I really want to give you a blow job. I've been thinking about it for weeks.'

Believe it or not, I said 'no'.

I said, 'Can I think about it for a bit? It's just, you know...'

'No problem,' Cheryl said. 'Things are complicated because of your wife, I know that, and it's fine.' But her expression suggested otherwise – that it wasn't fine at all.

I also thought about it for weeks, in fact it would be fair to say I got obsessed.

I wondered if Cheryl was good at it (something Dawn, who wasn't a fan, had not been). If someone, say Cheryl, was a blow job *expert*, then what would that *feel* like?

I also wondered if Cheryl would dump me if we didn't now move on to a sexual relationship, and how I'd feel if she did, and if I would ever have another chance to have sex before I died. I even snuggled up to Dawn one night just to check she'd still push me away. She did it tactfully, and with humour, but push me away she did.

Finally, I wondered if I'd look back from the decrepitude of old age and regret that I hadn't seized the day.

When I finally said yes, I fell in love with Cheryl instantly – fell in love while I still had my dick in her. Maybe that's why they call it 'making love'. At least, at the time I thought I loved her, though that probably only goes to show what a stupid word 'love' is. It was nothing like the way I'd felt about Dawn, way back when, and with hindsight it didn't have the depth or heft of how I felt about Dawn even during the lowest ebbs of our relationship.

But Cheryl was pretty and sexy and fun. She gave, it turned out, excellent head, and she gave it with joy. She arched her back and screamed the roof down when she came, too, and these were things that made me feel like a real man – whatever that means. It made my heart race to see her and sometimes it gave me a hard-on just to think about her – she was only the second woman I'd ever slept with, after all.

I'd be sitting, in theory watching *Gogglebox* with Dawn, in reality thinking about sex with Cheryl, and I'd have to position a cushion to hide my erection. That truly was like being seventeen again.

We started to go to her flat. She was single by then and, for shagging, the flat was both more comfortable and more discreet.

Her place was small, new and girly – a sort of opposite of home, where things had morphed into junk-store chic. Many of Cheryl's things were fake leather, and most of them seemed to be pink.

She had an enormous Samsung TV that was rarely switched off, and, for music, a shitty Bluetooth speaker that was rarely on. She had inspirational art on the lounge wall – *Live Well, Laugh Often* and, in the bathroom, *Life Blesses Us Every Day*. She had surprisingly expensive tastes in glassware but one hundred per cent plastic pot plants all over the place because she had, she claimed, 'purple fingers'. I'd questioned that the first time she'd said it and she'd explained, 'Well purple's the opposite of green, innit?'

This is going to sound stupid but, in the interests of honesty, I'll say it anyway: I loved all of it. Even her naff-ness. *Especially* her naff-ness. Being there to witness it felt young and fresh and attractive.

We started going away for weekends – a spa in the Lake District, a hotel in Edinburgh, one-nighters in Scarborough and Devon. As cover, I named business meetings, team-building sessions and conferences, and sometimes these were even real. It was simply that I rarely attended any of the events. I was too busy banging Cheryl in the shower.

For the most part, it wasn't that complicated to keep it all hidden. Dawn, as far as I could tell, was uninterested to the point that I sometimes wondered if she was conspiring to make it all possible.

Then one day as we were driving home – my knob actually sore from too much sex – Cheryl shifted in her seat and turned off the radio.

'Can I talk to you about something?' she asked. She slid one hand down my inner thigh.

'Of course,' I said. 'Anything.'

'So, you know how I'm on the pill,' she said. 'And you know how I'm nearly forty? Well, I'm thinking that maybe I want a kid.'

'Right,' I said. 'OK...' My breath caught in my throat. *Windscreen, air-freshener, Cheryl's hand.*

'I mean, you like kids, don't you?' she asked.

I laughed a bit at that. Lucy's horror years had flashed through my mind's eye the instant she'd said the word kid, but I'd countered them with images of her and Lou as cute toddlers on the beach. How could you even begin to sum up how you felt about all of that? Certainly not with a yes or a no.

'You don't?' Cheryl asked, confused by my snigger.

'It's just...' I said, glancing at her and smiling. 'It's a bit more complicated than that, isn't it?'

'I know *that*,' she said. 'I ain't stupid.'

'I didn't think for one minute that you were,' I said.

'And I know you've got two already, and I know you're pushing fifty and—'

'I'm fifty-four,' I said, interrupting her. I was surprised that she didn't know that.

'Oh,' Cheryl said, looking shocked, then, 'I thought you were forty-nine but whatever. And I know you're not gonna leave her...'

I glanced sideways at her and thought – genuinely, for the first time ever – *Well, I might*. The kids were long gone by then, with Lou working for Activision in London, and Lucy and Alek trying for babies over in Ashford. Dawn and I no longer seemed to share a great deal – though how much of that was my fault, it was hard to tell. But she no longer wanted to do anything much with me. The bike, the car, days out, sex, none of it really interested her. Most of the time she was so wrapped up with her mother or the kids, or Wayne or Shelley, or her latest lost cause asylum seeker, that I suspected she didn't think about me at all.

'You wouldn't leave her, would you,' Cheryl said – it was more of a statement than a question. All the same, she was daring me to contradict her.

I shrugged and looked back at the road. 'I don't know,' I said. 'I've never really thought about it.'

'I have,' she said. 'I think about it all the time.'

'I didn't know that. You never said.'

'But anyway,' she said. 'That's not the point. The point is that even if you never leave her, I'm thinking I might like to have a kid before it's too late. And at my age I'm cutting it a bit fine. So if it was, like, *mine* – if I promised never to ask you for nothing – would that bother you? Knowing it was yours and what-have-you? Or would that be too weird?'

'I don't know,' I said. 'I'm sorry. It's a bit... you know... out of the blue.'

'We've been seeing each other almost three years,' she said. 'So it's not that out of the blue.'

I thought, *Christ! Three years?* I counted them up, and it was true. It was just that if you took all the days we'd spent together and laid them end to end they'd add up to about two months – less, probably. Whereas Dawn – well, that was thirty years.

'You know what I mean,' I said. 'We've never talked about anything like this. We've never talked about having a kid and we've never talked about me leaving her, for that matter, either.' We never said Dawn's name. It was always 'her' or 'she' or occasionally, when Cheryl was annoyed with me, 'your damned wife'.

'No,' Cheryl said. 'That's why I'm talking to you now, innit? But no pressure. And I mean, I could shag any old bloke to make it happen. I could pick up some random on Tinder. It's just that I'd kind of like it to be you. I keep imagining this gorgeous little mini-you running around. I bet you were super-cute as a kid, weren't you?'

'Me?' I said. 'I'm not sure.' Certainly I had no memory of ever being told I was.

I worried about it a lot. I said 'No,' and then I said, 'Yes, maybe,' before switching to 'Probably not'. I changed my mind every time I saw her and, understandably, she started to get fed up.

'You're just stringing me along,' she said. 'I know it's a "no". It's just you won't say so cos you're worried I'll run off with someone else.'

But it wasn't that – it really wasn't. It was honestly that I couldn't decide.

It would have been good to discuss it with someone, I suppose, but there was no one I could tell. I could almost imagine going through it all with Dawn. We got on so well, we argued so rarely, that I could imagine her saying, 'Well, these are the pros and these are the cons' and being perfectly rational about helping me choose.

Yes, the only person I wanted to discuss it with was my 'damned wife'. Hard not to acknowledge everything I was risking.

* * *

One spring day, I turned up at Cheryl's and it was her mother who opened the door.

'Oh!' I said, blinking at the gust of perfume that hit me on the doorstep. 'Hello! Is Cheryl home?'

'I'm here,' she shouted from indoors. 'Don't mind Mum. She's leaving, *aren't* you, Mum!'

'Don't worry,' her mother said as she stepped aside to let me indoors. 'She's almost ready. She's been trying to get me to leave, but in truth I wanted to get a peek at you. Now it's getting serious and all!'

'Right,' I said, forcing a smile and turning to Cheryl.

'Mum!' Cheryl protested. Then to me, 'Don't take any notice of her. Serious indeed!' And then to her mother, 'Honestly, Mum, you'll scare him off!'

Cheryl's mother tottered over to the sofa and then lowered herself down gingerly. 'It's me knees,' she said, apparently answering some question suggested by my facial expression. 'Buggered from a lifetime of wearing heels.'

'Oh,' I said. 'Buggered knees. That sounds inconvenient.'

'It is,' she said. 'It's *bloody* inconvenient.' I glanced at her shoes then. They were big and pink and had the highest heels I've ever seen other than on a catwalk.

'Oh, I know, I know,' she said, following my gaze. 'But I just can't walk in flats. Plus, they look so much better, don't they? Feminine, like.'

. . .

Once we were finally on our way, I drove in silence, playing the images of Cheryl's mother over and over on the little screen inside my head. Because she'd shocked me, really, Cheryl's mum. She'd seemed so much like a man in drag that it was almost impossible to believe that's not what she actually was.

She'd had big bouffant Long Island hair and slightly off-centre make-up that looked like the printing process might have gone wrong and slipped half an inch to the right. She'd had a gravelly voice, and had been wearing a tight pink Chanel-style two-piece that made her look like a posh sausage. And the shoes, of course, those shoes! She was like the love child of Les Dawson and Eddie Izzard.

'So is she your birth mother?' I asked. It was the only way I could think of to ask the question. I mean you can't really ask, *Is your mum trans by any chance?* no matter how open-minded you are on the subject. Once you can ask that and no one gets upset, we'll really know attitudes have changed.

'What?' Cheryl asked, hesitating about being offended.

'You just don't look much like her,' I said, by way of an alibi. I assumed that she'd be flattered by that.

'Oh?' she said. 'Really? You don't think so? Well, good.' Then, 'No, she really is my mum, more's the pity.'

The truth was she *did* look like Cheryl, though. It's just she looked more like she might be Cheryl's *dad*.

'And your father?' I asked, casually. 'Is he still around?'

'You know he is,' Cheryl said, and it was true, I could remember her having mentioned him. 'He'll be at home drinking beer in front of the telly. I told you before – we're all worried he's going full-blown alcoholic. He drinks way too much these days.'

Ah! I thought. *I'll bet he does.*

'And her name?' I asked. 'I don't think you ever said.'

'Leslie,' she said. 'But everyone just calls her *Les*.'

I had to look out of the side window when she said that. It was as much as I could do not to laugh.

About three months later, I was working in our Margate branch doing a stock-take. The branch manager, Ryan – a lively, joyous, chatty young man I liked a lot – was having car trouble, so in the evening I offered to drive him home.

As we reached Westbrook, Ryan's phone rang, so he wriggled in his seat to extract it from his pocket.

'Hi,' he said. 'I'm almost home... No, my car's knackered, innit... I'm sorry sweetheart, but... Beer? What? Well it'll have to wait... A taxi? You must be joking? It'll cost more than the beer. OK, OK... I'll see what I can do.'

Once he'd hung up I asked what it was about.

'Major crisis!' he said, 'Grandpa's out of beer.'

As it was a stunning evening and we had the top down I offered to drive him out to his grandparents to deliver Coke, beer and crisps.

But when I pulled into the car park of the sheltered housing unit where they lived, I started to worry it had been a bad idea.

'I'll just stay here,' I said. 'You go.'

'Oh, come on,' Ryan said. 'I'll only be five minutes, but you should definitely come and meet 'em. They're lovely.'

The lobby made things worse. Two women in chairs were staring at a silent TV screen and all my anxiety from Wales washed back over me. *Wheelchair, piss, chipped worktop*, I thought. This time, counting in threes was making it worse.

But then we got to Ryan's grandparents' door and the feeling went away. Their little flat was lovely, and they were overjoyed to see their grandson arrive with beer.

'Here he is!' his grandad said. 'Our wonder-boy.'

'Can't have you out of beer, now, can we?' Ryan said, crouching down and beginning to stack the little fridge.

'Come in, come in young man!' Ryan's grandmother instructed. I was still lingering in the doorway. 'We don't bite.'

'Hello,' I said, edging over the threshold. 'I'm Rob.'

'He's my boss!' Ryan told them, sending me a wink. 'My car's broken, so I had to ask him to drive me. So you've got my millionaire boss delivering your beer in his Audi. I hope you're happy.'

'Ah, so you're the one!' his grandfather said. 'He tells us all the time what an ogre you are.'

'I do not!' Ryan said, and his grandfather laughed. 'You'll get me sacked, you will.'

'I'm only pulling your leg. He said you're the best boss money can buy,' his grandfather said.

'You're mixing up your metaphors, Bertie,' his grandmother said. 'You can't say that about a person.'

'Oh, he knows what I mean, don't you?'

'I do,' I said. 'So thanks.'

We didn't stay long, but by the time we left I felt that the visit had done me some good. It had at least provided me with an alternative image of old age.

'Nice little set-up they have there,' I told Ryan, as I drove him back.

'I know. That's all stuff from their house. They always had good taste, those two.'

'It's nice to see some oldies looking happy,' I said. I thought about the horror of having seen mine and wondered where they were now and if it was as nice as Craven Court.

'Dad's parents were a whole different story,' Ryan said. 'They didn't want to move, didn't want to pay for care, didn't want to pay for home help... it went on and on until social services had to go in and drag them out of their own shit. The new place is pretty 'orrible though. But they were well skinny by the time anyone intervened, so I s'pose they're better off. Dad was upset about it. But those two, they've always been lovely. They get on really well and they have bingo on Mondays and cards on Wednesdays, and a disco at Christmas. Gran still dances. Imagine that! And they take 'em to the beach in summer... Yeah, they're happy as Larry, really. But what they don't like is running out of beer. Gramps says that's his secret. His daily can of Guinness. He's convinced he'll die if he stops.'

'You look like her,' I said. 'But I guess you know that.'

'Gran?' Ryan laughed. 'Oh, I know. Everyone always says that. But you should see my mum. We're like two peas in a pod. It used to embarrass me when I was a kid, 'cos everyone always said it. But nowadays I kind of like it. I s'pose we all become our parents eventually.'

'Maybe,' I said. I thought, but didn't say, *I hope not*. I swallowed with difficulty.

'I worry about that, though,' Ryan said. 'Don't you?'

'Becoming like your parents?'

'No, not me, the wife. The mother-in-law's a bloody nightmare. So I'm hoping she won't be like her. Nag nag nag. That'd be my old age ruined good and proper.'

'Right,' I said.

'Bit of a cliché,' Ryan said. 'They kind of have to be awful, don't they?'

'Mothers-in-law?' I asked, as I pulled up outside Ryan's house. 'Mine's actually pretty nice, so I don't think it's obligatory.'

'Yeah? Dawn's mum?'

'Yes, she's funny and lively and actually still pretty fit.'

'Well then,' Ryan said. 'You'll be fine.'

As I drove home that evening, a little later than usual, I was thinking about everything I had back home. If I was ever to enjoy a peaceful old age then it would inevitably be with Dawn.

I walked in the door feeling both guilty and determined to make it up to her. But Dawn was in an angry fluster, in the process of cooking up a storm. The table was laid for six.

'Hey,' I said, leaning in the kitchen doorway. 'What's up? Why are the posh plates out? We celebrating something?'

Dawn, busy stirring some kind of sauce, froze and glared up at me. 'Don't tell me you've forgotten!' she said. 'I mean, I know you're late. I can *see* you're late. But you haven't *totally* forgotten, have you?'

'Oh shit,' I replied, pretending I'd remembered even though the truth was I still had no idea what she was talking about. I glanced around the room, hoping for clues.

'It's Mum's birthday, you bloody idiot! Well, tomorrow it is, but we're doing it tonight.'

'Oh yeah, I thought that was tomorrow though!' I lied.

'I... Jesus, Rob! I *told* you she can't do it tomorrow. I told you she's got a medical thing.'

I had no recollection of that conversation.

'And where's Lou?' Dawn continued. 'You were meant to pick him up from the station. D'you forget your own son as well?' At that precise instant my phone rang – a call from Lou, asking where I was.

'Sorry, dude, running late!' I told him. 'I'll be there in fifteen minutes.

'Unbelievable!' Dawn said. 'Absolutely un-bloody-lievable!' And I could see how for her it might be. She had no idea how much stuff was going on in my head. 'Go!' she said. 'Go now! And buy some bloody champagne on the way!'

As I drove to the station I thought about how Cheryl had been taking up every spare smidgen of space inside my brain. News about my own family had been rolling off me like dew, simply because I just didn't have the spare mental capacity to take it in.

At home, around Dawn, I felt numb. And she seemed angry with me all the time.

Yet when I was with Cheryl – sexy smiling Cheryl – I felt awake, appreciated and alive.

I thought about the retirement home again, about Dawn, Lou and Lucy being my real family. And I wondered if it was salvageable.

Cheryl, quite reasonably, wanted an answer, and in the end, after a few months of anguish, I said 'yes'.

It wasn't an unconditional yes, and I didn't say yes to everything, either.

I never promised, for instance, that I'd leave Dawn, even though I thought that I might. And I didn't say I'd be around for the kid either, though I think we both expected that I would.

But I thought, *This is a chance for a second, completely different life.*

To die having had one family, one daughter, one son, one wife – it seemed mean on the part of whoever had set the whole thing up that we only got one turn on the merry-go-round.

So refusing to accept a second life, when it had been served up on a plate like that, struck me as kind of churlish.

But the main reason I didn't just say 'no' was that the more I thought about it, the less I felt I had the right.

I could stop seeing Cheryl – I had that right. But to force her to choose between me or having a kid? That wasn't fair. And it especially wasn't fair when she'd reached a point in her life where she might not even meet another potential partner before it was too late.

As for telling her she needed to carry on taking the pill,

actually trying to dictate what drugs another human being did and didn't take, that struck me as something that would have been the worst kind of misogyny. When I thought about it I imagined Dawn telling me about some other guy saying it to one of her girlfriends. 'What an arsehole!' she would have said. 'Can you even *imagine* the gall of the guy?'

So I didn't say, 'Carry on taking the pills.' Instead, I said, 'OK.'

I said, 'It's your body and if you're happy to have a kid, no matter what I end up deciding about the rest, then that's totally your choice.'

'Good,' Cheryl said. 'Because I think I was going to stop taking them whatever you said.'

That whole debate had been fraught and emotionally charged and, as far as my potential future role as father and partner, nothing had been resolved anyway. And all that serious discussion, all that messy back and forth-ing, it made the whole thing feel a little bit less 'fun'. Sex, too, suddenly seemed less amusing when the result just might be a pregnancy. When Cheryl squashed her knees against her chest after I'd pulled out, a gesture she claimed made pregnancy more likely, it actually made me feel a bit sick.

Meanwhile, back home, Dawn and I glided around each other, barely touching, like champion ice-skaters.

Dawn was spending a lot of time with her mum. Tracey had some unspecified girly health issue but as she'd sworn Dawn to secrecy it all remained very mysterious. My guess was she was having a hysterectomy or something, but I honestly didn't have a clue.

They were both still busy with Home from Home too.

Since the Brexit vote, attitudes to refugees had taken a turn for the worse, and charities like theirs had more and more desperate cases to deal with. Add that to the fact that I was busy at work, and fake busy at fake work (read: spending time with Cheryl), and we weren't exactly seeing masses of each other.

But when we did find ourselves together, we got on fine. We were polite and thoughtful towards each other and disagreed only rarely. We were heavily into the Arctic Monkeys at the time, and more surprisingly perhaps, Lana Del Rey. The Arctic Monkeys CD had been a gift from Wayne, while Lana had been left behind by Lucy. So for a while those were the two albums we listened to. We agreed on our TV preferences as well, and were both addicted to *Chernobyl* and *Giri/Haji*, so when we weren't running around separately we'd eat takeaway Indian and catch up on those.

I thought a great deal about Ryan's grandparents around that time – that visit had really marked me. I imagined how easy it would be to find myself with Dawn in a little sheltered housing unit one day, listening to Arctic Monkeys and The Stone Roses.

Cheryl favoured reality TV and twenty-four-hour news channels – the same anxious stories going round and round and round. She liked Kanye West and Drake, Adele and Ed Sheeran, and favoured fish and chips over Thai, which she claimed 'burned her tongue'.

For the first time since I'd met her, the differences felt less exciting. If anything (though I refused to let myself think this clearly), they were actually beginning to grate.

TEN

LOSING TRACK (BY DAWN)

Mum had breast cancer. She was devastated about *losin' a boob*, as she put it.

Other than her inability to put up with any man for any length of time, she had very few faults, my mum. But one that she did have was vanity.

Not that worrying about losing a breast is vanity – I'm not suggesting that for a second. It's clearly one of the worst, most terrifying things that can happen to a woman.

But because Mum *was* vain and because she still liked to seduce – still *needed* to seduce, I suppose – I do think that it was even worse for her than it would have been for a no-shave-Shirley like myself.

'You're so lucky, being married,' Mum said one day. I was driving her home from a consultation with the surgeon, the one where he'd announced she was going to need a partial mastectomy.

'Lucky?' I repeated. 'Why?' I wasn't feeling particularly lucky in my marriage at that point. Rob felt too often like another a clingy child, hanging around and trying to get my attention. And because of what was going on with Mum, I didn't have the attention to spare.

'At least you've got someone no matter what happens,' Mum said. 'No one's going to want me after this.'

'Mum,' I said. 'You're catastrophising.' *Catastrophising* was Wayne's new favourite word and it was starting to grow on me too. 'The surgeon promised you'll look fine.'

'One, he didn't promise,' Mum said. 'And two, he said he'll *do his best* and the scar should *begin to fade* after six months.'

'It was *within* six months, Mum,' I said, reaching across to squeeze her arm, a gesture that, unusually, made her flinch. 'He looked like a boob man to me,' I said. 'I'm sure he'll make sure your tit looks even better than before.'

'If it does,' Mum said, forcing a smile that looked more like a death-rictus, 'I'll be all off balance, won't I? I'll probably go round and round in circles.'

But I understood totally why she was so worried. She's always been proud of 'Pinky and Perky'. Men had always commented on them too. For Mum, a partial mastectomy was about as traumatising as trauma can get.

We'd been out of Lucy's madness for a couple of years by then, and I was only just starting to relax when Mum got diagnosed. Suddenly I found myself playing support team all over again, only this time it wasn't to Lucy's drug-fuelled frenzy, it was driving Mum to scans and consultations, and then surgery; it was post-op check-ups, chemo, and wig-buying... it just went on and on. But beyond the actual process, which in itself was terrifying enough, there was something bigger and even more scary: the fact that my mother had become mortal.

On top of my fears for Mum, I'd suddenly found myself in the at-risk category too, so I had to have scans and blood tests and specialist gropings. My own boobs were, for the moment, cancer-free, so that was a huge relief. I'm not sure I could have coped with much more.

I wasn't allowed to tell anyone about Mum's cancer, and that included Rob.

'You can't make me keep secrets from my husband,' I told Mum. 'It's unethical.'

'Ooh, get you with your fancy words,' Mum said. 'Anyway, I think it's up to me who I tell. Don't you?'

'But why, Mum? It just makes everything so complicated.'

'Because I'm the one having my boob chopped off and it's not an image I want to share with other people.'

'They're not *chopping it off*, Mum, and Rob isn't just *other people*, either.'

'People change,' Mum said. 'Once they know, they change. Suddenly you're just another old bag with cancer. Larking around with your Rob's the only thing that keeps me going sometimes.'

'Yeah... Only he's not that larky these days,' I pointed out.

'No,' Mum said. 'He's not. What's that all about?'

'I don't know,' I said. 'I think we're going through a bit of a trough. But anyway, this is ridiculous! What am I supposed to tell him when I have to help you? When I have to drive you to the hospital or whatnot.'

'Then *don't* help me,' Mum said. 'I'd rather deal with it all on my own than have you tell all and sundry.'

'Again, Mother!' I said. 'Rob is *not* all and sundry.'

'Dawn,' Mum said looking grave. 'I'll make it simple for you, shall I? If you tell him... If you tell *a single bloody soul*, then I'll never speak to you again. And I do mean that. I really bloody mean that.'

'Christ!' I said. 'OK!'

Of course, Mum was right, too. It was *totally* up to her who she told. But it did make things difficult back home. I told Rob Mum had 'women's problems' – something that sounded so eighteenth century as to almost be laughable – but that wasn't enough to cover the hundreds of days Mum needed me by her side, so I still had to fib my way out of the family schedule on a regular basis.

At the beginning, when Mum's terror was most intense, Rob had been going through a needy phase, snuggling up against me in the hope of sex – sex I was too preoccupied to want. Sometimes he'd reach across to caress my chest. It was supposed to get me in the mood, I think, but in reality it made me think about breast cancer, and that, in turn, made me feel sick.

One night I remember in particular – I had an appointment to be professionally fondled the next morning. I pushed poor Rob away with a violence he didn't deserve or understand.

He had a weird sort of midlife crisis just afterwards and became strangely unpredictable. He bought tighter jeans than he'd ever worn before and some square-toed biker boots and a very expensive-looking leather jacket. He also bought a couple of Hugo Boss suits and I remember joking that he needed to choose one identity crisis and stick to it.

He looked gorgeous in a suit, as it turned out, but I never once managed to say so. I'd always associated suits with bad people, that was the thing. Suits were for dodgy estate agents and wanker-bankers and shifty politicians – all the people we love to hate. So I disliked myself for finding him so sexy dressed that way, and ended up being mocking and sarky, essentially to hide my own discomfort. Poor Rob. He was trying so hard, but I don't think he wore them more than twice.

He bought a very impractical sports car with such ridiculously small rear seats that we had to use my little Micra whenever we had company. 'I'll take yours,' Rob would say, if he needed to drive two people anywhere, or if I asked him to take something to the tip. I'd roll my eyes and reply, Lucy-style, 'Whatever,' and watch him squeeze his enormous body into the driver's seat.

He even bought a motorbike – I mean talk about midlife crisis! – and seemed gutted when I wouldn't get on it.

But motorbikes reminded me too much of Billy. I was scared, I think, that if I climbed on behind him I'd remember so powerfully how young and free and in-love I'd once been that carrying on with Rob would be impossible.

And then, around the time of Mum's chemo, Rob gave up trying to convince me and started doing things on his own. I'd wake up on a Sunday and find him gone – a note saying that he was off biking, or running, or cycling. Or I'd wake up to feel the bed gently bouncing and realise that my husband was beside me actually wanking.

But it suited me, that's the horror of it. His absence meant that I didn't need to find excuses not to have sex. I didn't have to find excuses to head over to Mum's, either. And I didn't even have to feel guilty about not wanting to take care of Rob, because Rob was too busy to care.

Did I suspect that he was having an affair? Well, *sort of*, I suppose is the best answer I can give, because I both did suspect and at the same time I didn't. It was a bit of a blurry monster at the edge of my vision, a monster I refused to look in the eye. Because if he was having an affair, if that really was the reason he'd stopped pressing his hard-on against my hip, then that suited me too. Is that a terrible thing to say? I expect it probably is, but, my God, it's true.

Anyway, by the time royal Kate had given birth to Louis Arthur Charles (at least they hadn't called him Gandhi), Mum's breast had been rebuilt and was healing pretty well. Her chemo was over and had been deemed successful, and her hair was growing back so well that wearing a wig was starting to get problematic. And it was only then, as the latest crisis started to wane, that I noticed how far apart Rob and I had drifted.

I worried I'd pushed him away too hard, and felt genuinely

sorry about it if I had. So I started suggesting mini-breaks; I started trying to drag him to the beach.

But he'd plugged all the gaps Mum's illness had created, with squash and motorbiking and work. The cracks that remained seemed somehow too small for me to fit back through.

Mum met a man at Home from Home – not one of the asylum seekers, but a helper. I'd got out of the habit of volunteering with her, probably because I'd spent so much of the rest of my time looking after her. Amazingly, Mum had continued to find the energy to stay involved, and it's just as well she did, because it was in the Home from Home kitchen she met Quentin. Quentin didn't mind her keeping her bra on, Mum said, and with her treatment over and Quentin to fawn over, she suddenly became far less present in my life. We'd been spending so much time together, it really was quite a shock. Obviously I was glad she was feeling better and was taking the time to live her little love story, but I'd be lying if I said I didn't feel a bit like she'd dumped me as soon as she found herself a man.

Anyway, time stretched. I started noticing how empty the house was. I started listening to the eerie silence that came from the kids' rooms during the afternoons. It seemed to drift down the stairs, like mist.

I'd open a book and tell myself to enjoy the peace and quiet. I'd remind myself how I'd just come out of years and years of madness during which I'd been gagging for an afternoon to read a book.

But no matter how much I'd craved it over the years, I couldn't quite convince myself calm was my 'thing'. Perhaps being needed was what made me feel best, after all.

* * *

In December 2019, Mum finally introduced us to 'Quin'.

Wayne, who was staying with me for a few days, had just been to pick his new girlfriend up from Ramsgate train station too, so the event felt pretty special.

But Rob wasn't home. He'd missed his train back from Manchester and it annoyed me more than was reasonable.

Just once, I kept thinking. *Just once, I actually ask him to be present, I actually tell him that it's important, and he's damned well not here.*

Of course, anyone can miss a train – it's happened to the best of us. But I think I suspected that he hadn't been where he said he was, and that's why I was so annoyed.

Anyway, both Quentin and Belinda turned out to be great, so we had a lovely meal all the same.

Quentin, who because of his name I'd imagined slightly posh and a bit theatrical, turned out to be a retired bus driver from Hackney. He looked vaguely like De Niro but with a shiny bald head. He was also funny and cheeky and visibly head over heels about my mother. Other than Pete, who at fifteen I'd been secretly in love with myself, I decided Quentin was the cream of the crop.

As for Wayne's new flame, well, what can I say? She was an absolute stunner in every way.

She was clever (she had her own advertising agency) and was helpful and funny too. But oh my God, she was pretty. She was so very very pretty that I remember wondering if it would be acceptable to ask if life was different for people like her. I wondered if things just always fell into place because no one she ever met could say 'no'.

Afterwards, as we were washing up – the dishwasher had given up the ghost – Mum leaned towards me, bumping my hip with hers, and said, 'You know, I suspect this might be The One.'

Because she'd never said anything like that about any of the many men she'd dated, I automatically assumed she was talking about Belinda.

'I know,' I said. 'She's gorgeous, isn't she? She reminds me of Freema What's-her-name. The one who used to be in *Doctor Who*. Martha Jones. D'you remember?'

'Never watched it,' Mum said. 'Can't stand it. But anyway, I meant me, stupid. I meant Quin. I think he might be the one.'

'Oh!' I said. 'Gosh!'

'You don't like him?'

'No, no, I do, Mum,' I said. 'I think he's lovely.'

'But?' Mum said.

'There's no buts at all. I'm just not used to hearing you say that.'

'I showed him my scar,' Mum said. 'I finally plucked up the courage.'

'Crikey,' I said. Mum had always told me she'd never show it to anyone. 'I'm assuming he didn't run a mile after all?'

Mum shook her head and paused wiping up. 'D'you know what he did?' she asked.

I'd noticed an unusual tremor in her voice, so I also paused what I was doing so that I could turn to look at her properly, and when I did I saw her eyes were glistening.

'Go on,' I prompted.

'He *kissed* it,' Mum said, her voice cracking. 'He kissed the scar, sweetheart. I get all tearful every time I think about it.'

'Oh, Mum,' I said. I released the dish I was holding into the soapy water and turned to give her a hands-free hug.

'Yes,' she said, when she could speak again. 'I definitely think he might be the one.'

'So you're in love,' I said. 'Like, properly, full-on in love this time?'

'I'm all over the place,' she said. 'Butterflies and everything. I can't believe it never happened to me before.'

'That's wonderful, Mum,' I said. 'I'm really, really happy for you.'

'You know what it reminds me of?' Mum said. 'Well, what *I* remind me of, really. I'm like you, when you were seventeen.'

I paused until Mum realised what she'd said.

'Oh, God, I'm sorry,' she said. 'I shouldn't have said that.'

'No,' I lied, 'it's fine. Moving on...'

'You know I saw him the other day?' Mum said. 'On the telly.' Apparently she wasn't ready to move on.

'Billy?' I asked, more shocked that she was continuing the conversation than that she had mentioned him in the first place.

Mum nodded. 'He's down in Suffolk or somewhere. Lives next door to Kate Bush.'

'Really?' I said. 'God! I thought he was in LA.'

'He's come back, apparently,' Mum said. 'Though it might be Devon, actually, not Suffolk.'

'Suffolk's over on the east coast, Mum. Ipswich, Bury St Edmunds, all that... Was it East Anglia or the West Country?'

'Oh, no, it's not over there. It was definitely down south but, you know, on the left.'

'So, like, Sussex? Or Dorset? Somerset, maybe?'

'Oh, I don't know, dear, do I?' Mum said, sounding exasperated. 'It's one of those down that way. *And* he's divorced.'

I shot a worried glare her way when she said that, because, though it was admittedly important information to me, I didn't understand how she knew that.

Mum pulled a face. 'What?' she said. 'He is!' Then, 'Oh, don't be daft I wasn't suggesting... I didn't mean anything by it. I was just saying. It's celebrity gossip, that's all. He lives down in Suffolk or Sussex or wherever next to Kate Bush and he's divorced, that's all.'

'Right,' I said. 'Well, thanks for the update. Again, moving on...'

'D'you think he can hear her singing?' Mum asked. 'I mean,

when she's practising and that. Because that would be my absolute bloody nightmare.'

I laughed out loud at that, and the laughter felt good. It
dispelled some of the tension in the room. 'I like Kate Bush,' I
said. 'You know I do. She's got a lovely voice.'

'Yeah, well,' Mum said. 'You just like her 'cos she sings even
worse than you.'

* * *

At first, I did my best not to think about Billy, but I was fighting
a losing battle. Suddenly, here he was again, popping into my
mind's eye while I was loading the dishwasher. What was Billy
up to? I wondered. Was he stacking his own dishwasher or
leaning over the fence chatting to Kate?

It started as idle interest, or at least that's what I told myself.
I wanted to see the Google Street View of his house. I wanted to
see how rich he was and laugh at him if he had bad taste. I kind
of hoped that he'd have a gold-plated toilet or something, some
taste crime that would put him beyond the pale. It has to be said
that I had quite a lot of time on my hands back then.

Anyway, despite many hours of internet searches, I could
not find Billy's address and nor could I find Kate's. And the
more I struggled to find it, the more the idea obsessed me.
Slowly but surely, my brain was going full-on-Billy all over
again.

I wished I could ask Lou for help because, as a fully certi-
fied geek, Lou could find out absolutely anything. But for
obvious reasons, I couldn't do that, so I just did my best on
my own.

Other than reading about Billy's best-selling singles and
some stuff on his divorce from Candice Rayner (all very amica-
ble, according to *the Mirror*, with Candice – in LA – having
custody of the kids), I didn't find much about Billy at all. The

only potentially useful information I could find was in the *Mail*, where I found a piece about the Bush house.

Kate, the article claimed, lived in East Portlemouth down in Devon, and her edge-of-clifftop house was at risk of plunging into the sea.

I looked for Billy's parents next, but, as I couldn't remember either of their first names, that was never going to work. It was only when I failed to find an address for them that I realised – or at least, *accepted* – that I really did want to see him again. i.e., it was the moment I found out that I *couldn't* find him that I understood that I'd really intended to.

Eventually, I explained the whole thing to Shelley. I do tend to tell Shelley most things, and we were in a wine bar and therefore pretty drunk, which definitely lowers my defences. But the main reason I told her was because I wanted her to still find me entertaining, and I knew it was the kind of intrigue she'd love.

'That's one dangerous game you're playing, sweetheart,' she said, her eyes sparkling with the excitement of it all. 'That's the sort of nonsense that can send a marriage up in flames.'

'Yeah,' I said, wrinkling my nose. 'But first you have to have something to send up in flames.'

'Oh, you're always so down on Rob!' she said.

'And you always defend him because you fancy him.'

Shelley laughed loudly at that and took another gulp of wine. 'True,' she said. 'Totally true. But he's still the nicest bloke I know.'

'Not nicer than Gavin, I'm assuming?' Gavin was Shelley's official long-term partner by then. By chance he lived six houses along from us, which turned out to be endlessly convenient.

'Oh, no, he is though!' Shelley said. 'Gavin's great, but I never said he was *nice*. I've never much liked the nice ones.'

'Right,' I said. 'Except for Rob.'

'Except for Rob. But I wouldn't like him either if he was available. You know how messy my brain is about that stuff. But seriously, tell Aunty Shelley what's going on. Because I can't see *at all* why you'd want to look up bloody Billy Fumble.'

I shrugged. 'I think we just got bored of each other, to be honest,' I said. 'Me and Rob, that is.'

'Oh, that happens,' Shelley said. 'That definitely happens.' She then proceeded to talk about someone I'd never heard of and didn't much care about – I think it was Ange's friend's sister-in-law and how bored she was with *her* husband – for a full half-hour.

But I wasn't really listening because I was thinking about Billy and wondering why I did still want to see him, and if a drive down to Devon might yield better results than Google.

A few days later the doorbell rang and I opened the front door to find Shelley on my doorstep looking excited. 'Ta-da!' she said, waving a Post-it in my face.

'Ta-da what?' I asked, then, 'Hello Shell. This is a surprise.'

'I stayed over at Gav's,' she said, 'but I wanted to see your face when I gave you this.'

I looked at the folded Post-it between her fingertips. '*This*, being...?'

'Lover-boy's phone number,' Shelley said.

'Lover-boy?' I repeated, then, 'Are you coming in or are you just going to stand on my doorstep being weird?'

'Can't stop,' Shelley said. 'Gav's taking me to Westwood. He's buying me a new bag for my birthday.'

'Right,' I said. 'Nice.' As she still hadn't handed over the slip of paper, I plucked it from her grasp. 'And whose phone number is this?' I asked once I'd unfolded it.

'Well, Billy Bumboy's, of course!' Shelley said, rolling her eyes. 'Honestly!'

'This is Billy's phone number?' I said, my eyes widening.

'Gav works for Orange, don't he?' Shelley explained with a

wink. 'Lucky for you, your Billy happens to be one of their star customers.'

'Christ,' I said. 'You didn't talk to Gav about this, did you?'

'Don't worry,' Shelley said. 'I didn't say why. He won't say anything.'

'All the same.'

'Oh. My. God!' Shelley said, sizing me up. 'You're going to shag him. You're *actually* going to shag Billy Ridiculous, aren't you? I can tell because you're getting all funny about Gav knowing.' She grimaced then and nodded in the direction of the hallway behind me. '*Is he home?*' she mouthed.

'No,' I said. 'Just me. Luckily for you.'

'Lucky for you more like,' Shelley said. 'Anyway, now you've got it, so use it wisely. Don't do anything I wouldn't.' And then she waved her fingertips at me and skipped back down the drive.

I waited a week before I texted Billy because I wanted to work out *why* I was texting him first. But – and I know this will sound daft – I couldn't work out why at all.

I could only work out, by elimination, all the potential reasons that didn't apply.

I didn't want to leave Rob for Billy, even though I'd admittedly fantasised about that in the past. Rob was the solid, good-natured rock I'd built my life upon. Rob was reliable, predictable, loving and kind. Rob had become a sort of *definition* of my adult life, and when I tried to imagine living without him I felt terrified

Meanwhile Billy was a famous pop star living next door to Kate Bush, for God's sake. That *clearly* wasn't on the cards. No, our lives had diverged too far for that to even be imaginable. So why was I even thinking about how unimaginable it was?

I didn't want to have an affair with Billy either. As for – I think – the majority of women, the idea of cheating, lying – of commitment-free sex – did nothing for me. My sex drive had faded after Lucy's birth and had dropped off a cliff after Lou's. Now I was heading for the menopause I seriously suspected the last vapours of it had vanished for good.

I didn't want Billy's fortune – I had everything that I needed – and I didn't want to share his fame either. I didn't want to be a casual friend – I'd spent too much time obsessing about Billy for that to be a possibility. So what was it?

Perhaps I just wanted to see what had become of him? Maybe it was sheer nosiness, I figured. But no, even that didn't seem to fit the bill.

But in the end, though I couldn't work out my end-game, I did it. I thought of Rob, wherever Rob really was, with whoever Rob was *really* with, until I got annoyed enough to convince myself it was about revenge (though it probably wasn't that either) and then I composed and sent the text message. It wasn't long, poetic or even elaborate but by the time I hit 'send' I was happy with it.

It said, *Hi Billy. I hope this is the right number. It's Dawn here from Margate, remember me? I was just wondering how you are. XX*

The hardest bit was choosing the number of kisses to put at the end.

I sat staring at the phone until it said, 'message delivered' and then 'message read' and then for another hour, until I accepted that whoever the phone number belonged to wasn't going to reply immediately.

The next morning when I got up, I had a reply waiting in my in-box. It said, *This is Billy Riddle's PA replying to you. I've transmitted your message to his personal number and he says he'll get back to you shortly. All the best, Joanna.*

* * *

I needed proof.

Once Billy had replied, I understood that I needed proof of Rob's infidelity.

Billy had sent me a text message from a new number saying, *Of course I remember! This is my personal number. Call me sometime. 7–8 p.m. is generally good. Billy x*

It was a normal non-committal reply to my normal, non-committal enquiry, but it made my heart race all the same, and I knew that my reaction – which had been as physical as it was emotional – meant there was risk involved in seeing him. So yes, I needed proof of Rob's philandering just in case things went wrong at my end.

I did all the usual clichéd things. I went through his pockets and checked his phone. I checked his computer and his bank statements and dug around in the glovebox of his car. And I found plenty of things that weren't quite right.

There were regular cash withdrawals (because other than spies and criminals on the run, really, who uses cash any more?). There were receipts from posh restaurants in towns we'd never been to, and I even found a credit card payment to a spa.

None of it was definitive – none of it would stand up in court, as they say – but it was good enough for me. The spa, specifically, was easily good enough for me.

I felt sick about going through Rob's stuff, and I felt sicker whenever I found something suspicious. But I also felt glad, and I hated myself for that. I hated that my husband's infidelity actually made me feel relieved because it potentially justified my own.

I had to wait for over a week to phone him, because though 7–8 might have been a perfect time for Billy, it was just about the most complicated time slot for me. Rob tended to get home around seven to find me cooking dinner – a dinner we'd eat about eight.

But 7–8 also gave me hope. Because 7–8 implied that Billy's

life was not like mine. From 7–8 he was alone, and bored. From 7–8 he was now hoping for a phone call from me.

In the meantime, I googled him endlessly, zooming in on photos until they pixelated. He still clearly favoured leather – something that, me being a vegetarian, should have repulsed me but didn't – but the silky jumpsuits had been banished long since.

He had a good head of hair – now salt -and-pepper grey – and looked fatter but tanned and happy.

* * *

'Did I tell you I'm away next weekend?' Rob asked. We were eating Thai noodles at the kitchen table.

'No,' I said, 'I don't think you did.' It had been weeks since Rob had been away 'on business' and I'd started to wonder if his affair was over or perhaps had never happened in the first place. And then I'd wondered if I would be glad, or disappointed, if one of those turned out to be true. *Best not to know*, I thought.

'Yeah, I've got a Samsung thing up in Newcastle.'

There had been times when I would have asked, through naivety, *What thing?* There had been times, also, when I would have asked him for details just to watch him squirm as he lied through his teeth. But that day, I just thought, *Wow, a whole weekend!*

'That's fine,' I said. 'When are you leaving?'

'Friday straight from work,' Rob said. 'Back late on Sunday night. That's OK, isn't it? We don't have anything planned this weekend, do we?'

'No,' I said. 'Nothing at all.'

'I'm sorry,' Rob said. 'But you'll be OK on your own, won't you?'

'Totally,' I told him. 'I'm used to it. I'll probably have Shell over or something.'

'Girls' night,' Rob said.

'Yeah.' It was surprisingly easy to lie.

As we ate our low-fat zero-pleasure yoghurts, I thought about how I'd finally be able to call Billy, and then it crossed my mind that if I managed to call him earlier in the week, perhaps I could use my free weekend to actually see him.

'Have you seen Blanche since you got home?' I asked. 'She didn't come in for her tea tonight.' This was another lie. Blanche never missed a meal, but Rob was clueless about such details.

'Probably snoozing upstairs,' he said.

'Can I let you clear up?' I asked, nodding at the table. 'I just want to check the garden, see if she's around.'

I walked around the perimeter calling Blanche's name, hoping that for the first time ever she wouldn't come running. And when I reached the bottom fence, I went behind the shed and pulled my phone from my pocket to call Billy. But as soon as I did it I realised it had been a stupid idea. Phoning from the garden was way too risky.

It was a surprisingly warm evening for late February, and I thought about the rumours everyone was talking about that we were going to be locked indoors because of Covid-19. Various European countries were already considering it, and the Chinese had been shut in their homes for weeks. It seemed like another reason to see Billy sooner rather than later.

I popped my head in the kitchen door and told Rob I was going for a walk.

'A walk?' he repeated, surprised. 'Is this about Blanche still? Because I'm sure—'

'No, it's just so nice out,' I said, interrupting him. 'And we're maybe going to be made to stay at home, so...'

'I don't think anyone's going to stop you going for *a walk*,' Rob said.

I shrugged. 'Whatever. I just fancy a stroll along the beach.'

'Want me to come?' Rob asked. 'Or...'

'Nah, you're fine,' I told him. 'I won't be long.'

I crossed the road and walked to the slope that led down to the beach.

A man was throwing a tennis ball for his dog, so I continued until I was out of earshot and then sat down on a rock to do the dreaded deed.

Billy answered almost immediately. 'Hello!' he said, 'I thought you'd never call.'

'You could have called me, too,' I pointed out.

'Yeah, except you're married,' Billy said. 'If my sources are correct.'

'Your sources?' I repeated.

Billy laughed. 'Oh, I just mean Joanna, my PA. Don't worry, I didn't involve the CIA.'

'So how have you been?' I asked. 'Taken any camping holidays in the New Forest lately?' It was a line I'd prepared in advance.

'God!' Billy said. 'Do you remember that? The awesome fun *that* was!'

'We were young,' I said. 'We were soooo young.'

'You were hot,' Billy said. 'You were smoking. Some of the best sex I've ever had.'

'Billy!' I protested. I could feel myself blushing. I felt flattered too.

'Well, it's true,' he said. 'If I'd known how rare it was to find that kind of chemistry...'

He didn't finish that phrase and for some reason I let him get away with it.

'You have half an American accent,' I commented.

'Do I?' Billy asked. 'Is it awful?'

'No. No it's actually quite nice. Makes you sound a bit like Lloyd Cole.' I was thinking about his singing, really, so the comment didn't make much sense.

'Oh,' Billy said. 'OK.' Then, 'You sound the same. Just maybe a bit posher.'

'Posh?' I laughed. 'Me?'

'I said Posh-*er*. Don't get carried away.'

There was an awkward pause. For my part I was remembering who I'd been all those years ago. I'm not certain what was going on in Billy's mind, but I sensed it was the same for him. 'Anyway, what's it like being a famous pop star?' I asked.

'Oh, it has its ups and downs,' Billy said.

'The ups being?'

'Oh, I dunno. Walking on stage. The roar of the crowd – all that shit. Having a Porsche and a garage to park it in is kind of nice too, I suppose.'

'And the downs?'

'I guess it's kind of lonely sometimes,' he said after a thoughtful pause. 'Hard to make a marriage work, too.'

'Yes, I read about that. I'm sorry.'

'And it's tough getting older,' Billy added.

'Why is it tough getting older?' I asked. It seemed an easier subject than his failed marriage.

'Oh, everyone expects you to stay the same, don't they? Everyone has this image in their mind's eye of how you were at twenty-five and the first thing they think when they spot you is *Christ! He's aged!* As if they haven't!'

'I suppose,' I said realising that even as I was speaking to him, I was still picturing Billy age twenty-one.

'How's your mum?' Billy asked. 'She's still around, isn't she? Tracey, is it?'

'Yeah,' I said. 'Tracey. That's her. She's still the same as ever.'

'She was brilliant your mum,' Billy said. 'I used to wish I had a mother like yours.'

'I used to feel pretty jealous of yours,' I told him. 'All those books. The records. The holidays in France.'

'The unlimited stash of weed.' Billy laughed.

'Indeed,' I said. 'Are they OK?'

'Nah,' Billy said. 'Not really. Mum died of lung cancer and Dad's in a home. Full-blown Alzheimer's. Can't tell his arse from his elbow.'

'Oh God,' I said. 'I'm sorry.'

'Yeah,' Billy said wistfully. 'It is what it is.'

We talked for almost an hour, and by the time it was over I was chilled to the bone.

When I got home, Rob looked up from the television and said, 'Oh, you're back. I was worried,' though it has to be said, he didn't look particularly worried. He *looked* like he was watching a Bruce Willis film.

I left him to watch the rest of his film and went through to the kitchen, where, nursing a cup of tea, I took the time to revel in my conversation. It had been absolutely gorgeous, and I was feeling flushed with joy in the afterglow.

We'd talked about the old days, mainly – our brilliant trip to the New Forest, and the garage he'd once lived in; Billy's friends from way back when. We'd talked about how exciting it had felt being young, and how being old and married was overrated, and how we both felt we'd lost our sense of self and how it was hard to feel any linearity, as Billy so marvellously put it, between who we'd been back then and who we were now. I'd forgotten how clever he was, how literary and generally good at expressing himself.

Then, we'd talked about ordinary life and Covid-19 and agreed that it was best to meet earlier, rather than later.

Once, finally, we'd ended the call, I'd sat and stared at the waves. I'd whispered, out loud, speaking to the sea, really, 'He was the one! All these years, and I really was supposed to be

with him all along.' It was silly, and I knew it, but it seemed true
to me in that moment.

* * *

My God, that week went slowly.

I filled the days studying Google Maps, wondering what to
wear, getting my nails done and my hair cut into a bob. Lord, I
even waxed my bush! In any other couple, that might have
raised suspicions, but Rob hadn't seen me naked in years.

Despite the fact that he really wasn't the suspicious kind, he
still sensed something was up.

'You OK?' he asked me on Wednesday night. 'You seem
kind of funny.'

'*Funny*?' I repeated, mockingly.

'Yeah, funny,' Rob said. 'Sort of happy but weird and edgy.'

'Well the happy thing's probably just springtime,' I said. 'I
always feel better when spring arrives.'

'Only we're still in winter,' Rob pointed out.

'You know what I mean,' I said. 'It's been lovely these past
few days.'

'Fair enough. And the edgy vibe?'

'Can't say I've noticed,' I lied. 'But it's probably all this
Covid-19 stuff. Everyone's a bit on edge, aren't they?'

'Sure,' Rob said. 'It is kind of scary.'

'Do you think they'll end up locking us all up, like the
Chinese?' I asked.

Rob laughed. 'Johnson?' he said. 'He couldn't organise it if
he wanted to.'

'They're talking about closing schools in Italy,' I said.
'They're going to ban non-essential travel, too.'

'That would bugger up my Samsung weekend,' Rob said.
'Not that I'd really mind. I'd much rather stay here with you.'

I didn't have time to think up a reply that wouldn't sound

like a lie, so instead I winked at him and offered to make him a cup of tea.

But the week eventually came to a close, and though Italy had decreed a kind of quarantine where everyone had to stay at home, and though the TV screen was filled with images of the deserted streets of Venice, life at home, for the time being, carried on.

Shelley came round on Friday night, bringing the gift of face masks. Ange had got their mother's sewing machine out and had churned out just over thirty masks made of children's curtain material.

'I'm not sure if they're virus-proof,' Shelley said, handing me two – one for Rob and one for me – 'but I s'pose it's got to be better than nothing.'

'Rob will never wear this,' I said.

'No,' Shelley said. 'Gav, neither. He says the day he wears a mask will be the day Corbyn wins an election.'

So we chatted about Covid-19 for a while, and then she told me some terrifying facts about the Spanish flu epidemic of 1918. She said that Gav's sister thought the whole 'Covid thing' was a hoax, like the moon landing, and then, because I had no idea what she was talking about, had to explain to me that there were people – fairly normal, clever people, she said – who believed the whole 'moon thing' had been staged in a film set out in Nevada.

When, eventually, that subject had run its course, Shelley swigged her beer and asked, 'So are you actually going to do The Deed this weekend?'

I pretended to be shocked. 'Of course not!' I told her.

Shelley pushed her tongue into her cheek and raised one eyebrow.

'Though I might have waxed,' I admitted. 'I'd forgotten how bloody painful it is. So maybe my subconscious has other ideas.'

'So it was your subconscious what did the waxing then, was

it?' Shelley asked laughing so much beer went up her nose. 'You crack me up, you do.'

* * *

I left the next morning at six.

Google Maps was telling me that the journey to East Portlemouth would take just under six hours, but I left eight so I'd have time to take breaks.

It was such a crazy undertaking, and I had so much time to think about *why* I was driving there, that there was no option really than to accept the fact that there was nothing casual about this journey at all.

By the time I'd joined the M3, I'd accepted the idea that I was probably going to sleep with Billy – at least, if the possibility occurred. This might be the last chance I'd get to do so, and it could even be the last chance I'd get to sleep with *anyone* ever again. In a way, it simply had to be done.

Around Ilminster my phone rang with an incoming call from Rob, so I had a major wobble there. I didn't pick up, obviously. What on Earth could I have said to him?

Following the beep indicating he'd left me a voicemail, I started to feel so bad about what I'd been planning that I seriously thought I might puke. I pulled into a service station and ate half a sandwich and drank a can of Coke in the hope that the combination might calm my stomach and when it didn't, when I continued to feel sick, I started looking at the map and considering whether or not I should turn back.

But then my phone rang again. This time it was Billy.

'Just checking you're really coming,' he said. 'It's OK if you're not, but I'd rather you just told me.'

I admitted I'd been having second thoughts, and was thinking about turning back.

'Why would you do that?' Billy asked.

'I don't know,' I said. 'I suppose I'm just worried this might be a really bad idea.'

'Either it's nothing, or it's something,' Billy said. 'It's a bad idea, or a really really good one. But either way, don't you think it's better to know?'

'Maybe,' I said.

'Where are you now,' he asked, 'exactly?'

When I told him, he laughed. 'You're almost here,' he said. 'That's less than two hours away. Come on! What have you got to lose?'

So, pumped up with caffeine and sugar from the Coke, I drove on, still trying to get my brain to settle on some definitive narrative about what was happening here.

Exeter came and went, and I admitted to myself that I was still hoping Billy was going to save me from my mundane little life in almost exactly the way he'd saved me that summer of 1990.

A sign for Newton Abbot slid past, and I accepted it was a ridiculous desire to have, but I couldn't quite shake it all the same.

Fritts Combe, Dunstone, West Prawle...

It was there, in West Prawle, that my revelation came. It felt so profound that it sent shivers down my spine.

I wasn't sure where the thought had come from, but when it came to me I knew it as truth: I had spent my life fantasising about Billy Ruddle, but had no idea whether my fantasy was based on a reality I'd experienced long ago, or a sort of madness that had briefly possessed me during my hormone-addled teenage years.

That fantasy, I finally saw, had pushed a wedge between Rob and me. It was the thing that had made me unable to relax into my relationship with my husband.

I was here, in my green Polo, shattered from seven hours'

driving, but on a mission to find out the truth, and there was nothing frivolous about that at all.

It would be nothing, or it would be something, as Billy had said. It would be a really bad or a really good idea. And the fact that he'd been able to put that into words so succinctly meant that he'd been having the same doubts himself.

So, today, I would find out, I decided. This had gone on long enough.

If I had to sleep with Billy to find out, then sleep with Billy I would. If the fantasy was real, and I had to leave Rob to be truly happy, then leave Rob I would, as well.

And if, after all, it was nothing more than a stupid teenage fantasy that had got stuck inside my head, then I'd be done with it, once and for all, and I'd go home and damned well be happy.

ELEVEN

CLOSING BRACKETS (BY ROB)

Have you ever been in love and then fallen out of it? Because if you have, you'll know that it's a strange, unpredictable process. Amazing how fast it can happen, too.

If she'd known the details, which of course she didn't, Dawn would almost certainly say that it was pure misogyny on my part. She'd say that I'd enjoyed no-strings sex with Cheryl but at the moment she'd become an actual person – an actual woman, with needs – I'd gone off her. And in many ways I suppose she'd be right.

If it had *felt* that way, if being like that, thinking like that, had been conscious decisions on my part, then I'd have to own up to being a right monster. But that's not how it felt to live through it. I swear to you that's not how it was.

How it *felt* was that I was *in love*, though perhaps, with hindsight, in lust might have been a better description. I was in lust for Cheryl's body, and in lust for sex in general. I was lusting for my lost youth – my *missed* youth, even – for fun, for change and for some plain old excitement to stave off death. And as Cheryl provided all of the above, she'd seemed totally irresistible.

What's perhaps most shocking, looking back, is that my infatuation lasted so long, because, all in all, it was almost four years. That last year was all about decline, though, so perhaps we should only count the first three. But ultimately, aspect by aspect, character trait by character trait, Cheryl began to grate on me, and once that process had started it seemed unstoppable.

Her make-up seemed to take longer and longer, so she was never on time for anything. Her heels – heels I'd once found so sexy – suddenly seemed a bit absurd, bad for her health, not to mention totally impractical. Specifically, we missed a train home from Manchester one afternoon because she refused to run in her heels, or indeed to take them off. The result was that I got home after midnight and had to put up with Dawn's fury for a whole week because I'd missed an important family meal.

Cheryl's music, particularly the rap, I found I suddenly couldn't stand. Her *think positive* platitudes made me sigh and roll my eyes. The way she touched me all the time in the car, the way her leg was always in the way of the gearstick, the way she could never seem to remember which of the bloody tooth-brushes was mine and which was hers, her snuffling with hay-fever at the breakfast table... These were all things that I'd loved about her at the beginning – even the snuffling – but now they became things that irritated the tits off me. And the list kept getting longer.

If she'd been my wife, if she had been the mother of my children, then I suppose we might have seen a couples' counsellor to try to work out what was going wrong. But she wasn't my wife, was she? She *wasn't* the mother of my kids either. Not yet. So in a way our relationship going wrong felt *right*, like it was perhaps a healing process rather than an illness to be cured. Like the closing of a set of brackets.

I saw her less and less often, and when we did see each other I found myself avoiding sex. I wouldn't have said no to a blow job, but Cheryl now deemed those a waste of spunk.

'Is it the kid thing?' she asked me one time I refused. 'Because I can always go back on the pill.'

I told her I didn't know what it was, and that I was just in a weird mood, and I was sorry, and these things all seemed true. All I really knew, the only thing I'd actually understood at that point, was that our relationship was losing its shine, but it hardly seemed fair to say that to Cheryl.

* * *

She got to the hotel in Newcastle before me, and I found her seated on the balcony smoking.

'Hello,' I said, dumping my case on the bed and shrugging out of my overcoat. I crossed the room and pointed to the 'No smoking' sign behind her and, when she shrugged and looked away, I sensed something major was about to happen.

'How was your trip?' I asked, sliding into the seat opposite her. It was cold on the balcony and I wished I'd kept my coat on, but as that would have looked like I was uncommitted to staying it was probably better to be cold.

'Terrifying,' she said.

'Terrifying?'

'I've probably got the Covid now, thanks to you. You can come and visit me in hospital on my deathbed.'

'Oh,' I said. 'Right. But you feel OK, don't you?' Cheryl looked pale and shiny and my immediate instinct was to flee.

She shrugged.

'OK,' I said, reaching for her free hand – a hand she pulled away. 'What's wrong?'

'Is it over?' she asked, speaking in smoke. 'Because if it is then I'd rather just know.'

'It?' I asked, obtusely. 'Is what over?' I don't know why I asked her that – I knew perfectly well what she was referring to.

'Us,' she said waving her cigarette around. 'You and me. Is it over?'

'Why d'you ask that?' I said, buying time and maybe hoping just a bit that she was about to express her own desire to move on.

'I haven't seen you for months, we didn't shag when I did see you, and you made me take the bloody train,' she said. 'And that's just for starters.'

'I told you, I had to bring a colleague with me,' I said, which had been convenient but also true. We'd listened to Steve's eighties pop all the way up the motorway and I'd thought about how much longer the journey would have been had the soundtrack been Adele or, heaven forbid, rap.

'So nothing's wrong?' Cheryl said. 'It's *not* over?' She neither looked nor sounded convinced.

Despite myself, I shrugged. It was an automatic reaction that came from my body rather than my brain and, as such, was maybe not entirely my fault.

'Christ!' Cheryl said. 'You *tosser!*'

'I don't know,' I admitted, my words catching up with my body. 'I'm sorry, I don't know what's going on.'

'Christ,' Cheryl said again, her eyes wide and shiny – her tone suddenly sharp. 'I thought you was just going to say "No, Ches, everything's fine." I really did. But no... You fucking fucker, you. Fuck!'

A lump formed in my throat. I admitted to myself that I didn't want to be with her at that particular moment, and yet neither did I want to make her sad. I thought I could probably make her stay or make her leave depending on what I chose to say next, and I was damned if I knew which was best. The whole thing felt impossibly complicated.

I shrugged again. It was the gesture that had upset her so much first time round, and, ouch! without thinking I'd done it again. So in a way a decision had been made. A lazy, selfish, badly expressed decision, but a decision all the same.

Cheryl understood everything. She crushed her cigarette on the marble tabletop and stood up. 'At least—' she said, but then stopped and with a shake of her head she left the balcony.

I followed her into the bedroom, where she was pulling her still-packed suitcase from the closet.

'Cheryl!' I said. 'Don't just leave. Surely we need to talk, don't we?'

'No,' she said. 'I don't think we do.'

'At least what?'

'What?'

'You said, "at least" something,' I reminded her.

'At least I'm not fucking pregnant,' she said. 'Thank Christ at least for that.'

'Please, just come back in and sit down and talk,' I said.

'Sorry,' she said. 'I don't do that. I've never done that.'

'Done what?' I asked. 'Talk?'

She pulled on her coat before she replied. 'I've never sat around waiting to be dumped,' she said, looking not at me but at the window. '... not my thing. I'd rather quit while I'm ahead.' And then she spun on one heel and left.

'Cheryl!' I said, as she vanished from view. But I could hear the weakness in my voice and I noted – as no doubt Cheryl did – that I hadn't followed her into the hallway.

Once the door had clicked shut, I threw myself onto the bed and stared up at the ceiling as I tried to work out what I was feeling. There was plenty of guilt there, that was for sure, and some sadness and a touch of relief too. But the overwhelming emotion was one of surprise that I actually felt so little.

Ceiling, air conditioning, sheets, I thought. *Light fitting, traffic noise, fingernail.*

But I was counting in threes out of habit, not need. I actually felt perfectly calm.

So I'm a cold-hearted bastard, after all, I thought.

That was a shock.

Because we all create these myths about ourselves, don't we? Mine was warm, helpful, generous Rob.

But there was also this other Rob, it transpired. There was *shag 'em and dump 'em, don't-give-a-damn-Rob,* too.

Who knew?

I ate in the hotel room that evening, and fell asleep in front of a film.

The next morning, I had breakfast in the room, alone, without Cheryl or Cheryl's snuffling. Plenty of people I knew would be down at the breakfast bar and I couldn't face the company.

I felt desolate and taut with stress, but also, deep within my chest, there was a strange pressure-cooker bubbling up of elation, as if change, endless change, was perhaps the spice of life after all. Cheryl and I had reached the end of a chapter, and that felt unbearably sad. But there was also a sense of excitement lurking about whatever was coming next.

While I was in the shower, my phone beeped with an incoming text message, and I just assumed it would be a 'good morning' text from Dawn or something from one of my colleagues. But once, suited and booted, I finally read it while waiting for the lift, I discovered that it was actually from Samsung. It said that due to rising concern about Covid-19 and the absence of a number of key speakers from Korea, all events had been cancelled. *Wow,* I thought. *That's a first.*

I went back to my room and turned the TV on, just in case I'd missed some major bit of news that might explain these dramatic changes. But Sky News was showing the same old images: deserted streets in Italy, tents going up for a field hospital, Johnson burbling on about 'herd immunity'. *He sees us as a herd*, I thought. *That's nice.*

I went and sat on the balcony and debated whether or not to call Cheryl.

Her cigarette butt had blown away but the marble table was stained where she'd stubbed it out, so I scratched at the stain with my finger and then licked it and rubbed at it repeatedly until it crossed my mind that indirect licking of tabletops during an epidemic maybe wasn't such a good idea.

I composed a text message that said, *Are you OK? All my events have been cancelled, so if you need to talk, I'm totally free.*

The first step was to change the ending from *totally free* to just *free*. The *totally* seemed to express a keenness on my part that wasn't entirely honest.

But then I thought about it some more and deleted all but the first three words, and sent them before I could change my mind.

Cheryl answered almost immediately. *We're done Rob*, her text message said. Quickly followed by, *If you ever leave your wife then let me know. Until then, there's no point, so just don't bother.*

I winced as I read it, because it was so real and so honest it felt like a slap.

Her message struck me as spot on, too. Because she was right, wasn't she? Continuing *would* have been pointless. Worse, we'd been risking creating a whole new situation – pregnancy. That would have been stupid, unpredictable and irresponsible... So yes, she was right: that was exactly the situation: unless I was going to leave Dawn, continuing was pointless. And I wasn't going to do that, was I?

A surge of love for Dawn, for the kids, for the life we'd built, came over me, taking me by surprise. Tears welled up to the point where one actually trickled down my cheek.

I'd put so much at risk, I realised, but by sheer luck we'd got through it all. I felt suddenly grateful to Dawn, to God or perhaps fate, that I hadn't been made to pay the price for what I'd done, that we'd survived long enough to allow the candle to burn itself out. That struck me in the moment as madly, undeservedly lucky.

My phone rang. It was Steve, the guy I'd driven up with. 'D'you see everything's cancelled?' he asked. 'It's crazy. Anyone would think it was Ebola or something. It's just a bloody cold, for Christ's sake.'

'It doesn't look like *just-a-cold* in Italy,' I said, glancing in at the TV screen. 'They're setting up army hospitals in tents.'

'Yeah,' Steve said, dismissively. 'Well, Italians...'

I didn't know what that was supposed to mean, but decided I didn't much want to either.

A sensation of... *foreboding* I suppose is the word, was rising up in me. I was thinking about Ebola and Spanish flu and crowded city centres and taking home some bug that could potentially kill my wife. It was dawning on me, I think for the first time, that maybe this was going to get nasty.

'Anyway, I've been looking up things to do,' Steve said. 'There's some museums and a place called the Biscuit Factory that looks quite cool – they sell art and stuff. And there's a cool waterside—'

'I think I'm just going to go home,' I said, interrupting his list. 'D'you want to travel back with me or...?'

'Nah, I'll stay,' Steve said. 'Samsung's still paying the hotel and stuff for the whole weekend – I checked. I can travel back with one of the other lads. I could do with a break from the kids, to be honest.'

'Sure,' I said. 'I remember that feeling.'

'Must be nice when they've all moved out,' Steve said. 'Must be like back at the beginning before they were born, right? Snuggling up on the sofa together. Going dancing and stuff. Christ, I miss all that.'

I laughed. 'Something like that,' I told him. 'Yeah.'

The drive home was six and a half hours, so I had plenty of time to chew things over.

To start with, I tried to avoid thinking at all, instead listening to the radio. But it was wall-to-wall Covid-19 and after a while I realised it was making me feel anxious. So I switched the radio off and allowed my thoughts to run their course.

I still love Dawn. That was the first clear thought I had.

She'd become spiky over the years and had made herself difficult to be close to, but perhaps that was my fault as much as hers. Maybe she'd known – though perhaps only subconsciously – about Cheryl, and if she had then that could, I supposed, make *anyone* spiky.

I thought about how Cheryl had started to grate on me, and wondered what a shrink would have to say about that. Something about my irritation didn't feel honest, I decided, as if maybe a bit of it was made up or at least exaggerated. If it was, then that was because it served a purpose. It made ending things that much easier.

It crossed my mind that perhaps I'd started to annoy Dawn in the same way Cheryl irritated me. I was surprised I hadn't thought of it before.

I thought about the way Dawn tended to react if I touched her, pictured her eye-rolls and her sighs when I attempted to pull her leg about something. It certainly all fitted the bill.

Did that mean we were doomed to separate too? Would there inevitably be a moment where I'd sit her down and ask if it was over? The thought was too hard to bear.

I let myself think about sex, then, and that was perhaps the hardest one of all.

Sex had never been an easy subject for me, but the surprise was realising that it maybe wasn't that simple for Dawn either.

First, I wondered if some kind of therapist could help us get back on the rails, but even imagining that was so embarrassing it made my teeth hurt.

I thought about sex with Cheryl and how unexpected it was that I found myself happy to give it up. So perhaps sex wasn't so important after all. Or perhaps it *had* been important before, but because I'd aged, or because I'd had my fill, it suddenly no longer was.

I pondered the fact that I'd gone off sex with Cheryl when she'd started trying to have a baby, and how that meant that sex could feel different depending on your motivation for doing it.

I remembered how Dawn had gone off sex after Lou's birth, then, and understood, in that moment, on the A1, for the first time ever, how a lack of desire for the outcome of sex – another child – might lead to a lack of desire for the act itself.

If she'd just explained it to me, I thought, *then I could have got a vasectomy*.

But of course, understanding why we feel the way we do is so difficult that none of us manage it very often... Who was to say Dawn ever even asked herself why she no longer wanted sex?

I bought flowers at the Medway services, and imagined myself handing them over on arrival. I'd have to be sweet enough to let her know I still loved her but not gooey to the point her defences went up. She'd never reacted that well to excess romance, whether in films or in real life. It tended to tip her into cynicism. Too much or too little romance had always been a fine line to tread.

Immediately I turned in to the drive, I saw that her car was missing.

She's out with Shelley, I thought. *Damn!*

I let myself into the house and made a mug of tea. I went

through to the sunroom at the back and sat listening to the silence of the house, which turned out not to be silence at all, but a series of creaks and groans laid over the barely audible electrical hum of the place. *This is how it would be if we split up*, I thought, and the image made me shiver as if I was cold.

I phoned and left a simple message. I said I was home, *surprise!* and asked when she'd be back.

The flowers would wilt, I realised, so I grabbed them and stuck them in a vase, then took them back out of the vase and emptied it and rested them in the sink instead. It would seem silly to pluck them from a vase to give them to Dawn just so she could put them back in the vase, but I wanted them to be a gift, not just some flowers I'd bought for the house. It seemed important to get that right.

At seven, as the sun was sinking, I called Dawn again and, when she didn't pick up, I had a brief angry frenzy of hitting the call button over and over – it went to voicemail every time. I called Dawn's mum but she didn't answer either, so I left a message on her voicemail as well.

Just to hear the sound of their loving voices I phoned the kids. Lucy was on her way out the door and Lou was at a crucial juncture of his video game so neither conversation lasted more than thirty seconds, but it reassured me to know they were OK.

I heated a frozen pizza up and ate it in front of the news.

France was closing schools and colleges from Monday. Italy had tens of thousands of cases. Things weren't looking good but Boris Johnson still felt optimistic.

I glanced at my phone again and frowned. *What if?*

I called Dawn for the third time and said, 'Call me back, I'm concerned.'

I phoned Tracey again, and this time she took my call. 'She's probably just out with Shelley or something,' she told me.

'I'm worried about her,' I admitted. 'Especially with all this Covid-19 stuff going on.'

'I know what you mean,' Tracey said. 'It's terrifying. But Dawn's fine, I'm sure of it. Don't worry. If she phones me I'll tell her to call you.'

I called Blanche for her supper – she didn't come – and then noticed Dawn had left her a massive bowl of crunchies. We only ever did that when we went away for a few days.

'Oh,' I said, out loud. 'OK.'

I didn't know what it all meant, but I felt pretty sure it wasn't good news.

TWELVE

BILLY II (BY DAWN)

On leaving the A roads, and after an endless series of twists and turns, I found myself on a long, narrow country lane that ran along Salcombe Estuary. The road weaved in and out, providing beautiful glimpses of the water through the trees.

Dotted along the way at regular intervals were houses, but none of them looked grand enough to be the sort of place where Kate Bush might live or high up enough to potentially crumble into the sea. So I wondered pretty much the whole way if I was going in the right direction.

Eventually, just after 3 p.m., Google Maps announced that I'd arrived. The nearest house was another thirty yards in front of me, so I continued until I was next to it, then pulled up at the roadside and phoned.

As the road ran above and behind the property it was impossible to see the actual building. The only things that were at street level were the grey doors to a garage, but you could guess, all the same, that the view over the estuary was going to be a good one.

Though I'd phoned Billy's personal number, it was Joanna who answered the call. 'Just park up in the garage,' she said.

'I'll be right up.' That surprised me, and I wondered if perhaps Joanna was more than Billy's PA. It was something I should have perhaps considered, and asked about, before coming.

The line clicked dead and I wasn't even sure if I was outside the right house, but then one of the garage doors began to roll smoothly up. '*Fancy, fancy,*' I murmured and I began to manoeuvre the car so that I could drive in.

It was a triple garage, but there were already two cars parked up, a mid-size Kia and an absurdly massive Porsche SUV, so it was lucky I only had a Polo. Fitting anything bigger between them would have been just about impossible.

A challenge, too, was extracting myself from the car once I'd parked, and I was glad Billy wasn't there to see me do it.

'Sorry, it's a bit of a squeeze,' Joanna said, surprising me as I closed the door. 'I always ask him to park further over, but you know Billy!'

I threaded my way past the cars to the corner of the garage where she'd appeared from behind a metal door. 'Joanna,' she said, offering a jingly-bangled hand. 'I'm assuming you must be Dawn?'

She was young – late twenties, at a guess – and brunette. She was pretty but had that austere PA vibe of efficiency about her. I noted the wedding ring on her left hand and suddenly wondered whether I should have removed mine, and then hated myself for even considering it.

Joanna was squinting at me, studying my face, and that made me wonder how much Billy had told her. What would Billy's uncensored take on Dawn be?

'Oh, I'm leaving,' Joanna said, as if I'd asked her a question. 'Don't worry, you've got him all to yourself!'

She pulled her keys from her bag and beeped the Kia, then squeezed past me and opened its door. But then she paused and made a little shooing gesture at me. 'Go on!' she said. 'Don't be scared! Billy's waiting!' And then she slid into the car and started the engine.

I pushed open the door and found myself at the top of a concrete spiral staircase.

Billy's waiting! I thought, repeating the words in my head as I descended. *Heaven forbid we keep Billy waiting!*

The staircase led directly to a wide modern lounge and the first thing that struck me was the view. The entire far wall was taken up by a huge picture window that offered a 180-degree view of the cove.

I glanced around the room to check it was indeed empty and then, because the window seemed to draw me to it magnetically, I crossed the marble floor to look out. A couple of small sailing boats were bobbing on the water just outside.

'Nice, huh?' I spun to find Billy leaning nonchalantly in a doorway.

'Huh! You made me jump!' I said.

Billy shrugged and puffed on a cigar. 'I live here,' he said with a shrug. 'So...'

Oh boy, had he changed! I wondered if I had aged that badly too. Perhaps I just wasn't aware of it.

I'd seen photos of Billy looking older, and even a couple of him looking a bit rough, snapped by paparazzi after a night on the town. But this was a whole different level, and I realised that perhaps those had been his *best* photos, not the worst – that they'd perhaps been the photos his publicity machine had *chosen*.

That particular day, he had a white ZZ Top shaggy beard and his pale grey hair was pulled back in a man-bun. His face looked red and bloated: it was the kind of face that makes you think, *high blood pressure*.

I thought about what Billy had said about getting older and how disappointed people were when they realised that he'd aged. Because despite the fact that I'd googled him, I'd still been stupidly picturing him aged twenty-one. I'd been imagining that I might be *attracted* the way I used to be too. I'd been thinking how wonderful that whoosh of love and desire would feel, anticipating it during the drive. But my only feelings on seeing Billy were horror and a sense of shock at my own stupidity.

'Gosh,' I said, lost for anything better to say. 'Look at you!'

Thinking I was commenting on his clothes, Billy glanced down at himself. He was wearing satiny white pyjama bottoms and an ornate embroidered smoking jacket, presumably chosen to go with the cigar. 'Sorry,' he said. 'I didn't quite get round to getting dressed today.'

I didn't believe that at all. My intuition was that he'd chosen what to wear with great care.

He smiled at me then, and I remember being shocked at how much a person's smile could change. He'd had a lovely smile in the old days but now his teeth were yellow, and his grin was lopsided and seemed a bit cocky, bordering on snide.

'You must be knackered,' he said. 'All this way just to see little old Billy Riddle.'

Ruddle, I thought but didn't say. *It's Ruddle.*

'Yes, it's a long way,' I replied. 'It's a bloody long way, actually. I don't think I've ever driven so far in my life. Didn't even know England *was* this big!'

'But worth it?' he asked, opening his arms in a weird Jesus-like gesture.

I noted the gold chain, the medallion, the white chest hair. 'Um, ask me later!' I replied, deciding to try to make a joke of it. 'I'll let you know.'

He winked at me then and crossed the room to wrap me in a hug – a hug I didn't much enjoy. The silky thinness of his clothing left too little to the imagination and he smelled like an ashtray after a party.

'So, drink?' he asked, releasing me and crossing to an actual bar on the left wall of the room, then slipping behind the counter. 'You're a whisky girl if I remember correctly,' he said, reaching for a bottle of Glenfiddich.

I took a discreet deep breath before crossing to join him and perching on one of the bar stools.

'Whisky?' I repeated. 'Um, no. Never. Hate the stuff. That must have been someone else entirely.'

He finished pouring me a whisky anyway but, when I shook my head and pushed the glass back, he shrugged and took a sip himself.

I glanced behind me, taking in the room. It was beautifully situated and generously sized, but the choice of furnishings – all leather, chrome, and brand new – made it look pretentious. There were massive paintings on the walls, and they were, I admitted, rather beautiful. But even these seemed somehow chosen to impress rather than to be enjoyed. The whole experience felt like being in a showroom or on a film set or in an ad.

'So?' Billy prompted. 'Beer? Wine? G&T? Bacardi and Coke? That's what the Margate girls drank back in the day, wasn't it?'

'Actually tea would be good, if you've got that,' I said.

'Tea?' Billy repeated, with a laugh. 'OK! Tea it is!' Then, puffing on his cigar and sipping at his whisky, he swaggered, over-casually, from the room.

Once he was out of sight, I felt able to think again, and the first thought that came to me was, *This was a mistake. A massive, horrible mistake.* I wondered how long I needed to stay before I could politely leave.

'Milk and sugar?' he called out.

'Just milk,' I said. 'Soy or something if you've got it, but otherwise normal milk is fine.'

I followed him through to the kitchen. It was all white gloss and stainless steel and looked more like a morgue than a room where anyone might cook a meal. 'Almond milk?' he asked, peering into a cupboard.

'Yeah, almond milk's great.'

'So what d'you think?' he asked, as he returned to the cup and jiggled the teabag around by the string.

I opened my mouth to reply but then closed it again because I wasn't sure what he was referring to.

'The house,' Billy said. 'Pretty cool, huh?'

'Oh, yes!' I agreed. 'Yes, it's lovely. Is it true Kate Bush lives next door?'

Billy laughed at that. 'No, she's way over the other side, on the cliffs,' he said. 'Why?'

'Mum told me,' I said. 'She saw something on TV about you and Kate being neighbours.'

'No, not me,' Billy said. 'But Steve Rider lives over that way, I believe.'

'Sorry, who?'

'Sports presenter,' Billy said. 'So how is she? Your mum?'

'She's fine,' I said. 'She had cancer, but she's OK now.' I wondered why I'd told him that, and then regretted that I had. It seemed unfaithful to have told Billy something Rob wasn't allowed to know.

'Cancer or heart trouble,' Billy said. 'It's always one or the other that gets you in the end.'

'Yeah,' I said. 'Maybe. But in Mum's case, not quite yet, thank God.'

There was an uncomfortable silence at that point, so I filled in with, 'Mum was worried you'd have to put up with Kate Bush singing. She thought you might be able to hear her from your place.'

'No,' Billy said. 'Luckily not.'

'I always liked her myself.'

'Yeah, well, your musical tastes were always dodgy,' Billy said, handing me my completed mug of tea. 'Come,' he said. 'I'll give you the tour.'

I slopped some of the tea into the sink so that I could carry it without spillage and followed Billy out the door. I noticed that my mug was emblazoned with the album cover of *Ears, Nose, Arse* and wondered if he'd had it made himself or if it had been a gift from the record company.

Billy led the way to the lower floor, which was only a few feet above the waterline.

'So this is my music room,' he said, pushing open a door.

Once again, the far wall was glass, and because we were lower the view was even more impressive. Rippling reflections of light dappled the ceiling. It felt like being on a boat.

'Wow,' I said.

'Yeah,' Billy agreed. 'I still say that every time I step in here. It's crazy, huh?'

There was a full-sized drum kit and a keyboard, and four guitars hanging on the walls.

'It reminds me of your garage,' I said.

Billy nodded and scanned the room as if he was looking at it for the first time. 'Maybe,' he said. 'Better gear though. That one's a Fender '57.'

'Sorry,' I said, 'what is?'

'The guitar,' Billy said, nodding. 'It's worth about ten grand.'

'Oh,' I said. 'Nice.'

'I've got a Moog, too,' Billy said. 'One of the original ones. But it's in storage. No room here, not with the drum kit.'

'Of course,' I said, though I had no idea what a Moog was.

Because Billy was slowly edging towards me, I crossed to the other side and made a point of examining his framed platinum discs. There were six of them on the wall.

'I really liked that one,' I said, pointing.

'*Ears, Nose, Arse*?' Billy asked.

'No, *Argy-Bargy*,' I told him. 'I had it on repeat for months.'

'Not my best,' Billy said. '*Ears, Nose, Arse* was way better. My latest stuff, too... Have you kept up?'

I shook my head. 'Sorry,' I said.

'I'd give you a copy,' Billy said, 'but they don't bother to send them any more. No one ever has a CD player these days, so...'

'I do,' I said. 'In my car. And...' I'd been about to say that Rob had started listening to vinyls again. I couldn't believe I'd been about to mention him to Billy.

'And?' Billy prompted.

'No, nothing. Anyway, looks like you've done really well,' I said, gesturing at the wall of framed discs.

'Yeah, it's been cool,' Billy said. 'To be honest it's mainly "Cherry Lips" that keeps me in cigars and whisky. The airplay stats on that one are *sick*.'

'That's great,' I said. 'You must be proud.'

He slid open one of the windows just enough to cast his cigar out and then closed it again. 'It's just a song,' he said. 'It's just a shitty catchy song, which, of course, is why everybody liked it.'

As he returned towards me he whacked the top of one of the drums with the flat of one hand, and then slipped behind the drum kit and sat down. He looked momentarily deflated and his shoulders slumped. He stared at the drum kit forlornly and for about ten weirdly long seconds he didn't make a sound. He actually looked a bit like a robot that had run out of battery power. But then I saw him make the effort to snap himself out of it. He reached behind and lifted an acoustic guitar from the wall. 'See if you remember this one,' he said, looking up at me.

Now this is going to sound a bit crazy, but as he started strumming 'Sunday Evening', everything shifted. His playing, humming, then singing that old song, made me remember with a jolt who he'd been, who I'd been, and how I'd once felt about him. It provided that sense of *linearity* we'd talked about on the phone, linking the me of here and now to the person I'd once been. I suddenly felt overwhelmed with emotion, as if I was grieving for someone I'd lost long ago, only the person I'd lost track of was me.

'Do you remember it?' he asked, interrupting his playing and looking up. 'I wrote that while I was with you.'

'Yes,' I said, my voice all crackly and weird. I slumped back in a tatty armchair in the corner of the room. 'Yeah, I remember. Carry on.'

Billy played 'Sunday Evening from beginning to end and, by the time he'd finished, I had tears in my eyes. The song had always been quite a good one, but it turned out to be far better without the drums and keyboards. I'd forgotten how beautiful it was to be sung to, one on one.

Billy sighed and then looked up at me. He saw, I think, my glistening eyes, and smiled. 'You really do remember,' he said.

I nodded. Out of the blue, as if the words came from my mouth doing its own thing, rather than from any decision my brain might have made, I asked, 'Why did you leave like that? Why did you just vanish out of the blue?'

Billy frowned vaguely at me as if he didn't understand. 'You mean, Margate to Manchester?'

I nodded.

'Well, I had to go back to college,' he said.

'I know that,' I murmured, looking down at my feet. 'But you could have said goodbye. You could have at least warned me. And I never understood why you didn't. Never.'

'I didn't know how to,' he said. 'I had a major crush on you but I couldn't take you with me. I was in halls of residence. Don't forget how young I was.'

'I was younger,' I said, lifting my head to briefly look him in the eye. 'And pregnant.'

Billy winced and tipped his head to one side. 'I did offer to send money for that,' he said.

I laughed sourly. 'I didn't need money.'

'No, I got that when you didn't reply.'

I realised that he'd misunderstood me and that I probably should have said, 'It wasn't money that I needed,' but the moment seemed to have passed.

I'd been about to tell him that I'd kept Lucy, but the thought that if he cared he might have asked – and hadn't – made me pause and then change my mind.

'Play something else,' I said, more to change the subject than anything else.

'What?' Billy asked, raising the guitar again.

'I don't know,' I said. 'Play your favourite from *The Weight of Diamonds*, whichever that is.'

'That was a shit album,' Billy said. 'We rushed it out because *Argy-Bargy* did so well.'

'No, it was great,' I protested. 'I listened to it so much, I knew all the words by heart.

'Nah,' Billy said. 'I hate that album. Choose something else.'

'OK, "Where Did You Go?" then,' I said. 'From *Argy-Bargy*. I loved that song.'

Billy sighed deeply and then started to strum. 'You sing, though,' he said. 'Seeing as you know it so well.'

I laughed, and my laughter was enough to make him remember.

'Christ,' he said, without interrupting his strumming. 'I forgot. I didn't believe you couldn't sing, did I?'

I shook my head and grinned at him.

'But you were right,' he said.

'Oh yes,' I agreed.

He smiled for a moment, lost in the memory, and then when his strumming came round to the right point he began to sing.

Where did you go?
Why did you leave me?...

The recorded version had been a rock-influenced pop song, but once again, with just his voice and the guitar, it was a revelation. It made the whole thing so soulful that tears sprang to my eyes instantly.

...I thought it was love
Where the fuck are you, Phoebe?

I jolted out of my trance and looked up at him with a frown. I raised one hand to interrupt him but he was too busy fingering chords to notice, so I spoke. 'Phoebe?'

'I'm sorry?' Billy asked, pausing his playing and looking up.

'Phoebe? Did you say *Phoebe*?'

'Yeah.'

'God, I always thought it was "Free Me",' I said. '"Where the fuck are you? / Free me!"'

Billy laughed. 'Free me would be OK too,' he said. 'It's actually quite nice.'

'But it's supposed to be *Phoebe*? I mean, it was *Phoebe* all along?'

Billy nodded and turned to hang the guitar back on the wall. 'She was Jake's girlfriend,' he said.

'Jake the drummer?'

He nodded again. 'Phoebe fucked off while we were on tour in France and he never saw her again. I'm not sure if he ever found out what had happened to her. We used to wonder if someone had abducted her or something.'

'Jesus,' I said. 'I was so certain I knew the words.'

'The joys of the misheard lyric,' Billy said. 'You know, Gandhi – my youngest – used to sing "We built this city on sausage rolls" whenever that came on the radio?'

'Really?' I said, smiling vaguely, but I guessed that my intonation had been wrong because I wasn't really thinking about what Billy was saying.

'We started printing the lyrics on the sleeve after *The Weight of Diamonds*.'

'Yes,' I said. 'I saw that.'

'God, you didn't think...?' Billy started to ask.

'Yes?'

'Never mind,' he said. 'Come on. Let's finish the tour.'

He extracted himself from behind the drum kit and I followed him out into the hall, still thinking about his unfinished question. *Had I thought the song was about me?*

The answer was, *not really*. But my misheard / Where the fuck are you? / Free Me! version had spoken to me in a way that enabled me to continue thinking Billy and I shared a connection. But the song was about bloody Phoebe. Talk about projection!

I reran that final snippet of conversation through my mind's eye. There had been a hint of a smile on his lips, hadn't there? The idea that I'd thought a song might be about me had been almost, but not quite, amusing to him.

'Guest room with en suite,' Billy said, pushing open a door. 'In case you want to stay over.'

I peered into the room. It was plain and had a smaller window with the same pretty view as his music room.

'Office,' Billy said, one door down. 'This is where Joanna lives most of the time.' It was a tidy office with a glass desk, a filing cabinet and a mustard chaise longue.

'She *lives* here?'

'Façon de parler,' Billy said, and, though I don't speak a word of French, I somehow understood what he meant.

'So you're not together?'

Billy glanced back at me and wrinkled his nose. 'Some drunken shenanigans in LA one night after a concert, but that's about as far as it went.'

'Right,' I said. 'Fair enough.'

'And last but not least,' Billy said. 'The master bedroom.'

He crossed the room to another large sliding window, but I remained hovering on the threshold, eyeing up the black satin sheets and thinking how clingy and uncomfortable they looked. How potentially threatening, too.

'Come look at the view,' Billy said. 'You can see even further along the cove.'

Still I hesitated, and, as I did so, a whole stream of different thoughts went through my mind.

I thought that entering Billy's bedroom was risky, but that the risk was of something happening that I had fantasised about for half my life.

I thought about the fact that Billy wasn't that attractive any more, but that I probably wasn't that much of a catch these days, either, and how I'd still found him surprisingly attractive when he'd been singing, and that perhaps if I could just get him to sing to me while we had sex... I smiled at that silly thought and then, deciding that my hesitation was looking worse than just following him, I went for it. I walked the length of the bed and stood beside him to look out at the view.

'Bedroom with a view, huh?' Billy said, bumping my hip with his.

I nodded. 'Yes, it's lovely,' I admitted. I wondered if I'd ever want to sleep with Rob again. I wondered if that was about Rob, or about me, and I wondered if sleeping with Billy would help me understand where the problem was.

'Looks even better at sunset,' Billy said.

'Cool,' I said. 'Must be nice.' I wondered if I'd ever sleep with anyone else in my life. Sex had been so simple when I'd been young. It became surprisingly complicated once you were older.

'If you stayed, you could see it,' Billy said. 'We could drink some champers and watch the sun go down. I wouldn't necessarily make you stay in the shitty guest room.' He slipped one arm round my waist as he said this, but I resisted him and pushed away.

'Come on,' he said. 'Don't be uptight.'

Uptight, I thought. *Uptight*. Something about that word annoyed me, but there wasn't time to analyse exactly why.

'Yeah, cheers, Billy,' I said, with fake flippancy. 'But maybe not today.'

I wrestled from his grasp then, and turned to head for the door, but as I did so he said, 'If not today, then when?' – which was another Argonauts song lyric – and then grabbed me from behind, throwing one arm round my waist.

In an attempt at making a joke out of it, I forced a laugh and continued on my way, dragging Billy behind me towards the door. But then he surprised me by pushing me sideways and, as my legs hit the side of the mattress, I lost my balance, and there was no option but to fall onto the bed.

As I pushed myself up onto my forearms, I caught a glimpse of Billy's bedside table and noticed a mirror on which stood a razor blade and a vial of white powder – no doubt coke. There was also a family photo that, under any other circumstances, I would have liked to study more closely. But as Billy was, by then, straddling me and trying to roll me onto my back, that simply wasn't possible.

I tried to crawl away from him, but he had blocked me between his thighs, so I went with the flow and rolled to face him.

'Billy,' I said, using the voice I use to reason with my children when they're being unreasonable. 'What do you think you're doing?'

He'd released the belt of his gown, revealing the full horror of his blobby stomach and white chest hair. He rubbed the not-inconsiderable bulge in his pyjama bottoms with one hand and asked, 'What does it look like I'm doing?'

'It's looks like you're pinning me to a bed against my will, and actually considering *raping* me,' I said. Lucy's self-defence teacher had told her that naming what was happening could be useful in making it stop.

But it didn't work on Billy. He lunged for my belt buckle, so I slapped his hand away.

'Rape,' he said. 'You'd like that, wouldn't you, you little slut!'

'No I wouldn't!' I gasped, struggling to speak through my outrage. 'And you know, many years ago, someone told me to never say "yes" to anything I didn't really want. Do you— Billy, *stop*! Jesus! Do you *know* who said that to me, Billy? Do you?'

'Nope,' Billy said, grinning inanely. 'But he sounds like a right twat.'

'It was *you*, Billy. It was you that taught me that incredibly important lesson.'

'So even I talk shit sometimes,' Billy said, laughing maniacally. 'Well, I did. When I was, like, a teenager. But now I'm all grown up, and I'm going to fuck you. Because despite all this play-acting you're gagging for it. I know you are.'

I slapped his hand from my belt a second time. 'Christ, stop, Billy. You've been watching too much porn, hon!' I said. I was trying to keep things fluffy because of my fear. 'I think it's fucked with your brain.'

'You always did like it rough,' he said, and I slapped his hand away a third time. 'Remember how I used to fuck you to kingdom come?'

I did remember, too, how rough the sex had been, and how I had, indeed, liked it. I remembered in that split second, too, how meek and boring I'd found Rob's lovemaking by comparison, and how disappointed I'd felt that he didn't bang me the way Billy had.

'It was a game back then, Billy,' I said, starting to get breathless from struggling beneath him. 'This isn't, Billy. I'm saying "no" here, so if you go any further this is rape. Let... me – Jesus! – go!'

He leaned down to try to kiss me, and by then the idea had become worse than repulsive, it had become terrifying.

I pushed his face away from me with the flat of my hand, so he grabbed my right wrist, then the left.

'I like a struggler,' he said. 'Little bitch.'

He still needed a free hand to undo my buckle – thank God I'd worn jeans – and he transferred his grip of my wrists to his left hand so that he could undo my belt with the right, and I thought, and for the first time believed, *I'm about to be raped*, closely followed by a rush of adrenaline and another thought, *No. I'm not. Not by Billy fucking Ruddle, I'm not!*

I writhed with all my might then, and managed to free my hands. I started pounding at his face with my fists but he was too close to really get a swing. He looked shocked, though, I remember that. He looked suddenly very shocked and very angry and I think I realised – correctly or incorrectly – that he was about to take a swing at me.

So I pushed him with all my might, and was a bit surprised when he actually toppled sideways.

Once he was off me, sprawling on the bed, I scrambled from the room.

'Dawn!' Billy shouted, behind me. 'Dawn, come the fuck back!'

I'd reached the bottom of the staircase before he'd even made it out of the bedroom door, and I was at the top of the stairs pushing my way into the garage by the time he'd reached the bottom. 'Dawn, come back and we can talk this through. I thought you were messing about. I thought you wanted to be slutty like the old days,' he said.

For a moment, in the garage, I panicked because I couldn't find a button to open the doors, but then I saw the panel of three controls on the wall behind Billy's Porsche, so I ran over and hit them all.

As I slid into my car, Billy appeared. The garage doors were still only halfway open.

'Dawn,' he said, 'for fuck's sake. I was only mucking around. Come back!'

I hesitated for half a second, wondering if I was overreacting. But then realising that the only way to find out was to stay, and that if I was right that might be catastrophic, I started the engine and put the car into reverse. The door was three-quarters of the way up.

When I glanced back at Billy, he was holding something in one hand and in horror I realised that it was a remote for the garage doors.

He grinned at me then – a sickly, horrible psychopath grin – and, with the theatrical gesture of a TV suicide bomber, he hit the button on the remote. The garage doors lurched to a halt.

I started to reverse out anyway, but as I did they began to descend again and the door scraped across the roof of my lovely little Polo, filling the air with a horrific grinding screeching noise.

Out on the street, I didn't look back. I crunched the gears and sped away but, as I was continuing further down the same lane, I had no idea where I was heading.

After a mile of random turns on country roads I arrived at an unsigned intersection and was forced to admit to myself that if I didn't look at a map soon I could quite easily end up back at Billy's. So I pulled into a scrappy field with a farm building behind which I could park out of sight.

When I pulled my phone from my pocket to check Google Maps, it was showing multiple calls and messages. There was a voicemail from Rob, asking where I was, a text from Shelley, warning me that Rob was home and looking for me, and one from Mum asking if I was OK. Just as I was deciding that I'd deal with all of that later once I was a safe distance from Billy, a message arrived from him as well.

It said, *You've broken my garage door you crazy fucking whore.*

It would have been better, no doubt, not to reply, or at least to wait until I was calm, but in the end the word *whore* was more provocation than I could resist. *Good,* I sent back. *I'm glad.*

I opened Google Maps, but then, realising that my reply hadn't been enough – hadn't even begun to encompass my anger, I sent another one.

You're a fat, red-faced rapist psycho, I typed.

Followed by a childish (but satisfying), *And* Ears, Nose, Arse *was shit.*

And then I began to cry.

It took ten minutes until I felt calm enough – could see well enough, even – to type Joss Bay into Google Maps, but as soon as the route came up I started to drive, still wiping the tears away with my sleeve. I needed to put some distance between Billy and myself quickly – I was still feeling physically threatened.

I remembered a Margaret Atwood quote about how men are scared that women will laugh at them, while women are scared they'll be killed. I wasn't sure if it was a reasonable thought but it had never felt truer to me than in that moment.

As I transferred onto the A38, I noticed the journey time in the corner of the screen and realised that I hadn't been thinking straight. It was showing five hours and thirty-nine minutes, and there was no way I was capable of driving it safely. So I pulled into a siding and hunted for somewhere to stay over, settling on a chain hotel just outside Exeter. I didn't know what I was going to say to them yet, but I decided I'd text Rob, Mum and Shelley from there.

As I drove, my emotions came and went in waves. I'd feel feisty or tearful, or angry, or scared and then, just seconds later, unexpectedly calm. I thought about the fact that I hadn't booked a hotel, and how a judge – specifically a male judge – might have said, had I not got away, that it was proof I'd been planning to sleep with Billy all along, and that therefore it couldn't be considered rape.

I thought about the term *premeditated*, and then *premeditated murder*. But of course, murder is only premeditated if you both plan it and go through with it. If you change your mind at the last minute and put the gun or the knife or whatever away, then it's premeditated nothing at all.

That seemed to be the whole point of the matter. Saying 'yes' is a continuous process, and saying 'no' stops that process instantly – whether it's a process that leads to murder or sex – no matter how premeditated it may have been. At least that's how it should work. But it's a concept that men – or at least, *some* men – don't seem to understand, specifically when it comes to sex.

I thought about Rob and how, at the beginning, he'd constantly asked me if everything was OK. Sometimes he'd been in the process of going down on me and I was on my back groaning, and he'd pause and look up at me from between my knees and ask, 'Is this OK?' and I'd hated him for that. I'd found his constant need for reassurance – though these days, one might call it *consent* – endlessly annoying, and, in an absurd way, a kind of opposite of manliness. That had been clearly incredibly unfair on my part when the alternative to ongoing consent was *rape*.

Men! I thought, then, *Sex, Christ, what an incomprehensible mess we've made of it all!*

.   .   .

The hotel was clean, generic and easy – it was exactly what I needed.

I paid for my double room (there were no singles), went up to the first floor, walked a long bleak corridor, and then pulled back the covers to lie down on the cool, crisp sheets.

I thought of Billy moving in to kiss me with his cigar-stained teeth, and shuddered. I thought of Rob and wondered if he really had a mistress and if he did if he called her a *dirty little slut*. I knew, even before I asked myself the question, that he didn't, that he never would or could.

I wondered why I hadn't loved him more for that – for his gentleness, for his constant search for consent, for his absolute reliability in the midst of the mayhem that was our family.

I fell asleep. It was only half past six, and my stress levels were sky-high, but I fell into a deep, deep sleep. Maybe it was the aftermath of all that adrenalin.

When I woke up it was dark both inside the room and beyond the window, and for a terrifying few seconds I hadn't the faintest idea where I was. But then my phone vibrated and the screen lit up and I realised I was in a hotel room and that it was my phone that had wakened me in the first place.

I lifted the phone and struggled to focus on the screen. It said, Rob: *Are you OK? I'm concerned.*

Christ! I thought. *Poor Rob.* The time was 22:25.

I started to type a reply but I couldn't think what to say, so I put the phone back down and went through to the bathroom, where I peed and washed my face.

Back in the bedroom, I sat on the edge of the bed with the phone. I sighed deeply and then typed, *Sorry Rob. I didn't know you'd be home today. I'm off on a little adventure. I needed a change of air. I'll be back tomorrow by midday.*

My phone rang just seconds after with an incoming call from him, but, because I didn't know what to say, I let it go to voicemail.

Another text landed: *If you don't want to talk to me that's your right. But are you definitely OK? Because I'm worried about you.*

I am, really. But I'm in a noisy restaurant, I lied. *Let's talk tomorrow when I get home.*

Am I allowed to know where you are?

Can we please talk about that tomorrow, too?

Sure, no problem. I love you. And CALL ME if you're in any kind of trouble.

His *I love you* made me feel a bit breathless. His *CALL ME* made me want to cry.

I love you too. I typed. *Talk tomorrow.*

My finger hesitated over the button for a second and then, at the dual realisations that it was true and that I'd actually let myself forget that essential fact, I clicked *send*.

When I went out to the car to get my tiny overnight bag, I realised how badly I'd scraped the roof. It looked like someone had started to squash the car in one of those car-crushing machines they use in breakers' yards. That was something else I would have to explain to Rob.

I found the half-sandwich I hadn't eaten on my journey up, so back in my room that's what I had for dinner. I was feeling sick and out of kilter anyway, as if I had jet lag or perhaps the beginnings of the flu. I just hoped it wasn't the Covid bug.

I desperately wanted to talk to Mum, to own up to what I'd done; to hear her reassure me that everything would be OK. Just the thought of hearing her voice down the line was enough to make tears well up. But when I imagined how that conversation might actually go, I could hear her expressing outrage on Rob's behalf. I pictured all the explaining I'd have to do to try to justify myself too – the conversation would be messy and emotional and endless and would end with her giving me a well-deserved telling-off.

So instead I sent her a text message saying I was fine and

that I'd spoken to Rob, and then ignored her incoming *Fine, but where the hell are you?*

Instead, I called Shelley, the only person who actually knew.

'You dirty dirty birdy birdy!' she said gaily, the second she picked up. 'I hope you've worked out what you're going to tell R—'

'Stop, Shell. Just stop. It's not funny anymore. None of this is funny.'

'Oh,' she said. 'What's up?'

'Everything's awful,' I said. 'I have so fucked this up, Shell.'

'Awful because it was wonderful with Billy, or awful because it was awful?'

'It was awful. It was beyond awful.'

'Christ,' Shelley said. 'D'you want me to come over?'

'I'm in a hotel, down by Exeter. So no.'

'Right,' Shelley said. 'Course you are. D'you want to tell me on the phone?'

'I don't think so. Not yet. But it was really, really, awful. I just needed to tell you that.'

'Right,' Shelley said. 'Awful how?'

'Rapey-awful.'

'Christ,' she said. 'He didn't... you're not saying... Did he?'

'No. I made a run for it. But it was pretty bloody scary.'

'Oh God,' Shelley said. 'Poor you.'

I blew through my lips. 'I'm gonna hang up now,' I said, 'because if I don't, I'm going to cry. And I can't be doing with that. I think I'm all cried out.'

'That's fine,' Shelley said. 'I get that totally. Call me tomorrow when you get home.'

THIRTEEN

PANDORA'S BOX (BY ROB)

Ceiling, laundry-detergent, scalp.

I couldn't sleep, or at least, not in any meaningful way.

I did keep dozing off, but almost immediately I'd wake up with the sensation of someone sitting on my chest. The bedroom was the worst place to have panic attacks, because there were so few things you could count in threes. It got very boring very quickly.

Lampshade, Dawn's pillow, my own chin.

Which was all very well, but where the hell was she? And who, if anyone, was she with? Had I really been so wrapped up in my own selfish adventure with Cheryl that I hadn't even noticed Dawn was doing the same?

I trailed through my memory banks, trying to remember whether I'd ever actually *known* that Dawn was here at home during my own trips away, or if that had just been what I'd chosen to believe. Sometimes, there had been signs – little gardening projects she'd accomplished while I was away, or a dishwasher full of dirty dishes from a dinner party. But for the most part the truth was that I simply didn't know.

I imagined her stepping in the door and saying, *So, look,*

Rob, I've met someone, and who could blame her if she had? I'd been so stupid I could barely believe it. I'd been massively, tragically stupid and I hated myself for it.

Then I'd do another round of counting in threes and switch to worrying about Cheryl. Not in a *poor old Rob, he's not gonna get his knob sucked anymore* kind of way... No it was much more of a *Poor Cheryl, I'm such a bastard* kind of thing. Because even though Cheryl had gone into the affair with her eyes fully open, knowing that I was married, she clearly deserved much better than me, too.

And then back to Dawn again, because, seriously, how could I even think about Cheryl at a time like this?

How had Dawn and I come to be so distant from each other anyway? Surely that couldn't be *all* my fault, could it? Everyone knows it takes two to tango, and if Dawn had wanted to tango, if she'd wanted to ride on the back of the XT to a beach and go skinny-dipping – and, frankly, who in their right mind would not want to do that? – then I'd never have given Cheryl a second glance. Or would I? Was I just trying to let myself off the hook?

She'd said – Dawn, this is – *I love you too* at the end of her message, hadn't she? I picked up my phone and read it again, and, yes, she'd definitely typed it. So that surely had to be a good sign.

Maybe she hadn't met anyone else at all. Maybe she'd just needed to get away to clear her head, but clear it of what? That implied she knew about Cheryl or at least suspected I was having an affair, so would it be best to deny or confirm her fears? No, I wouldn't lie. I wouldn't be able to live with myself if she'd worked it out and I lied.

Would things be salvageable if I did own up? Were there enough *sorrys* and *forgive-mes* in the world to make things right?

By then it was 5:50 and the sky was flaming red and my

tummy was rumbling, so I gave up and rolled from the bed. My body ached as if I'd spent the night in a boxing ring.

I didn't text her and I didn't call.

It seemed that whatever was going on was almost certainly my fault, so all I could do was be on my best behaviour, and wait. Giving her the space she'd said she needed seemed a no-brainer.

Finally, just after eleven, her car pulled up outside. I was sitting in the sunroom biting my nails – or rather the skin around my nails because there was very little chewable nail left – when I heard the crunch of tyres on gravel.

I stood. I felt sick to my stomach. I sat back down.

I thought of Cheryl waiting on that hotel balcony and wished that I smoked, and then thought of lung cancer and was glad that I didn't.

I stood again and looked through the kitchen and down the hallway to the front door. Her silhouette would appear behind the patterned glass soon. Was it better to go and meet her, or better to wait? Perhaps I should have involved myself in some household task so that I didn't look quite so bloody nervous.

I'd know, I decided. The second I saw her face, I'd know if it was all over.

But then the glass shimmered and coloured with the silhouette of her purple jacket and the door opened. She was in the hallway looking at me from a distance, and I didn't know anything at all.

She dropped a small bag at the bottom of the stairs – a bag that was no doubt full of clues – and then, avoiding eye contact, wriggled her way out of the jacket.

I met her halfway, in the kitchen, where finally she looked me in the eye.

She blushed, just a bit, but she definitely blushed, which

seemed strange. She reminded me of when she was seventeen, and at first I thought it was the blushing, but then I noticed she'd had a haircut, and realised a split second later that she'd had it done before I left for Newcastle, but that I hadn't consciously noticed. Actually, I had noticed something was different, but I hadn't taken the time to work out what it was because I'd been too busy thinking about Cheryl and whether or not I was going to have sex with her and risk a baby, or leave her, or maybe neither. More shame on me.

'Hello,' Dawn said, almost shyly.

'Hello,' I said.

I thought, *Christ this is uncomfortable. What's that all about? It feels like a first date with a stranger.*

'Shit this is weird,' Dawn said. 'It's like being on a bloody first date or something.'

I smiled at the fact she'd said almost word for word what I'd been thinking and stepped forward to wrap her in my arms.

For a moment I was fighting back tears, but then I realised that Dawn was actually crying and as my concern switched from myself to her, the pressure behind my own eyes dissipated.

'Hey, hey,' I said, squeezing her tighter as she shuddered. 'What's all this about, eh?'

'I've wrecked the car,' she spluttered. It hadn't been at all what I was expecting.

'The Polo?' I asked stupidly, because she didn't have any other car, and she nodded into my shoulder. 'Well, *that* doesn't matter,' I said. 'As long as you're OK, that doesn't matter at all.'

'I know,' she said.

'That's not why you're crying?'

She shook her head. 'No, I'm crying because of something else.'

'OK,' I said. 'Do you want to tell me, or...?'

'Later,' she said. 'Can I tell you later?'

'Of course you can,' I said. 'But you're OK, are you? You're not hurt?'

'No, I'm not hurt.'

'And everyone else is OK? Lucy's OK?'

'Yes, everyone's fine as far as I know.'

'Then whatever it is, I'm pretty sure it doesn't matter.'

She started to sob properly then – the full-on, snotty shuddering kind. My own eyes teared up again in sympathy.

'Oh, Dawn,' I said. 'Jesus, I'm sorry. Whatever it is, I'm sorry.'

'Me too,' she said. And then she moved her arms so that she could hug me back, and I started to smile. Because whatever was going on, and whatever was going to happen next, right then, at that moment, we were choosing to hug each other, and Christ that felt good.

Understandably, things remained strange all day.

We drifted around each other keeping busy, doing chores, filling and emptying the washing machine, all the time scrupulously avoiding eye contact. It really was as if we were both shy and that was the strangest feeling.

That evening we decided to rent a film – my idea, but one Dawn jumped at just a little too enthusiastically. I think we were both terrified that if we didn't fill the void we might have to actually speak to each other.

The next morning I woke up to find that Dawn was already downstairs. This was unusual enough to merit comment.

'Oh, I know,' she said, when I mentioned it. 'I've been awake since half past four. You were snoring like a... like something that snores very loudly.'

'Like... you when you were pregnant, maybe?'

'Yes,' she said. 'Exactly like that.'

'Well, I didn't sleep much the night before,' I offered in my defence. 'I was kind of catching up.'

I poured myself a coffee and sat opposite Dawn at the table. It would have been weird to sit anywhere else but also the atmosphere in the house seemed to have changed and I'd realised we were going to have to talk. The requirement for conversation seemed to be hanging in the air.

Dawn was texting on her phone, and when she saw me watching she waved it at me and said, 'Shelley. She was worried. I'm just letting her know that I'm home.'

'Fine,' I said. 'Of course.' I wondered how much Shelley knew that I didn't, and betted the answer was *all of it*. I thought about how strange it was that my wife's best friend might know her better than I did.

Once Dawn had finished and sent her text, I spoke, tackling things from the most practical angle possible. 'You don't have to tell me the details if you don't want to,' I said. 'But if we need to make an insurance claim, then we should do that pretty sharpish.'

'It's bad,' she said, 'I know. I went under one of those roll-top garage doors and it rolled down right on top of me as I was driving out.'

'Christ,' I said. 'What in, like, a public car park? Because if that's the case their insurance will pay. It's supposed to stop as soon as it sees a car.'

Dawn shook her head. 'Private, I'm afraid,' she said.

'But all the same. It still—'

'Can we just leave it?' she asked, pulling a face that made her look like she had toothache. 'I know it's going to be expensive, but can we just fix it ourselves? Or even just leave it like that? I really don't care. Driving round with a car that looks like an elephant stepped on it doesn't worry me at all.'

'But if we could get the insurance to—' I started.

'It's just that I really don't want to get into it all. Not with... Not with this particular person.'

I chewed my bottom lip and thought about those words. *This particular person.* I wanted to repeat those words in a sarcastic tone of voice, but by chewing my lip I restrained myself. I cleared my throat. 'OK,' I said. 'No problem. I've got a guy out in Ashford – a client. Does bodywork. I'll get him to look at it instead.'

'Is that OK?' Dawn asked. 'Are you sure?'

We both knew it was a rhetorical question.

She turned to look out of the kitchen window then, so I opened the *Guardian* web page on my phone.

Diving into the cool depths of my phone felt like safety, but she dragged me back out by saying, 'I suppose we're going to have to talk, aren't we? I suppose there's no way round it.'

'You make talking sound like torture,' I said.

'Well sometimes, it is. Don't you think?'

'I guess it depends what you need to say.'

'And what you have to hear,' Dawn said. 'What the other person says.'

'Uh-huh,' I said. 'Maybe.'

'So I have something I should probably tell you,' Dawn said. 'And it's not going to be a bundle of fun.'

'Oh,' I said. 'Crikey!' Dawn raised an eyebrow, and I regretted making light of it immediately. 'Sorry,' I added, 'just nerves...'

'But I need to tell you, *before* I tell you, that it was a mistake and I'm sorry and it's over.'

'Oh,' I said. 'OK. Same here, for what it's worth.'

'Same here?' Dawn said. 'Which bit?'

'All of it,' I said. 'I need to tell you something and it was a mistake and it's over and I'm sorry.' My eyes misted up as I said that, and I saw that Dawn had noticed.

'Is it?' she asked. 'Before we get into my one, is yours over? Definitely? Definitively?'

'It is,' I said, but my voice came out so croaky that I had to say it again. 'It is. So who goes first?'

'I suppose...' Dawn said, then, 'You know what? I actually don't need to know about yours at all. I just needed to know if it was over and if... I suppose I need to know if you still want all this.' She gestured vaguely at the kitchen and though I knew exactly what she meant, she added, 'If you still want me, really.'

'I do,' I told her. 'I never wanted all of this, all of *you* more than I do right now.'

'Right,' she said. 'OK. Well, me too.'

'Thank God for that,' I said, reaching for her hand, but she withdrew it out of reach.

'I should probably tell you mine first,' she said. 'Before we get all cutesy.'

I covered my mouth with one hand and thought for a moment. 'I'm not sure I need to know your details either,' I told her, realising that it was true only as I said it. 'Unless you actually feel you *need* to tell me?'

'No, I don't,' she said. 'I really don't.'

'Then it's OK,' I told her. 'Leave it at that. Really.'

'But I'll tell you if you need to know,' Dawn said. 'I'll tell you anything you want to know.'

'Same here.'

'So nothing?' Dawn asked. 'You don't need to know anything at all?'

'No, I don't think so,' I said. 'Not if it's over.'

'It is,' Dawn said. 'It never really got started, but it's definitely over now.'

'Is it, was it Billy?' I asked. 'Actually, don't answer that.' I didn't even know where the question had come from. I'd never consciously imagined she might be seeing Billy. Not after all these years. But the question had come from somewhere, and without considering it further I'd said it out loud.

'Yes,' Dawn said. 'Yes, it was Billy. But nothing really happened, just so you know. And I'll never see him again. I really hope I won't, anyway.'

'Christ,' I said. 'And I knew it was him. How did I know that?'

Dawn shrugged and shook her head sadly.

'It's always been Billy, hasn't it?' I said. 'It's always been fucking Billy, lurking in the background.'

'Only in my head, really,' Dawn said. 'I haven't, you know, seen him... *hadn't* seen him since... back then. Not once. And I'm sorry I finally did. But at least now I *have* and I can confirm that he's an arsehole. Worse than an arsehole. Much worse, actually. So... yeah.'

'So he's gone,' I said. 'Billy's out of the picture, once and for all?'

Dawn nodded and a tear ran down her cheek.

'Billy fucking Riddle,' I said. 'He's been like a bad smell for thirty years.'

'It's actually Ruddle,' Dawn said.

'I'm sorry?'

'His name's Ruddle, not Riddle. He thinks Riddle sounds cooler, I suppose. He's such a... But anyway, yeah. I'm really, really sorry, Rob. I'm sorry I had him on my mind. There was no... no point to it all, really, but he was. He was always hanging around in the ether, one way or another, like you say. Like a bad smell.'

'Until now.'

'Yes, until now.'

'Will we be better, do you think?' I asked. 'Now you know? Will we be better together?'

'Maybe,' Dawn said. 'I hope so. And you too? Now yours is over?'

'Yeah,' I said. 'Yeah, I'm pretty sure we will.'

'There's something else I need to tell you, actually. Something that's nothing to do with... all of this.'

Sink, flowers, tabletop.

I'd thought we'd glimpsed the end of the tunnel, but here we were plunging straight into another one. A proper calm gasp of air between the two would have been nice.

'It's not...' Dawn said, studying my features. 'It's nothing bad. But it has been...'

I raised my eyebrows as I waited.

'It has been a kind of lie, I suppose. And it hasn't helped us be close.'

'OK,' I said.

'Mum had cancer,' she said, and for some reason – perhaps because those words were so unexpected – it took me a moment to understand what she'd said.

'Cancer,' I finally repeated.

'Breast cancer. Back in... 2016 or 2017 I think. About three years ago, anyway. And she had to have a partial mastectomy. And then chemo. And then reconstructive surgery. So that's where I was, in case you wondered. In my head, I mean. And actually physically, too, a lot of the time.'

'A mastectomy. That's...' I gestured vaguely towards my chest.

'Yes,' Dawn said. 'They removed half of one of her breasts.'

'Jesus,' I said. 'But why—?'

'She wouldn't let me tell you,' Dawn said, answering my unfinished question. 'She wouldn't let me tell anyone. She made me promise. She's told a couple of people now it's all over, so I s'pose it's OK. But at the time she said that if I told you she'd never speak to me again.'

'But that must have been awful,' I said.

'Oh, it was. She was in pieces for weeks, months, years, really. It was terrifying for her.'

I hadn't actually been thinking of Tracey, though that was probably wrong of me. I'd been thinking about how awful it must have been for *Dawn*, worrying about her mother and not being able to share any of the burden with anyone else.

'And for you,' I said. 'That must have been hard for *you*.'

Dawn shrugged. 'It wasn't easy,' she said. 'But I just sort of battened down the hatches and sailed into the storm with her. I think I'd had plenty of practice with Lucy, if I'm honest.'

'Wow,' I said. 'I was so...' I shrugged. '*Busy*... I didn't even notice. I mean, I did, but I just thought... I don't know... that you were bored with me, I suppose. You seemed distracted. Which obviously now makes sense.'

'But that's a bit true, too,' Dawn said. 'I did feel a bit bored with it all. That's why I wanted to tell you. Because it wasn't only your fault. Your being "busy".'

She made quote marks with her fingers as she said the word 'busy' and I flinched at the memory of everything hiding behind that euphemism.

'That wasn't one hundred per cent your fault,' she continued. 'Because it suited me – and yes, I know that's a horrible thing to say – but as we're being so honest here, I need to say it: I had to be with Mum – I had no choice but to be with her all the time, and you being "busy" actually gave me some space. So I may have been a bit complicit.'

'Bloody hell, Dawn,' I said. 'You're amazing. Do you know that?'

'With amazing like that, who needs *awful*?'

'No, I mean, the way you know what you're thinking. The way you can just say it and be so clear. You do amaze me. You always did.'

Dawn smiled sadly. 'I thought about it a lot while I was... during these last few days... And I wanted to tell you it wasn't all your fault.'

'But you're wrong,' I said. 'My bit... well, that is, was, my fault. I just want you to know that I'm owning it. And I feel terrible about it.'

'Fine,' she said. 'Well, you own yours, I'll own mine.'

We looked at each other until we started, just barely, to smile, and then Dawn said, 'I need to go for a walk; get a breath of fresh air; clear my head. Do you mind?' She stood and pushed her chair back from the table.

'Not at all,' I told her. 'As long as you're coming back.'

She smiled properly then and reached out to touch my shoulder. 'I'll be back in an hour or so,' she said. 'And then we can take things from there.'

'Your mum!' I said. I couldn't believe I hadn't asked yet. 'Is she OK?'

'She is now,' Dawn said. 'Yeah, she's fine. She's in complete remission.'

'Thank God,' I said.

'Nah. Just thank the NHS.'

'Indeed.'

'And while we're on the subject, I'm fine as well. Boob-wise, I mean.'

'Why? Was there a doubt? Because if there was then you didn't tell me that either.'

'Yeah, there was a bit,' Dawn said. 'Because of Mum. These things can be, you know... whatever the word is. I can't think.'

'Genetic?'

'I was thinking of the other one, but *genetic* will do.'

'Hereditary?'

'Yeah, exactly. Only it wasn't, isn't, in my case. So that's good.'

'Yeah, that's the best news of all,' I said. 'I wish I'd known. I wish you'd told me.'

'And now I'm going for that walk,' Dawn said.

'Enjoy,' I said. 'I'll have lunch ready by the time you get back.'

'Wow,' Dawn said. 'Someone really *is* making an effort.'

The evening was a strange one and it still kind of felt as if we'd just met. We were polite and helpful to each other – *overly* polite and *overly* helpful – and the jokes were as unfunny as the smiles were fake. I hoped that we just needed time to bed back into our relationship, but I'd be lying if I said I didn't feel worried that something had been definitively broken.

The next morning I waited nervously to see if things would feel better over breakfast, but though I delayed leaving for work until nine-thirty, Dawn didn't appear and when I finally swiped my keys from the bowl I actually felt relieved. Her absence took the pressure off, though I also felt guilty that I felt that way.

During the drive in to work I listened to the radio and the coverage was all about the pandemic. France was entering a kind of preventive quarantine they were starting to describe as a *lockdown* from Tuesday morning onwards. It was no longer just a case of closing schools and hospitals. Everything non-essential would now shut down.

I wondered if electronics wholesalers might be considered essential and betted mentally that they weren't. I wondered how the business would survive if we had to close but continue paying salaries, and how our employees would survive if we didn't.

Employees. That included Cheryl. I tried to think something coherent about Cheryl but failed, so instead turned my attention back to the radio. A government epidemiologist was saying that it might be best to let the disease run its course. Yes, there had been outbreaks in some care homes, and yes, hospitals were being stretched, but for the moment it was nothing worse than winter flu.

I frowned at the radio when he said that, because as far as I

knew Italy, Spain, France, Denmark and, of course, China, had
never shut down for winter flu.

When I got to the Ramsgate office, I was surprised to find
Pete, one of our two customer-facing staff, wearing a mask.

'That's a good look, Pete,' I joked. 'Suits you.' Up until that
morning, with a couple of exceptions, the only people I'd seen
wearing face masks had been Asian.

His colleague, Sue, pulled a face at me. 'Can you tell him?'
she asked. 'Can you tell him he'll scare the customers off? Cos
he sure won't listen to me.'

'You'll all be wearing them in a week,' Pete said. 'Or you'll
be in hospital rigged up to one of them breathing machines.
Your choice.'

I shrugged. 'I don't know, Sue,' I said. 'I'll, um, try to find
out if there's any guidance.'

As I said that, the sliding door opened and customer
entered. He was an elderly man, and he was wearing a home-
made face mask.

'Hi,' Sue said, discreetly grimacing at me before turning to
face the client.

But the man, after freezing for a second to study both
myself and Sue from a distance, slipped past us in the direction
of Pete's counter at the far end.

'I think that may be your answer, Sue,' I said, lifting the flap
in the counter to enter.

Alone in my office, I ploughed through the weekend's
emails, sorting them into various folders and forwarding them to
the people concerned.

And then one from our Maidstone branch popped up with
a ping. It was written by the branch secretary. Cheryl. She was
resigning, she said simply. It was time to 'move on to fresh
pastures'. Her only question was if she needed to send me an
actual letter, and whether I was going to require that she work
her notice period.

I stared at that email for almost twenty minutes as I tried to work out what I was feeling.

But other than a sensation of sickness, of *physical* stomach-churning sickness, I honestly couldn't come up with a single reasonable thought.

At the end of the day, as I was packing up to leave, Ryan came in to see me. He suggested we order face masks for everyone. The delivery guys were requesting them, he said, and it seemed irresponsible not to supply masks for everyone.

'Meditech still have some,' he told me. 'But their sales guy says they're running out fast. They're made in China apparently, and all the factories are shutting down because of Covid.'

'Sure,' I said. 'Fine. Order some. Order them for every branch.'

'Like, how many would you say, though?' Ryan asked. 'One per person per day for a month?'

'I guess,' I said, though at that stage a month actually struck me as excessive. 'If they need to be binned daily. *Do they?*'

Ryan shrugged. 'No one seems to know,' he said. 'Some say you can wash them, but hospitals say they have to be binned.'

I drove home that evening listening to the radio again thinking alternately about Dawn and Cheryl and the pandemic.

The newsreader was describing new lockdowns throughout Europe and the inevitability of one happening here. Some of our own hospitals were already declaring 'critical events' – whatever those were – and soon, he predicted, we'd be opening hospitals in tents ourselves.

When I got home, Dawn was making dinner. She too had the radio on.

'Have you been listening to all this?' she asked.

I nodded. 'It's like being in some awful apocalyptic film.'

Dawn looked up from the pan she was stirring. 'That's exactly what it's like.'

'We're ordering masks at work,' I said. 'We're putting an order in for hundreds of them.'

'Bring some home if you can,' Dawn said. 'Apparently all the chemists are out of stock.' Then, 'Lucy phoned. She wants to come home this weekend. I wasn't sure what to say.'

'Why?' I asked. I couldn't remember anyone in our family ever saying anything other than "yes"'.

'Well, we're supposed to be reducing our social mixing and what-have-you, aren't we?'

'Ah,' I said. 'Yes, I suppose. Then tell her "no" if you're worried.'

'But what do you think?'

'I think it's unlikely that Lucy Boop will give us Covid.'

'They were out at a party on Friday with about thirty other people...' Dawn said. 'She got home at six a.m.'

'Then, like I said, if you're worried, tell her it's not convenient. Tell her we've got something on if that's easier.'

'But she's worried we'll get locked indoors,' Dawn said. 'And if that happens then we might not see her again for ages.'

'Then say "yes".'

Dawn stopped stirring and turned to face me. She put her hands on her hips.

'Rob,' she said. 'I need you to make this call. Don't ask me why, but I need you to choose. It's just too much... I don't know... responsibility.'

'OK,' I said. 'Then no.'

'No?'

I laughed. 'You asked me to choose.'

'But I thought you'd say "yes".'

'Then yes!' I said, trying to keep the exasperation from my voice.

'But you said "no". So you actually think it's dangerous.'

'I did say "no", but if I'm honest, it's got nothing to do with how dangerous it is. I just think we maybe need some time to ourselves.'

'Right,' Dawn said. 'You're right. We do.' Then, 'But I think I'm going to tell her to come.'

I laughed again at that. 'OK,' I said. 'Whatever.'

'Is that OK?'

'Yes, sweetheart, that's totally fine.'

By the time the weekend had come round we'd added Wayne (who wanted to see Lucy) and Tracey (who wanted to see Wayne) to our festivities. Having Tracey over also implied Quin's presence as he now rarely left her side.

It probably wasn't what our glorious prime minister had intended when he'd said to 'reduce social mixing to a minimum' but, as Lucy apparently pointed out, 'we might all be dead by summer'. Of course, it would later transpire that 10 Downing Street was party-a-go-go during the lockdown, so perhaps that's *exactly* what the PM meant.

Anyway, we were happy to catch up with them all and happy for the distraction too. Our week alone had not been an easy one. The tiptoeing on eggshells had continued all week, so Tracey-and-Wayne's hilarious mother-and-son sniping was most welcome.

Other than some excitement about Wayne getting back together with Belinda – now two years and four girlfriends previous – and raised glasses at the good news of Alek's new job as a bar manager (the reason he couldn't be present), virtually all the talk was of Covid. How bad would it be? Were the government over- or underreacting? How long would a vaccine take to be developed?

I remember hoping it wouldn't all go on for too long because otherwise the conversation about it alone would become exhausting. But when I imagined what *too long* meant, I was thinking in terms of weeks, or at worst a few months. We still had no idea...

Once we'd waved everyone off on Sunday afternoon, Dawn and I found ourselves at a complete loss for subjects of conversation, so we rehashed the conversations of the weekend and ran through the obvious choices of how well Lucy looked and how happy Tracey seemed with Quin and when even those subjects ran out we sat and ate in silence.

'Lucy picked up on it, you know,' Dawn said eventually, waving a spaghetti-laden fork in the space between us.

'On what?'

'This,' she said through an ugly mouthful of spaghetti. 'Us. She said we had a *quote* weird vibe going on *unquote*.'

'Oh,' I said. 'Well, I suppose she's right. We do.'

We ate in silence for a moment longer and then I asked, 'Do we need to see someone, do you think?'

'See...?' Dawn started, then, 'Oh! You mean like a shrink?'

'Yeah,' I said. 'A guy at work's been going to couples' counselling with his wife. It made me think, that's all...' This was an out-and-out lie, but I felt that I needed an excuse to bring the subject up.

'Brave,' Dawn commented.

'Seeing a counsellor?'

'No, talking about it,' she said. 'I didn't think you straight boys discussed that kind of stuff. I thought it was all cars and hi-fi and porn.'

'Well,' I said. 'We don't much, you're right. I'm not even sure how it came up, now.'

Dawn filled her mouth with pasta but once she'd swallowed, instead of replying as I'd expected, she actually fed herself another forkful.

'Should I take that as a "no" then?' I asked.

Dawn laughed at that and gestured at her mouth. Once she

could speak again, she said, 'No, I was just wondering what we'd talk about.'

'This, I suppose,' I said. 'Us. Our *weird vibe.*'

'That conversation wouldn't take long.'

'No,' I agreed. 'Unless we talked about what led to the weird vibe. Unless we talked about all the stuff we decided we didn't need to say.'

Dawn pulled a face as if she was in pain. 'In front of some stranger?' she said. 'Makes me feel queasy just to think about it.'

'Yeah,' I said. 'Me too, really. So you think we just wait? You think the vibe will just blow over?'

'Hopefully,' Dawn said. 'Yeah, hopefully it will.'

But the awkwardness did not go away, and, if anything, as time passed it got worse – though that may have been simply because we had so much time to think about it.

Within a week, I and half my staff were working from home, and, within two, two-thirds of them had been furloughed, meaning that the government paid eighty per cent of their wages so they could go crazy, locked in their homes. Every single one of our retail customers had been forced to close shop, leaving only our professional clients – electricians and fitters and the like. Even they found their workload drying up. The whole planet was grinding to a halt.

The only good thing to come out of any of it was that I was able to ease my guilt just a touch by helping Cheryl. After the exchange of a few frosty emails, she agreed to cancel her resignation and be furloughed instead. After all, she was hardly going to find another job in the middle of a pandemic.

By week three, Dawn and I were putting on weight and getting cabin fever, so we started walking together, an hour every morning and an hour every evening, and it was on one of these walks, one Saturday morning, that Dawn again broached the subject of our 'vibe'.

'You know, I've been thinking about what you said before,' she said, out of the blue.

We were sitting on a bench in King George Park – a sporty forty-five-minute walk from home.

'What I said when?' I asked.

'About how edgy things are,' Dawn said. 'About maybe seeing someone.'

'Oh,' I said. 'That. It's not getting better, is it?'

'No,' she agreed. 'No, not much. I feel like I can't breathe at home half the time.'

'Me too,' I said. 'But I don't know how much of that is due to lockdown. It's all pretty stressful. Just watching the news makes me feel breathless.'

'Yeah, that's definitely part of it,' Dawn said. 'But the other part is this weird vibe we have going between us. It's exhausting trying to think of things to say.'

'I think it might be because there's an elephant in the room,' I said. 'It makes it hard to talk about anything else.'

'That's exactly what it feels like,' Dawn said. 'It feels like there's an elephant stealing all our oxygen. Two elephants, actually.'

A little Basset hound came running up to us, followed by an elderly lady wearing a face mask.

'Please don't,' the woman said, as Dawn reached out to pet the dog. 'They can carry it from one person to another, you know.'

'Oh,' Dawn said, snatching her hand back. 'Sorry.'

Once the woman had clipped the lead onto the dog's collar and dragged him away, I murmured, 'They carry it from one person's ankles to another, you know.'

Dawn snorted. 'Talk about paranoid!' Then, 'You know Mum washes her shopping when she gets home? Do you think we should start doing that? Surely you can't catch it from shopping, can you?'

I shook my head. 'Probably not,' I said, then, 'Maybe. They've got it in Ryan's grandparents' care home, you know, out in Westgate? Did I tell you that? Five cases already, apparently.'

'No,' Dawn said. 'You didn't say. They OK?'

'So far,' I said. 'But he's worried. I hope they're OK. I met them once and they were lovely.'

'God,' Dawn said. 'What a worry.'

'Anyway, you were saying. About our dodgy vibe. Do you think that we need to see someone after all?'

'I don't know,' she said. 'I mean, I'm not even sure how easy that would be at the moment. We'd probably have to do it over a bloody webcam or something. So I was thinking... what I was thinking, really... is that maybe we need to do it ourselves.'

Trees, cut grass, wooden bench. I gulped a mouthful of air trying to find some O_2, but it seemed unusually scarce.

'Are you OK?' Dawn asked. 'You look kind of sweaty. I hope that dog didn't just give you ankle Covid.'

'Just, you know... One of my panic things,' I said. 'It'll pass.'

Grumpy woman, barking dog... Dawn reached out to take my hand... *wife's hand.*

'We can do this,' she said. 'We still love each other, right?'

I nodded. 'Totally. No doubt about that.'

'Good,' she said. 'Then we can do this. Let's go home and watch shite TV.' And with the realisation that she wasn't going to open Pandora's box right that second, I found myself suddenly able to breathe again.

Though lockdown had blurred the line between workdays and weekends to the point where I'd sometimes have to check my phone to work out what day it was, we did try to keep Sundays special.

I'd skip breakfast so that I could have brunch with Dawn and then we'd FaceTime the kids and phone Tracey and Wayne to check everyone was OK. In the afternoon we'd generally settle down to watch a film.

That Sunday went pretty much to plan, but as we sat in the lounge Dawn said, 'You know what? Can we skip the film today? I think we've seen all the decent ones anyway.'

I turned and frowned at her. 'OK,' I said doubtfully. 'What you thinking of?'

'How about we try that talking business,' she said.

'Oh,' I said. 'OK.' I clicked the TV off. 'Here?' I asked. The lounge somehow didn't feel right for that kind of conversation, but I couldn't think where might be better. Perhaps the kitchen. Somewhere with cold clean surfaces would maybe help keep emotions in check.

Dawn shook her head. 'Let's walk,' she said.

I nodded towards the window and pointed out that it was raining.

'Barely!' she said. 'Come on. Talking's easier outside. I think it's because there's more air.'

We pulled on raincoats and boots and headed in the direction of Margate, and the drizzle felt strangely refreshing. I couldn't remember the last time I'd actually chosen to walk in the rain.

When we reached Cliftonville we automatically made our way to our old house, where we stood side by side on the wet pavement looking up at the tatty façade. The paint was peeling and one of the windowpanes on the top floor had been replaced with board, but the house next door had been recently and rather beautifully repainted.

'Maybe the neighbourhood's finally making a comeback,' I said, nodding.

'Maybe,' Dawn said. 'It'd be about time.' Then, 'That house was the most amazing thing anyone's ever done for me and I don't think I ever even thanked you.'

I smiled and nodded as I scanned the windows, remembering seeing Dawn and baby Lucy through them when I used to get home. 'I was so happy in that house,' I said, a lump forming in my throat. 'I loved you both so much. I still do of course, but back then I felt like I'd been blessed. I felt like I'd won some sort of lottery.'

'I should have been happier too,' Dawn said. And I'm sorry that I wasn't. I'm really, really sorry.'

'Hey, you were OK,' I told her, bumping hips.

'Nah, I wasn't,' she said quietly. 'I did my best, honest, I did. But I was still in love with Billy.'

We walked to the lido and then down and along the broad promenade to the harbour, and by the time we got there the drizzle had stopped. The sea was grey and oily, as if made of something far more viscous than seawater, and even the seagulls seemed subdued.

We sat on a damp wall at the end of Margate harbour and it was there Dawn told me everything.

She explained how much she'd loved Billy (something I knew already) but also why she'd loved him (something I did not). She explained how she believed that the girl I'd met and fallen in love with was, at least in part, Billy's creation.

I told her that I thought she was giving him too much credit, but she insisted that no, her confidence to dress the way she had, her love of indie rock and Britpop – even, obtusely, her feminism – these things had all come from Billy. 'His parents gave me the first books I'd read since school,' she said. 'Without them I might never have read another book again. Seriously. My books, politics, music, all of it came from that one summer with Billy.'

I remained unconvinced, but ultimately what did I know? Some experiences certainly change who we are and some even end up defining us.

'But he was never a nice person,' Dawn added.

It sounded like the subject might be coming to a close, and

that would have been welcome because my tolerance for all things Billy was reaching saturation point, but Dawn went on, 'He was shiny, like a diamond. He drew people in. He drew me in. But he never deserved anyone's love like you do. So I'm sorry. I really am.'

We sat in silence for a moment staring out at the sea and then I said, 'So I suppose it's my turn now?'

Dawn sighed. 'Almost,' she said. 'But not quite.'

She went on to tell me about her trip to East Portlemouth and, when she reached the part of her story where Billy had pinned her to the bed, I got so angry that I could have killed him had he been present. I literally had a flash of the red curtain and understood how it came about that people committed murders. The mystery of the crushed Polo was finally revealed too, and I forced myself to laugh along with Dawn. She seemed to have decided to find that bit of the story amusing, and I didn't want to take that away from her. I knew from experience how she used laughter to transform anything unbearable into a joke.

But I did genuinely consider driving down there and smashing Billy's face with a hammer. I imagined how satisfying that would feel.

'So what do you think?' Dawn asked, once she'd finished.

'Well, I totally get why you don't want to hang out with him anymore,' I said, aping her strategy of joking about the unbearable.

'Yeah,' she agreed. 'It was awful.'

I watched her feet for a moment. She was banging her heels together like clackers.

'If he'd actually been nice, would you have left me?' I asked.

'Oh!' Dawn said, then, 'Christ!'

'That's a "yes" then,' I said. 'That's OK.' I wondered why I had said that. It clearly wasn't OK at all.

'The truth is, Rob, he was a fantasy,' she said after a moment's thought. 'It's not easy to explain... But I'd made him into this fantasy man in my head. So if he had been that perfect person – if the fantasy had been real – then yeah. I probably would have. Anyone would have. But it wasn't. He wasn't. Because he couldn't be.'

'Because?'

'Sorry, because what?'

'He couldn't be because…?'

'Oh, because fantasies aren't real, are they? That's why they're so appealing. Real relationships are with real, imperfect people like… well… us, I suppose. Real relationships look like this. They're about arguing and negotiation and skidmarks and who does the washing and… I don't know… All that shit. They're not about perfect brilliant sexy pop stars who never say anything stupid. Because that's all just fantasy. Is any of this making any sense to you at all?'

And it did make sense to me. It made a lot of sense, actually. All I had to do was think how attracted I'd been to my fantasy version of Cheryl.

'Anyway, there's one final thing,' Dawn said. 'And I've been umm-ing and ahh-ing about this one – about telling you, I mean. But if I don't, I'm worried we'll still have an elephant. So I think it's maybe better to get rid of it.'

'Go elephants!' I said theatrically, to mask how nervous I was feeling. I was pretty sure this was going to be about sex, and very probably about how bad I was at it. 'Elephants be gone!'

'Exactly,' Dawn said. 'So here goes.' She turned away from me then and when she looked back I could see she had fresh tears in her eyes. 'I think Lucy is Billy's child,' she said. 'I'm sorry. But I'm pretty convinced.'

'Oh,' I said. She'd knocked the wind right out of me with that one. It wasn't what I'd been expecting at all.

'He had a photo,' Dawn continued, 'on his bedside table. He also had quite a lot of cocaine as it happens, but that's a different... Anyway, this photo, it was of his kids. The ones he had with Candice Rayner. A little boy and a little girl.'

'OK...?'

'I didn't get much of a look at them. I mean, I was kind of busy fighting him off. But for a split second I thought it was Lucy, that's the thing. The little girl... she looked so like Lucy, I actually thought it was her.'

'Right,' I said. 'OK. That must have been... disturbing.'

'And I just thought you should know. Especially what with all the... Billy-like problems we've had with Lucy. I thought you should know that's probably not your fault.'

'I never thought it was,' I said.

'No?' Dawn asked. She looked bewildered.

'No, I always thought that half of that was *Lucy's* fault,' I said. 'And the other half was just Lucy's... *illness*, really. Like any other illness.'

'Really. You never felt guilty?'

I shook my head. 'She is an actual person with her own brain, you know. She didn't come with some secret remote control I keep in my pocket.'

'Oh, gosh!' Dawn said. 'That must be nice. I wish I could say the same.'

'You felt guilty? You actually felt like it was your fault?'

'Of course,' Dawn said. 'How could I not?'

'Wow. You never said.'

'No. Maybe I didn't.'

'But anyway, you're wrong, you know, what you said before...'

Dawn frowned at me. 'Which bit?'

'That Lucy is Billy's child.'

'It's just that the photo—'

'No, I understand what you're saying, Dawn,' I said. 'And he may even be the guy who provided, you know, the little spermatozoid or whatever that wriggled its way in back in 1990. I mean, he also may *not* be and I guess we'll never know. Hopefully, we'll never know.'

'But—'

'No, shush,' I said. 'Listen. She's not his child. Lucy will never be his *child*. Being someone's child, being a parent, that's a relationship, not just a one-off event. That's hours of work. It's thousands and thousands of hours of work, actually. It's nursing them through chickenpox and driving them to dance class and bloody violin even though they play like shit; it's parents' days and dragging them out of squats and taking them to rehab. It's worrying about them and crying about them and saving them and then doing it all over again and again and again until it works. So no, you're wrong. Billy's never even met her, for Christ's sake. At this point... at the point we've got to now, Lucy is very much our child. We made her, we saved her, Dawn, not Billy. She wouldn't even be *alive* if it wasn't for you.'

Dawn pinched the bridge of her nose to stem the tears. 'Thanks,' she said. 'You're right.'

'I'm assuming Billy doesn't know about this?' I asked. 'You didn't actually tell him, did you?'

Dawn shook her head and sniffed. 'No, he didn't ask,' she said. 'He never even asked if I kept the baby.'

'Nice,' I said. 'Classy guy. The more I hear, the more I like him.'

'I know,' Dawn said. 'I can barely believe I ever looked at him. Oh, and, for what it's worth, you've aged far, far better. He looks dreadful.'

I nodded. 'I actually saw him on TV a couple of years ago and I have to say he didn't look particularly attractive. My guess is too much booze.'

'My guess is too much coke.'

FOURTEEN

PANDORA'S BOX (BY DAWN)

We started to walk home and almost instantly it began to drizzle again – a drizzle so fine that it was little more than a mist, but it soaked my jeans and left my face shiny and wet all the same.

As we walked, Rob told me his half of the story, the fairytale of Rob and Cheryl.

Was it better to know, or not to know? While he spoke, that was the question I kept asking myself.

Because, knowing something had happened but not *what* had been so hard, I'd caved in to the idea that we needed to talk. And yet the details were pretty unbearable too. Specifically the duration – learning that his affair had gone on for *years* – was particularly hard to hear.

But I tried to understand. We'd decided on honesty and non-judgement, so I really did my best.

It had started with the motorbike, Rob said, and I could see how that could be true. He'd had a classic midlife crisis – if wanting to have fun again *was* a midlife crisis – but I'd said no. I *hadn't* wanted to get on it, or have fun, and not for any sensible reason I could name. I hadn't wanted sex with Rob for years either, though even now, when he asked why (which he did), I had no real explanation to offer. The beaches he'd gone to with Cheryl, the trips to spas and distant hotels... well, he was right when he said I would have refused. Because I'd been with Mum all that time, hadn't I? I'd been holding her hand while they trickled chemo into her veins. And Rob hadn't known that. So what was more natural than finding a companion who *did* want to do all these things?

But then he asked if I hadn't been with Mum, would I have wanted to do any of those things with him, and the only true answer I could give was 'no', and that made me realise that it hadn't only been about Mum. It had been about my own midlife crisis, my own resentments about the life I'd led and the person I'd spent it with and, in an awful way, Mum had been a convenient distraction from my doubts about my life with Rob. And about Billy, of course. Always bloody Billy.

So yes, I tried really, really hard to understand. And to be fair. And I tried to listen without resentment. But I couldn't really do it. The best I could manage (something that was largely facilitated by the fur-lined hood of my parka) was not letting my resentment show.

By the time we got home, Rob had finished and, by way of an excuse to avoid being in the same room as him, I ran a bath. I was chilled through from our rainy walk, I explained. I needed, quite desperately, to get warm.

But the truth was that I needed space to think about it all – without Rob studying my face for clues. I needed time to work out whether knowing was better than not knowing; to consider whether my anger was temporary or whether it might be a new, permanent state of being. To consider whether I now knew enough to decide once and for all if I would stay or go. Because we were running out of time here. I was heading for fifty. If I chose Rob again this time, then it would almost certainly be until death do us part. There was a thought! It was truly now or never.

Once the bath was ready I took a deep gulp of air and slipped beneath the surface of the water. Was I really considering leaving him? Just acknowledging it was a shock.

Because how absurd would that be? Staying with someone during the lies – my lies, his lies, everyone's lies – only to leave him because of his honesty.

Eventually, with nothing resolved, I climbed out of the bath. The water was starting to go cold and my fingers were turning pruney.

But as I dried myself I suddenly realised there was something else I needed to know. There was a whole chunk of Rob he'd kept secret, and it was perhaps another part of the reason we'd drifted apart. If we were doing honesty, I thought, then we might as well go the whole hog.

I found him in the lounge reading something on his phone. He'd changed into joggers and a rust-red fleece and looked cosy and just a bit cuddly.

'Good bath?' he asked.

I nodded. 'Yeah,' I said. 'I drifted off for a bit, I think.'

'Good,' he said. 'That was one wet walk. Don't want you catching a cold and having to worry about whether it's Covid, do we?'

'I need to ask you something else,' I said, without further ado. I knew the subject was taboo, and I knew it was risky to ask. If I waited, I feared my courage would fail me.

'OK,' Rob said, sounding suspicious. 'Fire away.'

'Your parents,' I said. 'What happened?'

'Oh,' Rob said.

'And that damned box. What was in that bloody box? Because I know it wasn't just rubbish. I always knew that wasn't the truth.'

'Ah,' Rob said. 'OK.'

'Was it?'

He smiled sadly and shook his head, then got up and walked from the room.

Oh, I thought. It had not been the reaction I was expecting.

I covered my mouth with one hand and wondered what would happen next. Had he gone to lock himself in another room? To pack a suitcase? To throw up? To find a weapon with which to club me to death? All utterly ridiculous imaginings, of course, but leaving the room without a word, without eye contact, had been inexplicably strange and, above all, most unlike Rob.

I heard a noise, a loud clanking noise, and it took me a few seconds to understand where it was coming from. But then I realised it was the sound of the attic ladder being unfolded. Of course. He'd hidden the contents of the box in the attic.

I climbed the stairs and by the time I got there he was above me, hopping about on the rafters. 'Here,' he said, eventually, so I climbed the ladder until I could see the box he was holding in his hands. 'Take it,' he said, 'and I'll come down.'

By the time he'd joined me on the landing, I'd examined the box from all angles. It hadn't been tampered with. It hadn't been opened at all.

'You're right,' he said. 'I lied. I'm sorry. I just couldn't face opening it. I didn't realise it was such a big deal. Not for you, I mean. Obviously it's a big deal for me.'

'OK,' I said. 'But why? What do you think is in it?'

'I've no idea,' Rob said. 'But memories, probably. Or at least some memory-joggers. And none of those are going to be good.'

'I shouldn't have...' I said, handing the box back. 'It's for you to decide, isn't it? I'm sorry. It was just that I could tell you were lying when you said you binned it, so I've been wondering about it for years..'

'No, you're right,' Rob said. 'Let's do it. It's time.'

.   .   .

He carried the box downstairs to the kitchen, where he placed in on the table. I went to the kitchen drawer for scissors, which I solemnly handed over.

Rob took them from me and studied the box. He was chewing his bottom lip and looked pale and somehow waxy. The tension in the room was unbearable and just looking at his twisted features made me feel nauseous. 'If this is too much for you,' I said, 'then I respect that. You mustn't do this for me.'

'No,' Rob said. 'No, it's got to be done. I don't know why but it has. And it's got to be done right now.'

He opened the scissors to use them like a knife and dragged them across the top of the box in a single determined swipe and then repeated the gesture across the left and right corners. The brittle layers of ancient masking tape gave way easily.

Rob looked skywards and took a conscious noisy breath, and then with tears in his eyes he started to lift the flaps.

I moved to his side and tried to put an arm round his waist, but unexpectedly he shrugged me off. 'Sorry,' he said, 'but I can't do this and... *that*... at the same time.'

I wasn't quite sure what *that* was really, but respecting his need for space I moved to the opposite side of the kitchen table.

Once he was able to see inside the box, Rob's first reaction was a sigh and a sad smile. The only thing visible was a folded red cable-knit jumper.

'Favourite jumper,' he said, taking it from the box, laying it on the table, and then sliding it in my direction.

I lifted it up by the shoulder seams and said, 'Very long, skinny favourite jumper.'

Rob sniffed. 'Yeah. It's from when I was fifteen, sixteen,' he said. 'I was tall but skinny as hell.'

I looked at the jumper again and imagined sixteen-year-old Rob wearing it and wished I had known him back then.

Next up was a photo album. He swallowed with visible

difficulty and barely opened the cover before closing it and handing it to me. 'Later,' he said. 'I can't do that one yet.'

I took the book from his grasp. It had a blue padded plastic cover printed with a map of Cornwall and thick gilt-edged pages. 'Can I?' I asked.

Rob nodded. 'But don't ask me to... you know.'

I nodded and, positioning myself so that I could do so discreetly, I opened the cover.

The rigid pages had cellophane covers that were supposed to keep the photos in place but, as they had long since lost their stickiness, the first two photos fell to the table.

One was a classic family-type photo of Rob and his parents standing in front of a caravan. They had what appeared to be genuine smiles and I felt relieved that he'd at least had moments like that during his childhood. I'd feared his entire upbringing had been a horror story.

The second photo was of Rob, aged about ten, standing next to a similarly aged little girl, and I saw Rob catch a glimpse and wince as I picked it up. Who was the girl, I wondered? His sister? That must be it, I decided. He'd had a sister who had died. But I didn't dare ask. Instead, I slipped the photos back beneath the cellophane and closed the album. Without Rob's commentary the photos were meaningless anyway.

When I looked up to see what was next from the box I saw that Rob had slumped onto a chair.

'What is it, sweetheart?' I asked, and he nodded in the direction of the box.

So I rounded the table to his side again and peered in. Laid on a folded pair of bleached jeans were two dolls, an Action Man dressed in military garb and a girl's doll with reddish hair.

'Can I?' I asked.

Rob nodded again, so I reached into the box for the Action Man, which I briefly studied and handed to Rob before reaching for the doll.

'Who's was this, Rob?' I asked. I thought of the little girl in the photo and felt certain he was going to say, *my sister's*.

'Chrissy,' Rob said, quietly.

'And Chrissy is...?' I asked.

'The doll,' Rob said. 'The doll's called Chrissy.'

'Oh,' I said. 'And who did Chrissy belong to? Do you have... *did* you have a sister or...?'

Suddenly tears were streaming down Rob's cheeks, dripping onto his shirtfront, so I put Chrissy down, first on the table, then back in the box out of sight, and pulled a chair up beside him. This time he let me wrap an arm round his shuddering shoulders and press my head against his.

We sat like that for a few seconds before I started to cry too in sympathy. It was the strangest feeling because I didn't know what I was crying about. But Rob's distress was so real, so visceral, it just seemed to grab hold of my guts.

Eventually, after a couple of minutes, Rob wiped his face with his hand, dropped the Action Man back into the box, and stood.

Without a word, he went to the kettle and switched it on, but I could hear from the hiss it made that it was empty, so I jumped up, switched it back off and pushed him towards the sunroom. 'Go sit down,' I said. 'I'll do the tea.'

By the time I'd made two mugs of tea and carried them through, Rob seemed calmer. 'Thanks,' he said, as I handed him his mug.

I placed my own mug on the coffee table and pulled a chair up so that I could sit right opposite.

'So the doll,' Rob said. He sniffed and cleared his throat loudly. 'The doll's called a Chrissy doll. It used to speak when it was new. It said, oh, I dunno... *I don't think so* and *tell you tomorrow*... Shit like that. You pulled a string and she spoke. But the string broke, so...'

'Right,' I said. 'OK.'

'We used to swap them. My Action Man and her Chrissy doll... Used to drive Dad crazy, me playing with a doll, a *girl's* doll, but...' he shrugged. 'My Action Man didn't talk, you know? I thought Chrissy was cool. You could talk to her and pull the string and pretend you were having a conversation with a friend.'

'Right,' I said again. 'Sounds fair. But whose doll was it in the first place?'

'It was...' Rob said, but his voice failed him. 'It was...' he tried again, his voice wavering. He turned his eyes towards the ceiling, then blew through his lips and said, 'Christ, this is hard.'

Then he closed his eyes and gasped a gulp of air and said, 'It belonged to Julie Sturgess.'

'Julie Sturgess,' I repeated.

'My friend,' Rob said. 'My... best friend, really. The neighbours' kid. We were best friends from... well forever really... They were there, next door, when we moved in, so... You know.'

'Sure,' I said. 'And then?'

'Well, they were there until the end.'

'The end?'

'Yeah,' Rob said. He blew through his lips and looked out at the garden and sighed. 'She got pregnant. That's the thing.'

'Pregnant?' I said. 'Oh.'

'Yeah,' Rob said, quietly. 'And they made... they made me... Oh God...' He started sobbing loudly then, but between sobs he continued to try to speak. 'They made me say it was *me*,' he finally managed to say, speaking in a high-pitched childlike voice. 'But it wasn't. We never even... I hadn't ever... not with anyone. She was my... she was my bloody *friend* for Christ's sake.'

I swiped tears from my eyes and moved to the edge of my seat to that I could touch Rob's knee. 'Someone made you say *you'd* got her pregnant?' I said, still struggling to understand.

Rob nodded. He pushed my hand away then and went to

the kitchen, returning with a roll of paper towel. Once he'd sat back down and blown his nose loudly, he went on, sounding terribly sad, but calmer. 'She was fifteen, you know? She was still *fifteen*. And I was only sixteen – it was just before my birthday. So it was... horrific. I mean, it was absolutely *horrific*. The police got involved and everything.'

'God,' I said. 'I can imagine. But *who* made you say it was you? And why? I don't understand, Rob.'

'My parents,' Rob said. 'My parents made me say it was me.'

'Your parents! OK, but why?'

Rob covered his mouth with one hand in an attempt to stifle a fresh bout of sobbing, but he couldn't help himself. He said something through the sobs and my guess was that he was answering my question, but I honestly couldn't make out what he was saying.

So I left my chair and draped myself across the arm of Rob's armchair so that I could take him in my arms, and he let me hold his shuddering body.

After a minute or so I thought I'd perhaps worked out what he'd said after all, but the idea was so horrific that I didn't want to believe it.

When, eventually, Rob's tears had subsided, I said, gently, 'Rob, I think I heard what you said, but you were crying so hard, honey...'

'Um, I'm sorry,' he said, softly. 'It's just so hard. It's just *still* so bloody hard. That's what's so crazy. Nearly forty years later, and I still can't even say it. I'm sorry.'

'Don't apologise,' I told him. 'Please don't *apologise*. But maybe you do need to say it. Maybe you do need to tell someone.'

'It was Dad,' he whispered, nodding slowly. 'Dad got her pregnant. But they made me say it was me.'

FIFTEEN

JULIE STURGESS (BY ROB)

We moved from Cardiff in 1971 – a move that was as unexpected as it was sudden.

I was six and had no understanding whatsoever of why we were moving. I have a vague recollection that Dad had lost his job as school caretaker, but I may have learned that later on. In retrospect I can take a pretty good guess at why that was, but at the time it was a surprise. One day we were living our lives and the next we were loading belongings into a Transit van, Margate-bound.

I was happy to move, so I didn't think too much about why. I thought the whole adventure was exciting. I'd been having a hard time at school anyway, being bullied for being taller than everyone else (yes, even at six, I was tall) for being what the meaner boys liked to call a *beanpole*.

Mum said it was a 'fresh new start for all of us' and that sounded pretty good to me. I was even happier when I discovered that our fresh new start would take place in a town with a funfair, mile-long beaches and a seafront of shimmering amusement arcades.

My father's new job was as caretaker out at the Hornby

factory, and I remember that was a subject of conversation between my parents. Snippets of those conversations bubbled up years later when I saw a school psychologist – stuff about how it was *safer* than working in a school.

Anyway, at six, I thought Dad working for Hornby was great news. I imagined him playing with Hornby stuff all day, and at Christmas he got staff discount on trains, Scalextric and more.

The Sturgesses were our first neighbours, and Julie and I hit it off instantly. Our gardens ran side by side and as we were still small enough to fit though the gaps in the rotten wooden fence, keeping us apart was pretty much impossible.

Mum didn't like Julie coming to ours – something I didn't understand until much later – but going to Julie's suited me anyway. Life at the Sturgesses' felt far more relaxed – the undercurrents somehow less emotionally charged. As both Julie and I were only children, we became like brother and sister.

It was Christmas '72 when Dad bought Julie the doll – we'd been in Margate less than a year. Coming from Dad, who was stingy even with his own, a gift that wasn't a heavily discounted Hornby product was a shockingly generous gesture.

I was considered an oversensitive *mummy's boy* by then, something my father was openly concerned about, so my own Christmas gifts were unrelentingly masculine. I got guns and soldier outfits and train sets. I got chemistry sets and Airfix kits that were beyond my capabilities to stick together.

So when he gave Julie that doll I felt unreasonably jealous. Chrissy had hair that you could brush and clothes with tiny buttons you could undo. And when you pulled the string she spoke! I got to know the order of Chrissie's replies and, aged seven, would lie in bed beneath the covers, pulling the string, pretending she was my friend.

'Are you ready for bed?' I'd ask her.

I don't think so.

'Do you want to play a game then?'

Why not?

'Hide and seek or shops?'

I'll tell you tomorrow.

'Don't tell Dad that Julie lended you me, will you?'

I'll never tell.

The Action Man was intended as my own virile alternative to the Chrissie doll, but to Dad's dismay Julie and I swapped them back and forth all the time.

Julie liked Action Man's muscular chest and Eagle Eyes, while I liked my secret night-time chats with Chrissie.

Was Dad concerned I would turn out gay? Could someone so twisted actually see that as a concern? Perhaps. Probably. Almost certainly.

But he needn't have worried anyway: I liked girls. It was just that I liked them so much more than boys I wanted girls as my friends, too. Boys were inexplicably cruel aliens. They stamped on worms and pulled the wings from butterflies. They taunted Welsh beanpoles like myself endlessly. Girls, specifically Julie Sturgess, were far nicer to hang out with. So yeah, a mummy's boy, a massive beanpole girly boy, that was me.

'Will you get out from under my feet?' my mother would say twenty times a day.

But if you hung around Mum you might get a sugar sandwich, or the chance to lick out the cake bowl, or even – if the positions of the stars were just right and Mum was in a good mood – the first of the scones from the oven. Beside the swish of Mum's skirt was where I felt happiest, where I felt safest, while Dad's lap made me inexplicably queasy.

Children understand nothing. Children understand everything.

And then one day, if you're both lucky and incredibly unlucky, you get to put the two halves together and understand everything you always knew but didn't know. That's how you become whole but also consciously damaged. Self-knowledge comes at huge cost.

So yeah, my father was a paedophile. There. I finally said it.

There is no specific moment you realise a thing like that. Instead, it's something you grow up with, a horror that hangs in the air. And then at some point, if you're lucky but also unlucky – usually because you're trying to understand what's wrong with you, or, in my case, why you can't breathe – you realise that you always knew, but also that you didn't know. You honestly, truly *didn't know*. But you also did, because that's where the queasy feeling came from. Only then do you understand why you've always felt broken in two.

By the time I was thirteen, I agreed with my mother. I didn't much like Julie coming to our place either, though I couldn't have told you why.

By fourteen, I knew I felt jealous. My father preferred the neighbour's kid to me, and, because she was everything he didn't want me to be – because she was feminine and pretty and soft when he demanded that I be hard and boyish and cruel – I didn't understand how that could be. His preference for Julie made no sense to me.

By the time I was fifteen, their friendship was making me feel uncomfortable. I'd come home to find fourteen-year-old Julie on the sofa watching TV with her head laid on my father's lap. Officially she was just waiting for me, so why did she look embarrassed that I was home early?

Dad continued to buy Julie more stuff than he ever bought me. 'She's like a sister to him,' he would say, when Mum criticised his generosity – generosity we genuinely couldn't afford. He'd turn to me then for backup and ask, 'Isn't she? Isn't she like a sister to you?'

I never knew how to answer that one, because I never knew which answer – sister or stranger – would be the answer that made my friend safe.

That realisation – the joining of the halves – came to me while talking to the school psychologist, who I was seeing because of my panic attacks. It was there, in the middle of an unrelated conversation, that I consciously realised the thing that I'd always but never quite known: what my father and Julie had been doing.

Of course, with adult hindsight, that should be rephrased as *what Dad was doing to Julie*. Because at fourteen or thirteen, or perhaps earlier – because I have no idea when it started – Julie certainly could not have given consent. And that's why it's called abuse. And that's why it's called rape. But at fifteen, I blamed them equally. Sad I know, but true.

That day, the day it came to me, I sat there, sweat pouring from me even though it was winter, watching the shrink's lips moving, trying to push images of my father and my best friend from my mind's eye. Trying not to throw up, too.

We drifted apart after that, Julie and I. Oh, we'd exchange a few words if I came home and she was there. We kind of had to really, because she'd pretend that she was there to see me. But she wasn't, we both knew that. She was there to see my father.

Then one day when I was almost seventeen, I came home from my job as an apprentice electrician to find my mother red-eyed at the kitchen table.

'I need to talk to you, Son,' she said, solemnly. 'I need to talk to you about something serious.' She'd never talked to me about something *serious* before. She'd never called me *son* either.

'Julie Sturgess is pregnant,' she said, once I'd taken off my jacket and sat down. 'And a man is coming in a bit – a policeman – and I need you to do something important for me. I need you to say that it's yours.'

At first I didn't understand what she was saying, and then once I did I didn't understand why. But there was no time for explanation because the doorbell had rung and the policeman had entered, and was sitting down at our kitchen table with a notepad.

'Your husband?' he asked, glancing around as if he might be hiding in the corner of the room.

'Away on business,' Mum said, 'and he doesn't know, which is just as well, as he'd beat the living daylights out of him.'

I realised in that moment that we were lying, and then with a shudder, with a hair-bristling shiver, I worked out why. Pennies can be slow to drop, especially when you don't want them to.

When the policeman asked me how long I'd been sleeping with Julie Sturgess, Mum said, 'Must be, what, six months, Son? He shouldn't have done it – we can all agree on that – but if we're being honest, that girl's always been a bit of a slut.'

It took everything I could muster not to gasp. I felt as if my head was exploding.

'I'd rather Rob answered, if you don't mind,' the policeman told her.

I looked at her, no longer My Beloved Mother, now suddenly The Great Paedophile Facilitator. Her eyes were steely blue, commanding me to obey...

This is the last thing you'll ever hear me say, I thought. *This is the last time we will ever sit together.*

'Yes,' I said. 'About that. About six months.' *You are dead to me.*

The policeman said that Julie's parents weren't pressing charges but that I wasn't to go within a mile of her.

'She lives next door,' I pointed out, quite reasonably. 'How can I not go within a mile?'

'She's gone away,' the policeman said. 'She's gone away to sort out the pregnancy.'

'I hope she's getting rid of it,' my mother said. 'No point bringing another little bastard into the world.'

The policeman coughed, then cleared his throat. 'I believe that is what her family have decided,' he croaked.

'Good,' my mother said. 'And by the time she gets back, we'll have moved anyway, won't we?'

'Well, at least they're not pressing charges,' she said, once the policeman had left. She sounded like she thought I should be relieved.

I'd known that my father had an evil streak, but I'd wanted to see my mother as his victim. Now, suddenly, I understood why they were together. They were cut from the same cloth. The realisation made me feel sick to the core.

Different questions went through my mind:

– *Did you know?* But I knew the answer to that one was, 'Of course I knew.'

– *How long have you known?* 'Since Cardiff.' At the very least.

– *How could you stay with him? Why don't you leave him?* 'Because I don't want to. Because I'm scared. Because I'm a monster. Because I never cared about the little sluts anyway.'

I found my mind knew all of her answers already. There was no need to even involve her in the conversation.

'Are you really moving?' was the only one I asked out loud.

'Yes, we thought it was time to go back to Wales,' Mum said. 'We thought it would be nice if we stayed by the coast though. We're thinking Anglesey, perhaps. What do you think?' She seemed to really think things were going to carry on like normal.

But I was already standing, I was already leaving, and in my head I was already gone.

It wasn't a *decision* to get away from her, from him, from that house, it was a *need*. It was impossible to stay a minute longer.

They left about a week later, probably in another hastily

rented van. I say *about* and *probably* because I wasn't there to witness any of it. I didn't help them pack and I didn't say goodbye.

I rented a room for six months from Alan, my electrician boss, paying him and his wife £25 a week, and then, once I'd saved a deposit, I moved into a grubby little bedsit opposite The Oxford pub.

Eventually I heard through the grapevine that Julie Sturgess had returned from wherever it was she'd been and then three months after that I saw a *for sale* sign outside their old house and learned that her family had moved too.

I never once tried to contact her and that wasn't only because it was forbidden. I felt so ashamed of what had happened that even thinking about Julie made me want to die. And I do mean that quite literally. It made me want to *die*.

But for the most part – incredible, *shameful* as this will sound – I managed very efficiently to not think about her at all. Until, of course, Dad phoned me about that box.

SIXTEEN

AFTER THE STORM (BY DAWN)

By the time Rob had finished telling me about his parents we'd moved back to the kitchen. We were seated at the kitchen table holding hands.

We were both red-eyed and pretty much cried out by that point and when Rob released my hand it was simply to go upstairs for a snooze.

After he'd gone, I sat and stared out of the kitchen window at the fading light and tried to think about everything I'd just learned. But there was too much of it all, really, or at least that's how it felt. It all seemed too massive to be logically thought about so all that was left was emotion – an almost overwhelming rush of compassion and sadness and love. My husband was upstairs and he was sleeping and I loved him. That was as far as logic would take me.

After half an hour or so, I moved to the lounge and turned on the TV. I was hoping it would provide some sort of relief from trying to think thoughts that refused to be thought, but the noise of it just irritated me. So with the realisation that what I needed was simply to sit and let myself be with this new reality, with these new feelings, I switched it back off and did just that.

Rob came back downstairs about nine. He stood in the doorway behind me and whispered, 'Are you sleeping?'

'No,' I said, 'Not at all.'

He entered the room hesitantly and perched opposite me on the edge of the armchair as if he perhaps hadn't decided if he was staying. His eyes looked bloodshot and he had the imprint of the seam of the pillowcase right down the middle of one cheek.

'You OK?' he asked.

I nodded and blinked slowly. 'Yes, I'm fine. But how are *you*?'

Rob shrugged. 'Tired,' he said. 'Exhausted, actually. The truth of my family is exhausting.'

'Yes,' I said. 'I can imagine.' Then, 'Though, actually I can't. I can't even begin to imagine living with that.'

'Um...?' Rob started.

'Yes?'

'Are...? Sorry, but I feel I need to ask this, OK? So don't, you know...'

'Go on, Rob,' I said. 'Anything.'

'So...' He cleared his throat and scratched his chin. 'Do you think you're going to leave me now?'

'*Leave you?*' I repeated in shock. Nothing could have been further from my mind.

'Yeah, now you know what a freak I am.'

I actually laughed a little at that. 'You're not a freak, Rob,' I said. 'God. I don't think that *at all*.' I patted the seat beside me and said, 'Come here.'

'In a bit,' Rob said. 'So you're not? Going to leave me?'

'No!' I told him. 'Don't be ridiculous!'

'It must have changed how you feel about me though. Surely it must, a bit.'

'No,' I said.

'You *were* pretty young when I met you,' Rob said.

I frowned. It took me a moment to work out what he was implying.

'God, Rob,' I finally said. 'You can't think... You don't... You *can't*! That's not the same thing at all!'

'No?' Rob asked.

'No! Jesus! To start with I was legal, I wasn't a child. And easily old enough to decide what I wanted. And secondly, you weren't my first. Not by a long, long stretch. And thirdly, you were in your twenties.'

'I was twenty-five.'

'Yes, twenty-five. You weren't forty or fifty or whatever. Plus, I made it happen, not you. You didn't *groom* me, for God's sake. So no! God, no! Don't ever say anything like that again. That's just...'

'Sorry,' Rob said.

'And stop apologising.'

'But it doesn't change how you feel, then?' he asked, after a moment of silence. 'Not at all? Be honest.'

'Actually, yes, OK. I suppose that if I'm honest, it does.'

'You see,' Rob said.

'I feel like... like... I don't know,' I said, struggling to put words to so many feelings. 'Like I know you... *properly*... maybe. For the first time.'

Rob frowned at me and then raised an eyebrow comically.

'It's as if... sorry, I'm not that good at this... but it's like, maybe there was this half of you that I didn't know. Or that I didn't understand at any rate. I mean, I *knew* you. But without context, half of you didn't make sense... Actually, I'm not sure *I'm* making any sense.'

'No, you are,' Rob said. 'You really are. I used to feel the same way about myself. That there was half of me I didn't understand.'

'But now I do, that's the thing. Now the whole of you makes sense. It's like... having a bigger screen or something – I can see the whole picture. And all that gentleness, all that softness you have... it seems... well... miraculous, to me, really. *Courageous*. I mean, you could so easily have become hardened and cold and awful. But you didn't, did you? You stayed sensitive and open and gentle. And I love you for that, Rob. God, I love you so much for that. For what you did with all of this... this hurt.'

My eyes were watering so much that I couldn't see, and when I wiped them with my sleeve I saw that Rob had his head in his hands. So I stood and once again crossed the room to join him by sitting on the arm of his chair.

'I thought you'd leave me if I told you,' he said through his fingers. 'I always thought that. That you'd leave me if you ever found out.'

'Oh, Rob!' I said. 'Christ, no! No, I don't think I could ever leave you now.'

'Because you feel sorry for me.'

'No! Because I *love* you,' I said. 'I love you so much, Rob. You're the most honest, kind, loving person I've ever met. And I'm sorry for everything that's happened between us, but I think – if you'll have me, that is – I think you're going to have to put up with me until the end.'

'Christ,' Rob said. 'Thank God.'

* * *

That first lockdown lasted until May, eased almost to the point of non-existence in September, toughened again in November, and went full-on prison-break all over again from January through to March.

Rob's business ended up reduced to a skeleton crew of six people working three branches while the other two were closed – closures that were intended to be temporary, but which a Brexit-plus-Covid-plus-War-in-Ukraine-inspired   economic downturn would prevent from ever opening again.

Because over two hundred thousand people died in the UK, because it wrecked the economy, routed the public finances, exhausted the poor nursing staff and deprived people of seeing aged, often dying relatives, what I'm going to say next will sound awful, but I'm trying to be honest here, so please don't hate me for it: for our family, the lockdowns were a godsend.

For Rob and I, it wasn't just that we hadn't spent time together recently, it was – as thanks to lockdown we finally came to realise – that we'd *never* spent much time together.

When I'd met him he'd been working flat out trying to pay for our first house and after that I'd had a screaming newborn to take care of, closely followed by a second. In the gaps when I might have had some free time, Rob had been setting up a business then organising its expansion, and by the time that had calmed down we had the move followed by Lucy's madness, Mum's illness and Rob's affair... The list of events that had happened to us, plus events we'd ourselves created to avoid spending time together, just went on and on. But suddenly, here we were, locked up together and bored, and it happened at one of the most crucial moments of our lives.

At the beginning, out of habit, we found things to do. Rob cleared out the garage and built shelves to organise everything properly, and I planted a vegetable patch, which despite hundreds of hours of back-breaking work would produce almost nothing at all. I did not, it turned out, have green fingers. While my plants failed to thrive, I redecorated our bedroom, and while Rob installed air conditioning in the sunroom I took up online yoga classes. When Rob finished his last DIY project he started running again – you get the picture.

But these lockdowns went on for *months*. They went on for so very long that ultimately we had no choice but to spend time together, and I mean not just in the same house but *together*.

The process of talking to each other was already under way,

but as the months went by we found ourselves talking like never before.

I dared to ask Rob how he felt about his parents and he did his best to convey the mixture of hatred and shame that he felt about them.

I'd always assumed that he must secretly feel a smidgen of love too – that, for a parent, seemed to me to be something that was unavoidable, even if it was perhaps impossible for him to admit. But then in January 2021 Rob's father died of Covid, followed just a few days later by his mother, and Rob genuinely didn't seem affected.

About a week after their online funeral – a funeral that Rob declined to 'attend' – I asked him if he had any regrets, any sadness – in fact, any feelings at all.

'You know – and this is gonna sound a bit monster-ey,' he said. 'But I really don't. Does that make me a bad person, do you think?'

I told him that, no, it didn't make him a bad person, at least not in my eyes.

'I wasn't sure if I would or not,' he said. 'I honestly thought I might suddenly get this rush of sorrow or grief or whatever. But it hasn't come yet, that's for sure. The only thing I feel is relief. Relief that I never have to see them or hear from them or hopefully even think about them again.'

'OK,' I said. 'Well, good.'

'It's the gift that just keeps on giving,' he said.

'What is?' I asked.

'Covid.'

'That does sound a *bit* monster-ey,' I told him. 'Maybe don't share that joke with anyone other than me.'

By the time we came out of the final lockdown, Lucy was pregnant, Wayne and Belinda had named a date, Lou had settled down with his girlfriend, Mum had moved out of her place and in with Quentin, and Rob and I were more in love than we had ever been in the entire history of our marriage. None of us spoke of lockdown as being a negative, though that wasn't a reality that was shareable with anyone outside the family.

Shelley (who'd split up with Gavin in the middle of lockdown) wouldn't have wanted to hear it, and nor would Trudy (who had long Covid) or Ryan (both of whose grandparents had been horribly ill, but survived) or indeed any of Rob's laid-off staff.

So we kept our little explosion of joy within the walls of the family unit. We had raucous meals and wore posh clothes for the first time in years to Wayne's wedding and had a baby shower for Alek and Lucy.

In March Lucy gave birth to a beautiful baby boy – seven pounds and eight ounces or 3.4 kilos if, like Lucy, you prefer your babies metric.

Arriving at the hospital, I crossed paths with Mum, who had already visited and was on her way out.

'It's one at a time,' she explained. 'So I'll wait for you outside. There's something I want to discuss with you anyway, so...'

Only half an hour later – slots to see baby Tom were in great demand – I found her sitting on a wall eating a Snickers and drinking Diet Coke. It was a beautiful spring afternoon.

'Healthy diet!' I teased, jumping up onto the wall beside her and reaching for the can of drink.

'Oh, I know,' Mum said. 'It's the special *keeping-cancer-at-bay* diet. Haven't you heard of it?'

'Isn't he gorgeous?' I asked, once I'd taken a sip from her can. 'He looks like Alek already.'

'It's the eyes,' Mum said. 'It's those ice-blue eyes. Though that might change. Yours were pretty blue when you were born and then they went all sludgy and green.'

'Thanks!' I said. 'Lucy looks dreadful though, doesn't she?'

'So did you,' Mum said. 'So did every new mother, ever.'

'Luckily, there were no mirrors,' I told her. 'So I never realised.'

'I have photos somewhere,' Mum said. 'I'll show you.'

'So you said there's something you want to talk to me about?' Perhaps it was the fact of having been in the hospital, but while I was with Lucy I'd started worrying that maybe Mum's cancer was back. 'You're OK, aren't you?'

'Yes,' Mum said. 'I'm fine. No, this is more about you really. Well, indirectly it is, anyway.'

I'm not sure why, but I suddenly thought that she was going to tell me who my father was. I thought she was going to say that it hadn't been Bert the minicab driver after all. Seeing baby Tom with Alek and Lucy had made her regret all those years of making a stupid story out of something so important. I braced myself for a revelation.

Instead she said, 'I wondered if you'd heard the news.'

'The news?'

'About your Billy?'

'Oh,' I said, simultaneously disappointed and annoyed. 'Please don't call him that. He's not my Billy at all.'

'Sorry,' Mum said. 'But have you? Heard?'

'No, I haven't heard anything at all. What's happened? Did the idiot get Covid?' I'd read about how anti-vax Billy was.

'No,' Mum said. 'He's been arrested.'

'Really?' I said. 'Why?'

'For rape.'

'Rape?' I repeated. 'Oh, wow.'

Mum nodded. 'Apparently there's a whole flock of them crawling out of the woodwork now.'

'A flock of...?'

'Supposed victims,' Mum said.

'Don't call them that,' I told her. 'Don't say *supposed* like that.'

'I just mean they're probably gold-diggers,' Mum said. 'It's what the papers are saying, anyway. I mean, he must be worth a bit, mustn't he?'

'And where did you hear this?' I asked.

'In the *Mail*,' Mum said, prompting me to roll my eyes. 'I know you don't like it,' she went on, 'but I like a bit of celebrity gossip myself. And the proof of the pudding is that you wouldn't even have known about Billy otherwise.'

'OK,' I said. 'Thanks. I'll have a look.'

For few months I broke my own rules: I started to read the *Daily Mail*. And their coverage of Billy Riddle's trial was as exhaustive as their judgements about his victims were dubious.

He was being sued, it transpired, by an American woman called Jennifer Styles who claimed to have had his child after he'd raped her. She was from an Evangelical Texan family who'd refused to let her have an abortion, so now her lawyers were trying to get Billy extradited to the US so that he could stand trial. The publicity had nudged six other victims into making themselves known, one of whom was Joanna, Billy's PA.

Had I had any doubt that he'd be found guilty, I might have forced myself to get involved, but, with seven victims describing almost exactly the scenario I'd been through, it seemed pretty much a foregone conclusion. And yet eventually, a year later, he wriggled out of it all by settling out of court – something men with money always do seem to manage one way or another. He'd paid an undisclosed amount to each of the six women and set up a trust fund for Jennifer Styles's child and as a result the case had been dropped.

Mum phoned me a couple of days afterwards, when she finally stumbled upon an article about it. 'I told you he was innocent,' she said. 'I told they were gold-diggers.'

So I was forced to tell her my own horrific Billy story and to explain the difference between an out-of-court settlement and innocence.

'You could have been rich,' she said once she finally got over her shock. 'You could have taken us all on a cruise.'

But knowing that I'd made the right decision that day when I'd crashed through those garage doors was enough for me. I hadn't overreacted after all.

I didn't want Billy's money. I didn't want anything from Billy. Rather like Rob, with his father, all I wanted was to never have to think of Billy again. Or at least not for a very, very long time.

EPILOGUE

There's a knock on the door and then almost immediately it eases open. 'Are you decent?' a chirpy feminine voice calls out. 'Can I come in?'

'We are,' Dawn says. 'Yes, come.'

The door opens to reveal Miriam's rosy-red features. 'We're starting in five minutes,' she says, 'and I just wanted to check you haven't forgotten.'

'But we've got a visit this afternoon – my grandson,' Dawn says. 'Didn't I say?'

'Oh, lovely,' Miriam says. 'Maybe he'd like to come too? We've got a juggler coming today and everything. It should be fun. You can always join in halfway through if you want. It's nothing formal.'

Dawn wrinkles her nose and shakes her head. 'Tom wants to talk to us,' she says. 'He wants to interview us actually. It's for his sociology project or something. He's at Nottingham Uni.'

'Oh!' Miriam says. 'OK then! We'll, I'll just leave you to it and I'll see you tomorrow.'

Just as she leaves, Dawn hears the toilet flush, followed by the steady hiss of a tap. She turns towards the bathroom as the door slides open and Rob returns.

'Miriam,' she tells him, answering his unspoken question, a question asked by merely glancing towards the door. 'They've got a juggler today apparently.'

'A juggler is it?' Rob says. 'D'you want to go?'

'No, we've got Tom coming in a bit, silly.'

'Oh, is that today, then?' Rob asks.

'Yes,' Dawn says. 'Yes, it's today.' She refrains from pointing out that she's reminded him of this three times already. She knows his forgetfulness isn't intentional.

'I'm going to go sit on the balcony for a bit,' Rob says. 'It's a lovely day. Are you staying there?'

'No,' Dawn says. 'No, I'll come.'

She presses a button on the armchair and it gracefully lifts her to a standing position. It's not that she can't get up without assistance, but it does tend to make her lower back twinge, and lately that twinge can last all day.

Outside on the balcony it is indeed a beautiful sunny day, but then most days now are sunny days. The youngsters only get excited when it rains.

Once they're seated opposite each other, Rob asks, 'So have you decided?'

'Decided what?' Dawn asks.

'What to tell him.'

'Tom?'

Rob resists the desire to say, *No, the Pope*, one of Dawn's favourite jibes. 'Yes, Tom,' he says, flatly.

'Not really,' Dawn tells him. 'I'm still hesitating between just us or, you know, the whole shebang.'

'By *the whole shebang*, you mean Billy,' Rob says.

'Yes.'

'He *was* quite a big one,' Rob says. 'I think you might have to leave out quite a lot if you don't mention Billy.'

'Because?'

'Because there are things that won't make sense... that you won't be able to explain otherwise.'

'D'you think?' Dawn says.

'Don't you?'

'Maybe. I don't know. I mean, I was thinking I could still tell him about meeting you, having Lucy, having Lou, Mum's death. Moving houses. Having to move into this place. That virus thing that had us all shut indoors.'

'Covid?' Rob offers. 'Or the pig one?'

'Not the Covid one. How long did that last anyway?'

'The whole thing, or...?'

'No, the bit when we weren't allowed out.'

'A month, maybe a bit more,' Rob says.

Dawn laughs. 'It was much longer than a month. *Much* longer.'

'If you know then why ask me? Anyway, I'm sure Tom can look it up.'

'Yes, I expect even Hubble knows.'

In the corner of the room a picture frame glows bright green and the screen lights up with the animated image of a young man's face. A smooth male voice says, 'I'm sorry, do I know what?'

'We weren't talking to you, Hubble,' Rob says.

'Sorry,' the voice replies. 'I'll be quiet.'

'So Covid is one of your big events, is it?' Rob says.

'Yes, that was a big one for me. A massive one really. You'd just split up with your bit of—'

'Cheryl.'

'Yes, if you prefer, *Cheryl*. And I'd just been to see Billy and realised what a twat he was. And the Covid thing sort of threw us back together.'

Rob nods thoughtfully. 'But you see, there he is again. How can you talk about one bit without mentioning Billy?'

'Oh,' Dawn says. 'Yes, I see what you mean.'

'And if you don't mention Billy, I'm not sure I want you mentioning Cheryl either, to be honest. I mean, that would kind of put me in a bad light.'

'And so it should!' Dawn says.

'Butterflies!' Rob says, pointing.

Dawn looks in the direction Rob is pointing and sees them, two beautiful blue butterflies fluttering together in the sunlight. 'Gosh,' she says. 'How lovely!' She hasn't seen a butterfly for almost a decade.

'Maybe it's working,' Rob says. 'Maybe the insecticide ban is finally working.'

'Maybe,' Dawn says. 'I hope so. But they're probably just some of the bred ones they've been talking about releasing.'

'But you know you're right,' Rob says. 'I remember that too.'

'You remember what?' Dawn asks. She's used to Rob's butterfly brain.

'How the Covid thing threw us together. I think that was when I actually realised I wanted to grow old with you.'

'Christ you took your time, didn't you?' Dawn jokes. 'You were in your fifties by then.'

'No, I know. And you know that I always loved you. But I was thinking about getting old around then. Worrying about it. And when we got... what was it they called it?'

'Lockupped,' Dawn says.

'Yeah,' Rob says. 'When we got lockupped – actually I'm not sure that is... but anyway – I remember thinking that being locked up with you would be OK. And here we are.'

'You thought it would be OK?' Dawn says, arching an eyebrow.

'Lovely, then,' Rob says.

'And was it?' Dawn asks, a cheeky grin on her face. 'Did it turn out to be lovely, darling?'

'Yeah,' Rob says, stifling his own grin. 'Lovely might be over-stating it a bit, but yeah, it's turned out OK-ish.'

'Better than with Cheryl?'

Rob guffaws at this. 'God!' he says. 'I can't even imagine. Did I ever tell you she liked rap music? That really shouty stuff when they go on about cop killers and what-have-you. She knew all the words.'

'Yes,' Dawn says. 'Yes, you told me.'

'And the TV. God, her TV was on all the time. She used to watch that thing where all the youngsters have to fall in love. I can't remember what it's called now but it made my brain go numb.'

'*Love Island*,' Dawn says. Rob has told her that story before as well.

'That's the one.'

'Still, at least she gave good head,' Dawn says wryly.

'Yes,' Rob says. 'Yes, she really did. But don't tell Tom that, will you?'

'All right,' Dawn says. 'I won't. Probably.'

'But anyway, yes. We had fun during the lockup, didn't we? D'you remember how we got all the old CDs out?'

'You forced me to listen to Duran Duran.'

'But you liked Japan, didn't you? And OMD.'

'That's true,' Dawn said. 'I still like OMD now. Actually Duran Duran wasn't as awful as I made out. I always thought it was a bit fluffy but it was OK. I just said it because it annoyed you. But I ended up hearing them so often over the years...'

'No more than you made me listen to Sonic Youth.'

'But I was bored with it all, at one point,' Dawn says. 'Did you ever realise or did I hide it too well?'

'Bored with what?'

'With everything, really. The lack of... I don't know... conflict... I can't think of the right word. Friction, maybe? It started to get on my nerves. I started craving someone who might disagree a bit. Someone I could argue with. Like when I was young and I used to argue about everything. Life just felt so predictable.'

'Actually, I know exactly what you mean. I felt the same way. But it was more like a lack of options for me.'

'Options?'

'Yeah, I don't know... a lack of possible paths, perhaps. I mean, when you're young, there are all these different lives you can live, aren't there? And for a while, the possibilities just seem endless. There are so many possible turn-offs you can take when you're a teenager, it feels terrifying. You can do anything, be anything, date anyone, live anywhere... But suddenly you're married, and you're getting older and all those possible futures seem to just get less and less until there aren't any turn-offs left. There's only one straight road. And that feels kind of scary. Claustrophobic.'

'But what you realise,' Dawn says, 'if you're lucky, like we were, is that those other paths, the turn-offs you didn't take, the changes you could have made, they're all still there. I mean, you *can* still leave, can't you? You can still go looking for someone new. Or live somewhere else. Or whatever you want to change, no matter what your age is. It's just that you've learned the other options *weren't* better. Still aren't better. You get the... the wisdom, I suppose, to appreciate the path you've chosen. To choose the life you already have. To re-choose the person, ultimately, that you're with. Because in the end you work out that there's nothing to be achieved after all. Except maybe peace, and harmony, and being happy and whatever.'

Rob nods thoughtfully. 'Maybe. I never thought about it quite like that, but maybe.'

'I mean, that's what we finally realised, wasn't it? What a whole life together had done for us. The fact that we'd sort of... merged until we agreed on everything.'

Rob laughs. 'Not sure about everything, but on most things, sure.'

'And that's...' Dawn says. 'I don't know. Something to be treasured, isn't it? I thought I was bored with it, back then. I thought I wanted other options. I thought I wanted to rewind and choose a different, more exciting path...'

'With Billy.'

'Yes, with Billy. And so did you. But when we came back from our little...'

'Detours?'

'I was going to say adventures, but yes, detours is good. Because that's what they were. And when we came back to each other, and even more when we were squashed up together by that pandemic, I realised that the way we get on, the way we'd ironed out all the kinks, well, in the end, that was the most amazing thing of all. No other path could really compare. And it had taken a whole lifetime together to manage that. There wasn't *time* to do it all again with someone else even if I'd wanted to.'

'I couldn't believe I'd almost thrown it away. I was so angry with myself for risking everything.'

'Yes,' Dawn says. 'Me too. The thought of being locked up with anyone else...'

'With Cheryl... God!'

'Or with Billy... terrifying.'

'D'you remember you gave me those weird books to read?' Rob says. 'During the lockdown? Ah! That's what they called it. *Lockdown*.'

'Weird books? What weird books?'

'The ones where all the men are bastards.'

Dawn laughs. 'Oh!' she says. 'Fay Weldon. Yes, I loved those books. I actually quite fancy reading them again.'

'They were good,' Rob says. 'But full of unhappy relationships. They kind of made me realise how lucky we were, too.'

'Maybe I gave them to you on purpose. I don't remember, really.'

'It was cosy though, just the two of us, wasn't it? With our books and our music and our walks.'

'We did get on well. It was a surprise.'

'We still *do* get on, don't we?' Rob says.

'Yeah,' Dawn says. 'And it's *still* a bit of a surprise. But anyway, we're getting sidetracked here. We need to decide what to tell Tom.'

They discuss how much to tell Tom all afternoon, but because the issue is so complex they fail to make a decision.

Lucy – Tom's mother – still doesn't know that her biological father may be the late William Ruddle. Dawn has always thought she might tell her about Billy at some point, but it's just never seemed like the right moment.

The truth, perhaps, would hurt her, but then does anyone have the right to deny another the truth? As Rob always points out, whenever they discuss it, the truth never did them any harm, in fact if anything it's the thing that saved their marriage.

The truth. The truth about everything. Repeated over and over for thirty years until none of it had the power to shock or to cause any more pain.

But as Dawn always counters, the fact that it worked for them doesn't mean it works that way for everyone.

And then it's five past three and Tom has arrived and still they haven't decided.

* * *

They chat with their grandson until almost four.

Tom, always fresh-faced and optimistic, reminds Dawn so much of young Rob that every time she sees him she has her doubts. But then a quick request to Hubble will pull up photos of Billy's daughter Julianne and it would be hard for her to look more like Lucy.

Once they've caught up on family news and discussed jugglers, Alek's upcoming retirement and Rob's dodgy shoulder... Once they've talked about butterflies, the ethics of lab-grown fish and Tom's love life, he takes off his Hubble wristband and lays it on the table between them.

'That's to record the conversation, right?' Dawn asks.

'Yeah. It types it for me too and sends it to my college account.'

'Of course it does,' Dawn says. 'So clever.'

'So, do you want me to remind you what this is all about before we start?' Tom asks.

'No,' Dawn says. 'I remember.'

'Actually, I do,' Rob says. 'If that's OK.'

'Of course,' Tom says. 'So it's a group project, recording tipping-point events in various long-term relationships, some successful and others not – we interview the divorced ones separately of course. Then we're going to use Artificial Intelligence to try to identify key events that change the course of a long-term relationship. It's as much about testing the AI as the relationship stuff really, but anyway.'

'OK?' Dawn asks, glancing at Rob. 'Ready?'

'Yeah, I understood at least the first three words,' Rob says.

'It's—' Tom starts.

'Just ignore him,' Dawn tells Tom. 'He understands perfectly. It's fine.'

'But... to be clear...' Rob says solemnly. 'Are you assuming ours has been a *successful* marriage?'

'Oh,' Tom says. 'Yes, I kind of *was* assuming that.'

'That's maybe a bit of a leap of faith,' Dawn says, grimacing.

'Indeed,' Rob says, looking dour.

Tom's smile starts to fade. 'Oh,' he says, looking crestfallen. 'OK. It's just that Mum said—'

Only then do Rob and Dawn allow themselves to crack smiles.

'You two!' Tom says. 'You're terrible.'

'We are,' Dawn agrees.

'We've always liked a joke,' Rob says, nudging Dawn. 'Haven't we, Dawney?'

'You should study *that*,' Dawn says. 'That's what makes a marriage work. A sense of humour.'

'She's right,' Rob says.

'*And* that,' Dawn says.

'I'm sorry?' Tom asks.

'Having a husband who always says you're right. That helps a lot, too. Massively, actually.'

'She's right about that too,' Rob says. 'Telling her she's right all the time definitely helps.'

Tom smiles and blinks slowly and shakes his head. 'Anyway!' he says, sounding determined to get on with the proceedings. 'Who's going first?'

'She is,' Rob says, nodding in Dawn's direction. 'Always.'

'OK then,' Tom says. 'And have you decided what your first event is, Gran?'

'So these are events that changed—'

'That influenced the trajectory of your marriage,' Tom says.

Dawn glances at Rob and raises an eyebrow. By way of reply, he just shrugs.

'You don't mind though?' she asks him. 'You're sure?'

'No,' Rob says, reaching to take her hand and giving it a squeeze. 'I don't mind at all. It's entirely up to you.'

'OK, so I suppose my first one will have to be meeting a man called Billy,' Dawn says. 'There's no way round it, really. His name was William Ruddle, but he went by the name of Billy

Riddle. You may have heard of him. He was a singer in a band. They were quite big back in the day.'

'Oh, exciting,' Tom says. 'What was the name again?'

'Billy Riddle,' Dawn says. 'His band were called the Argonauts.'

Tom pulls a face and shakes his head. 'I think it must have been before my time.'

'Oh, it was *definitely* before your time. They were big in the 1990s.'

'Wow,' Tom says. 'So, like, fifty years ago. Ancient history. And who was this Billy Riddle? To you, I mean?'

'Well, Billy, was my first proper boyfriend.'

'OK.'

'I met him at the Harbour Lights, a biker pub in Whitstable, where my best friend's brother liked to hang out. At seventeen I shouldn't have been in a pub at all, let alone a wild, druggy, biker pub like the Harbour Lights. But Derek's Kawasaki had a flat battery, forcing him to take his mum's old Hillman Imp. He'd offered a spare seat to his little sister, Shelley, and Shelley, being both my schoolfriend and too much of a scaredy-cat to go alone, invited me...'

The End

A LETTER FROM THE AUTHOR

If you enjoyed *The Imperfection of Us* and would like to join other readers in keeping in touch, stay in the loop with my new releases by signing up to my personal email newsletter on the link here:

www.nick-alexander.com/signup-for-updates

I'd be delighted if you sign up to either – or both!

If could spare a few moments to leave a review that would be hugely appreciated. Even a short review can make all the difference in encouraging a reader to discover my books for the first time.

The idea for *The Imperfection of Us* came from a conversation I had with a friend who, rather like Dawn's mum, constantly dumps his partners. I was trying to explain how giving up the excitement of constant change is hard, but that it opens the way to a different set of advantages that a long-term multi-year relationship brings. The way two people can grow together, for example. The way they come to agree on so many things and learn when to help and when to step back. The way one comes to feel safe and supported by the everyday reliability of a long-term relationship. It clearly isn't as exciting as constantly swinging between being in love/being devastated, but it's almost certainly a more profound kind of happiness and one that fits more comfortably with the wisdom that comes with getting older.

It crossed my mind that these things – these qualities of long-term relationships – are rarely exploited in fiction, which so often go for the immediate (and easier to write) excitement of falling in love/break-up drama. So I set out to write a novel that would attempt to contrast that constant excitement/upheaval, the drama of being obsessed and in love, with the humdrum but not insubstantial qualities of a long-term year-on-year relationship. Initially, I began writing about a middle-class couple in Cambridge, but I quickly realised that I'd used that trope too often and that I was feeling bored with my characters before I even started, so I stopped and tried again, setting it in a Margate council estate instead, whereupon the whole thing came to life.

Spunky Dawn and her generous, cheeky mother are based on a friend's girlfriend I briefly met when I was seventeen. I'd been down to the New Forest with a bunch of friends on a motorbiking camping trip and when we got back we really did camp in his girlfriend's mother's garden, bang in the middle of the Millmead estate. While the bit about the sausages and chips she served everyone is also true, the rest is pure fiction.

Anyway, thank you for choosing to read my latest novel. I do hope you enjoyed it.

Thank you so much. Nick x

www.nick-alexander.com

ACKNOWLEDGMENTS

My thanks to the wonderful late Fay Weldon for taking the time to encourage me right at the beginning of my writing career, to Rosemary for being my touchstone since this whole adventure began and to Lolo for putting up with me day to day as I slog out all those words. Thanks to Claire and everyone else at Storm Publishing for all their hard work on this novel. It's been quite the pleasure working with you!